COLLECTOR
of SECRETS

COLLECTOR
of SECRETS

RICHARD GOODFELLOW

Copyright © 2015 by Richard Goodfellow
Cover and jacket design by 2Faced Design
Interior design by E.M. Tippetts Book Designs

ISBN 978-1-940610-33-7
eISBN 978-1-940610-45-0
Library of Congress Control Number: 2015941257

First hardcover publication: August 2015
1201 Hudson Street, #211S
Hoboken, NJ 07030
www.PolisBooks.com

POLIS BOOKS

I kill an ant
And realize my three children
Have been watching

Kato Shuson

ACKNOWLEDGMENTS

A well-known proverb say it takes a village to raise a child, which feels similar in many ways to my multi-year journey toward the publication of this first book. And, of course, there are numerous people who must be acknowledged and thanked for their valuable participation:

The many fearless editors – Crash Davis (your take-no-prisoners style was much needed at the beginning); Ann Harmer (smoother of words and creator of flow); Arlene Prunkl (teacher of Point of View and other writing rules); Joan Goodfellow and Bill Goodfellow and Susan Stubbs (my wonderful family and biggest cheerleaders); Sheila Davis; Tracy Beresford; Stephanie McNulty; Kikine Capier; and a host of other friends and family who kindly read early versions and provided valuable feedback and insight.

My cousin Clayton Goodfellow who ventured to Manhattan with me to provide his guidance and assistance in finding an agent. This would never have happened without you, my friend.

The amazing Jennifer Weltz (and all the hard-working staff at the Jean V. Naggar Literary Agency) who provided the light at the end of the tunnel, and even when I was losing faith, continued to support and believe in Collector of Secrets.

Jason Pinter, founder and publisher of Polis Books, who has enthusiastically embraced Max Travers and his continuing adventure.

And finally, my brother and business partner, Chris Black, whose steadfast refusal to read the book's printed version has encouraged Audible to publish an audio version.

This is my village and I am so grateful.

PROLOGUE

1945 – Luzon, the Philippines

THE JUNGLE raised its hand to strike back. Oversized fern leaves smacked against the truck's windshield as it lurched and bucked on the dark, narrow road, the branches screaming as they cracked and tore. From childhood, Ginto had roamed beneath this lush, green canopy, but now the old familiarity felt askew, as if twisted through his present actions. By all rights, he should have been asleep in his hammock, not helping the Japanese invaders. The jungle knew his betrayal, and it was shouting its anger.

He wiped the sweat from his tanned forehead and pressed harder on the truck's accelerator. The engine groaned and pulled against the weight of the cargo. The side windows were closed, making the cab stifling, but better the heat and humidity than the insect hordes attracted by the dancing headlights.

Glancing over at his young son watching warily from the passenger's seat, Ginto mustered a crooked smile, attempting to reassure the boy that everything was fine. He shouted over the noise of the laboring engine. "Now remember what I said. When we get there, you hide on the floor. Understand?"

The boy nodded his head in acknowledgment.

"Don't worry, Benjie. Everything will be all right."

The night before, outside the village café, the foreigner had whispered the delivery instructions, telling him to drive into the hills—alone. But ever since the slaughter of Ginto's wife and the disappearance of their daughter, Benjie had refused to leave his father's side. The horror was too much for the eight-year-old, and he often lay motionless on the dirt floor of their hut, as if imitating death. Little seemed to lift the almost permanent haze that clouded the boy's eyes, and at times Ginto was sure he was losing his son to madness.

The boom of distant explosions pulled Ginto's focus briefly from the road ahead. When his gaze again flicked forward, he saw that a man was standing in the pathway. A submachine gun waved in the air, motioning the vehicle to stop. Ginto grabbed Benjie and pushed him frantically to the floorboards while struggling to slow the lumbering truck. The gunman leaped backward, swallowed by the foliage as the shuddering vehicle bounced past the spot where he'd stood.

Quickly reappearing, the shouting soldier raced forward, banging on the driver's door. Ginto clambered down from the cab, his shaved head bowed. He stuttered, trying to explain as the strike from the gun butt caught him on the side of the neck. He dropped to one knee, his hands raised in a vain attempt to protect himself from the blows that followed.

NINETY feet to the south, hemmed in by jungle on three sides, Prince Takeda's tent rested in a forty-foot-wide clearing, visible only from the sharp, desolate peaks of the surrounding mountaintops. Under camouflage canvas, the prince gazed up from his diary. He leaned back in his chair before crossing white-uniformed arms over an ample belly. Adjusting his slim, round spectacles, he motioned slightly with a flick of his wrist. The lieutenant, standing nearby, ran and knelt before the chair.

The prince spoke in a gentle but authoritative voice. "See that those men get moving. We have very little time to finish this operation, and the cargo needs to be inside the cave."

"Yes, Your Highness. And when I return, shall I secure the official map and inventory list?"

"No . . . that won't be necessary this time."

Lieutenant Tetsuo Endo's downcast face edged up, registering confusion and surprise.

"Did you misunderstand?" Prince Takeda flared his nostrils. "I said, 'not this time.'"

As the lieutenant rose and began to turn, the prince spoke again. "And make sure the truck driver is with the others when everything is complete."

"Yes." The lieutenant stole a brief glimpse of the prince's dark brown eyes before he bowed again. Exiting hastily, he cut across the muddy, open ground.

For a man of royal stature, the prince could on occasion show extraordinary kindness, but this was not one of those moments. With the Allied army advancing throughout the Philippines, time was quickly running out. He reflected that the emperor would not reward failure, even from a favored cousin. For three years, the prince had spent his life in these jungles, scouting for locations and overseeing construction. It all came down to completing the final tasks just hours ahead of the enemy.

The epic 1942 battles of Midway and Guadalcanal had turned the tide of World War II in the Pacific. Now, two and a half years later, the few weakened Japanese troops led by General Yamashita were sacrificing themselves to slow the Allies' progress. But the enemy forces were too strong, and the area would soon fall into American hands.

BROKEN slivers of moonlight reflected off the scattered pools of water that had formed in the open earth. The lieutenant cursed the mud as he marched toward the truck. Drawing closer, he motioned. "Soldier, get back to your post. And you!" He pointed at Ginto, who was rising from the sludge. "Get this truck inside!"

Ginto stared over the officer's shoulder at a cavernous opening in the mountain's rock wall. The dimly lit entrance appeared large enough to swallow two trucks. Shadowy figures moved around the breach; their voices were barely discernible against the explosions from the village over the ridge.

Lieutenant Endo moved closer and drew his handgun, pressing it to Ginto's chest. "Are you going to drive, or do I have to do it for you?" he bellowed.

"No, no, I'm very sorry. Yes, right away," Ginto said as he backed away, trembling, bent at the waist. Turning, he scrambled into the truck's cab, closing the door with great haste.

PRINCE Takeda watched with satisfaction as the truck finally rolled into motion. It would be his honor to seal the last of the hiding places before making his escape. Suspended in the deep blue waters of the nearby Pacific Ocean, an I-55 submarine waited silently, ready to surface at the appointed hour.

He glanced at the final tan-colored map lying on the desktop before folding it between the pages of his diary. There was no need to pass this one on—he would keep it to himself. He retrieved his chocolate brown satchel; a golden sixteen-petal royal chrysanthemum, the size of a palm, was clearly embossed on both front and back. While packing away the inventory list, he ran his hands over the corners of the Italian leather satchel and thought of how pleasurable it would be to soak once again in the steaming pools of Hakone and feel the chill of *sake* sliding down his throat. Nearly three years of drawing maps and digging holes was enough. The emperor should let him rest.

Lieutenant Endo returned and began to stomp the mud from his boots. Following the noise, the prince turned and stared blankly. "Why are you not supervising the unloading of that truck?"

"My post is to provide guard for Your Highness."

Smooth voiced, the prince replied, "No, your post is to do as I ask, and my instruction was to get that truck unloaded. We are behind schedule and your boots can wait. I need the bags from that truck placed along the entrance walls. Once you are done, bring it here and load this tent for immediate departure. Is that clear?"

"Yes, Your Highness," Lieutenant Endo turned and splashed toward the cave.

FROM within the truck's cab, Benjie peered cautiously over the edge of the driver's side window. Outside, his father was laboring along with several soldiers, carrying sacks from the truck bed in order to pile them along the inner walls of the rocky entrance. He could feel the ache in his stomach as he turned to look through the front windshield at the tunnel stretching deep into the cave. The lone overhead bulb did little to illuminate the cavernous darkness, yet he could still see the outline of crates stacked deep inside.

Suddenly a green jacket covered the driver's side window. An officer had leaped onto the sideboard, shouting orders. Benjie slithered quickly onto the floor near the passenger's door. The memory of soldiers standing over his mother's lifeless body flooded his mind and his breathing became rapid. He wrapped his arms around his bare knees, shivering involuntarily. The officer's head moved from side to side and each time it did, Benjie was sure the man would turn and look directly at him. With a groaning whimper, he willed himself to slide up and crack open the passenger's door. Gripping the seat, he inched out and slipped to the ground before dashing into the tunnel.

Pressing himself against the rock wall, he drew closer to the back of the cave, his eyes adjusting to the darkness. Ahead, beyond the crates, a group of more than twenty seated men were bound. He didn't know if they were alive or dead until one man lifted his head and cried out. A nearby soldier hammered the butt of his rifle, breaking bone, and a shriek of pain rose then faded.

Staying low to the ground, he turned back toward the entrance, his body quivering. Four more men were entering the cave. They were struggling to carry a box the size of a small casket. Swaying in a side-to-side motion, their cargo hung from slings of webbing gathered over their hunched shoulders. As the men entered the darkness, they passed the spot where he lay frozen.

Without warning, one of the men stumbled on a rock and collapsed. The box's impact on the cave floor sprung the lid open, and the contents tumbled into the dirt. Benjie's eyes widened, transfixed at the astonishing sight.

Cursing loudly, the men shouted for assistance from the nearby guard.

The commotion provided cover to turn and dart back the way he'd come. As he neared the truck, Benjie watched his father drop the last sack into place while the officer in the green jacket stepped down from the truck's sideboard and grasped his bare arm. The man waved toward the dark end of the passage, but his words were drowned by the truck's engine roaring as it backed from the cave.

Benjie watched silently while his protesting father was forced past him, deeper into the cave. He wanted to shout and run into his papa's arms but fearing a scolding, he remained invisible.

Soon, the soldiers near the entrance moved outside and Benjie followed, cautiously drawing close to the mouth of the cave. The men appeared busy, so with his heart pounding, he raced out, running south along the outer slope of the mountain, stopping only when shielded by the leaves of a low-lying fern. Crouching in the darkness, he watched the entrance, awaiting his father's return.

Mere moments passed before the green-jacketed man exited the cave—

alone. He began rolling lines of wire toward the roadway leading into the jungle. Approaching a man in a white suit, he bowed low before handing over a device attached to the wires' end. Together, accompanied by the far-off sound of explosions, the two men disappeared behind the truck.

Seconds later the ground shook, and flames roared from the cave's mouth. A plume of thick dust choked the air as the roof and sides of the opening collapsed into a heap of jagged rubble.

Benjie screamed and stumbled backward, throwing up his arms to protect his head from the debris raining down. He strained to see the cave through the smoke, but only a jumble of rock lay where the entrance had once been. His only thought was that he would be left behind in the frightening jungle.

The noise of revving engines drew his attention. Across the clearing, the truck and a black, six-wheeled touring car began to depart. Benjie sprang from his hiding place. Muddy water splashed his legs and arms. He ran forward, screaming, "Papa . . . *Papa!* . . . I'm here! Don't leave me! PAAAAPAAAA!"

Brakes squealed and canvas flaps flew open as half a dozen soldiers sprang from the truck bed with guns drawn. Desperately trying to stop, Benjie slipped and fell in the mud. The first man caught him easily and pinned his face down before dragging him to his feet. "Prince Takeda will want to speak with you."

Climbing from the touring car, the prince held a silk scarf to his face and waited while the soldiers returned.

Benjie cowered with his head down, nostrils frothing with mud, tears pouring from his eyes, as Prince Takeda bent slightly forward. "Did your father drive you here in this truck?"

The boy nodded yes as the prince placed a finger under his chin and lifted his grimy head, forcing Benjie to meet his stare. "Do you know where we are?"

"No." He sniffed, shuddering.

"You are a brave boy—in the jungle all alone." Prince Takeda addressed the nearest soldier. "Clean him quickly and put him with me in the car."

"Where's my papa?" Benjie cried out, afraid to gaze again into the dark, piercing eyes.

The prince stared down with a wry smile on his face. "Guarding the emperor's things," he said.

CHAPTER ONE

Thursday, April 19, 2007

F LAMES OF brilliant orange daylight burned through the morning haze and came to rest on the timeless sprawl of Tokyo. Reflected beams of light swept across the towering glass skylines of the former sixteenth-century castle town, working their way into the maze of streets and narrow alleyways below. The low nocturnal hum of dawn gave way to the buzz of daytime as the city woke from another brief sleep.

Max Travers cracked open a groggy eye and peered at his Westclox pocket watch. Despite its age, his grandfather's battered timepiece had proven remarkably reliable. He rolled from his futon before stumbling five steps to the closet-sized bathroom of his dilapidated wooden share house. A handful of cold water smoothed the bed-head hair over his forehead and ears as he hurried back to his room. Pulling on jeans, Skechers, an untucked button-down, and grabbing his briefcase and Hollister hoodie, he charged down creaky stairs and out the front door. Heading for the Sugamo station on foot, he picked up his pace to a near run. Timed to the minute, he would catch the next train, meet his girlfriend, and arrive promptly at his English lesson.

Two schoolgirls walking past him giggled and whispered as they pointed. Even after a year of living in Tokyo, Max was still caught off guard by how shocked some Japanese were to see his sandy blond hair and clear blue eyes.

A lean, six-foot frame also made him stand out from the crowd. But being gawked at was still annoying, especially since there were so many foreigners living in the city.

Such status had once seemed amusing, but the unusual treatment wore thin within the first few months. Max heard it best described as Exotic Pet Syndrome—when befriended by someone, you could never be sure of their motivation for wanting to know you. The few people he trusted belonged to the eclectic group in the foreigners' house he called home.

Known affectionately as the Tokyo Poor House, or TPH, it was a cultural blender of five people, sometimes more, in four cramped bedrooms on a little side street in Kita-Otsuka. The two-story wooden structure was wrapped in unpainted wooden shingles, and its slowly rotting timbers caused it to lean heavily to one side. By all appearances, it was one of the few buildings that had miraculously survived the World War II fire bombings. Inside, the house was no better—the musty smell was overwhelming. But foreigners came and went in rotating cycles, so little care was taken of the place. Most of the furniture had been plucked from the garbage. A spray-painted Christmas tree decorated one of the panel-board walls in the cramped second-floor living room. The closet-sized kitchen was a haven for crawling life. Roach traps left overnight were always filled by morning.

Max paused at a mailbox and deposited an envelope. The international money order addressed to his mother was meant to arrive before the first of the month, the same as always. A bit of frugality was required on his part, but at least he could be sure her rent was covered.

Checking for traffic, he crossed from the side street onto a wider roadway. A stretch of cherry trees, just beginning to show their pink buds, ran down the lane parallel to the train tracks nestled in the concrete ravine below.

Eventually reaching the main street, he dashed across the wide stripes of the intersection crosswalk and entered the brown-tiled Sugamo train station. He fought through the crowd of people inside before nodding to the attendant at the turnstiles. The uniformed man was obviously bored, staring blankly into space.

I know how you feel, buddy. I was headed for a lifetime of boredom myself.

Max raced down the stairs to the platform of the Japan Rail Yamanote train line with a full two minutes to spare. Putting on his hoodie against the cool April breeze, he thought back to the day, almost a year before, when he'd made the snap decision to leave his dead-end job. Junior college was meant to ensure a better life, but it hadn't really worked out. The best accounting jobs went to the CPAs, with their pinstriped suits and smug attitudes. The scraps were thrown to the less educated dogs. Even now, Max liked to savor the memory of "D-Day," as he called it.

That day, just like so many others, he had navigated a sea of identical beige cubicles, while nameless coworkers stared blankly at glowing screens. Slipping off a corduroy sports jacket, he unconsciously moved to hang it on his chair back. But this time his hand refused, as if it had a will of its own. Instead, he paused to look at the humble brown desk with its neat piles of paper, and a thought rose up, a familiar notion that amplified and thundered and refused to be silenced any longer. *There's gotta be more to my life than this!*

Typing the resignation letter took all of five minutes.

Three weeks later, he was living in Tokyo.

THE flashing blur of the green railway car snapped Max from his thoughts. As the train slowed to a stop, crowds of people formed on either side of the sliding doors, waiting to pour into the space left behind by those exiting. He lined up behind a half-dozen businessmen and a slender Shinto priest.

Three gangly teenagers cascaded from the train. Dressed in khaki army pants and torn black shirts, they sported a surplus of facial piercings topped with impossibly spiked hair.

Oh man, not these guys again. The punks seemed to have nothing better to do than loiter aimlessly near the station's entrance, mocking passersby and dispensing trouble.

The leader of the group veered sharply to the right, hammering Max's chest, spinning him backward into the side of the train. The youth sneered aloud, *"Ira-ki mu-ru-der!"* and stood defiantly with his snickering entourage.

Max rubbed his aching sternum as adrenaline and anger rushed to his limbs. He stiffened, momentarily bracing for a brawl, but three against one was lousy odds. It was clearly best to back down and turn the other cheek. He wished he could be braver for once and stand up to them. But this wasn't his country and dealing with them wasn't his battle.

The punk's threatening movements were unexpectedly cut short by the billowing robes of the nearby priest who inserted himself with a flourish into the conflict's center. The man's sharp voice and raised hands drove the group into a hasty retreat before he turned and vanished into the train. Since nothing other than his pride seemed damaged, Max followed suit, withdrawing to the safety of the car's interior before exhaling loudly.

Glancing down the length of the car, he noticed all eyes staring at him—the trouble-making foreigner. The only available seat was next to the Shinto priest, and Max took it quickly, squeezing his briefcase between his feet as he sat down.

The priest appeared to be thirty years old at most, and his calm demeanor offered an aura of peace that defied his youthful age. Black layered robes covered him, except for a hint of white at the V-neck collar and the tightly bound cloth around his wrists. His slender face sported a thin beard running downward from the bottom of his lower lip and extending out along his chin, like an inverted *T*.

The train's soft female voice floated into the air—"*Doa ga shimarimasu. Go chui kudasai*"—before switching smoothly to English. "The door is closing. Please be careful." The doors rolled shut and the train shuddered into motion.

Max waited a moment, unsure whether he would embarrass the man by directly acknowledging the intervention. But the opportunity to interact with a priest proved irresistible, and he followed tradition, bowing his head while expressing his gratitude. "*Domo arigato.*"

"You're welcome. I am sorry for those boys." The priest responded in a clear English voice. "You are American?" He pocketed a Nintendo DS into the folds of his robe, while a wooden string of prayer beads remained clutched in his right hand.

Max was impressed by the near-perfect intonation. "Yeah, I'm from California."

"Aaaah," the priest said knowingly. "Where did you grow up?"

"I . . ." The guy seemed uncharacteristically straightforward for a Japanese—perhaps a common trait of religious figures—but Max wasn't about to reveal to a stranger that he had spent his childhood shuttling between a dozen towns and cities. "I lived in L.A."

"I went there once, while attending school in San Francisco." The priest pressed his palms together as he spoke. "My name is Toshi."

Max knew the routine of questions that would follow. It was always the same: *What do you think of Japan? Are you an English teacher? Do you speak Japanese?* Even so, he chose to play along. Meeting an English speaking Shinto

10

priest was a rare opportunity indeed.

The twenty-six-minute ride passed swiftly. Finally, Toshi stood as the train slowed on the approach to Hamamatsucho station, and Max couldn't help but feel a twinge of disappointment. "My English school is just one more stop," he noted casually. "Do you work around here?"

"No. This is where I live." Toshi leaned against a pole to brace himself. "Please come visit me anytime." As the train ground to a halt, he bowed and held out a black business card with both hands.

While accepting the card, Max caught a brief glimpse of the priest's pinkie ring, the prayer beads having covered it until now. The rapid movement made it difficult to clearly discern, but the image was of multiple gleaming petals, like those of a golden flower.

The priest vanished into the swirling bustle of the platform's crowd, accompanied by the soothing female voice announcing the train's departure.

Soon, the station disappeared into the distance while Max stared at the embossed lettering on the card—Suzuco Games—and the map to Toshi's house on the back.

CHAPTER
TWO

I T WASN'T really an English lesson, but Takahito Murayama knew it was
supposed to be. At least that's how the Thursday meetings with Max had
begun nine months earlier. They were located at his office on the third floor
of a narrow five-story building squeezed between two other structures of
equally slim proportion. Built in the late 1970s and situated in Tokyo's Minato
ward, the brown tile exterior was frosted with big-city grime. The Plum Tree
Restaurant occupied the ground floor. A cramped staircase leading to the
floors above could only be accessed with a nod to the building's owner, who sat
entrenched at an outdoor table. The laconic man was surly at best. Unshaven,
he smoked an endless chain of non-filtered cigarettes while consuming a
bottomless cup of green tea.

The first few lessons had been filled with quiet tension, despite
reassurance that Max was the best teacher at his school. Mr. Murayama had
decided beforehand that he wouldn't cooperate with the young American,
who he assumed would be overly talkative, poorly educated, and vastly
overconfident. He didn't care that his daughter, Yoko, had insisted he keep up
his linguistic skills, even at ninety years old. Her mask of concern only served
to remind him that she simply wanted him out of the way. Her English school
was transforming into a corporation, and she didn't appreciate his meddling.

She told him the language training would keep him sharp, and she was not a woman to take no for an answer.

At their introductory meeting, Mr. Murayama had made a point to sit with arms folded and a dour look on his wrinkled face. However, surprisingly, the boy was not at all as he had presumed. In fact, Max was bright and articulate, with a great interest in history and an even greater number of questions. His infectious curiosity about Japan's past—the Glorious Empire—grew on the old man, who now looked forward to the Thursday meetings. It was a time to relive old victories and remember friends and places long since gone.

Setting down his pen, he ran his fingers along the latest entry in his personal catalog. Goose bumps prickled his aging arms. A sweet and familiar sense of satisfaction rushed down his back. Gathering rare and beautiful artifacts had been a childhood hobby that had grown into a full-time passion. The addition of new possessions never lost its youthful thrill. Unable to resist temptation, he flipped the pages backward before his eyes came to rest, yet again, on the most significant entry—all those years ago.

The diary—when I'm gone the world will finally know its truths.

He shuddered and slammed the catalog shut.

Rising from the desk, he shuffled into the hallway, turning left toward the kitchen, intent on setting the kettle. From the window of what had been the secretary's office, he watched the buzz of traffic along the two-laned street below. Soon, the steaming whistle caught his attention. After pouring water and adjusting his black, square-framed glasses, he opened a hidden door. With a firm grip on the tea tray, he shuffled his slippers back into the office sanctuary.

Faded cherry-wood paneling and an assortment of filing cabinets framed the room. Cavernous by Japanese standards, the office was thirty-five feet deep and twenty feet wide. Near the front, a black leather sofa and two matching chairs huddled around a wooden coffee table, set before a row of street-side windows. Several feet back, in the center of the room sat a gray metal desk, buried beneath an avalanche of loose paper. Behind the desk was a waist-high beige drafting cabinet, while on the side wall opposite the hallway door, the years of his distinguished diplomatic service were displayed in hundreds of pictures hung above an unbroken row of two-drawer cabinets.

Setting down the tray, Mr. Murayama lowered himself slowly into the first of the soft leather chairs. It wouldn't be long, he thought, before his slippers stopped bringing him to this office, which had been his shelter for twenty years, since the end of his career.

Looking up, he let his gaze roam over the long wall, and he wondered what would eventually become of the many framed pictures. He considered all the treasures filling this office and the storage room at the far end of the hall. They were overflowing with artifacts he'd gathered. Once he was gone, Yoko would take the art prints in the drafting cabinet, but she would throw away or sell the rest. She moved too quickly, wanted too much, and didn't know the true value that the past could hold. That's why he kept the key ring to himself. Even if Yoko was in her mid-sixties, he could still see in her the same little girl, desperately trying to prove herself superior.

A picture on the end table caught his eye, taken in 1961, during his first posting to Washington, D.C.. Distant memories sometimes felt more real than the present, and at other times they drifted away like smoke in the wind.

There I am, and the man next to me is . . . who is he?

A wave of panic washed over him.

I'm already losing my body—please don't let me lose my mind.

He commanded himself to remain calm.

Focus! Pull all the pieces together before trying to solve it.

He let his mind's eye wander back to the Georgetown house on Reservoir Road. Lush trees surrounded the three-story light-brick federal-style home. A cocktail party was underway and he was standing on the grass. The wife of a guest appeared with a camera and asked the three men to cluster together. She asked the banker to move to the group's center.

That's right. The man was the chairman of a bank, a Rockefeller, perhaps. The other man, with the mole above his lip, is Kazue Saito—my old friend's protégé.

Silently, Mr. Murayama congratulated himself on piecing together the puzzle and once again defying the relentless hands of time.

CHAPTER THREE

ACROSS TOWN, Kazue Saito took a single step into the green park space. He paused to adjust his Burberry coat and black-brimmed hat. Only his skittish eyes roamed above the white surgical mask covering his face. He didn't have a cold.

On the sidewalk behind him, the intermittent flow of office workers increased as the clock drew toward noon. To the east stood a cluster of sparkling white pine trees belonging to a nearby shrine. Finger-sized fortune papers were wrapped around the protruding limbs, as if coating them in a thick blanket of hoar frost. Sacred wishes for money, health, happiness, long life, and true love covered every branch, twig, and bud.

Today, at last, Kazue felt that his prayers would finally be answered. Living on a pension was agony, and now the suffocating burden of his gambling debt would be lifted. He knew it was wrong to offer the secrets for sale. They weren't really his to sell, after all. But constant threats from the loan sharks overrode reason, forcing him to post the "For Sale" item on the Internet.

It didn't take long to receive a bite. The reply simply gave a time and place, along with instructions to look for a single tree branch. The cryptic nature of the message indicated it was likely mafia—the *Yakuza*—but he was past the point of caring. His life needed to change.

Kazue glanced at the lone oak in the center of the park, not thirty feet away, and then he saw it. Sunlight flashed on the single strip of white tied to one branch of the otherwise barren tree. Rushing forward, he sent a dozen gurgling pigeons flapping upward. He glanced around nervously as he untied the message—a job usually reserved only for priests. The message within held a phone number and his whole body shook as he dialed it.

A female receptionist confirmed his internet post before forwarding the call to a gruff voice that answered on the second ring. "Oto Kodama here."

He knew the *Yakuza* leader's name from the media. The aging man was reputed to be ruthless and sadistic, and the timid words stuck in Kazue's throat. "Y . . . You left me a message on a tree."

"The book I've been searching for? Do you have it with you?"

"No . . . not exactly, but I have information on where you can get it. It is easily obtainable."

"Meet me tonight—11:30 p.m.—at the shrine of the honorable dead. You get half the money when you deliver this information, and the other half when I have the book."

The loan sharks would want all their money, half was unacceptable "But I need the full amount."

Kodama shouted, "My way, or there is no deal. Am I clear?"

"Y . . . Yes."

The connection went cold.

THE *Yakuza*'s youthful eyes watched from behind the bushes ringing the park. Like the lethal gaze of a tiger stalking skittish prey, they followed Kazue Saito as he hurried back toward the sidewalk. A primal grunt of anticipation escaped the hunter's thick lips. Cigarette smoke curled slowly from each of his nostrils.

CHAPTER
FOUR

D ASHING FROM the train station exit, Max scanned the bustling crowd in the concrete plaza below. Finally spotting her, he made his way down to street level. Tomoko had happened onto his school just five months earlier, and when Max had first made eye contact, it was all he could do to speak his native tongue. Her slender five-foot-nine-inch frame was taller than the average Japanese woman, and her long, straight black hair fell halfway down her back. She didn't carry herself in the typically demure Japanese manner, but with an uncommon grace and self-assurance. Most of all, what had attracted him was her striking smile and her nontraditional manner of refusing to cover her mouth when she laughed. She was seeking the nuance of the English language. Tomoko's marketing position with Ralph Lauren's Polo brand demanded it.

She was leaning against a wall, waiting, giving him a familiar look that told him he was pushing his luck being late. As he neared, she called out, "Did you go drinking last night? Or is there another woman I should know about?"

Max stopped just short of her and waggled his eyebrows in jest. "Hey, a guy's gotta keep his options open."

"You better not!" She swung her purse playfully at his shoulder and he ducked sideways, laughing, before grabbing her in his arms to kiss her.

"You look amazing." He caught the scent of honey in her hair.

"Yes, I do." She grinned. "But don't try to . . . *nande-ke?* What's the phrase? Butter me up."

He couldn't hold back a playful grin. "I'm shocked you think I would try."

Tomoko laughed. "I think you're playing me?"

He rested his forehead briefly against hers. "Mr. M is gonna love meeting you. Come on—we need to get moving." He draped an arm across her shoulders, directing them toward the street's endless grinding traffic.

"Max, wait." Her face grew serious as her steps slowed them. "There's something important I have to tell you."

Tomoko was remarkable; more so then any of the handful of girls he'd dated. Maybe he had pushed his luck too far, after all. Maybe she'd finally caught on that he wasn't in her league. He tried to appear calm. "Okay. What is it?"

She leaned in close to his ear. "The front of your jeans is open."

Tomoko giggled as his briefcase hit the ground. He glanced around self-consciously, thankful that nobody seemed to be watching. "Damn. I got dressed so quickly." His face felt flush. "I thought everyone was staring at me because I'm *Gaijin*." He closed the offending fastener and bent down to recover his fallen briefcase.

"Give yourself a break. You don't need to always try to be perfect." As he rose back up, Tomoko stepped in close, pressing herself into him. "I like you just the way you are."

"Really?" He was unsure if she was simply teasing him. "You sure?"

"Yes." She swept away the loose blond hair covering his eyes. "Perfection is boring."

"Well, if that's the case. Hmmm . . ." He playfully tapped an index finger across both lips as if contemplating a deep thought. "I could just 'fly low' all the time."

"No." She laughed gently and pulled at his arm. "Come on. You're right—there's not much time. We need to hurry."

MAX knocked loudly before opening the office door precisely at noon. Sidestepping through the entrance, he moved to the exposed back of the sofa. "Good to see you, Mr. Murayama," he said with a respectful bow of his head.

"Sit down, my boy." The older man waved for him to take his regular seat, facing the street-side windows.

"Well . . ." Max lowered his blue eyes, then shot a self-conscious look back over his shoulder toward the partially open door. He could clearly see Tomoko's outline through the frosted safety glass. The English class rules were few, but privacy topped the list.

Mr. Murayama squinted in the direction of Max's gaze and his voice sparked. "Who is that?"

Seeing the flash of anger, Max spoke quickly. "I know you like the afternoon to just be us, but my girlfriend really wanted to meet you. It won't take long, I promise."

Pausing as if to allow the flattery to sink in, Takahito Murayama adjusted his cardigan before nodding. "If only for a minute, then please invite her in."

Max opened the door to the narrow hallway, and Tomoko stepped inside. She was dressed casually in jeans and a long-sleeved top, and her shimmering hair cascaded forward from her shoulders as she bowed low from the waist. "Murayama-*sensei*, it's an honor to finally meet you."

"She can only stay for a minute," Max interjected. "She's off to Hokkaido this afternoon."

From his seated position, the old man watched with interest; Max could see he was captivated by her beauty. "I love the North Island. Wonderful place."

"I've heard the same," she replied, "but it's all work."

Max took Tomoko's hand, guiding her forward to the long wall of photos. He spoke over his right shoulder. "I mentioned all your amazing pictures."

Tomoko moved from photo to photo, floating her slender fingers over them without touching. "Amazing," she exclaimed. "There are so many famous people. This is the White House . . . and . . . that's you with Ronald Reagan!"

Mr. Murayama beamed. "Yes. That was during my second posting to the Washington Embassy."

"How did you get so many?"

"During a thirty-year career, there are plenty of meetings and dinners." His old eyes watched her examine the photos with keen interest before he spoke again. "Which do you think is my favorite?"

Tomoko looked taken aback. "I don't know how I could guess that."

Mr. Murayama's face took on a mischievous grin. "I think you can. Take some time." He pointed a bony finger at Max. "And you—no helping her."

Tomoko looked at Max, who shrugged, then perched himself against the edge of the desk in the center of the room. She turned and slowly walked back and forth along the length of the wall. Several minutes of focused attention passed before she finally stopped at the room's far end, with the drafting cabinet at her back. "It's this one," she said confidently, pointing to a simple matted photo in a slim copper frame.

Mr. Murayama leaned forward, serious. "Why do you think?"

Max perked up. "Yeah, why?"

"This copper frame has changed color only on the side edges—the two spots are the size of thumb prints. I think this picture has been held many times." She paused, seeking confirmation. "Am I right?"

Mr. Murayama clapped his appreciation. "Very well done." He let out an audible sigh. "Yes, that photo of John F. Kennedy—" He stopped speaking, appearing to catch himself in what he was about to say. "—JFK was a good man."

Tomoko beamed and laughed before glancing at her watch. She returned to Max's side. "I'm sorry, but I have much to do before my flight. *Domo arigato*, Mr. Murayama, for your time."

"You're welcome. Next time please give a warning, so I can prepare three cups of tea." He shot Max a look.

She ran a hand along Max's face while whispering, "I see why you like him so much." Seeming uncertain how to act, given the setting, her thumb stopped to rest in the dimple on his chin as she placed a light kiss on his cheek. "See you soon."

"*Trunk-u hitotsu dake de,*" Max whispered back, cupping her elbow tenderly in his hand. Even though only the two of them knew the meaning, Tomoko blushed slightly. The phrase "with a single trunk" was from the song "Romantic Airplane." Soon after they'd met, he had spent a maddening week memorizing the Japanese words. One night at a karaoke club he had calmed himself, swallowed his pride, and taken the microphone for the very first time. Much to Tomoko's delight, he dedicated the performance to her. A foreigner covering a local song was unheard of, and although he missed most of the notes and a few of the words, the bar went crazy with applause. Ever since, it had been their song.

Neither man spoke until they heard Tomoko's footsteps begin the descent down the stairwell.

"You never told me," Mr. Murayama stated while he poured tea into the two cups.

Max dropped onto the center of the sofa. "Never told you what?"

"How beautiful she is."

"Really? I'm sure I mentioned it. I didn't mean to upset you by bringing her."

"No need to worry. Let's move on. I have something very personal to show you today." Mr. Murayama reached into the breast pocket of his suit jacket and withdrew a series of interlaced rings laden with dozens of keys. His shaking fingers leafed through them. "And since I have seen you carry one, I am sure you'll find the items interesting." At last he selected a key. Handing over the ring, he gave Max instructions to go to the wall at the far end of the room, to the second of the five tall cabinets. "In the bottom drawer, you'll find a wooden box. Bring it here."

"No more rifles please." Max recalled their previous class with an uneasy chuckle. An accidental discharge of gunpowder had made his ears ring and sent him ducking for cover.

"No, no. They were returned to the bank's vault."

Max quickly located the cabinet, thinking how incredibly satisfying it must feel to have gathered so many artifacts over the years. Murayama had a life well lived. Already Max had seen dozens of samurai swords, stacks of ancient scrolls, and crates of marvelous wood-block prints. And yet they had barely scratched the museum-like storage room in the building's back room.

The requested drawer slid open easily, revealing the dark polished box. "I can see it."

"Me, too." Mr. Murayama sighed. "Finally, I can see why you were brought to me."

"Huh?" Max was down on one knee, trying to figure the best way to retrieve the tight-fitting box without damaging it. "What is that supposed to mean?"

Mr. Murayama replied. "Just keep the box flat."

Max thought the comment odd but let it pass, choosing instead to listen to the old man's raspy cough, which seemed to be growing more persistent lately. "Why? What's in here?"

"Something I've wanted to show you for a while . . . and . . . I have a favor to ask."

Max played along, amused by the old man's desire to begin each session with a sense of mystery, noting that it was a small price to pay for something that clearly provided a great deal of joy. He returned to the front of the room. "Are you sure you're okay?"

Mr. Murayama nodded silently as the box came to rest on the coffee table. The wooden case was a perfect cube, one foot square. An inch-wide light wood inlay decorated the perimeter of the top, while the center was the same dark wood as the rest of the box. He slid his handkerchief into a pocket as he shifted forward, studying the box before moving it one-quarter turn. Then he pressed the inlay four times in a clockwise motion, starting with the right side. On the fourth push, the dark center of the top made a light popping noise and rose slightly. Grunting with satisfaction, he removed the lid.

"How did you know which side to press first?" Max examined the box closely, but each side of the inlay appeared identical.

"If I told you, then I wouldn't have any more secrets, would I?"

Max sat back with arms folded. He had learned that the silent treatment was the best and only way to pressure an aging diplomat.

Mr. Murayama relented as expected. "All right. All right. In the game of Mahjong, there are tiles representing the four winds. The East wind always goes first. To open this box, the single thing that matters is for East to go first, then South, then West, and last, North."

"Then why'd you turn the box once before pressing down the first time?"

"To appear more complicated."

Max laughed.

Mr. Murayama's self-satisfied grin washed away as he lifted a crimson velvet cover, revealing a tray of antique pocket watches. He selected a shiny silver timepiece and lifted it tenderly from its resting place before handing it over.

"Like my grandpa's . . . " Max examined it carefully. The script on the back was similar to the calligraphy used throughout Japan. The difference was the extensive use of circles in many of the symbols. "I don't recognize the writing. What language is it?"

"Set that one down on the cloth. Here is a beautiful one."

Together they reviewed the contents of each tray in the box, and soon more than twenty timepieces covered the table. Finally, Mr. Murayama lifted out the last tray, revealing the lowest level in the box. "Here is the most special one. Notice the pearl dragon behind the hands."

The fine gold metalwork was stunning, and the inlaid design was vibrant with colors and intricate detail. Max took the antique in both hands. The mysterious language etched into the gold back appeared similar to many of the other watches on the table. He looked up to address his unanswered question and was surprised to see the old man wiping tears from his eyes. "Are you all right?"

Mr. Murayama nodded but seemed choked with emotion. He struggled to retrieve the handkerchief from his pocket. "I have something to tell you." Pausing, he blew his nose. "I received these during the war. They are Filipino or Korean, some Chinese."

A distinct feeling of unease settled over Max and he squirmed in his seat, praying that the moment would fade quickly.

Mr. Murayama's shaky voice continued. "I thought it was important to have them." His drooping eyes appeared to transport him backward in time. "Many years ago, I served in Manila . . . the Philippines, during World War Two. Many terrible things happened—it was war." He paused again, lost in thought.

The mantelpiece clock ticked steadily on the nearby desk, seeming to grow louder with each passing second. "When people wanted things done, they gave me gifts—I could get papers signed by the Admiral's Office. I don't know where the gifts came from. But I'm sure they weren't purchased. Do you understand what I mean?"

Shifting restlessly and nodding his head, Max dared to speak. "So, why are you telling me?"

"I won't be around forever, and these watches should go back to the families they were stolen from. Everything I have spent my life gathering will be passed to museums when I die, but this one task must be done sooner than that, by someone I trust. I need some peace of mind before I go." An uncomfortable silence descended on them, blanketing the room.

Mr. Murayama's pleading eyes flicked upward, drilling into Max. "I want you to return them."

CHAPTER
FIVE

I N THE darkness, retired diplomat Kazue Saito ran across the open stone courtyard of the Yasukuni Shrine. A sliver of moonlight cut the sky. Passing beneath the Torii Gate, he could make out the broad open doors of the Great Gate just ahead. The late hour meant that the lone guard was asleep at his post. Saito and his attacker were the only two awake in the shrine's compound.

Glancing backward as he fled, Saito tore the white medical mask from his face and wiped the trickle of blood at the corner of his mouth. Behind him, illuminated, he could see the white exterior curtain of the Hall of Worship skirting the arching rooftop jutting into the black sky. Below its wooden eaves, facing the open hall, stood his attacker —revealed only as Jun— in silhouette with head bowed as if in silent prayer.

Drawing closer to the Great Gate, Saito chanced another glimpse backward. What a terrible mistake, he thought as his burning lungs urged him to rest. *I should never have tried to sell the diary to the mafia.* To his horror, he saw that the attacker was now striding in pursuit. At sixty-eight, he was no match for the speed of the shadowy figure approaching.

The man was right behind him now. He was broad-shouldered with a shaved head, and his deep voice carried easily in the thin night air. "You promised information. Where is it?"

"I told you . . ." the former diplomat wheezed, "I need the money first. Please!"

"Your price is too high, Mr. Saito, but you will give me what I want." Drawing closer still, the burly attacker pulled a *Surujin* chain from inside his leather jacket. On one end was a round metal orb the size of a baseball. Swinging the chain in a circular motion, he launched it toward Saito. The weighted end wrapped swiftly around the older man's neck, then back around the chain itself. Jun yanked backward abruptly. Saito's feet shot outward, and he shrieked in pain before striking the hard ground.

Saito felt a massive hand grasp his trench coat by the collar. He was dragged to the edge of the wide stone causeway before being propped into a sitting position beneath the golden chrysanthemum set high on the Great Gate. Crouching, the younger man leaned in close so that his foul breath was only inches away. "I want the information you agreed to give to my Father."

Saito stared at the jagged scar running down the right side of the man's face from the outer edge of his eye to his lip. "Oto said he would meet me. He said he'd give me money . . . I need the money." Saito coughed violently and rubbed at his throat.

"Things have changed." A rigid finger poked Saito hard in the forehead. "Tell me what I want to know, and you might live. That's the new deal."

"Please, can we speak with your master?"

The young *Yakuza* scowled and then sprang to his feet. Grabbing Saito's trench coat, he again dragged the kicking diplomat over the rough stone until they were well behind the Sacred Water Basin.

Jun paced back and forth, making grunting noises. He bounced the weighted end of the *Surujin* chain in one palm while fingering the heavy silver links with his other hand. The bladed end of the chain swung free.

Saito realized with a sickening sense of dread that there would be no reasoning with the *Yakuza*. He fumbled to open his coat and pulled a business card from his breast pocket. Rolling onto his back, he held it in the air with a trembling hand. "Murayama . . . is the man who holds what you're looking for."

Jun turned and snatched the prize from the outstretched arm, then caught the chain's bladed end and plunged the attached knife into the center of the diplomat's chest. Saito's eyes shot open, and a look of confused horror crossed his face as he lay dying on the ancient stones.

Appearing almost gleeful, Jun's mouth mimicked the roaring dragons at the end of the causeway. "You would have been better to tell me inside the sacred shrine. I would never have killed you in there." Pocketing the card, he turned and disappeared into the night.

Saito pressed both hands to the wound. The end was near. He could feel his lifeblood flowing out, yet his greatest concern was the name on the card.

What have I done to my old friend? There's no time to warn him. No time to explain.

Despite the searing pain tearing at his body, a glimmer of an idea took hold in his mind. He retrieved his cell phone from a coat pocket. The case was visibly cracked.

Please let it work.

His bloodied fingers struggled to open it, and as he pressed the On button, a familiar cold blue glow illuminated the dark ground around him.

Maybe there is a way . . .

CHAPTER
SIX

"MAXWELL EARNEST Travers, you're officially mad." Zoe tugged nicotine-stained fingers through her spiky platinum hair and laughed hysterically. In her usual blunt British style, she got right to the point. "You've kept on working for that nutter Yoko, and now her father wants you to carry World War Two junk into the Korean and Chinese embassies?"

"I couldn't find another school that would sponsor me for work." He took a gulp of beer.

The living room of the Tokyo Poor House had seen better days. The tatami floor's straw was fraying thin, while against the edges of the room lay stacks of decrepit pillows. Dark panel board covered the walls, and the cool late-night air crept in around the open window frame where the sliding plastic panels no longer fit. A battered television sat on a shaky table between the two open entranceways joining the room to the hallway and the tiny kitchen. Peeking out from beneath the table was a rusty breadbox-sized heater. Its red glowing coils hummed in a vain struggle to warm the room.

The two roommates were seated facing each other on the floor, their feet nearly touching in the center of the cramped space. Max was only half absorbed in coiling his rope, getting ready for a trip to Yugawara in two weeks' time. His fascination with rock climbing hadn't yet rubbed off on

Tomoko who preferred instead to spread a blanket on the ground and watch the activity from a safe distance, tucked behind the pages of a novel.

Max knew he needed to find the right time to discuss his return plane ticket with Tomoko, but he set aside the thought along with his rope. "You're making the situation sound worse than it is."

"Am I, really? Wasn't it you who told me that Yoko was changing her English school into a corporation so she could sell shares to the naïve parents of her students? She's stealing their money, but not really, since each of the daft women are willingly handing over a million dollars. And the other day she sent you to fetch a three-thousand dollar outfit she bought in Ginza?"

Max's reply was cut short.

"No, no, I'm not finished." Zoe's eyes brightened. "Let me quote you from the other night—'The Dragon Lady is nuts. She's robbing good people of their money, and they don't see it. I've got to do something'—and now you get this bizarre request from her father. You should just get another job."

"Okay. Yeah. I may have said some of those things."

Zoe hopped up and walked four paces into the kitchen to check on the midnight meal. "You said all those things, you wanker."

Protesting was pointless since she was right; instead, he leaned back against the corner pillows and watched her rakishly thin arms chop vegetables. At times her mind was sharp, like now, and he felt as if he really knew her, but then she would unexpectedly disappear for days, only to reappear, high and disoriented. Zoe Pitman had moved into the TPH six months earlier, but nobody had seen her for the initial weeks while she dried out from a Thailand heroin addiction. She had stayed in her ground-floor room, screaming and bouncing off the walls. When she finally appeared for the first time, her hollowed cheeks, worldly manner, and the deep dark circles under her eyes all served to hide the fact that she was only twenty-nine years old.

Max refocused his attention on Zoe's inquiring face. She was standing in the kitchen doorway. "Are you bloody listening to anything I'm saying?"

"Sorry, no . . . but I'm all ears now."

"I said, you should gather all those lovely parents and explain what the hell's going on."

"And then what? Have Yoko chasing me? She's crazy enough to do it, you know. There's something strange about her past. Nobody knows anything about it, including her assistant, Kenji."

"So just quit and walk away." Zoe turned back to the stove.

"Yeah, that's pretty much what I'm thinking." He paused before raising a lingering concern. "But what about money? Can I get another school to sponsor me a work visa?" The critical question had been silently gnawing at him for weeks.

"Possibly. Once you get through all the bureaucratic bullshit. But it's a huge hassle, and you'll likely have to leave the country while it's being processed." Moments later, she emerged with two steaming bowls, setting one on the floor before handing him a pair of chopsticks. "Better get to that before the roaches do."

Max slurped loudly while Zoe ate quietly.

"You're such a boy."

He grinned like a contented ten-year-old, a thin line of juice trailing down his chin. "Hey, it's customary here—the noisier the better."

They quickly consumed the meal and flopped back against the pillowed walls. Max organized his draws and carabineers by clipping them together. "So assuming I tell my students' parents what Yoko's up to with their money . . . what should I do about Mr. M's request? I know you think he's using me as a fall guy, but most of his friends are dead and I think he trusts and respects me. Maybe I should—"

Zoe's voice snapped. "Are you simply going to natter on and answer your own question?"

"No, no. I want your opinion. I do. Talk."

Seeming satisfied with his response, she proceeded. "Fine, but you won't like it." She took a drink. "If you walk into some embassy carrying bits of old World War Two paraphernalia, I have a feeling the police will come round for a visit to find out where you got it. So go ahead and tell the nice people that Yoko is stealing their money. She seems a bit nutty, but I doubt she's dangerous. As for the old man . . . I don't know, tell him to have a yard sale or something."

Max formed his thoughts. "I get what you're saying, but after my English lesson today I did some research and learned some incredible stuff about Japanese history. Some of it I'd already heard from Mr. M, but his recollection was a bit watered down, at least according to what I read." Max packed the gear into his climbing bag and pulled a knee toward his chest with his arm. "Did you know that this country's military conquest of Asia started as early as

29

the 1890s when they invaded Korea?"

Zoe shook her head.

"China, Taiwan, Singapore, and the Philippines—all brutalized until 1945. Millions of people were stripped of everything—turned into slave labor. Hundreds of thousands of women were forced into prostitution. And they called them 'comfort women' to make it sound better." He swallowed away the sympathetic lump forming in his throat. "The Rape of Nanking was vicious. Tens of thousands slaughtered." His back slumped against the pillows. "There was so much more, but I couldn't read it. Way too depressing."

Max was surprised by Zoe's contemptuous snort. "Is this all new information to you? That's shocking, considering you're usually a bit of a know-it-all." She propped herself up on her elbows. "Don't they teach anything in American schools? It's called imperialism. Every major country's done it. And it was the same back then as it is now—if there aren't Americans getting killed, it doesn't make the news, does it? It's just a footnote after the sports page. The world's a shitty place, so get used to it."

"I know, I know. It's just that I thought I was beginning to understand this strange country. It finally started feeling like a place I could belong, for the long term." Max stared at the water-stained ceiling, half wishing he hadn't begun the conversation. "Now I'm not so sure anymore."

"Oh, don't be a big girl's blouse." She kicked his foot. "Get me another beer."

He grinned and rolled to his feet. "Anyone tell you you're a slave driver?"

"I guess I should give you credit for being one of the few Yanks making an effort to see the big, scary world." She pulled herself up into a higher sitting position. "But I can't figure what this history lesson has to do with the old man."

Max's bare feet padded back across the tatami floor. Handing over a fresh Kirin, he sat down beside her. "Never mind, you'll just give me shit like always."

She elbowed him lightly in the ribs.

Max stared at the condensation forming on his bottle, for a moment unsure whether he should go on. But friends like her were rare. "I just thought that by returning those watches, it might make things better." He looked at her world-weary face. "Help bring closure for people and undo some of the crap that's been done. I mean, couldn't things stand to be just a little better?"

He knew it sounded naïve as soon as the words left his mouth, so he shrugged with mock disdain. "See, I told you it was dumb."

Zoe smirked. "You sound like the bloody Dalai Lama." Then her eyes darkened and her face turned serious. "Some people try to change the past, Max, but in my experience, you can't undo the bad stuff. As hard as you try, you can't wash it completely clean." She ran a cracked fingernail down the needle marks on her arm. "It just is what it fucking is."

CHAPTER
SEVEN

Friday, April 20

LATE MORNING sunshine filtered through the partially opened blinds covering the office's street-side windows. Takahito Murayama could feel the warm streams of light angling across his lap as he sat on the black leather sofa. Holding a steaming coffee cup—the only one of the day—he inhaled the aromatic scent, anticipating the first sip. The other hand retrieved a freshly pressed edition of the *Yomiuri Shimbun* newspaper.

The first page held little new information. The Japanese Congressional Diet was still debating whether to amend article nine of the 1946 Constitution, renouncing the right to wage war. The Constitution, drafted with American help, forbade Japan to create land, sea, or air forces. The newspaper described the supposedly peaceful crowds of people gathered outside the Diet's legislative building to demonstrate both for and against the change. Photographs showed hundreds of competing protestors with yellow and orange banners. A legion of paneled trucks with enormous loudspeakers could be seen in the background. Rows of well-armed riot police stood between the protesting hoards and the columned gray stone of the government's Diet building.

On page two, a headline blared: **FORMER DIPLOMAT MURDERED**.

The old hands shook as he stared at the two black-and-white photos beneath the headline. The top one clearly showed a body lying face down on stone-covered ground. A single dress shoe lay next to the shrine's water basin, while dirt streaks were evident on the back of the man's trench coat. The diplomat's arms lay over his head, which faced away from the camera. The bottom photograph was an official government headshot, showing a solemn and much younger Kazue Saito dressed in a pinstriped suit. The left side of his face was angled toward the camera, but the mole above his lip was clearly evident in the photo.

At the Yasukuni Shrine in the Asakusa district of Tokyo, former Diplomat Kazue Saito, of Toyama prefecture, was found murdered. A caretaker discovered the dead man at about 1 a.m. near the entrance to the grounds. Mr. Saito entered the diplomatic corps in 1960 at the age of 20 and assumed postings in Washington, D.C., England, Canada, and Spain. He was divorced in 2001 and retired in 2004 at the age of 64. Robbery does not appear to have been the motive for murder, as police claim to have a wallet with cash that was found at the scene. A shop owner near the shrine reported seeing a young man running from the dark pathway around 11:45 p.m. The shop owner's description was vague, but he did recall the young man riding away on a "very loud" motorcycle. A smashed mobile phone was lying next to the body, but no weapon was found. Police are awaiting autopsy results in order to establish the time and cause of death. The shrine's guard was not available for an interview.

Setting the paper down and turning to the end table, Mr. Murayama stared anxiously at the framed photograph of Kazue Saito and himself.

They'll surely come looking for me next.

Closing his eyes, he listened to the knocking of his heartbeat and thought back to the first time the two had met. It was Washington, D.C., the summer of 1961, and the heat and humidity had brought the city to a standstill. Kazue had entered the Japanese Embassy with a white cotton dress shirt plastered to his body. He refused the invitation to sit and asked instead to take a walk. It was an odd request, but Mr. Murayama remembered agreeing out of concern for the younger man, who clutched his briefcase while pacing anxiously.

One week earlier, Mr. Murayama's old friend and World War Two comrade, Lieutenant Tetsuo Endo, had passed away from lung cancer. Because of official ceremonies in Washington, it had been impossible for Mr. Murayama to return to Japan to attend the funeral in person. A late-night call to his Georgetown residence had informed him that Tetsuo's protégé would be visiting Washington shortly.

As the two men walked under the oak trees in Rock Creek Park, Kazue appeared to be sweating from more than just the stifling heat. Before long, he broke down and described how Tetsuo Endo had called him to his bedside on the night of his death and given instructions to personally deliver a package and a message—a regular diplomatic courier could not be trusted.

Mr. Murayama recalled, as if it were yesterday, the sunlight filtering through the trees while children splashed in the nearby creek. They sat on a bench while Kazue spun an incredible tale that could only be a lie, or a final deathbed joke. But the younger man finally convinced him that the words were indeed true.

He remembered removing the diary from the satchel and taking note of the yellow leather cover, the fine texture of the paper, the masterfully crafted handwriting, and finally the prince's authenticating seal. The two men talked for hours until the shadows grew long. Agreeing it would not be wise to speak about this to anyone else, they formed a pact of secrecy—never to be shared until the time was right.

A hesitant breath filled Mr. Murayama's lungs, bringing him back to the inconceivable horror of the present. *Had they killed Kazue for what he knew?* He could not help but feel a sense of both loss and panic. The murder left him the only guardian of the dangerous past, sole gatekeeper to information so powerful that, after that first meeting in the park, the two men had spoken of it only in code.

Finally rising, he shuffled toward the windows and pulled the strings to raise the blinds, allowing the morning light to spill in. He stared out, priding himself on the fact that it wasn't death itself he feared, but only what would happen to the diary. It had to be protected at all costs.

They seek to destroy knowledge. Will they find me next?

From behind, the linoleum floor creaked sharply and he turned toward the sound. He could see a shape—the outline of a man—in the office doorway. *Have they come so soon?* The sudden contrast of shade and bright light caused his vision to blur and waver. He stepped away from the window and found himself losing balance. Stumbling several steps before falling to his knees, he collapsed in heavy fog.

A trail of warm coffee ran from the table's edge onto his face, and he felt a hand on his cheek. A voice was calling his name, and then he was being lifted to the nearby chair.

"Mr. Murayama! Say something."

Forcing weak eyes open, he peered up to see Max's concerned face hovering overhead.

"Stay still. I'll get Yoko." Max jumped up.

"No . . . no . . ." Mr. Murayama croaked a reply. "Don't! Please just give me a minute to rest."

Max paused in a half turn, unsure of himself.

"I was not expecting you. It's not our normal day." The old man drew himself up in the soft chair. "Please, a cloth."

MAX moved swiftly through the nearby office door, briefly forgetting the purpose for his visit. He made a sharp left in the hall. Entering the street-side kitchen, he grasped a towel and located the nondescript round picture hanging on the wall. He turned it forty-five degrees to the right and a latch gave a distinctive pop, revealing a hidden doorway in the wood paneling. He ducked down and slipped through the opening, reappearing in Murayama's office to crouch beside the leather chair before handing over the towel.

Mr. Murayama spoke, astonished, as he wiped his face with shaking hands. "Two surprises," he said hoarsely. "First you come without warning, and then you walk through my secret door. How did you know?"

Max hesitated, now wishing he hadn't panicked and used the short-cut to return. "On a break, a few weeks ago, I came down here. You were in the kitchen but then you just disappeared. I waited in the hall, and could hear you moving in your office. So I figured there must be a hidden passage."

"That entrance was made for a secretary to bring tea." Mr. Murayama paused, his expression gaining strength. "From your story, you must also have come back later for a closer look."

Max knew it was pointless denying the truth, and he grinned. "Busted."

"Never mind, never mind. It's good to be curious. But keep it our secret, my boy." The old man let out a sigh and dabbed at the coffee that had run into the folds of his cardigan. "So why did you come today?"

I really should tell him that I'm quitting the school, but this is gonna be hard enough. "I considered your request to return the watches." Max remained crouched next to the chair, but found himself unable to maintain eye contact, afraid to view the inevitable disappointment. As much as he had repeatedly justified the decision in his head, delivering the message was proving more difficult then anticipated. "It's an admirable thing, for sure. But, I just can't do it—it's too risky."

The cloth in Mr. Murayama's hands twisted into a tight spiral as a moment passed in silence. "I see," he finally choked out. "Well, thank you for letting me know."

"I just—"

"No need to explain." The reply was swift and final. "I understand that I asked too much of you."

Max rose and stepped back, longing for the awkwardness of the moment to dissipate. Desperate to change the subject, he glanced at the newspaper lying on the center table. "Hey, I saw those same pictures in today's English paper. It said a retired diplomat was murdered yesterday. Did you know him?"

Mr. Murayama looked up, catching Max in a direct stare before responding with a definitive shake of his head. "No."

CHAPTER
EIGHT

THE PRIVATE elevator had only two buttons, one for ground and the glowing one indicating the thirty-first-floor penthouse. Jun Hirano wiped the sweat from his shaved head with a massive paw of a hand. The Yebisu Garden Terrace tower, with its clean marble floors and bright lights, made the twenty-eight-year-old feel uncharacteristically anxious. The setting blazed in sharp contrast to the gambling halls and dark alleyways of Shinjuku, where he felt most comfortable running card games, drinking whisky, and chasing after lovely girls out for a day of shopping. The streets, after all, were where he had grown up since being orphaned at the age of nine.

It wasn't clear why the head of the family had extended him a personal invitation. The honor was usually reserved for the senior advisors of the *Yakuza* gang, but the caller's words had been clear: tell no one of the afternoon meeting, and come alone.

Two guards were waiting as he stepped into the penthouse foyer. Dressed in matching black suits, they stood stone-faced, their feet shoulder-width apart with hands clasped overtop their enormous bellies—former sumo wrestlers by the look of them. Standing slightly shorter then his own five-feet-ten inches, they easily outweighed him by fifty pounds each. Their imposing presence didn't help to settle his uneasiness.

The marble foyer was open to the floor above, with a grand, sweeping staircase rising to the second level. An ornate Western-style chandelier hung from the ceiling, while a dozen historic wood-block paintings adorned the surrounding walls. Jun felt as if he was entering a Hollywood movie set.

He removed his black loafers and followed the two men as they moved down a side hallway. The décor soon adopted a Japanese feel, with light wood and clean lines. Approaching a door on the right, they entered what appeared to be a changing area for a *sento* bath.

One of the guards spoke as if he'd already anticipated a question. "Father prefers tradition, but he also requires privacy. A public bathing house won't do." The expressionless man gave Jun instructions to place all his clothing in one of the wicker baskets provided before proceeding into the next room.

Resisting the temptation to respond with a cocky comment, Jun stripped off his leather jacket, long-sleeved dress shirt, and jeans. Removing his boxers revealed the full extent of the patterned tattoos blanketing his muscular shoulders, back, and buttocks.

Entering the second room alone, he noted that the white-tiled space was about twice the size of the first room. To his left, on the wall adjacent to the door, were five square wooden stools positioned in front of matching silver faucets. Directly ahead, covering the entire back portion of the room, was a waist-high bathing pool ten feet wide and six feet front to back. Steam rose from the pool and created a thick layer of moisture that swirled around Jun's naked body and condensed on his skin.

He shuffled to the farthest faucet. Squatting, he perched his two-hundred-pound body on the tiny stool and began washing himself. Dripping, he stared at his round-faced reflection in the mirror. Slowly he ran an index finger down the old scar that traced the right side of his face. He had earned it in a weapons training camp when he was a teenager, and he relished the intimidating appearance it lent him.

Jun moved to the pool and dangled his legs into the heated water.

A shot of cooler air made him glance up as a slender blonde woman entered the room and held the door. Wrapped only in a white terry towel, she looked as if she'd stepped straight from the cover of a *Playboy* magazine. Behind her was *Yakuza* Father Oto Kodama.

Instinct took over, forcing Jun to slip into the pool, standing, in order to bow respectfully. Finding himself suddenly up to his hips in the scalding water, he winced in pain.

Oto's gruff voice echoed off the tiled walls. "Don't burn yourself, my boy." He pointed into the water below Jun's waistline. "You'll find that thing useful on occasion." Slick black hair edged with silver covered the Father's head, framing his dark eyes and permanent scowl. Two dog tags suspended on a silver chain hung halfway down his bare chest.

The leggy blonde towered over the five-foot-five mafia leader. She removed the older man's towel, revealing the tattoos painted across his sagging belly. Intricate drawings of dragons and samurai covered his entire body except for his feet, hands, jowly neck, and face.

The woman removed her own towel and placed it next to Oto's. Jun remained standing, his eyes lingering on her body, watching transfixed as a train of silky hair fell down her back to her perfectly formed hips.

Oto spoke while shuffling across the tiled floor. "She is something, isn't she? I bought her in Singapore. I hate Americans, but for her I've made an exception. She can't understand a word we're saying, but who cares?" The older man clambered into the hot water, followed by the elegant blonde.

Jun sank down to his neck, choosing to remain silent, unsure of how to appropriately respond.

"You're probably wondering why you're here."

"Yes, Father." He knew that he should focus on Oto, but he couldn't stop his focus from drifting toward the pink breasts peeking above the water line.

"I wanted to commend you for obtaining the information last night at the shrine."

"Thank you, Father."

"But did you really need to kill the diplomat?"

Shamed, Jun lowered his eyes. A story needed to be quickly created. "The man threatened to inform the police. I couldn't let that happen."

"But you must understand that his death raises questions with the authorities, and smoothing these things over costs a great deal of money."

"Very sorry, Father."

Oto ignored the apology. "However, I've used the information from the business card you obtained. A cleaning crew will bug Murayama-*san*'s office tonight, after which I want you and Hiro to take the van and start listening."

"For what?" Jun sat up higher.

"I'm looking for a brown leather satchel containing a priceless old book.

I want you to recover it." Oto's dark eyes burned bright. "But—I don't wish to coerce Murayama-*san* directly. He was a diplomat and the police could surveil him as well after the unfortunate shrine murder. It will be slower this way, but less obvious."

Jun felt a swell of pride. *I'm being asked to carry out duties directly for the Father!*

"And I have another task." Steam rose into the already moist air as Oto continued speaking. "I'm growing concerned about your *Yakuza* brother, Hiro. I'm hearing reports that he's acting strangely again. I believe he's been tainted by weak Western influences." Oto's flat nose wrinkled. "All foolishness! The family is what matters. And his heart may not be with our family anymore. Do you understand?"

Jun's chin dipped into the water as he nodded.

"He tried to leave us once. It was years ago. He was young, and I thought he learned his lesson, but perhaps not," Oto said. "Let me know if you see anything unusual in his behavior."

"Yes, of course, Father."

The blonde woman whispered into Oto's ear. He splashed a hand, giving approval for her to leave the bath. "These Americans can't take the heat."

Rising up and swinging her long, smooth legs up over the tiled edge of the bath, the woman fully exposed her entire body. Jun could feel himself becoming aroused, and in an attempt to avoid being noticed, he clasped his hands together in his lap while his gaze followed her every move.

Oto cleared his throat and the two men briefly locked eyes. "I too was once a young man."

Jun felt a hot rush of guilt spread over his face.

"Don't be ashamed, my boy. It's only natural to be attracted to her. In fact, I'm feeling generous. You may have her for a few hours."

Jun wiped his brow with a single wet hand, marveling at the father's generosity.

"Woman-u!" Oto's English word boomed and echoed in the little room. "Give-u him-u good-o time-u."

She wrapped herself in a towel and showed her perfect white teeth in a dazzling smile.

Jun rose rapidly, sending a wave cascading over the pool's edge and onto the floor. He bowed while keeping his hands folded tightly over his groin, attempting to awkwardly scale the bath's edge.

As the door closed, the aging leader drew a napkin-sized white terry cloth out of the water. Folding it twice into a small square, he placed it on top of his head and settled deeper into the warm water, dreaming of the diary that would soon be his and the riches within.

CHAPTER NINE

I T WAS meant to be a pleasant evening of traditional *Kabuki* theater, and normally Max would have been excited about trying something new. But as he pressed down the crowded sidewalk, surrounded by bright neon-crowned buildings, he felt a clear sense of trepidation. Yoko, the Dragon Lady, was waiting for him, and her reaction was going to be unpredictable at best.

Delivering his resignation letter just hours before had lifted a huge weight from his shoulders. Yoko had been on the phone, planning an upcoming art exhibit, with her back to the door. Her vicious cat, Luciano, reclined on a guest chair, hissing as Max entered the office. Tossing the sealed envelope onto the desktop, he dashed out before she could spin around her high-backed chair.

He knew he would miss teaching the kids, but he was weary of Yoko's lies and her ever-changing stories. She'd successfully seduced him with a position on the new board of directors, however in the end she was simply placating him. Having his school expansion ideas repeatedly agreed to, then ignored, had shown her objective wasn't to create a viable business. And as if to add salt to the wound she had insisted he run her errands. The expensive purchases of clothing, along with the growing pile of Tiffany's boxes, were a constant reminder of her true objective. Their once close friendship dissolved into silence, and as the quiet tension escalated, he grew confident that Yoko's true agenda remained hidden behind a well-crafted layer of deception. She'd manipulated him, treating him like her blond poster boy, just so she could gather more investors. He was merely someone to distract the students' mothers while Yoko reached her greedy hand into their purses and robbed them of their life savings.

In a country where he could barely manage the language, Max felt powerless to stop the wheels in motion. But his resignation was one thing he could still control. Tonight would be the last night he would play the part of Yoko's Exotic Pet.

Walking a jagged line through the sea of strolling shoppers, he adjusted his blazer, which was beginning to show its age. Reaching into an inside pocket, he glanced at his grandpa's pocket watch and saw that it read 7:10 p.m.

Damn. Ten minutes late already.

He had seriously considered backing out of this choreographed event. But he'd agreed to the outing a month ago and costly tickets had been purchased. His students' mothers would be waiting. Expectations would be high, and he could not bring himself to disappoint them.

From the opposite side of Ginza's Harumi-dori Avenue, Max could see the white *Kabuki-za* building a block away. Dramatically bathed from below in brilliant light, the recessed center of the historical façade created the impression of a sixteenth-century Asian castle with matching east and west wings. The vision was striking, and he wondered what it would have been like to attend the original opening in 1889.

Crossing at the busy intersection, he stared up at the overhanging clay-tiled roof. Dual blood-red banners flapped in the evening breeze. Adorned with thick black *kanji* lettering, they hung past the matching third-floor balconies and framed the downward-sweeping lines of the black and gold second-story marquee. As he drew closer to the building, he could see Yoko's unmistakable bobbed haircut near the entrance. She was attending to her entourage of ladies. Gathered near the front pillars, they stood chatting beneath a string of glowing red lanterns.

He tried hard to ignore the nervous sweat soaking into his undershirt.

As if she heard his quickened heartbeat approaching, Yoko turned toward him and dipped her head in a slight nod. "Thank you for showing up." Her lips, which normally arched downward, lifted at the corners into a forced smile that didn't match the dark tone of her eyes. "You're late."

"Yeah . . . well," he muttered, looking away.

She raised a single pencil-thin eyebrow. "I assumed you'd be early, since you left the office in such a hurry." Not allowing him time to respond, she turned back to address the dozen women clustered together, holding her hands outward like a maestro conducting an orchestra.

He watched the ladies nodding heads while they drank in her animated narration—lies, he was sure—punctuated at the end with a noisy laugh. *Why don't they see through her?* It was clear she was hard at work, since the only two terms he'd been able to understand were his own name and the word for "corporation."

Max took a step backward as Yoko finally broke away from the group and moved toward him.

"We're just waiting for Mrs. Hirano before we go in," she said.

"Fine." He made a point to avoid eye contact. *She certainly can't overlook her wealthiest contributor.*

Reaching into her Prada handbag, Yoko drew out the resignation letter and thrust her manicured hand toward him. "You forgot this."

It was clear the envelope had been opened, and he heard himself bite back. "I didn't forget that letter. I quit."

Her eyes grew even darker. "I don't accept." The paper shook in her outstretched hand. "You can't take a board position and then simply resign."

Glancing over Yoko's head, Max caught a glimpse of several women curiously eyeing them, and he made a point to temper his rising frustration. "We shouldn't talk about this here."

Yoko waved dismissively and her tone grew curt. "They can't speak English and have no idea what we're talking about."

"I want my passport back."

"Is that what this is about?"

"It's not the only thing, but you've had it for weeks, and I've asked for it at least three times."

"I told you the lawyers need it for the legal paperwork."

What bullshit, Max thought. "Really? Is that the latest story?" His body tensed—he hated arguing. "Last week when I politely asked you it was another excuse, and the week before that something else. I'm surprised you can keep all the lies straight in your head sometimes." He waited for the explosive fireworks, but they didn't come.

"Max, please." She drew out her words and softened her tone. "Something has upset you, and we need to talk about it." She folded the letter back into her purse. Lifting her head, she smoothed the sides of her hair. "Let's have brunch tomorrow. It's Saturday. We can discuss whatever is bothering you."

He had witnessed this bait-and-switch tactic before, and he wasn't about to fall for it again. "I have plans with Tomoko all day." He stared with rigid eyes. It was only a partial lie.

"Well, then, Sunday, perhaps." She stepped closer. "We were so close. Let's mend the fences."

Well, she does seem sincere.

Before he could respond, the moment was broken by a braking taxi. Mrs. Hirano was finally arriving. Yoko's change from conciliatory friend to money-hungry parasite was instantaneous. She pressed Max backward with a sharp elbow and stepped on his foot as she rushed to the cab door.

Watching her at work, Max was astounded at himself. She had almost beguiled him again. What was it about her personality that blessed her with the ability to charm and control? A few more seconds and he would have agreed to brunch with a simple shrug of his shoulders. He resolved to grow a thicker skin, become tougher. In the meantime, however, he would have to find a way to get his passport back while attempting to avoid her for the next two weeks.

Max followed while Yoko ushered her wealthy little flock past the bowing attendants and into the red-carpeted theater lobby. She was unlike anyone he had ever met—a master of manipulation. And as the closing doors blocked out the bustling street noise, he couldn't help but wonder who had taught her to play this high-stakes game.

CHAPTER
TEN

Saturday, April 21

TOMOKO COULD see her breath as she perched against the low wall in Sapporo's Odori Park. Her cell phone was pressed to one ear as she left an answering machine message.

"Hi Max. I'll be on my way home to Tokyo soon. Meet me in Roppongi tonight, instead of Shibuya. I miss you. Bye-bye."

The jeans she was wearing offered scant protection against the chilly stone, and she rocked from side to side, shivering in the early morning sunlight. A few more minutes of this and she would be taking the coat from the bum sleeping on the bench behind her. Miki was fifteen minutes late, and Tomoko felt ready to kill her.

Certain she heard her name being called, Tomoko attempted to block the glare from the bright eastern sunrise. In the middle of the park plaza, she could see the outline of someone jogging toward her. She desperately hoped it was Miki, but it couldn't possibly be. The person heading her way was wearing a pair of thigh-high black-and-white striped stockings and pink Converse Chucks. Her friend was much too conservative for an outfit like that.

"Oh no, you're freezing! I'm so sorry," panted a familiar girlish voice.

Tomoko stood to get a better look, and her jaw dropped. "Wow, I can't believe it!"

Miki's flattened, shoulder-length, bleached blonde hair was held in place at the front with three pink plastic barrettes. A white T-shirt covered in large black stars peeked out from under a red Betty Boop jacket, and her pleated miniskirt almost covered her leggings. She was a five-foot-tall billboard begging for attention.

"You like?" Miki spun around. "Here, put this on." She handed over a silver goose-down coat.

"Thank you. I'm so cold." Tomoko's voice rose close to a whine. "And you're really late." She could barely take her eyes off her old college friend.

"Hey, you're the one who came this far north without warm clothes." Miki stepped closer to help. "This sticks sometimes." She twisted the zipper and it finally moved.

"Well, it's spring in Tokyo."

"Which is five hundred miles south of here,. Come on, let's walk and heat you up." Miki's bracelets rattled as she adjusted her shiny pink purse.

"All right, but you need to explain your outfit."

"So you don't like it?" Miki placed an index finger on her lower lip and stared up with a pout as they both broke into hysterical giggles.

Morning traffic was light, and they crossed the street to the next section of the park. "You try working in a boring government job. I have to wear this awful uniform and the work is so, so, so boring." Bitterness edged into her voice. "I didn't get an exciting job like you."

"I know," Tomoko conceded. "But you deserved it."

"Well, some of us are short and a bit on the fat side." Miki snickered self-consciously, before holding up an open hand. "You don't need to say anything. I'm happy you got the job. And besides," she said, throwing her blonde head back, "I've decided that I'll simply compensate with style."

Tomoko nodded and enjoyed the warmth beginning to build up inside the jacket. "So why are we meeting here? My hotel is only a few blocks from the TV Tower."

"I was worried about handing over private government information with too many people around. I could get in trouble, you know." Miki scanned the area. Several other couples could be seen, but nobody was paying them any attention. "I know my job is bad, but I can't lose it."

"Well, if you're playing secret agent, you're not exactly blending in with those stockings."

They both laughed.

"It took me about a week, but I did get most of what you're looking for. Although, if you don't mind my asking, why do you want the information?"

"I just have a strange feeling about Max's boss, Yoko. Something isn't right."

"You're really crazy about this American guy, aren't you? Tell me what he's like."

Tomoko beamed as she spoke. "He's tall, with amazing blue eyes."

"No, not that. I've seen pictures already. You know what I mean. Most white guys are bad news—they come here for a while and then they're gone." Miki snapped her fingers. "I want to know what he's like. Does he have money? Do you love him?"

"Don't worry. It's only been a couple of months, and we're taking it slowly."

"You're avoiding the question."

"Fine. If you must know, he's kind-hearted and he makes me laugh. I know that sounds dumb, but it's true. You remember the guys we went to school with? They got jobs with big companies and became exactly like all the boring businessmen we used to ridicule. Well, that's not Max. He's spontaneous and willing to try new things. I know it sounds ridiculous, but I've always pictured my life as an adventure. I think it can be that way with him."

Miki pressed on with the line of questioning. "So what about his family?"

"He hasn't said much, really, other than that they moved around a lot. His mother lives somewhere in California. She's extremely religious, a Christian, but we've only talked about his father once—sounds like a drinking problem— he changes the subject whenever I ask." They crossed another street and continued strolling east. "He's mentioned his grandfather a few times. They were close before he died . . . I get the feeling that's why Max likes spending time with Mr. Murayama."

"You know that guys from bad families usually have hidden issues." Miki clicked her tongue for dramatic effect. "Lots of emotional baggage."

"Seriously? Did you just quote that from a magazine?"

"It's true! You need to be careful that he doesn't become another one of your 'I can fix him' projects. You remember how the last three guys turned out."

"This is different. He's different."

"If you say so." They both took a little step to the right as Miki nudged her friend gently with her hip and changed the subject. So what's it like to have sex with a *Gaijin*? You know what they say about a guy with a big nose!" Miki mockingly licked her lips.

The two stopped next to an ornate dry fountain, and Tomoko turned to confront her friend. "I can't believe you!" Attempting to appear angry, she couldn't help but grin a little at the same time.

"Oh, don't be a prude. Here's the deal. You tell me about the sex, and I'll give you the information you asked me to find."

"No."

Miki put a finger to her bottom lip and rolled her eyes upward. "Okay, but some of the material is quite . . . mmmm . . . interesting."

Tomoko folded her arms across her chest. "This is not fair."

"No, turning twenty-six and being called 'Christmas cake' to your face because nobody wants you after the twenty-fifth—now that's not fair." Miki patted her purse with her free hand. "This is just called creative negotiating."

"Fine." Tomoko held out a half-thawed hand, and they shook on it. "But can't we go inside somewhere?"

"Sure." Miki pointed back the way they had come. "There's a breakfast place—Rope 101—just on the other side of the fountain. We can go . . ."

Tomoko was already on the run, moving before Miki could finish speaking, and as she charged around the corner and across the street, she could hear her friend laughing while jogging to catch up.

GRIPPING the cup of hot tea with both hands, Tomoko felt the tingle of blood finally reaching her fingertips. She blew on the steaming liquid. "So what did you find?"

"Well, there's plenty of information about Mr. Murayama. He was a public servant in the diplomatic corps, so there's a bunch of boring stuff. Postings to embassies and things like that. I'll give you the folder later."

"Thanks." Tomoko sipped her tea while Miki picked at a croissant.

"However . . . there were a couple of interesting things that stuck out."

"Like what?"

"Well, there was information about his daughter, Yoko Murayama, but only back to 1985."

"What do you mean?"

"I found some post-1985 newspaper articles about a Tokyo art showing, but nothing before 1985. It's like she just didn't exist before then."

Tomoko wrinkled her forehead and frowned. "But how is that possible?"

"I don't know." Miki adjusted one of her feather earrings. "I'll keep looking, but I'm telling you, if there was something to find, I would have found it by now. Plus, everything is digitized these days. There should be records," she said, shrugging, "but there simply aren't."

"Was there anything else?"

Miki appeared slightly uneasy as she looked around the empty, rundown café. The owner, perched next to a ceramic good-luck kitty, was hidden behind a newspaper. "There was one other thing." She motioned for them to move closer together and her voice became a whisper. "According to diplomatic records, Mr. Murayama never had any children."

CHAPTER
ELEVEN

D UTY-BOUND, HIRO sat on the hard-padded bench that ran the inside length of the Toyota Dyna van's windowless cargo area. The gray vehicle was parked in a string of bumper-to-bumper cars lining the street opposite Mr. Murayama's office. Late-afternoon traffic was sporadic, but apartment dwellers out for a Saturday stroll flowed by in an unending chain.

He adjusted the padded headphones that sealed his ears, pressing down his permed, curly black hair. Beside him, Jun was shifting ceaselessly. Squeezed elbow to elbow with his partner, Hiro was growing increasingly annoyed at the younger man's inability to remain still. The nearby police box concerned him. Jun's massive size and constant movements shook the van and threatened to expose their listening post. The last thing they needed was for a concerned citizen to alert the police to the strange rocking vehicle down the block.

Hiro pulled the left earpiece away from his head and whispered through thin lips. "Little brother, could you please stop moving?" The traditional *Sempai-Kohai* relationship of mentorship, reciprocated with respect and obedience, had never gelled between the two men. Forced together only through circumstance, they labored on common tasks, but would never truly mix.

Jun's grunt barely acknowledged the request; his eyes remained glued to the pages of the phonebook-sized *Manga* he was holding. *What garbage*, thought Hiro. The comic was disgustingly low-life, but he knew the young thug eagerly awaited new issues of *Berserk*. The violent fantasies centered on the life of an orphaned warrior named Guts, who led The Band of Hawks mercenary group. Every tale spun a bizarre story of heroism and glory, a life for which Jun clearly longed.

Hiro glanced at the detailed bloodshed depicted on the *Manga* cover. He felt a look of disdain creep across his slender, hawkish face. He would never relate to Jun's propensity for violence, but then their childhood experiences were so different. Jun had been orphaned in the late 1980s—raised on the streets, while Hiro had grown up with four older sisters. His mother would tell him how she had prayed to the *kami* spirits to send her a son. She knew his father wouldn't rest until he had a boy to carry on the *Yakuza* traditions.

Feedback from a transmitter in the office squealed as Hiro snapped forward to adjust the controls on the sound console running the length of the van's opposite wall.

The first hour-long shift had gone to Jun. It was now hour number eight, and there wasn't much going on inside Mr. Murayama's office. Two radio microphones had been planted by a night cleaning crew. Hiro could hear the sound of sliding drawers accompanied by the shuffling of feet. The old man was likely moving things around, but little else appeared to be happening.

Hiro slid the pile of Coke cans and empty Styrofoam ramen bowls to Jun's end of the counter where they belonged. The cleared space exposed several translated novels. He reviewed the stack, trying to decide which one to read once it was Jun's turn to listen again. A classic, like Shakespeare's *Romeo and Juliet*, wasn't the kind of story that could be read while crammed into the back of a van with a two-hundred pound gorilla. He fingered the outside of his dog-eared edition of the classic American tale, *On the Road*. It was a possibility, but his interest in it had waned for the moment. So the choice was between *Cry Freedom* and Che Guevara's *Motorcycle Diaries*.

Abruptly, the office telephone rang, and Hiro listened closely as Mr. Murayama answered.

"*Moshi-moshi?*"

"Hello, Murayama-*san*. It's Rikyu, from the Mizuho bank. I'm very sorry for my slow response to your message. I was at the park with my family."

"No need to explain. I wish to move some things to my safety deposit box. It's quite urgent, and I would like you to send a truck on Monday morning."

The line crackled with static as Rikyu sucked in air between his closed teeth. "Is that so?" The snakelike noise continued. "I'd like to but the trucks require advance notice of one business day, which means Tuesday at the earliest. If it's urgent, I could drive over myself on Monday."

"The items are very valuable. Do your best to send a truck, otherwise come yourself with a security guard at 8 a.m."

"Absolutely, Mr. Murayama, and thank you for your business."

Hiro pulled off the headset and tossed it on the console. "That's it. We're done here." He interlaced his fingers and reversed his hands over his head, leaning forward to stretch his lithe, but muscular, five-foot-six frame in the cramped space.

Jun remained engrossed in the pages of a raging life-and-death cartoon battle.

Impatiently, Hiro kicked him sharply in the shin. The blow caused the big man to spring up, striking his head on the low metal ceiling. He unleashed a blistering yelp and dropped the *Manga* on the floor. The sound was much louder than necessary, in Hiro's opinion. For a comic book warrior, he could be such a baby at times.

Jun glowered as he rubbed his bald head, his eyes flooding with loathing.

Ignoring the reaction, Hiro slid open the van's front curtain. "I said, let's go!"

IN the twilight of evening, the van's front tire rammed the curb while attempting to park near a FamilyMart convenience store.

"Watch your driving!" Hiro snarled, slamming the passenger's door before heading to a nearby pay phone. He unfolded a scrap of paper in his nicotine-stained fingers and inserted a stolen calling card. Cradling the receiver against his ear, he dug around in his jacket pocket and pulled out a package of Marlboros.

On the third ring, Oto's gruff voice answered. "Is there a problem?"

"No, Master, but Jun should take driving lessons . . . and to learn to sit still for five minutes."

"He's your apprentice. It's your responsibility to teach him." Oto paused. "And remember, even you have been known to make mistakes sometimes."

Hiro ignored the dig and took a drag on the freshly lit cigarette. He blew a smoke ring into the Plexiglas NTT phone casing. "The old man called Mizuho Bank to come retrieve some items for his safety deposit box. He didn't indicate what he's moving, but the appointment is for Monday morning."

"Are you prepared to carry out the break-in, then?"

"Yes. We'll go to the office tomorrow night. It should be quieter then. But I don't know exactly where the leather satchel is. From the plans I saw, there are dozens of filing cabinets."

"So open them all! You've got the equipment." Oto's deep voice rattled with impatience.

"Yes, Master."

"Do you expect difficulty from the building owner?"

"No. He's a drunk." Hiro took another drag of his cigarette.

"Well, that's good for you, then."

"But I want to do the job without Jun," Hiro blurted. "He's too unpredictable."

"Out of the question!" Oto barked. "And don't even think about leaving with my satchel."

The verbal blow was direct, and Hiro's posture snapped rigid. It didn't seem fair that he should continue to pay for an attempted escape, especially one that happened so long ago, but he swallowed his thoughts, forcing dutiful words from his clenching throat. "I understand, Master."

"And make sure that your *Kohai* doesn't kill anyone else. At least not right now, anyway." A harsh click on the line ended the call.

Slamming the green receiver into place, Hiro snatched the phone card from its slot.

I better not forget this. There are a lot of thieves out here.

CHAPTER
TWELVE

M AX STOOD in the dim evening light below the pink-and-white candy-striped awning of the Almond Café. The busy corner on Roppongi Street was the most popular meeting spot for nightclub revelers to gather, and on a Saturday night, the rendezvous point was swarming with life.

The once-quiet Six Trees district had sprung to life in the late nineteenth century when Japanese soldiers were housed in the area. Young men with a combination of testosterone and money spawned the growth of cabarets and nightlife. Post-World War Two American troops fueled the party tradition, and the district now teemed with Western shops, restaurants, and nightclubs. Roppongi Street's eight lanes were lined with traffic, while overhead the roar of vehicles on the multistory Shuto Expressway intensified the congested feeling of the overpopulated area.

The distraction of the swirling circus helped Max drown out his growing feelings of unease. How much longer could he keep chasing after Yoko for his passport, and now that he had resigned, would she ever give it back? Soon enough, he was going to have to consider more drastic measures.

Max's pulse quickened as two hands covered his eyes from behind. "Finally! The *Geisha* I ordered. It's about time." Reaching back, he grabbed the wrists pressed against his ears and spun around to see Tomoko's lovely face. She laughed while they wrapped their arms around each other, melting together. It was at just such moments, when he was warmed by her glow, that Japan felt the most like home.

He whispered, so only she could hear. "Is this like ordering a pizza? More than twenty minutes late and the next *Geisha's* free?"

Tomoko pulled back, smiling. "Speaking of pizza, I'm so hungry. They didn't give us anything on the plane. Come on." She grabbed his hand, dragging him around the corner and down the street. Directly ahead, the glowing figure of Tokyo's "Eiffel Tower" soared into the night sky. The ambient noise changed as they fought their way through clusters of barking salesmen balanced on the sidewalk, pressing on past the folding tables covered in a smorgasbord of cheap clothing and silver jewelry.

"I have so much to tell," Tomoko shouted.

A hawker waved a reggae T-shirt as they made a sharp right turn into a quieter side street. "Let me guess." He pulled back against her arm and rolled his eyes. "Tony Roma's again? How about *sushi* instead? Or even *shabu-shabu*? Heck, I'd settle for *Okonomiyaki*."

Tomoko tugged him forward. "I'm the one who hasn't eaten today. I should get to choose."

"Kenji got time off from the school and we're supposed to meet him and his friends for drinks in an hour." He watched her mouth shape itself into a little frown and he found himself grinning defeat. "Okay. If it's what you want. But you need to get us past that lineup."

"Not a problem." She squirmed her way to the front of the dozen waiting people. The flash of her business card and a brief dialogue with the hostess had them moving inside within moments. The place was packed, so they sat in the back under a sign blaring Best Ribs in America.

Onion rings, ribs, and beers arrived while Tomoko described the Sapporo television shoot in detail. Max licked sweet barbecue sauce from his fingers while listening intently. He loved to hear her talk, especially about work. Her eyes would grow fiery with passion while her cheeks would flush, and although it seemed impossible, she was even more radiant than usual.

Finally full, Tomoko stopped and took a deep breath. "I have to explain . . . there's something I need to tell you." She bit at her lip.

Max pushed away his now decimated plate. "What do you mean?" He hated confessions—they usually meant bad news.

Unsure of his reaction, she began cautiously. "I have a university friend who works for the government in Sapporo, and she did some research for me. Well, I mean that . . . I asked her to investigate Mr. Murayama and Yoko."

Stunned, Max gaped at her for a moment before speaking. "Are you kidding? If she works in government, that's a massive invasion of privacy." He fought to temper the agitation he felt flaring up. "And why would you do that without talking to me?"

"I know, I should have, but Miki found out some very interesting things."

"Such as?" His chair squeaked as he sat back.

"There is no information about Yoko before 1985. It's like she didn't exist at all."

Max thought back to the little history he knew about Yoko. "Well, did you know she lived in Dallas and New York? Maybe she was there until '85." He wiped his fingers before tossing the napkin to the table, just a little too hard. "I can't believe you'd do that without discussing it first. I never would have agreed."

"I want to help you. I know I've only met Yoko a couple times but there's something strange about her. And the feeling is getting stronger based on your missing passport, and the money she's getting the parents to give her. Something isn't right." Tomoko reached across the table and clasped his hand. "There's more and it gets worse. According to Miki, Mr. Murayama never had any children."

"Okay, that's just crazy."

"It's not a mistake," Tomoko said emphatically. "Something's wrong, and this proves it."

Downing the last of his beer, he paused before replying. "Mr. M is a good friend. Why would he need to lie to me? He wouldn't do that. It doesn't make any sense."

"I don't know. He seems like a nice old man, but it could still be true."

"So, if he isn't Yoko's father, then who is he? And why would they both lie?" Max shifted irritably in his seat, his voice rising. "We should leave."

The waitress appeared at the table, popping the balloon of escalating tension. She handed over the bill before hurriedly gathering the dishes. Tomoko took the opportunity to head for the door. "I'll meet you outside."

"Yeah, fine." Max walked slowly to the till, paid, then forced his way through the ever-present crowd huddled at the doorway. Standing in the fresh night air, it dawned on him that maybe he needed to take a break and get out of the country for a while. Away from all the weirdness—from the Dragon Lady, the unrelenting city, and the drug-addicted roommates. Tomoko was standing at the curb with her back to him as he approached and spoke abruptly from behind. "I need to go traveling for a while."

"What?" Eyebrows raised, she turned to stare at him.

He could read the shock on her face, and his mind raced to explain what could only appear to be an irrational outburst. "It's not what it sounds like. I quit my job yesterday."

She threw a hand to cover her mouth, but said nothing.

"Let me explain. My work visa is tied to the job, and Zoe told me I'd have to leave the country to get a new one. " He struggled to choose the right words. "I'm not sure if that's true, but why not use it as an opportunity?" He tried to move closer. "I just thought of it now. We could travel together for a few months. Maybe backpack around for a while."

Tomoko stepped back, out of reach. "That's crazy—I can't take off months to travel."

"You could quit your job, too."

"This is unbelievable. How could I have been so stupid?" Her eyes fell to the sidewalk, refusing to meet his gaze.

"But we could—"

Icy frost crackled in her voice as she interjected. "My brother is dead, Max. I'm an only child now. You know that. My parents are getting old and they expect me to care for them. And I can't leave my job. It's my duty." Head down, her long hair swung to and fro. "My girlfriends were right."

He knew well enough that her friends were afraid of foreigners; that they'd been whispering against him. "I want us to be together."

"Doesn't matter." Eyes glistening, she looked as though she wanted to cry but was too proud. "I need some time to think, alone."

"I'm not leaving you." He was trying to explain things to himself as much as to her. "I want you to come with me."

"So this is my fault—for not being able to drop everything."

Nearby, rising above the hum of the surrounding city, Kenji's voice was shouting their names, struggling to grab their attention. Max glanced over his shoulder toward the nearby McDonald's, and in the brief moment it took him to wave a greeting, Tomoko sprang away into the mouth of a waiting cab.

The taxi door snapped shut as Max rushed forward, tapping repeatedly on the window. "What are you doing?" He banged on the glass with the palm of his hand, frantic, stumbling over his feet as the vehicle accelerated. "Where are you going? Please, Tomoko, let's talk." The glass barrier and the car's rising engine muffled her words, but she allowed herself one hurtful glance that tore at his gut before the car pulled away.

Max swore in despair and punched the air as the taxi's taillights disappeared up the street, only to be lost in a blur of neon.

CHAPTER
THIRTEEN

H ER EYES slowly panned the inside of the car, and she wondered how she'd gotten there. The emblem on the glove box read Cadillac Series 62. The driver seemed familiar, but a murky shadow clung to him, and she couldn't quite see his face. The car stopped in a dark, wooded forest heavy with fog. The man handed her a brown envelope. She peered inside and saw that it held tightly packed bundles of U.S. currency. The man's instructions were muffled, and she strained to hear the words as he leaned across her to grasp the chrome door handle.

Yoko instantly found herself standing in the outdoor dampness. The car's tires crunched over gravel as the slender, fin-shaped taillights disappeared into the haze. She was struck by the strangeness of it all, yet for some reason she didn't feel frightened.

Looking down, she noticed she was wearing a sleeveless black satin cocktail dress, with white gloves that rose to her elbows. Clutching the envelope to her chest, she began to walk down the road. The mist cleared and the ground changed to the lawn of a luxurious estate home. Four immense pillars at the front of the grand building were spiraled in lights of sparkling green and red. Cars filled the driveway. A smiling butler motioned her toward the warm glow of the front door, and she entered.

The foyer held a brilliant Christmas tree that reached up to the second floor. People drifted about, laughing and talking as a string quartet played "Deck the Halls." Passing a full-length mirror, she caught a reflection of herself. Touching her black bouffant hairdo, she noticed how incredibly young she looked.

In the living room, a handsome man stood in the far corner. She walked toward him. He was slim and youthful, with short brown hair, lime-colored eyes, and a pouting lower lip. He smiled without showing his teeth. Looking across the room toward the fireplace, she noticed an olive-skinned woman sneering at her.

Blinking, she found herself on a backyard patio. The handsome man followed her as she walked away across the grass. Turning to face him, she handed over the envelope and he suddenly grasped both her arms and his warm lips pressed against hers. She felt herself almost give in, but then swiftly pushed him away.

Immediately he was gone, and she found herself watching a car driving slowly through a crowd of hysterical people. As it passed she could just make out, in the back, the tortured face of a weeping lady in a pink jacket and hat. From behind, a finger tapped her shoulder, and she turned to see the familiar young man grinning and holding a rifle. Suddenly his mouth twisted in pain as a scarlet spot grew quickly in the center of his chest before he slumped to the ground, disappearing from sight into the angry crowd swarming around him.

The world reformed itself, and she was in a room with high ceilings, paneled chestnut walls, and worn hardwood floors. An imposing oak table ran along the far wall. Behind it sat four pale men dressed in suits, each with greased hair and slim black ties. In the center of the room was a lone wooden chair. She felt herself smoothing her satin skirt before sitting. The men fired question after question, and she wanted to answer them, but no sound came forth. They grew increasingly angry and pounded the table with their fists. Her chair slid continuously closer, and the men's faces grew larger and angrier. Red-faced, they shouted repeatedly. She felt hot tears on her cheeks and wanted to rise and run, but she seemed glued to the chair, unable to move.

Yoko screamed and bolted upright in bed. The tabby cat resting beside her hissed. Breathing in sharply, she clutched at her chest, heart pounding in her ears as sweat trickled down her back. *It's only a nightmare.*

She rocked back and forth, willing her racing pulse to slow.

When will I be free of the past?

When will all the lies end?

CHAPTER
FOURTEEN

Sunday, April 22

A PHONE WAS ringing in the distance—three, five, seven times. Max's mind climbed from its short slumber. He smelled straw. A tangle of sheets bound his feet together. His right eyelid came unstuck, and he saw the blurred tatami floor pressing against his face.

Pale light edged through a set of closed blinds, illuminating the meager room. A tousled sheet and a second wafer-thin mattress lay a few feet to the left. Kenji, Yoko's assistant, had been sleeping there, but the bed was now empty.

Outside, a metallic squeak preceded the *whoomf* of a door pulling shut. Footsteps approached. The room's wall slid open a few inches, and Max yawned. "Man, it's way too early to be up. Where'd you go?"

Kenji's familiar spiked hair and chubby frame entered the room. His voice carried a slight lisp as he spoke. "I went for hangover medicine." He dug into a plastic bag and pulled out a pair of battery-sized brown bottles. "If you want one, there's 'Real Gold' or 'Go For It, Mr. Liver.'"

Max rolled onto his side. "Hey, I only had a couple of beers. You calling me a lightweight?"

"No, I just thought . . ."

"Just kidding. I don't need any. Thanks." He sniffed tentatively at his armpit. "But, phew, I could really use a shower."

"*So desu ne.*" Kenji nodded in agreement as he lifted the blinds to open the window. "I'll make breakfast."

THE two sat facing each other at the corner table in the apartment kitchen, drinking coffee. Max struggled to force his ruminating mind away from his now damaged relationship with Tomoko. "Have you ever seen any photos of Yoko and Mr. Murayama together?"

"Yes. Of course."

"Any old ones?"

Kenji stopped chewing his toast. "A few. Why?"

"Any before 1985?"

"I don't know—the pictures in the office don't have dates." A puzzled look replaced Kenji's almost permanent grin. "That was the year I was born."

Max pressed on, refusing to reveal his motivation. "All right, so how about pictures of Mr. Murayama with Yoko when she was little?"

"Hmmm . . ." Kenji pondered awhile longer. Finally he shook his head. "No, I don't think so."

Max took another sip.. It wasn't conclusive proof either way. But why lie about Mr. Murayama being Yoko's father? Max decided there was no point pressing the question. In two weeks, when he was finished teaching at the school, it wouldn't matter, anyway. "Never mind. Forget about it."

Kenji shrugged. "I need to clean up the beds. My parents are coming to stay for a few days." Lifting his jacket from the kitchen floor, he emptied the pockets into a ceramic bowl next to the sink before continuing the conversation from the next room. "So why did you quit the school?"

"You've dealt with Yoko a lot longer than I have. I should ask why you bother to stay. You know, she won't give me back my passport."

"Yes, I know." Kenji reappeared, wearing a sheepish expression on his cherub face. "I feel very bad. It's not right."

Max stared at his friend. "It's not your fault. You didn't make her into what she is."

Kenji mumbled something half coherently at the ground.

"Excuse me?" Max was sure he'd heard a confession of sorts, but he needed to clarify.

"I said she's keeping your passport in the drafting cabinet in Mr.

Murayama's office—fourth drawer from the top."

"Are you serious?" Max set down his coffee. "How long have you known?" He couldn't help feel betrayed, and it showed. "You know how much this has been driving me crazy."

"I only learned last week. She thought you might look for it in her office. She said you would get it back once the investors paid all their money." Kenji's slender eyes suddenly grew round. "You can't tell her I told you." An unspoken apprehension of the Dragon Lady passed between them.

"No, don't worry. I won't say anything." Max shook his head. "I can't believe it's been sitting right there."

Kenji ducked back into the living room and a vacuum roared to life.

Max stood to place the dishes in the kitchen sink and his eyes came to rest on the adjacent ceramic bowl. The plastic Ferrari keychain was familiar—he'd watched Kenji pocket it after locking up the office. *I would just be borrowing it.* He tried to push away the wicked thought blooming in his mind. It was immoral, and a feeling of guilt gripped him. But everything about the whole situation with Yoko seemed wrong, and besides, he would only be retrieving what was his already. Plus, Kenji owed him—and maybe, in this case, two wrongs would make a right. Holding his breath, Max slowly closed his fingers around the keys. They slid easily into the pocket of his jeans. Instantly, he was overwhelmed by the urge to depart, and he shouted over the noise. "I'd better get rolling." Stepping into the nearby alcove, he bent over, wriggling his feet into his tennis shoes.

The vacuum's roar died down as Kenji reappeared. "I'm sure Yoko will give you back the passport soon."

"Yeah, for sure. And thanks for the karaoke last night, and for letting me crash here. I needed to take my mind off things." The gratitude was delivered with a quick head bob. "Didn't feel much like going home after everything that happened with Tomoko." He tried hard to push the memory of the disappearing taxi from his mind.

"*Douitashimashite.*"

Max opened the door and made it halfway down the hallway before Kenji's shout forced him to a stop. He cringed and turned around, the office key weighing heavily in his pocket.

"Wait! There is one picture of them both on the office wall. It's Mr. Murayama pushing Yoko on a swing—I recognize the birthmark on her arm.

She looks very young."

"Thanks buddy. See you later."

The apartment door clicked shut.

If Kenji was right, there was concrete proof that Yoko was Murayama's daughter. But he still needed to retrieve his passport. And now, thanks to Kenji, he knew exactly where to find it.

CHAPTER
ELEVEN

THE OFFICE lady's perfect hips swayed rhythmically while she maneuvered a rolling cart through the islands of desks. With a demure smile and soft touch, she loaded and unloaded neat stacks of National Police Agency case files.

As she passed through a group of seated detectives, they stared at the lines of the navy blue polyester skirt that hugged her slender waist and curved over her well-formed buttocks. Shoulder-length black hair, a long-sleeved white blouse, matching blue vest, and short-heeled pumps completed the uniform. Like paper dolls, office ladies, or OLs, were normally clone-like, unknown in identity. However, this woman's appearance was something special. She had a perfectly tight body, dazzling almond-shaped eyes, and flawless cheekbones.

On the same floor, Masami Ishi, superintendent of the Criminal Investigation Bureau, sat behind his desk in one of the few private offices in the NPA's Tokyo head office. Outside the window behind him, low gray clouds spread into the distance over the sprawling city. He normally didn't work on the weekends, but this was an exception. Already, more than forty-eight hours had passed since the murder of Kazue Saito, and the first official report was just being delivered. It was a pitifully slow performance for the Agency in such a high-profile case. Several phone calls had already been received from prominent government officials. They were making rumblings about the need for a Senate investigation. He would have to personally reprimand the officers involved, but first he wanted to see the results.

The superintendent adjusted the thick, wire glasses resting against the pockmarked skin of his round cheeks. His shoes barely touched the floor. The comb-over on his balding scalp slid down his forehead, and he swept it back into place. Leaning back in his chair, he opened the Sunday newspaper. The OL quietly entered Masami's office, holding a single file in the crook of her slender arm. Walking with her eyes cast down, she moved robotically toward the oversized mahogany desk and gently placed the file down before bowing and backing out of the room.

She was definitely above average, and he'd have to see to it that she was transferred to the weekday shift. Masami Ishi's overbite showed more prominently as he smiled to himself.

Opening the file, he scanned the page. He'd already seen most of the summarized details from the crime scene, and all the forensic evidence. The information he was specifically looking for was the results of the cell-phone analysis. SoftBank Mobile was notoriously slow at providing call-record details, so the police lab had been tasked with extracting information from the smashed remains of Kazue Saito's cell phone.

The last connection had been made at 11:41 p.m. on Thursday, April 19, to a cell phone registered to Takahito Murayama. He was curious to see that it wasn't a call, but a text. Flipping the page, he read the message. It was brief— just three numbers followed by two Latin characters—but it spoke volumes.

Masami Ishi leaned back in his chair. Rubbing his forehead with the palms of both hands did little to reduce his creeping anxiety. This situation was growing uglier by the minute.

Grabbing a marker, he paused, then blacked out the contents of the short text message. Under no circumstances could the politicians see this information right now, at least not until he could piece together why the dead diplomat had shattered his cell phone before dying.

CHAPTER
SIXTEEN

M AX'S SHORT letter described the situation in clear and simple terms. The first line read, "To the Dear Ladies." It would need to be translated into Japanese. It detailed the false, excessive invoicing of school tuition and expenses, personal spending of investment funds, and suspicion of planned fraud on Yoko's part. He acknowledged that he couldn't prove it all, but they needed to be warned. Sealing the envelope felt like purging something evil from his soul. After tonight, Max knew there wouldn't likely be a chance to speak again with his students' mothers. If everything went as expected, he would have his passport back and Yoko would be furious beyond words.

"Why not wait until tomorrow and just ask the old man to get the passport for you?" Zoe was propped against the floor pillows in her usual corner of the TPH living room, eyes glazed from the previous night's drug-fest. The nearby electric heater, nestled beneath the television, buzzed and clicked as a subtitled Matt Damon recklessly raced a car through a Moscow tunnel.

"Murayami doesn't go to his office every day." Max lay shirtless, soaked in sweat on the living room floor. An hour-long run, intended to clear his head, had served only to give him a painful side-stitch. "What if the Dragon Lady moves it in the meantime? Now that I know where it is, I don't want to miss my chance to get it back."

"You're paranoid."

Max craned his head to take a gulp of Pocari Sweat. "I have the office key, but that's it. Once I smash the lock on the drafting cabinet, it'll be breaking and entering, whether it's my passport or not."

Zoe's contemptuous snicker prompted him to lift his head quizzically. "What was that for?"

"You—Saint Max, the patron saint of the Tokyo Poor House—are actually going to break into a locked cabinet? Yeah, right."

"I'm only perfect when compared to you," he retorted. "And besides, I really upset Tomoko last night. Not very saintly."

Zoe shrugged. "So you'll apologize like you always do."

"Advice from someone whose longest relationship is with a needle?" He turned onto his side and faced the wall. "Your own words, not mine, remember."

Behind him, he heard Zoe rise and descend the squeaking stairs to the main floor.

Moments later the stairs shuddered again, and Zoe flopped down. "You may not appreciate my wisdom, but you can thank me for this."

Max felt something solid strike the back of his head. "Ow, what the hell?" He rubbed the spot of impact before turning back over. He retrieved a thick, shiny pen from the straw floor.

"Nice Waterford knock-off, but you've lost me."

Zoe crawled forward, taking the pen from Max's hand. She unscrewed the two halves of the burgundy casing and let the slender silver contents scatter on the floor. "This is a 38-gram ballpoint pen, lock-pick special. The carbon steel 'tension wrench' is the clip—here—and it holds nine different steel picks."

"You're joking, right? Where'd you get this?"

"Never mind. You want to know how to use it or not?"

"Yeah. Of course."

Zoe demonstrated with an old lock. "Most have a pin-and-tumbler design. Visualize a lock like a solid metal pipe surrounded by a metal tube. There's nothing stopping the pipe from spinning freely. Now imagine you drill a line of five holes through the tube and into the pipe. You place five pins into all five holes. Can the pipe spin freely anymore?" Max was sure it was a rhetorical question as he watched her shake her head. "Pull out all five pins, and the pipe is free to spin again. That's the basic concept."

"That's it?" He shifted into a sitting position to better view the demonstration.

"There's a bit more to it, but picking one is simply a matter of moving the pins without a key." She dropped the lock in Max's palm and raised her eyebrows. "It's a bit more challenging if it's a wafer lock, double-wafer lock, or even a tubular lock."

"Yeah, which means I'm back to using a crowbar."

Zoe gave a slightly malicious grin. "Odds are it's a simple pin-and-tumbler, which I can show you how to 'rake.' You'll have a good chance."

"Thanks." Max tried to read her face. "But where'd you learn all this?"

"My step-father." Her eyes dropped, avoiding his gaze. "Fear is a fantastic motivator."

THE cutesy Pokemon recording instructed Max to leave a message at the sound of the bell. Tomoko was obviously screening her calls. Each of his half dozen attempts had gone unanswered.

He knew the frustration in his voice would be evident—he hated fighting with anyone, but most of all her—so he chose his words carefully. "What happened last night, Tomoko, and what I said . . . I'm so sorry. I didn't mean what you think. Give me a chance to explain." He paused briefly. "Things are about to change, big time. Call me back."

Lowering the receiver, he stared at the return portion of the plane ticket in his hand, reflecting on the fact that he had kept its existence to himself. Purchased almost a year earlier, it was a "use it or lose it" deal that was set to expire in less than a month's time. He knew he could choose to toss it away, but each time he tried he remembered shelling out the hard-earned cash, believing in the moment that personal choice and calculated risks could rise above circumstance, that all the books he'd read about having a "can-do" mantra were really true. That maybe he wasn't just like the rest of his family, and would actually make something of himself. The past year had been about new beginnings, exciting and fresh, but now the cracks of reality were showing through, as they always did. Was it possible that every place was the same, after all? Maybe his dad was right—maybe it was just best to keep moving and never look back.

He folded the ticket and exchanged it for the loose door lock lying on the floor next to his futon. Only a few hours remained for some final practice before a night trip to the office.

CHAPTER
SEVENTEEN

THE LATE hour meant little foot traffic. Max used exit A1 of the Mita subway station to approach the office, since it avoided the police box at the intersection to the west. Cars and taxis rolled by from time to time. Thankfully, most cab drivers already had fares and were just taking a shortcut through the area. A group of rosy-cheeked businessmen staggered along the sidewalk after exiting a nearby pub, and he kept his head down in order to avoid drawing undue attention.

The air smelled fresh for a change. Light drops of rain flecked the concrete sidewalk. Max pulled the black-and-orange Yomiuri Giants ball cap down farther over his eyes and stooped a little to appear shorter. A black hoodie and blue jeans allowed him to blend more easily into the patchwork of dark and light between the intermittent overhead street lamps. Cold wind swirled down from the buildings above, nipping at his nose and ears.

Forty feet from the slender office building, he could see that the Plum Tree Restaurant's rolling metal shutters were pulled down. This was a good sign; it meant he wouldn't have to deal with the gruff owner. The man's mess of stained teeth and his shaggy appearance were alarming enough in the daytime. He certainly wasn't someone Max wanted to encounter on a stormy night.

Zoe's wrong. I can do this.

He paused next to the metal door at the building's front, his breathing shallow and underarms wet. The Ferrari keychain felt smooth as he played it between his thumb and forefinger.

Just get the passport. It belongs to you, anyway. No big deal.

Steeling himself, he twisted the key in the lock. The deadbolt was oddly sluggish, and he tugged it a few times before it finally turned. The door pressed open and he was inside.

Gradually, his eyes adjusted to the dim glow of an emergency exit sign. The closet-sized entryway was empty. To the right was a locked glass door leading into the restaurant.

Ascending the twisting flights of stairs was difficult in the dark, so he moved cautiously, cursing as he tripped and caught himself on the second landing. The baseball cap fell off, but he found it and stuffed it into a pocket.

Swinging open the third-floor door, Max slipped into the short central hallway. *Odd that it's unlocked.* Shards of street light cut along the edges of the half-closed kitchen blinds and stretched past him down the corridor. He could see Murayama's office was open, and he stepped toward it. In the stillness, the free-moving stairwell door slammed closed, resonating with an echoing thud. Ominously, from behind him, a deep Japanese voice spoke.

Max whirled around. He could see a shaft of light dancing on the wall of the open storeroom in the back. The deep voice spoke again. He couldn't make out the words, but they masked the sound of his squeaking shoes as he charged forward into the kitchen and ducked to the right. The beam of approaching light bounced against the kitchen blinds as the voice came down the hallway. Max held his breath and prayed that the man would turn left into the office.

A second voice with a harsh but hushed edge resonated from within the office. *"Jun! Damare!"*

Max understood the demand to "shut up," but the remainder of the men's conversation was lost on him as he hunched anxiously in the shadowy kitchen. He suddenly found himself wishing he'd paid more attention in Japanese language class.

"JUN, get to work!"

"There are at least forty filing cabinets in the back storeroom and thirty in here. How the hell are we supposed to open them all?"

"If you'd stop wandering around and focus on this room, we could find the satchel and leave."

"I can't pick locks like you."

"That's why I brought a metal bar for you. And try not to make so much noise—at least not with your mouth."

"Give me the bag. If I have to do this much work, I'm taking anything that looks valuable."

"I don't care. Just do something."

CROUCHED in terror, Max listened to the screech of twisting metal as cabinets were wrenched open, their contents tossed carelessly to the floor.

Beads of sweat formed on Max's forehead, and he wiped them away. Any chance of recovering the passport was gone now. No building security meant there wouldn't be a rescue. He needed to find help.

Peering out of the kitchen, he could see that the door to the office was wide open. Flickering light escaped from the dimly lit room. It would be risky to attempt passing the open entry on the way to the stairs. Max grabbed the kitchen door and prayed it wouldn't squeak. Slowly, he pulled it to the point of closing. He needed time to think. Remaining motionless for what seemed like an eternity, he fished out his pocket watch, squinting to see the face. It was twenty minutes after midnight.

Thunder cracked in the distance and raindrops began tapping against the window.

The two voices in the office grew animated. It seemed they'd found what they were looking for. Summoning all his courage, Max decided his only chance was a quick retreat. Waiting would mean they could corner him in the kitchen. Taking a deep breath, he pulled open the door and edged into the corridor. His muscles tensed as he got set to run.

Then, from nowhere, a disembodied head poked out of the dark stairwell and looked straight at him. Max felt his racing heart tearing a hole in his chest. He pulled back and dropped to the floor. The figure of a crouching man skulked into the twilight of the hallway. A baseball bat rested on his sinewy shoulder. In the thin light, the grim face was unmistakable. The owner of the Plum Tree had awakened from a booze-soaked sleep, and he was pissed off.

The restaurateur inched toward the kitchen before he stopped and his head flicked to the left, appearing to listen. Seconds dragged by while he remained coiled in place. Then, without warning, he charged into the office. His screaming battle cry soon joined with other voices in a chorus of angry shouting.

Awestruck, Max watched as the owner was immediately driven back into the hallway, entwined with a lunging thief. Both men hammered into the wall before toppling into a heap on the floor. The second thief leaped from the office doorway and joined in the scuffle, which became a sea of swinging arms and kicking legs.

Max knew he had to move fast. Reaching up, his shaking hand groped the wall until it felt the familiar round picture frame. A quarter turn, and the hidden doorway popped open. Without rising, he slithered into the adjacent office. He could hear the owner still swinging viciously as the action moved down the hallway to the kitchen. The secret doorway pressed closed just in time, shuddering with the weight of a violent body blow.

The leather chair was next to him and he pressed against it for support, his heart beating wildly. Other than the dim glow of the desk lamp, the only light entering the room was through the partially open blinds. Directly in front of him, leaning against the edge of the end table, lay the thieves' daypack. But it didn't make any sense. Why rob the place with such a small bag?

This is Mr. Murayama's whole life. I can't let them get away with it.

The owner's screams of pain rang out. The sound of shattering bone galvanized Max, and in one swift movement, he leaped to his feet and grabbed the daypack. Managing to get it over one shoulder, he flew into the hall. The polished floor was smooth, and his feet slipped under him. Slamming into the stairwell door, he looked up and caught a brief glimpse of a thick-necked man in the kitchen.

With his pulse drumming in his ears, Max plunged down the dark stairs, racing to reach the door. Footsteps thundered behind him while he fumbled with the front latch before stumbling blindly onto the sidewalk. Charging across the empty street, he chanced a look back. The shorter thief was just steps behind, while the thick-necked guy was now running the opposite way.

Max tripped on the far curb and his pursuer lunged, grabbing at the daypack, pulling downward. Instinctively Max freed himself by spinning sideways and knocking the grasping hand away. The sudden release sent the thief tumbling to the ground.

The piercing sound of a whistle ripped the air. Max glanced up, with the sidewalk still flying by, to see a night patrol officer standing just thirty feet ahead. The man was pointing excitedly while fumbling with something on his belt: a gun.

Max made a sharp left turn into a laneway as he popped the daypack's second shoulder strap into place and broke into a sprint. Flying past rows of silent shops, he continued down the lane before making another left along a side street. There was no need to look back. He could hear both pursuers close behind.

An approaching bicyclist zagged wildly. Ringing his bell in complaint, he barely avoided colliding with the pursuing thief. The short-lived delay allowed Max the chance to dart right, squeezing into a passageway between two buildings. It was barely wide enough for his shoulders, and with the daypack on he couldn't turn sideways. His hands gripped the walls and he slowed, moving cautiously forward. Close behind, the thief hit the mossy clay ground and stumbled to his knees, cursing. A second later, the policeman entered the passageway at full speed, both legs shooting out from under him. His shout of surprise was followed by the thud of his skull as it hammered the ground.

The next laneway was just a few feet away, and Max charged to the right after his feet touched the pavement. Ahead, blinking lights outlined a nighttime road crew at work. A flagman was waving a glowing yellow baton as Max approached. Just before they collided, he dashed around the shocked man before leaping over a construction crew standing in a narrow hole in the road's center. Seconds later, he heard the flagman shouting again. Looking back, he saw several other workers now standing together, blocking the road.

What the hell was I thinking?

From Max's last ominous glimpse of the thief, he appeared to be texting with his both hands.

Turning left, working his way deeper into the maze of narrow streets, Max slowed his run as light from the next major roadway grew brighter. In the distance, he could hear, drawing closer, the rising whine of a high-pitched engine. A lime-green motorcycle flew past. The thick-necked man had overshot the entrance to the road. With sickening certainty, Max realized that he'd been herded into a trap. The noise of the engine became guttural as the sports bike geared down to turn around.

The barren fronts of the surrounding single-story shops closed in like a collapsing vice. Max knew he had mere seconds. Desperately, he spun around, searching for somewhere, anywhere, to hide, but there was little choice. He raced forward, vaulting upward off a bike rack, slamming hard into the front edge of a flat concrete roof. Hanging precariously from his torso, his feet kicked wildly, searching for a spot on which to gain purchase.

Dual headlights tore open the darkness, searching, seeking. Again and again, the piercing engine shrieked as the bike crept forward. The undulating sound reverberated off the surrounding buildings like a baying pack of hounds. Rubber ground against asphalt as the driver twisted the handlebars back and forth, using the light to sweep the vacant edges of the laneway.

Gravel bit into Max's back. Lying prone on the flat rooftop hiding spot, he lifted his head slightly as the noise moved past. From his vantage point, he could see the man's enormous upper body wrapped in a muscle shirt, a reflected pool of light illuminating the patterned tattoos running from his shoulders to mid-forearm.

Instant terror charged the air.

Holy shit! He's Yakuza*!*

Minutes ticked by as Max lay pulsing with fear in the darkness—plenty of time to ponder the awful question: why were the *Yakuza* in Murayama's office?

CHAPTER
EIGHTEEN

Monday, April 23

THE POINTED nose of the Ninja ZX-10R sports bike poked out of the alleyway's deep shadows. From his vantage point three blocks away, Jun could see the echo of flickering red police lights against the dark buildings. There would be no going back to finish dealing with the restaurant owner. With any luck, the injuries the man had already suffered would buy his silence. He was a drunk, but he likely wasn't stupid enough to point a finger at a gang of organized criminals. If not, accidents could occur when they needed to.

The scattered rain increased its tempo. Jun flexed and rubbed his hands against the droplets forming on the muscles of his bare arms. Beating a hasty retreat had meant leaving behind his new motorcycle jacket and riding gloves. The *Gaijin*—probably an American—would have to pay both in cash and in pain.

Closing the visor on his helmet, he revved the engine to a purr. Within seconds, Jun's screaming bike vanished into the wet night.

THE taxi navigated the empty 2 a.m. streets, its windshield wipers intermittently rising and falling. The driver glanced down every so often at the map on the business card he'd been handed.

Max periodically caught the driver's questioning eyes as they drifted to the rearview mirror, and he knew the man must think him a crazy foreigner. He slouched in the backseat, his chin pressed against his chest, positioning his head well below the lace-covered headrests. It felt insane, but completely necessary.

The motorcycle had moved up and down the laneway repeatedly, and he'd remained on the damp rooftop hiding place until he was sure he couldn't hear the engine any longer. Pulling his warming hand from his pocket had produced the forgotten business card. The moment seemed strangely fateful; priests were meant to provide sanctuary, and Max had nowhere else to go. Heading home to the TPH was out of the question—the police could easily determine where he lived, and it likely wouldn't take long for the gangsters to find out the same. And Tomoko wasn't returning his calls. His nerves felt exposed and raw. He needed somewhere safe to think.

The daypack lay beside him on the backseat. Unzipping it, he pulled out an old, soft-shelled leather satchel. Dual cinches attached to simple brass buckles held the overhanging front closed. A symmetrical gold emblem was stamped onto the leather—it looked familiar, but he couldn't recall where he'd seen it. Undoing the tarnished clasps, Max lifted away the front flap and peered inside, noting the spine of a book. As he withdrew the volume, he saw that the yellow cover was embossed with a cresting wave over a distant image of Mount Fuji. An ornate red seal was pressed into the center, but the streetlights flickering periodically through the taxi's window made it impossible to read the fine script.

Opening the book's pages close to his face released a light, musty smell, the familiar scent of libraries and fine paper mixed in the blender of time. Leafing through it, he flipped past pages filled with handwritten Japanese symbols.

Eventually, the cab entered a side street and slowed to a stop in front of a two-story house. The place was astoundingly large by local standards. It would have garnered little attention in a new American suburb, but in the center of Tokyo, it was most unusual. Although reluctant to leave the warmth of the cab, he paid in cash, grabbed the daypack, and climbed out.

Standing before the grandiose home, Max wondered if he was making a mistake, but the steadily increasing rain pushed him toward the locked metal gate. Behind it, a flight of stairs rose sharply to the entrance. A flash of lightning illuminated intricately carved wooden doors guarded by a pair of security cameras mounted overtop.

The brick column to the left of the gate held a panel with a buzzer, a keypad, and a monitor. Max wiped the gathering rain from his face. He pressed the buzzer and waited, shifting his weight nervously from foot to foot as he kept a wary eye on the street. No answer. He pressed the buzzer again, silently wondering if a backup plan would have been a smart idea. Just then, the screen in front of him glowed to life and Toshi's sleepy face appeared.

A gust of wind blew droplets of water against the glowing monitor, drawing twinkling translucent lines down the screen. Both men stared as seconds ticked by with neither saying anything.

In a hesitant voice, Max finally spoke. "My name is Max Travers. I met you on a train—"

Toshi interrupted, "Yes, I know. You need help. Come in right away."

Max's elation mixed with the rain as the sanctuary gate sprang open. Dressed in a patterned cotton robe, Toshi opened the carved door, beckoning him upward.

Once inside, Max stared wide-eyed at the vaulted foyer rising to the second floor. A wooden staircase on the right ascended and turned ninety degrees before meeting the upper landing. On the wall to the left, a yard-wide scroll hung two stories from the high ceiling to the polished floor. Two white marble urns rested beneath the fabric's brush-stroked surface.

"You're hurt. Let me get a cloth." Toshi disappeared.

Turning to a nearby mirror, Max saw blood feathering from a cut above his left eyebrow into the hair over his ear. It was apparent now why the taxi driver had been staring so intently.

Footsteps echoed as Toshi returned. "You're much taller than me. Please, I need you to sit."

Max moved to the flared bottom of the wooden staircase, feeling grateful that the door to a stranger's home had been opened so quickly at such a late hour. The Shinto priest knelt down and dabbed gently at the cut with a cloth. The warm water felt soothing, almost healing, as if in his hands it was able to wash away the violence of the night, replacing it with calm and tranquility.

Toshi formed gauze into a makeshift bandage, then fixed it in place with medical tape. "That should stop the bleeding."

"Thank you." Max had been sitting motionless, facing the two white urns and engaged by their simple beauty. He pointed to them, curious. "What are those?"

"My parents."

Max cringed. "I'm so sorry."

"Don't be embarrassed. It's always better to face reality. My parents were victims of terrorism. They were on the subway during the Sarin gas attacks more than ten years ago." Toshi stood. "Now, please follow me. You need rest."

Suddenly, Max could think of nothing other than sleep. He felt completely drained, exhausted from the ordeal. Toshi led him to an upstairs guest room. The spartan space held a single mattress in the center of the tatami floor. Wheat-colored linens were folded down at one corner as if a visitor had been expected. Max wanted to express his gratitude and explain what had happened, but the question was, where to begin? "There was a robbery." Unzipping the damp daypack, he withdrew the brown leather satchel and pressed it toward Toshi.

The priest accepted the offering and held up his free hand. "Please. There is no need to rush." His face was relaxed, and his voice serene. "No need to say anything."

"But there's a book in this satchel. I need to know what's in it."

"It can wait until morning. For now, you must rest." Then he dipped with a bow and was gone.

Max needed no further encouragement. He removed his wet clothes and dropped them in a heap before kneeling onto the mattress and rolling under the covers. Soft flannel arms wrapped around him. The last thing he recalled was a vision of hundreds of glowing stars. The fog of dreams rolled in. Sleep came swift and sure.

TOSHI stared at the satchel's gold embossed emblem—a beautiful flower. He ran his fingers over each of the sixteen chrysanthemum petals. Since the nineteenth century, the symbol had represented the power and majesty of the Japanese royal family. It seemed impossible to think that he was actually holding it in his hands. He lifted the overhanging leather flap and carefully removed the book. The stamp of a red *Hanko* seal was pressed onto a coin-sized paper circle in the center of the cover. The signature gave the name Tsuneyoshi Takeda.

Toshi partially opened the cover, then closed it hastily. His wiped his sweaty palms against his robe. Reading a document belonging to another member of the royal family felt wrong. It felt like a sin against the emperor himself. But the cover seemed to burn hot in his hands, almost as if the book desired to be opened and understood. Eventually the urge became too overwhelming. Turning to the first page, he read:

> Year 16 of the Shōwa reign—This is the chronicle of my honorable journey to places yet unknown. The tide of righteous war has temporarily shifted, and our glorious nation is being tested. The emperor's brother Prince Chichibu called to me, and as I knelt before him, he asked for me to serve Amaterasu. The Sun Goddess's lifeblood must be protected. Temporary places of safekeeping must be found. Prince Chichibu will be the chief architect, while I shall execute the masterful plans. I look forward to the hardships and challenges that lie ahead. My heart is pure with obedience. Duty is asked of me, and I will deliver it.

CHAPTER
NINETEEN

FOUR POLICE cruisers monopolized the roadside parking in front of the
Plum Tree Restaurant. Bookends of bright yellow security tape blocked
the sidewalk on either side of the skinny office building. Rain poured from
the dark gray sky, driving a pair of surly uniformed officers to hunker under a
stunted eave near the building's front doorway. Seven-thirty Monday morning
traffic inched by while drivers peered wide-eyed through foggy windshields.

Scarcely taking in the scene below him, Mr. Murayama stared from
the rain-soaked third-floor windows. Upon arriving at the office, he had
been dumbstruck at the sight of open drawers and twisted metal cabinets.
Contents on one side of the room were stacked neatly on the floor, while on
the other side they lay smashed and strewn in jumbled piles. A lifetime of
searching, collecting, and cataloging lay in shambles. It seemed as if a two-
headed monster had stormed through the room. His insistent pleas for the
police to leave had fallen on deaf ears. Charged with a duty to determine the
attackers' identities, the officers had stated emphatically they were not about
to go away, even if he insisted through teary eyes that nothing was missing.

STANDING in the room's center, Yoko's mind seethed with clear, unfettered
rage. Bad publicity and a loss of confidence were the last things she needed as

she fought to finalize the sale of the school's shares. Years of meticulous work lay in the balance. She needed just a few more weeks to wrap things up. Her chance to start over again was so close.

The police had been most uncooperative in providing any information. Thankfully, however, one officer liked to talk. He let it slip that two men—one blond—had been seen running from the building, and the injured restaurateur had managed to utter the word *"Gaijin"* before lapsing into a coma. Since the building's lock was undamaged, the "foreigner" in question could have been only one person: Max. But she couldn't check to see if his passport was still hidden in the drafting cabinet. The detective and two police officers in the room were not allowing anything to be touched. If Yoko could have breathed fire and destroyed everything in sight, she would have done it.

"Excuse me, are you all right?" The detective was now standing almost directly behind her.

"Yes, I'm fine. This is all so upsetting." She turned and pursed her lips into a half smile, meant to convey fortitude in the face of hard times.

"If you will sit down again, we can finish up sooner."

"Yes, I understand."

"Your father isn't handling this well. He should probably go home."

Yoko glanced at the pathetic old man slumped sideways in the black leather chair. His normally slicked-back hair hung like fuzzy gray twine around the outer edges of his wrinkled face, framing his square-rimmed glasses and puffy, red eyes.

The detective excused himself to answer his ringing cell phone.

Movement to the right caught Yoko's eye, and she turned to see Kenji's arrival. He stood stoop-shouldered while his eyes swept slowly over the carnage in the room. With a fortune-teller's skill for reading people, she could see the culpability in his face like it was a blinking sign. Since the detective appeared engrossed in his call, she took the opportunity to cross to the doorway.

Her lips barely moved, and her voice was whisper-soft to avoid being overheard. "You know something. Tell me what it is."

Kenji's mouth hung open. He stared at his Adidas. "I'm not sure—"

"Out with it!" she hissed through clenched teeth.

"I think Max took my building key yesterday."

Anger coursed through Yoko's veins.

Returning to the couch, the detective motioned for Yoko to join him and she complied, sensing that her veil was wearing thin. His tone had changed from that of a moderate inquisitor, and he now spoke with new authority. "Mr. Murayama, I've just received instructions from headquarters to collect your cell phone."

Ashen-faced, the old man stared into space, his chest rising and falling in hesitating spurts.

"Mr. Murayama, please. Where is your phone?"

Yoko interjected. "This seems silly. How is his cell phone tied to all this?"

"I've been asked by the superintendent of the Bureau himself to request it." The detective glowered. "Sir, are you going to comply?"

Mr. Murayama's silver head edged upward and ticked slightly from side to side. His glazed eyes were accompanied by a raspy, hollow voice. "I don't know where it is."

Yoko interjected again. "He probably left it at home. Kenji can run over and get it for you."

"That's not necessary. I'll have an officer take your father home. He can assist in locating it."

Murayama groaned and rubbed the top of his left arm. He began to stand but slowed as his face twisted into a grimace. Frozen in a half stance, he gasped, sucking in great gulps of air before collapsing forward onto the coffee table. The wooden cube rang hollow with the weight of his body, and it was the detective's quick reaction that stopped him from falling a second time as he pitched toward the windows.

Bolting around the table and lowering the limp body to the floor, the detective slapped Murayama's cheeks. There was no response. He threw off his suit jacket and barked at the officers, "Call an ambulance! He's having a heart attack!"

The detective hesitated and threw a glance at the two wide-eyed officers before he began CPR. He covered Murayama's mouth with his own and puffed three times. His shaking hands landmarked the chest before he leaned onto his straightened arms, thrusting forcefully downward. The room resonated with the sound of snapping ribs.

KENJI stared at the ensuing chaos, certain no one was paying him any attention. He took several stealthy steps backward toward the drafting cabinet.

Thankfully, the long, narrow drawers had been left open. Slowly, he pressed the top three drawers backward with the edge of his left hip. They couldn't be closed completely, or there would be an audible click. As the top of the fourth drawer became exposed, his left hand slid into it. Without looking down, he probed with his fingertips beneath the layers of tissue paper and artists' prints, his heart beating a little bit faster when at last he felt the passport's smooth exterior. Finally free, it slipped smoothly into the back pocket of his Levi's as he breathed a hushed sigh of relief on his way to stand behind the sofa.

The commotion in front of him continued. Looking down, he thought how odd it was that Yoko didn't appear upset or even engaged by the life-or-death scene playing out before her. Instead, she looked like someone waiting for a train or passing time in a doctor's reception. What past event could make a daughter care so little for her father?

CHAPTER
TWENTY

THE STARS no longer glowed, but Max could detect their outlines on the bedroom ceiling. He supposed a child must have put them there. It would be easy to lie quietly for hours and ignore the sliver of hallway light creeping in under the door, announcing the morning.

He tried desperately to drift back to sleep, but reality crept in and clawed him back with each failed attempt. Soon enough he succumbed to wakefulness and admitted it was time to get up and face his problems.

His wet clothes were missing. Beside the daypack lay a plaid house robe folded overtop a pair of bedroom slippers. Pulling upright into a sitting position, his back muscles sparked, and the ribs on his right side ached. As much as he wished the *Yakuza* ordeal had been a sleep-induced nightmare, his body wasn't about to let him forget what had really happened.

Max pulled on the robe and ran a hand through his nest of scratchy hair while surveying the almost bare room. Other than the futon it held only a neglected wooden shelf topped with dusty baseball trophies and a framed diploma: "Toshi Suzuki, Master's in Business Administration, Stanford University."

With the daypack over his shoulder, Max shuffled into the hallway and down the smooth hardwood steps. Hazy light filtered through a pyramid-shaped skylight overhead. The drumming of rain on the glass echoed in the still air. Following the stairs' ninety-degree turn, he could see across the foyer directly into the living room below. It bore Moroccan influences. An embroidered rug covered the floor, and a glass-and-silver *sheesha* stood guard in one corner. Oversized posters shouted from the walls. The artwork was covered in Japanese writing, but a few spoke in English: "Mongolian Invasion," "Combat Unit One," "Roman Conquest." Toshi was reclining on a white L-shaped couch in the far corner of the room, still wearing the same blue robe from the night before. The yellow leather book lay closed on his chest.

Max tiptoed toward the wide, arched entranceway.

"Where did you get this book?" Toshi's clear voice cut through the air.

Max jumped. It was too early in the morning for surprises, and his response registered mild annoyance. "Bit of a long story."

Setting the patterned book on the granite coffee table, the Shinto priest sat up and rubbed sleep from his eyes. "You must tell me where you found it."

Max needed to ease into the conversation. "I will, but first tell me about the posters."

"My company makes these video games."

"Seriously? On the train, when you said you owned a game company, I thought you meant a store or something."

"Do you like video games?"

"A few, but I don't play much. How'd you get into the business?"

Toshi stood and pointed at a framed black-and-white photo of a conservative-looking middle-aged couple. It was an old studio portrait with the man in a suit standing behind the seated woman; both wore solemn looks. "My father held a Ph.D. in history. When I was a young boy, we played many games. We would dress in costumes and make up stories like 'Alexander the Great in Japan' or 'Jerusalem Siege.' He had a great imagination. After my parents' death, I wanted my father's stories to live so that others could enjoy them. I was surprised when the games became so popular."

Max thought of the two white urns in the hallway and quickly attempted to change the subject. "So how can you be a Shinto priest and have a video game company?"

"Most priests are volunteers. We don't do it for money, but because we believe in something. My mother loved the shrine. I do it to honor her." Toshi smiled but his eyes were serious. "I will get tea. Then you tell me the story of how you found that book. *Wakarimashita?*"

Max nodded in resigned agreement, knowing that revealing the whole story would mean explaining his own part of the break-in. "And thanks again for letting me stay."

"My pleasure." Toshi exited to the kitchen through a smaller arched doorway while Max unzipped the daypack. He laid the contents on the coffee table: a cell phone, a velvet bag filled with silver bracelets, several loose ornamental daggers, and a well-worn copy of *The Motorcycle Diaries.* Max recognized it from the photo on the cover, the defining journey of Che Guevara across South America, and thought how odd it was that he would be reading a couple of pages of the same book each night before falling asleep.

He picked up the cell phone, flipping open the front in order to power it on. It was a similar model to Tomoko's. *I sure hope it doesn't have GPS. If this was Thick Neck's phone, he would hate to make it that easy for those goons to find him.*

Max shuddered at the thought of the *Yakuza* in the dark office kitchen and again in the alley. The phone made two shrill chirps before falling silent. He recognized the noise—a text message—and scrolled to the inbox: **893O.K.**

What the heck does that mean?

Toshi entered from the kitchen, carrying a tray with steaming cups and bread with jam. The smell of food made Max realize just how hungry he felt. He turned off the phone before tossing it into the empty daypack.

The food made him talkative, and between bites Max recounted the story of the stolen passport and his quest to recover it. He detailed the encounter with the *Yakuza* as well as the building's drunken owner, the race to escape from both the thief and the police, and finally the chance discovery of the business card in his pocket.

Toshi sipped his tea and listened without interrupting.

As Max reached the story's end, he stretched out sticky fingers to grasp the yellow book.

Springing forward, Toshi stopped him. "Please wipe the jam from your hands first."

Max laughed with nervous surprise. "Okay. But tell me why it's so important."

An inexplicable weight seemed to descend on Toshi's slender shoulders.

He sighed and squeezed the bridge of his nose. "How much of my country's history do you know?"

"Not as much as I thought, but I've certainly been learning. Why?"

"Have you ever heard of Prince Takeda?" Toshi paused, but Max's returning gaze was blank, so he continued. "Prince Takeda was first cousin of Emperor Hirohito, also known by the name Emperor Shōwa after his death. Hirohito ruled for more than sixty years, from 1926 to 1989. Many foreigners think he had no real authority, but this is not so. In truth, he was the highest power in the government—before America took away much of his control. Until 1945, he was said to be a child of the Sun Goddess, Amaterasu. The red circle in the center of our flag is the Rising Sun, after all."

Toshi paused to sip his tea. "Countless stories tell of empires growing, then falling. This is a fate most countries suffer at some time in their history. My country is no different. For many years before World War Two, we controlled Korea, Taiwan, Singapore, parts of China, and other countries." His tone grew solemn. Pain tinged the edge of his voice. "Many sad and shameful things happened then. Millions of people were made into slaves. Others were raped, tortured, or worse—murdered."

Max felt himself being drawn backward into a past that he wasn't sure he cared to know.

The priest continued. "Shinto and Buddhism do not teach us to do these things, but greed listens to no religion. Many people were hurt, and lives were destroyed. Also, much wealth was taken from these countries and brought back here. This happened for almost fifty years, and it continued during World War Two. The government would like to erase this history from our memory. They make half apologies with one face while the other face is in school and on TV, teaching us that it is a lie and the stories of other countries are exaggerated. But I have studied these things on my own, in America."

"I get what you're saying, but I don't see the significance. If everything you've said is common knowledge, then why is this one book so special?"

"The thing this book speaks of—the thing that is not common knowledge— is that when America began to win the war, it became more difficult to bring the stolen goods back to Japan. This book claims to know how that wealth was protected. It says that years were spent hiding the foreign treasure in hundreds of secret places in the Philippines. According to the words here, thousands of slaves, including American war prisoners, were used to do this. Most of them died while working or were buried alive. This book clearly states that all of this was planned and directed by the emperor's brother, Prince Chichibu. The secret project, named Golden Lily, was managed by one of his closest cousins, Prince Takeda." Toshi edged forward on the sofa, his eyes full of noticeable apprehension. "Max, if these writings are true and this became public, the effect on Japan would be terrible and the royal family would be ruined."

"So someone wrote a book with details about all this?"

Toshi's grim face nodded. His voice rose in urgency. "Not just someone. These appear to be the words of Prince Takeda himself . . . his personal diary."

CHAPTER
TWENTY-ONE

T HE SWISH of the sliding glass doors was drowned out by the tidal wave of noise, a clamoring resonance of falling metal balls competing with a disco beat and the bells of a hundred Vegas slot machines.

Hiro stood outside in the drizzle as the grating sound swirled onto the sidewalk. He loathed *pachinko* parlors. His recalled the childhood terror generated by the awful machine-gun noise as the stream of balls bounced down through spinning gates and clacking levers.

Twenty-four hours a day, seven days a week, metal balls are exchanged for prizes, which find their way to nearby alleyways, where the merchandise is exchanged for cash through slots in unmarked doors. Like most *Yakuza*, Oto Kodama worshiped *pachinko* not only as a national obsession, but also as a way for people to gamble in a country where it was otherwise illegal. Over time, vast fortunes grew ever larger, with money accruing not to the passive players, but to the crafty facilitators.

Each Monday afternoon, Hiro knew that Oto reviewed the revenues of his immense *pachinko* parlor in East Shinjuku. He had left a message demanding a meeting at 3 p.m. sharp.

Pushing against the initial sound waves, Hiro sidestepped his way past the businessmen and bleary-eyed teenagers slouched in the tunnel-like rows of machines. Reaching the back of the cavernous room, he spoke briefly to the leering youth behind the counter before being buzzed into the back through an adjacent steel door. The cacophony slowly faded as Hiro moved deeper into the bowels of the aging building.Soon he stopped before the looming presence of Oto's two giant bodyguards before being ushered inside the office.

The bright interior contrasted sharply with the dingy hallway outside. Pristine walls met a white marble floor in the fifteen-by-twenty-foot room. Three stainless steel tables ran down either side of the room, holding stacks of cash organized by denomination. Observing the room's perimeter, Hiro gawked at six identical females dressed only in bras, panties, and high heels. Each of the slender women had shoulder-length black hair and an excess of makeup, culminating in candy-red lips. They clutched clipboards and made tallies, accounting for the mountains of cash.

Ahead, Oto sat alone in the center of a sofa against the far wall. Dressed in a gray pinstripe suit with a peach-colored shirt stretched over his protruding stomach, he was smoking a stubby cigar and talking on a cell phone. Jerking his hand, he motioned for Hiro to stand in the empty center of the room, next to the mouth of an open floor safe. The leader's cell-phone conversation dragged on.

Hiro ruminated as he stared at his cheap dress shoes and shifted his weight from foot to foot. He was sure that being made to stand on ceremony was just another way for the fat man to humiliate him.

Jun is always talking about "Father this" and "Father that," but you'll never hear me call you Father. You're just an old slavemaster. He remained glued to the spot.

Finally, Oto ended his call and spoke. His gruff voice dripped with disdain. "I asked you to do one simple task, and you failed again."

Hiro's sweaty palm smoothed the curls on his head. "We were surprised by the owner of the restaurant. Jun was making so much noise. I wanted to . . . asked you . . . it would have been better doing this job on my own."

"Careful where you place blame!" the *Yakuza* leader growled.

"Forgive me, Master. It was my fault entirely, and I will do whatever I must in order to correct things."

"That's a better attitude." Oto took a puff on his Cuban before reaching into his inside breast pocket and withdrawing a folded piece of paper and a photograph. "I spoke with a contact this morning at the police department. I want you to find and follow Tomoko Asano. She works for Polo."

Hiro stepped forward and took the offering as Oto continued speaking.

"She's the girlfriend of the American who, the police tell me, ran off with my prize. She lives with her parents in Chiba prefecture. Find her, and chances are you'll find the foreigner."

"And what should I do with the American?"

"Just scare him into giving you the satchel. I don't need any more attention, and I'm sure he won't put up much of a fight."

Hiro stepped backward in preparation to leave. "Understood."

"My patience is wearing thin. Fail again, and you may find yourself without a family. And we all know what happens to *Yakuza* without family." Another puff on the cigar let the moment sink in. "Go!"

Hiro quickly left the sterile room and exited the rear of the building. Stepping into the flat gray light of the overcast afternoon, he paused to look at the photograph. It had been taken outdoors, in front of the green patina of the Daibutsu, the thirteenth-century Great Buddha in Kamakura. A group of people in the background, standing close to the aging bronze statue, were dwarfed by its massive height. In the foreground was a smiling older Japanese woman—beside her was the American. It had been difficult to get a clear view of him during the chase, but from the photo, he looked to be mid-twenties, about six feet tall, with a full head of blond hair. Picking him out of a crowd would be easy.

Hiro's slender, knobby fingers opened the folded piece of paper—a portrait ripped from a Waseda University yearbook. Tomoko was dressed in a graduation gown, and her long black hair framed a clear-eyed face with a relaxed, confident smile. The breath caught in his throat. She was one of the most beautiful women he had ever seen, a woman that most men only dreamed about. The kind of woman he knew he would never have.

Carefully refolding the paper, he hurried down the alley.

CHAPTER
TWENTY-TWO

M ASAMI ISHI exited his government-issued car and climbed the stairs to the brown building's fourth floor. Standing quietly, he peered from the English school's hallway at the woman seated behind the office desk. Her skin was wrinkled and the jet-black hair was likely dyed, but there was no mistaking the face. It had been more than twenty years, but it was indeed her.

He straightened his tie, adjusted his thick glasses, and brushed his comb-over back into place, before rapping on the open door. "I need to speak with you about the burglary last night."

Yoko gave a slight start, and her mouth pursed into a frown. "I told everything I know to the detective this morning."

"Oh, I think you do have more to say," he said gently, but firmly, as he stepped into the office.

Yoko rose up behind her desk. "Excuse me? You can't just come in here!"

"You may run from your past, but it will eventually catch up with you." Masami Ishi stepped forward again. "Don't you recognize me?"

Her hand flicked the air. "I think you need to leave!"

He had pondered this moment on the drive over from the National Police Agency, and it was unfolding just as he'd expected. "Think back, Yoko—back to the time before your last name changed, before you disappeared in 1985, back to when I knew you as Yoko Endo and not Yoko Murayama. You were one of the best grifters I ever caught. Your ability to make people open their wallets was astounding. Even to this day, I've never encountered a con artist with more skill and personal charm."

Yoko's face held a look of blank surprise and hint of a gasp escaped from her burgundy lips.

Masami Ishi watched with pleasure as the recognition flooded her eyes, like a bursting dam thundering down an abyss.

YOKO sank back into her chair. The shock was so great that she almost failed to push the button hidden beneath her desk. The video camera in the room's corner blinked silently to life, along with an audio recorder.

"The police report I read a few hours ago was very interesting, considering your past—our mutual past, really." Masami Ishi casually removed his tan trench coat while he sat uninvited in a guest chair facing the desk. "It seems that you're about to make this school into a publicly traded company. It will likely be the biggest financial deal of your sordid career. One that will make you very wealthy, I'm sure. I suspect this burglary couldn't have come at a worse time, could it?"

Yoko felt the pressurized past rush into the room, making it vibrate and sway. In a flash, she relived her father's death and the discovery of his massive loans. She felt again the angst and heartache of learning to survive regardless of the cost. Her horrible nightmares were coming back to haunt her. This simply couldn't be happening.

"But . . . how?"

"It is an odd coincidence. You have to imagine my surprise when I saw a photo of you in a burglary case that wouldn't have reached my desk except for its extraordinary link to a high-profile case. How could I ever forget your lovely face, even twenty years later? The report noted your name as Murayama, and then I realized how you had slipped away from me all those years ago. You didn't run—you simply used a name change to sweep away your past and create a fresh start. You were hiding in plain sight. But the thing I still haven't figured out is why—why—a diplomat of Takahito Murayama's standing would agree to lend you his last name? You must have something really good on him. Perhaps you'll tell me in time, as we get reacquainted."

Yoko's bloodshot eyes jerked up to meet his icy stare. She clenched her teeth and her jaw became rigid. "I would rather choose prison than let you put your greasy hands on me again."

Masami Ishi chuckled. "You've aged well, but I'm not here for sex."

The muffled sound of giggling children could be heard in the classroom next door as she eyed him warily. "You must want something. After all these years, you wouldn't have come here simply for conversation."

He pressed his palms together as if to pray. "You're right. I do want something else. It's not sex, but that other thing that most of us can never get enough of."

She nodded with understanding. "You want a cut, don't you? You want to steal my money!"

"Those are very strong words coming from someone in your position. I'm simply looking for a charitable donation to my upcoming 'retirement fund.' Perhaps two wrongs can make a right."

Yoko stroked her bobbed hair and straightened her shoulders while struggling to regain her composure. Pressing her chair back, she crossed her legs and smoothed her skirt. Regardless of what he said, he was still a man, after all. "What size of charitable donation are you looking for, Masami-*kun*?"

"Fifty percent of everything you get from the sale of shares."

Her shoulders stiffened, but she refused to allow her face to flinch. "That seems a steep price."

"You can settle for it, or you can get nothing . . . except some jail time."

Yoko counter-offered. "Crimes require proof. I'll give you twenty-five percent—and your wife never has to find out that I'm aware of your unusual birthmarks."

A smile spread across Masami Ishi's overbite. "Thirty-five percent, and we let my birthmarks offset your criminal past."

Her sense of the room began to stabilize. It wasn't a perfect arrangement, but seemed necessary if she was to survive another day. "Fine, but I have one additional request." She raised a single index finger. "The police report of the burglary will point to a teacher at this school—Max Travers. However, until the sale of shares is finalized, nobody can know about Max's involvement. The investors would lose confidence, and everything I've worked for would instantly fall apart."

"So what do you want me to do?"

"I want you to double the number of police needed to catch him, then I want you to hold him quietly until after I finish selling the shares. It should be complete in the next couple of weeks."

"Are you insane? Hold an American without announcing his capture or formally charging him?" Masami Ishi's voice rose in pitch. "That's kidnapping. As superintendent of the CIB, there are limits to what I can do. My actions are closely watched by the National Public Safety Commission."

She leaned forward in her seat. "I remember you being very resourceful Masami-*kun*. You wouldn't have risen to the position you're in without having some influence. I'm sure that for the sake of your 'retirement fund,' you can find a way."

"I'll do what I can, but I can't make any guarantees." His cheeks reddened, and he rose to his feet. "Either way, when this deal goes through, I want my thirty-five percent." He turned and left the room without looking back.

Yoko breathed a sigh of relief as she listened to the stairwell door slam shut.

From the hall, Kenji peered into her office. "*Sensei*, is everything okay?"

"Yes. It was just a salesman, but I sent him away." She waved a tired hand. "And one more thing before you go. You need to cover Max's classes. The story is that he's on a trip with his aunt who is visiting from America."

"But *Sensei*—I'm no good at lying."

"Please don't argue with me. I'm not going to put up with it."

"Yes, *Sensei*." He dropped his head.

"Good. Now, I need some quiet. Don't let anyone else come in."

As the door closed out the unforgiving past, Yoko reached for the bottle of Tylenol in her desk drawer. She needed relief—something fast. Something that would stop the throbbing pain threatening to split her skull wide open.

CHAPTER
TWENTY-THREE

"IT'S ALL GONE WRONG!" Max's voice stammered as Tomoko played his message again. Etiquette dictated that she shouldn't use her cell phone on the train, but she couldn't help herself. He sounded distressed, although it might be just a ploy just to get her to talk. Tomoko closed her phone, noting the blinking low-power warning, and stood up as the subway car braked. She briefly contemplated sticking to her plan to let him suffer a while longer. But he sounded genuinely upset. The message said to meet at 6 p.m. near the statue of Hachiko the Dog. It had been a hectic afternoon at the office, and she checked her watch—6:55.

Climbing the stairs to the cavernous western gallery of the Shibuya train station, she wove through the throng of high-tech Bit Valley workers and tanned *Kogal* girls loaded with shopping bags. Having spent a summer in San Diego, she had described the unusual female subculture to Max by comparing them to California's Valley Girls. It really wasn't much of a stretch, since there were so many similarities: rampant materialism, lots of attitude, and a style all their own.

Several *Kogals* stopped directly in front of Tomoko as she hurried toward the exit. Pressing her way through the group resulted in one teenager dropping a shopping bag, its contents scattering across the floor. A mistaken attempt to stop and help only subjected her to a chorus of swearing and catcalls. Throwing up her hands, Tomoko sneered at them before turning and continuing on her way outside. "Stupid girls," she spoke to herself. "Where have all the smart ones gone?"

AS the blonde *Kogals* gathered their strewn merchandise, one of them, dressed in a flowery miniskirt and matching platform boots, chased after the last of the runaway parcels. Before she could reach it, a muscular man bent down and picked it up. He stretched out a tree-trunk arm to return the package and she caught a glimpse of the intricate tattoos beneath the rolled-up sleeve of his dress shirt. Biting her frosted lower lip, the giggling young woman batted her heavily blackened eyelashes. The thick-necked *Yakuza* winked at her and continued on his way out the exit, following a shorter, pinched-face man.

RISING overhead, massive video screens blinked and glowed atop the central Shibuya intersection. The entire area was flooded with people and, as much as he tried, Max couldn't watch every direction at once. He glanced quickly into the daypack. The diary was still there, along with his own expiring plane ticket. Together, they felt like a lead weight pulling on his shoulder as he paced under a darkening sky.

Despite Toshi's dire warnings, Max had departed the house around noon. Aware that the *Yakuza* gangs were likely on the lookout for him, he had avoided the trains and subways. Instead, he spent the afternoon walking an indirect course from Hamamatsucho to Shibuya, which stretched the distance from four miles to eight. He told himself not to be afraid, yet he caught himself repeatedly checking to make sure that he wasn't being followed. During the brutal office assault he had seen what the mafia thugs were capable of doing.

For a fleeting moment he'd considered going to the police, but he had no intention of rotting in a Japanese prison. The cops had probably already pointed an accusing finger in his direction, explaining to Mr. Murayama that he'd been casing the place all along—planning the robbery—waiting for the best time to strike. The authorities were benevolent enough to well-behaved foreigners, but stories occasionally circulated of *Gaijin* being persecuted for unsubstantiated crimes. He'd once read a magazine article detailing how the authorities and the *Yakuza* often worked together. A call to the police might just end up delivering him straight to the bad guys.

His phone calls to the TPH had gone unanswered, but then it wasn't unusual for his nocturnal roommates to sleep away most of the day. He'd also thought of phoning home to the States, but it was a different world altogether—how could he possibly explain everything taking place and make it sound even remotely plausible? He had even considered calling his buddy Jeff in Okinawa—they'd been tight once, before Jeff moved away—but there was nothing the guy could do to help him from so far away.

Taking sporadic breaks throughout the afternoon, he'd killed time in the back of coffee shops. He paid only in cash, always mindful to keep an eye out for anyone focusing too much attention in his general direction. He had to keep thinking. There had to be a solution, but after a wearisome afternoon he was forced to admit that the answers still eluded him. He was on his own, adrift.

An overhead screen showed that it was almost seven o'clock. Tomoko was an hour late, if she was coming at all. Against the advice of her friends, she had chosen to give him a chance, and Max realized now that he'd been too self-absorbed to pay attention. He hated the idea that he might have permanently screwed things up, and the pressure of waiting made the brick in his stomach grow heavier by the minute.

Max muttered his upset as he stomped toward the row of pay phones next to the intersection. He slid into the first available booth and inserted a calling card.

Tomoko answered on the third ring. "I was delayed." Her voice sounded cold, detached.

"Where are you now?"

"The corner by the Tokyu Department Store. I can see the statue."

Max gripped the phone while he turned to scan the crowd outside. Picking out anyone else would have been difficult in such a busy place, but he quickly spotted her tall, slender figure and confident stride. She was approaching the statue from the far side of the plaza. "I can see you now."

"Fine." Her voice remained monotone.

Then he saw them. Max gasped into the receiver at the sight of the *Yakuza* rounding the corner thirty feet behind her. They were the same two from Mr. M's office. "No . . . No . . . *No!*" His pulse rose to a throbbing beat.

"What do you mean, no?" Tomoko stopped walking and the two men behind her followed suit. "You asked me to come here."

"I . . . I . . . didn't mean you." He worked to calm his rapid breathing. "Oh my God."

"Max, what's going on? Where are you?"

He turned to face the back wall of the booth, crushing the receiver to his face. "You have to trust me. You have to do what I tell you."

Her voice rose in obvious frustration. "Is this some kind of joke? I—"

"It's *not* a joke, Tomoko. Two men are following you. Don't turn around. *Don't.* But they're right behind you." He peered back over his shoulder.

Tomoko's voice cracked and he could hear her choking back tears. "I don't know why you're doing this, but it's not funny. I'm going to the Starbucks. I'll wait ten minutes, and if you don't come, I'm leaving."

The line went silent. Max sprang from the booth and watched in horror as the idling men mirrored her movements. Her path cut around the bronze statue. Then, twenty yards away, she stopped dead in her tracks, turned ninety-degrees to her right, and looked directly at him from across the plaza.

Max suddenly felt the world shift into slow motion. He yelled and waved his arms frantically, shouting for her to run, but her face was unreadable, confused. Tomoko took only a few steps toward him before the blurry streaks of the two *Yakuza* surged past her. Max watched her mouth drop wide with shock as she stumbled in the wake, but he couldn't stay still any longer.

He turned away and raced toward the crowded intersection. A human wall blocked the path before him. Terrified words tore from his throat as he plowed forward without slowing. "Get out of the way! Move. *Move!*"

It didn't take long for the noise of the surging crowd to drown out the sound of his name being screamed in the ever-increasing distance.

MAX rubbed his aching ankle and stared out a black glass window onto the T-intersection of two narrow laneways. The hostess pressing against him didn't seem to care that he was out of breath and still partially soaked in sweat. In fact, he knew the only thing that concerned her was that he was nursing a beer. It was her job to get him drunk and make him spend his money—a scarcity in the lukewarm economy—and she was clearly growing frustrated.

Topping up his glass, she pressed it back with a demure smile. "Prease to drink," she insisted.

Max thanked her and turned his face back to the window. His eyes darted up and down the streets in all three directions. Thinking back, he realized he'd stood at the Shibuya pay phones far too long. It had been a harrowing escape. His only saving grace was that the intersection's four-way scramble had changed to allow pedestrians the right of way. He'd been able to bury himself in the mass of people swarming the crossroads. At least a dozen innocent bystanders were steamrolled in the process, but there had been no time to stop.

The hostess spoke again. "It Japanese custom to drink to pretty girl. When you come to Japan?"

He took a sip, then set it back down.

"Keiko!" From the back of the room a woman's harsh voice rang out. The hostess excused herself and slunk away.

Relaxing slightly, Max turned to take in the room for the first time since he'd stepped through the doorway. It was a typical karaoke lounge—narrow and long. The bar sat near the back. Light from a sparse row of halogens glinted off the chrome bar stools and was being absorbed by the dark carpet and burgundy velvet walls. Three men in suits sat toward the far back corner. Two hostesses poured drinks into them and giggled while the fourth salary-man stood in front of a glowing monitor, warbling his way through "I reft my hard in Sun Frunsisco."

Max had thought this to be an amusing cultural activity. But over time, it grew increasingly embarrassing: the same red-eyed employees and sweaty-faced patrons, with ties half undone, desperately trying to forget their self-appointed prisons—the "lifetime" jobs they hated so much.

Keiko returned and slid into the booth. A whiskey bottle was clutched in her hand. "Prease drink or *Momma-san* ask you to reave!"

Max grabbed his beer and shot-gunned the glass. The prospect of leaving wasn't in his best interest. He had barely outrun the two mafia goons, and they were probably still out there searching for him at the train stations and taxi stands. No, he needed to kill some time before he could lose himself in the crowd. It would be suicide to try to move anywhere for a while. But they couldn't check every bar in the area. There were thousands of places on a hundred identical streets. He would sit tight, wait for a while, try to call Tomoko again, and then figure out what to do next.

This is all my fault. Dear God, please let her be okay.

Keiko slid a full glass of whiskey onto the table and jostled him with her elbow. The imitation Tony Bennett had finished crooning, and Max clapped in half-hearted appreciation.

CHAPTER
TWENTY-FOUR

THROUGH THE blanket of his own cigarette smoke, Hiro could see the enormous glowing red numbers and the round multistory column of the 109 Department Store rising into the night sky over the Shibuya intersection. The floodlights at the bottom of the colossal silver silo illuminated the poster of an alluringly posed model. Her sexy fifty-foot legs were in perfect proportion with the rest of her lingerie-clad body.

Across the bustling road, he could occasionally make out Jun, who was leaning against a wall at the entrance to a pedestrian-only street. They had been waiting and watching for over two hours. The girlfriend was nowhere to be found, nor was there any sign of the American.

Hiro knew it was a stupid, useless effort. Seven streets intersected at Shibuya Crossing's *Center-Gai*, making it the busiest intersection in the world. There were so many ways in and out of the area that it was impossible to ensure the American didn't get past them. He could have taken a cab, but Oto's other men were following up leads with the taxi companies. He could also have walked to another train station ten or fifteen blocks away and hopped onto one of a dozen trains. Hell, he could be halfway to Osaka by now.

The longer Hiro pondered these thoughts, the more agitated he became.

What made him even angrier was the truth he knew about himself: that regardless of whether he agreed with the plan, he would stand under the blinking neon signs for as long as Oto told him to do it. What else was he supposed to do? This wasn't America, where a man could be anything he chose. This was Japan, where fate set the path he was required to walk. No amount of anger or wishing could change that. He rubbed the filtered end of his cigarette against the missing digit on his left hand, a youthful attempt to leave the gang and a lesson learned the hard way.

Jun's sudden movement from across the noisy road caught Hiro's attention and snapped him from his thoughts. The no-brained oaf could move with startling speed, and before Hiro could see what was happening, Jun had disappeared around the corner.

Hiro charged into the headlights of the oncoming traffic with only the thought that an honorable death would be better than losing the prey. A van slammed on its brakes and skidded to an awkward stop. The van's horn and its driver's angry shouting were quickly followed by the crunch of metal as a white Camry slid into the van's rear. The commotion increased with a chorus of squealing tires, accompanied by an irate symphony of horns as the crowded intersection transformed into a snarl of halted vehicles.

Hiro darted through the chaos and tumbled over a sedan's hood before making it to the far side of the street in front of the giant Tsutaya music store. Glancing back over his shoulder, he could make out the officers who were already hurrying from the nearby police box. Hiro made a quick right turn, then disappeared down a side street.

Despite the glare of blinking signs, he could see Jun about seventy-five yards ahead—the massive shoulders bobbing and weaving through the throngs of people. Ten yards farther, a blond head rose above the crowd. Jun covered the distance in short order and, with a great leap, sent himself and the foreigner tumbling to the ground. Sharp screams erupted from a nearby group of teenage girls, who scattered and moved away like a school of frightened fish.

Hiro raced forward.

Jun stood over the curled-up foreigner—his cell dialing a waiting driver. Hiro arrived and in one swift movement he pulled the man's hands away from his face, which was crimson and contorted in pain. Tears were rolling down his pale cheeks, and it was immediately clear that an awful mistake had been made. This *Gaijin* wore a nose ring and had an old scar on his forehead. The one they were looking for was conservative and bore no scars . . . yet.

The squeal of tires around the corner on Hands Street and the shouts of approaching foot police broke the momentary pause. Hiro grabbed Jun's arm and dragged the confused idiot down the block. A black Mercedes appeared from nowhere. The door flew open and the two sailed in head first.

As the car sped away, the sirens and buzz of the chaos outside disappeared into the pounding sound of blood in Hiro's ears. He would be lucky to keep his other nine fingers when Oto learned of this mistake.

CHAPTER
TWENTY-FIVE

MAX'S HEAD rose just far enough so that his eyes were flush with the sidewalk. He scanned through the metal railing in all directions around the Kawasaki subway exit. A pale yellow glow from a row of streetlights stretched the length of the block. The place seemed deserted. He limped up the remaining stairs and across the concourse before slipping into the shadows of a row of alpine fir trees along the west side of the open area.

He rubbed his throbbing ankle while crouching in the darkness for what seemed like hours. Finally, a slow-moving SUV appeared. It had to be her. The vehicle came to an abrupt halt as he stepped into its path. The driver's door opened and Tomoko jumped out, dashing the dozen paces to his waiting embrace.

Max spoke first. "I'm so glad you got my message to meet here. I was worried those guys had caught you.

"No," she said. "What's happening?"

"I can explain, but not here."

"I was so scared!" She let out a small yelp as he squeezed her hard. "I waited at the Starbucks, but my phone was out of power."

Max pressed his cheek against the top of her head. "I'm sorry about the other night. I never mean to upset you." Skittish, he glanced around the empty street, wary of any threatening movement, concerned over the ominous silence. "C'mon, we should go, just in case."

"Okay . . . but where to?"

His mind was still racing. "They're probably watching my house. We need to put some distance between them and us. Let's go to that *onsen*—you know, the hot springs resort your mom's friend owns on the Izu Peninsula. It's not too far, right?"

"About three hours. But I don't know if that's a good idea. It only has a dozen rooms. What if it's full?"

"Then we'll find someplace else. Trust me. We need to go."

Max limped on his way to the vehicle and Tomoko pointed. "What happened to your foot?"

The pain was stabbing now, shooting upward to his knee, but he didn't want her to worry. "It's nothing. I just twisted my ankle."

"Then I'll drive and you talk. We can take the Higashi Kanto Expressway. I'll call the hotel right now." Tomoko took the wheel and they headed southwest.

It took thirty minutes to reach the bright floodlights of the enormous Yokohama Bay Bridge, about the same amount of time as Max needed to explain about Kenji's keys, the office break-in, the escape to Toshi's house, and the surprise of Prince Takeda's diary. They were almost halfway across the bridge's 2,500-foot span when he paused the story. "Pull over here for a minute."

Tomoko wore an incredulous stare. "I can't stop in the middle."

He unclipped his seatbelt. "I'm serious. Stop the car and give me your phone."

"Did you only hurt your ankle?"

"Oh, you're funny. No, really. Your cell phone has a GPS chip. I checked it out. Meaning that with the right technology, someone can find or follow you."

The SUV slowed to a halt. Tomoko reached back for her handbag, eyeing him suspiciously. "This is stupid. Just because someone has tattoos doesn't make them *Yakuza*." She retrieved the compact silver bundle before handing it over with reluctance.

Cold air whistled into the vehicle's interior, whipping Max's hair around. His voice rose in order to be heard over the noise. "I'll get you a new one." He limped toward the edge of the bridge as several passing cars angrily blasted their horns.

Darkness soon swallowed the phone on its plunge toward the icy waters of the Pacific Ocean.

SEVERAL hours later, the SUV's headlights swept over dense shrubs and a row of purple and pink azaleas as Tomoko turned into the U-shaped driveway of the Fairlady *onsen*. The familiar single-story building always reminded her of a Swiss mountain chalet, with a white Tudor exterior and dark wooden beams.

"My mom's friend doesn't speak English, so let me handle this," Tomoko said.

Mrs. Kanazawa's plump figure shuffled out of the hotel's sliding front door. She was wearing her trademark grin. "*Konbanwa!*"

Exiting the vehicle and bowing politely, Tomoko replied, "Kanazawa-*san*. It's so kind of you to make room on such short notice."

"Your call was a surprise, but you know you're always welcome." Mrs. Kanazawa's words ended abruptly, and a look of surprise crossed her face as Max slid out of the passenger's door.

"This is . . . this is my boyfriend, but it's not what you think. There's been some trouble . . . "

"Your boyfriend? A *Gaijin*? You know your parent's opinions." Mrs. Kanazawa wiped her hands on her apron. "And what kind of trouble?"

"I'm fine. Really. Please don't say anything. I'll tell my parents everything later."

A painful silence lingered while Mrs. Kanazawa weighed the situation, looking Max up and down. "All right," she blurted with a swipe of her finger in the air. "But separate rooms. If your mother found out I let you have a room together, it would never do."

"Thank you so much," Tomoko replied while bowing sharply. She looked at Max and motioned to him with a flick of her head.

"*Domo arigato*, Kanazawa-*san*," he mimicked in Japanese, but the older woman turned away with no reply.

THEY removed their shoes before stepping onto the hardwood floor in the antiseptically clean lobby. Max could see a garden through the opposing wall's plate-glass doors. The hotel appeared to be built in the shape of a horseshoe.

Beyond the central garden, through a pair of open wooden gates, was a steaming pool of water; a bamboo wall separated the pool into two distinct halves. Lights from beneath the surface of the glowing water illuminated the overhanging trees. Wooden walls fenced in the right and left sides of the property, with the far unfenced edge offering the unobstructed clifftop view of the ocean that made the Izu famous.

Mrs. Kanazawa handed over two keys and directed them down a corridor on the right side of the lobby. As they approached their rooms, Max whispered, "I understood enough of that conversation to know that you haven't told your parents about us, like you said you would."

"You don't understand. I need more time. They're good people, just not very open-minded." Her voice became strained. "Please, can we talk about it later?"

Mrs. Kanazawa was observing them while attempting to appear busy at the front desk, and Max watched Tomoko fumble with her room key as she glanced back toward the lobby. He knew she was nervous and realized he should be grateful, especially after the events of the day and how well she'd handled it all. "Sure." Aware of the distant scrutiny, he resisted the sudden temptation to hold her in his arms. "And thanks for everything today."

He was already in his room and out of sight when Tomoko's voice drifted through the closing door. "You're welcome."

MAX lay on the bed. He withdrew the yellow diary from the daypack and stared at its outline before placing it on his chest. It rose and fell with his breathing.

For a brief time, before exhaustion claimed victory, he lay anxiously, eyes open in the dark, unable to shake the feeling that both his and Tomoko's lives, their fate, had somehow become fused with that of Prince Takeda himself.

CHAPTER
TWENTY-SIX

Tuesday, April 24

THE JAPANESE politician set down the National Police Agency report on the "Shrine Murder." He'd read it over at least half a dozen times. The information made him nervous. Something needed to be done. But he knew that his actions, if discovered, would never be forgiven nor understood. This thought played in his brain as his shaky fingers fought with the buttons on his dark gray suit. These telephone calls, rare as they were, filled him with anxiety.

The aging politician was forbidden from using his home phone to dial the Washington, D.C., number, so he left his apartment early. Exiting the exclusive brick-and-glass tower, he shuffled into the dappled morning sunlight. His uniformed driver stood attentively next to the navy-blue BMW and held his withered arm as he climbed inside the plush interior.

In the thirty years of receiving payments into his Swiss bank account, he'd dialed area code 202 only four times. It wasn't up to him to decide whether a situation warranted action; he was simply required to call the number if he saw or heard anything that might justify concern.

What was it about April 24 that seemed to make this call necessary? It was eighteen years ago to the day when he had last dialed the D.C. number. The height of the "Recruit" bribery scandal was bringing the Japanese government to its knees. Phones were ringing, protestors were shouting, accusations were flying, and Ihei Aoki was talking too much. If only the foolish man had stayed silent, perhaps he would still be alive. Being secretary to Prime Minister Takeshita had entitled Aoki-*san* to detailed knowledge of the government's inner workings. It was truly regrettable that he had became so vocal, telling friends that "Recruit" was a minor matter compared to another scandal he was about to make public. Two days after the last telephone call to Washington, Ihei Aoki had become just another suicide statistic. Suspicions of foul play swirled for months, but a Senate investigation proved nothing.

The BMW crept up a freeway on-ramp and merged into traffic. The Shuto Expressway's morning rush hour traffic seemed to grow more congested by the day. Seated in the back, the politician rubbed two fingers back and forth across his Sacred Arrow tie clip. His eyes stared vacantly out the tinted windows at the passing towers.

He was aware that opponents would call him a traitor if they knew of his U.S. connection, but he would argue that the ends justified the means, and that keeping the Liberal Democratic Party in power was the best thing for Japan. Look at the mess that had to be cleaned up after they'd briefly lost power in 1993. It was the LDP, after all, that had shepherded the rebuilding of the country since 1955. Things would fall into chaos without them. Heaven forbid that the Socialists or Communists ever gained power. In fact, that had been the U.S. military's main concern when it started applying secret money to the problem in the 1950s. Interesting to think that even back then, the American leaders were unaware of what their own government was really doing.

Exiting the crowded expressway, the car finally reached the manicured trees and sweeping driveway of the forty-story Akasaka Prince Hotel. As the BMW slowed at the hotel entrance, a red-jacketed valet ran out.

Crossing the lobby's white marble floor, the politician passed through the elevator vestibule. He checked his watch, calculating it would be seven o'clock Monday evening in Washington. A lone man was occupying one of the phones to the left, so he chose the bank of phones on the right instead. In an age of mobile communications, these telephones were seldom used, and he assured himself he could not be overheard. No amount of caution was too great in such a hazardous venture. He picked up the receiver and noticed his hands shaking far more than usual.

Dialing the number, he listened. The ring tone sounded strange and long. A man answered after the fourth chime. "Hello?"

The politician hesitated. The voice on the other end seemed different. Was it a slightly French accent? But it had been so long since the last call, and his mind wasn't what it used to be.

The voice on the other end repeated the greeting. "Hello?"

"*Moshi-moshi. Elgin-san onagaishimasu.*"

The Washington voice switched immediately into fluent Japanese. "How may I help you?"

"I have information for Mr. Bob Elgin."

"I'm his brother, Lloyd Elgin. You can talk to me."

The politician relaxed. The key phrase and its response were confirmed. He had dialed the correct number. "Lately, I have heard tell of a diary and a map for sale. The items were said to be direct evidence of things that should remain confidential. I didn't file a report because it was unsubstantiated. Then, more recently, it was also rumored that a secret buyer had come forward. Since then, two unusual things have taken place. Someone murdered a former diplomat named Kazue Saito several days ago at the Yasukuni Shrine. Then yesterday the office of another retired diplomat named Takahito Murayama was robbed. The thieves ransacked his extensive files. He is an avid collector, and over the years he's accumulated a number of official and unofficial documents. The police do not know what was taken. You will find that these men knew each other, and they both knew of the 'Black Eagle' and the M-Fund—among others. Separately, these events may mean nothing, but together they could warn of a coming problem."

"Is there anything else that could explain what's happening?"

The politician glanced up to confirm. The man at the other phone was gone. "I don't know what's happening. Perhaps nothing. But I can tell you that after almost forty years in politics, I know when something doesn't feel right. Call it intuition or call it experience, Mr. Elgin, I don't care. Should you choose to investigate, I have left copies of the police reports for the two incidents. They're in the designated safety deposit box. My part is complete, and now it is up to you."

"Agreed." The line went dead without a goodbye.

LLOYD Elgin closed his next-generation satellite phone. The Code required him to research any calls within six hours, determine if action was necessary, and file an encrypted electronic report; nothing was to be written on paper. Checking his watch, he considered his options. A concert with Emanuel Ax and Edgar Meyer was a rare opportunity he didn't want to miss. There would still be just enough time to deal with this after the performance.

Adjusting his bow tie, he rejoined his wife and a group of friends standing beneath the majestic pillars of the Kennedy Center. The men were all uniformed in tuxedos, while the women radiated elegance in evening gowns and luxurious furs. He assured them there would be no more delays, then motioned for the group to continue inside. His blonde trophy wife took his arm and fell into step next to him.

"Is everything all right, darling?"

"Yes. But I have work to do later, so you'll have to go for drinks without me."

She tugged his arm more tightly into the speckled brown fur of her jacket. "You work so much. I'm just glad you could come tonight." Stopping in the foyer, she ran a manicured hand across his dark, smooth hair and stared at his strong angular jaw, full lips, and kelly-green eyes. "This means a lot to me, Vincent, and I want you to know how much I love you for it."

CHAPTER
TWENTY-SEVEN

THE MORNING call from her childhood friend came early, but Mrs. Asano expressed her relief upon hearing that Tomoko was staying at the Fairlady *onsen*. She commented that it was strange since Polo advertising shoots were generally scheduled well in advance.

Mrs. Kanazawa assured her friend that it was probably just an oversight, and she would call again once Tomoko left. She made no mention of the American—Max—for now.

Upon ending the call, Mrs. Kanazawa heard a single click followed by a buzzing noise, then a second distinct click. Telephone reception on the Izu Peninsula was sometimes unreliable—the big-city customers always received the best service.

AT the same time, another call was being made from a private room at the hotel, the third attempt at the same phone number.

Miki couldn't concentrate. The cell phone strapped to her inner thigh continued to vibrate. The caller was extremely persistent, whoever it was. Brushing a stray blonde hair into place, she rose from her desk and bowed to her scowling boss, who sat opposite her in the huddle of six metal desks. Excusing herself, she hurried down the hallway to the ladies' room. Entering the closest stall, she retrieved the phone and hesitated—the number wasn't familiar. She answered with a whisper, "*Moshi-Moshi.*"

"Miki—it's Tomoko calling. What took you so long?"

"We aren't supposed to take personal calls at work."

"Sorry, but I need you to help me again, and this time it's extremely urgent."

Miki's voice rose with excitement. "Really? What's happening?" A loud cough from another stall made her cringe, and she pressed the phone closer to her ear.

"I can't explain everything right now. I'm still trying to figure it out myself, but Max is in danger, and there may be *Yakuza* involved."

"How exciting." She could barely contain her voice in a whisper.

"Maybe in the movies, but not for real. I'm scared, Miki-*chan*."

"Don't be afraid. Tell me what you need."

"I want you to do some research for me on Prince Takeda."

Just a minute." Miki paused while the nearby toilet finished flushing and the other woman in the bathroom washed her hands. The high heels passing Miki's stall stopped as if to demonstrate they were aware that rules were being broken. Finally, the other woman left the room. "There was someone else in the bathroom. Probably that old cow who sits next to me. Anyway, did you say Prince Takeda, the first cousin of Emperor Shōwa?"

"Sure, if you say so. I know he's a prince, but that's about it."

Miki felt confused. "But you can find information about him in any library or on the Internet."

"They won't have what I'm looking for. I want to know where he's living."

Sitting back on the toilet, Miki giggled. "Well, if you're planning a visit, make sure to take me along. I've never met a real prince."

"I'm serious. Can you find out where he lives?"

"It'll take me some time, but you know I can find anything."

"Thanks, Miki-*chan*. I'd really appreciate it if you could do it quickly."

"All right, but you have to call me later and tell me everything that's happening."

"I will. I promise."

The slim phone was slipped back in its thigh-mounted carrying case. Exiting the bathroom, Miki dropped her gaze to the floor, wiped the smile from her face, and relaxed the tension in her shoulders. As much as her mind was racing with excitement, she knew she needed to blend back into the group, at least until the end of the workday.

H IRO LIFTED his head briefly from the pillow before snorting with disgust and dropping it back down. The pounding from the hallway was relentless. He'd slept only a few hours, and already it seemed the game was starting again.

Clad in striped boxer shorts, he shuffled to the apartment door. Opening it, he found Jun leaning against the outside wall. The younger *Yakuza* was dressed entirely in black and sporting a vicious grin.

Hiro squinted into the bright hallway lights. "What are you smiling about?"

"Get dressed, *Sempai*—I received a call from Father."

"You? Why would Oto be calling you?" He rubbed his eyes as Jun's massive form squeezed past him into the cramped apartment.

"You'll have to ask him yourself, but I'd say that right now you're not his favorite person."

Hiro was growing irritated with the smug attitude. "All right, so what did he say?"

"A phone call was made this morning to Tomoko Asano's house. It came from the Fairlady *onsen* on the Izu Peninsula. The Polo girl and her American boyfriend are hiding there. Father wants us to go and finish the job." Jun's smirk grew even wider. "And another thing—he told me that this time, I'm in charge."

CHAPTER
TWENTY-EIGHT

A FISHERMAN AND his wife worked diligently alongside the Pacific Ocean shoreline of Sagami Bay. The tiny woman stood mending the net while her husband sang aloud as he loaded supplies onto their once white twenty-foot vessel. His croaking voice blended in harmony with the seagulls' cries. Dressed in a fraying burgundy shirt with dark overalls and claw-toed rubber boots, the fisherman adjusted the knotted towel he wore like a headband. His wife's face remained hidden beneath the large, bill-like rim of her cap, which lent her the appearance of an exotic bird.

Max was sitting a dozen paces down the shore on a water-smoothed rock, the *onsen* nestled in the trees on the hill behind him. Elbows on knees, he rested his chin on his hands. The daypack sat below in the sand. Brilliant sunlight shone in his face.

The previous night's sleep had been short and restless. Visions of the past few days had surfaced with the first light that crept in the window. He desperately needed fresh air and some time to think. Now, sitting next to the water, Max tried to keep his mind off the past and focus on what to do next. But there were too many questions. His mind jumped from one to another, then circled back again. Supposing he could solve the immediate problem with the *Yakuza*, he had to consider that he was no longer employed. Finding another job without a passport or work visa would be next to impossible. And since the police had likely identified him by now, there was no telling how badly it could end. Worse yet, Mr. Murayama might well think he was the cause of the fiasco, and would never forgive his seeming treachery. It all seemed overwhelming, and he wished he could just sail off in the fishing boat and leave the mess behind.

A familiar voice roused him. "I thought you'd be down here."

Tomoko was standing nearby. Her hair was pulled neatly back into a ponytail. In her hands were two cups of coffee. Max took the drinks and balanced them on the rock. Reaching up, he pulled her down toward him and kissed her. "Thanks for rescuing me. You are my knight in shining armor."

The comment produced a snicker as her head came to rest on his shoulder. "You're welcome."

They sat staring at the water, Max trying and failing to ignore the feeling that this was simply a fleeting moment—the eye of a growing storm. Tomoko reached for a coffee as he motioned toward the fisherman and his wife. "You think they're happy?"

"I don't know. Should I ask them?"

"No, no—I was just wondering if having a simpler life makes people happier. Does that sound crazy?" He knew there was no clear answer.

She took a sip from her steaming cup. "Not crazy. It's probably true for some people." The morning light was bright, and she gripped his hand before squinting to look into his face. "I'm surprised you broke into Mr. Murayama's office. It's not something I expected from you."

"Hey, it's my passport after all." He knew he sounded defensive. "Why? Do you think I was wrong to do it?"

"No, but you're not so . . . not so . . . *nanda-ke*? Not usually so forceful."

"Yeah, well, I was sick of being a hostage to the Dragon Lady."

Tomoko paused before asking the question he was most hoping to avoid. "So what now?"

He exhaled sharply. "I've been thinking about that a lot, and none of the options look great."

She pressed on. "I think we should go to the police and explain about the robbery and why you were there. We could also give them the daypack."

Max knew what she was really saying. Hidden between the words lay the fact that she wanted things to return to the way they were, although he was pretty sure that was no longer possible. "The cops saw me at the office. They'll charge me with the break-in, for sure and, besides, I've also read that the police are all tied in with the *Yakuza*."

Tomoko clicked her tongue. "You've been watching too many movies. Are all American police linked to the mafia?"

Max realized the prejudice in his comment. "Okay, you're probably right, but I still don't want to go to prison."

"You used a key to get in the office, remember? Besides, the two other men were probably regular thieves. We don't even know if they're *Yakuza*. Lots of people have tattoos."

"You're kidding, right?" His voice grew louder. "You mean that having tattoos all the way down both arms shows they weren't *Yakuza*?"

"I'm just saying they may not be part of a gang."

Max pulled away and put both hands around his coffee cup. "Whatever." He didn't bother trying to hide his frustration. "So if it was just two lone crooks, tell me how they found you in a single day. It's not like they followed me to Shibuya. How did two small-time crooks determine my identity, figure out that you were my girlfriend, find your office, and then follow you?"

Her eyes widened, and she looked at Max. "What if it was Yoko? That has to be it!"

"Okay, now that just doesn't make any sense." The rising sun slipped behind a cloud. "Why would she have people break into her own father's office? What would be the point?"

"I'm not sure, but I've never trusted her . . . and only Yoko or Kenji know where I work." Tomoko snapped her fingers. "That has to be it."

He toyed with the insane idea. "Seems unlikely, but I guess anything is possible, especially with her." The fisherman eased the boat from the shore. The smiling man gave a shout and a wave as he revved the motor, and Max returned the wave, glad of the diversion. While the vessel shrank from sight, the fisherman's faceless wife clambered to take a seat next to her husband's standing figure.

Tomoko slid down and rested her back against the sun-warmed rock. Max reached for the daypack, unzipped it, and retrieved the pale yellow diary from the brown satchel. It felt old and rich with history. "You should see this." He handed it over for her inspection. "But don't get it dirty."

The warning triggered a short burst of laughter. "When did you become the guardian of Japan's past?" Her hands ran over the raised leather surface. Opening it to a random page, she read the Japanese writing.

THE brilliant morning light greeted my eyes after another sleepless night. Yesterday, the tunnels of Teresa, south of Manila, were finally closed. Entombed alive were nearly one hundred laborers and foreign combat prisoners. It is the same each time a vault is closed. Huddled together in the damp caves, they wail and cry for mercy, which never comes. The sound of their collective voices echo inside my brain. The sunken faces and hollow eyes haunt my dreams and keep me from sleep.

Earlier, I sent word to Prince Chichibu, begging him to let me spare their lives, but he denied my request. The reply stated simply that we must guard the emperor's belongings and protect them with absolute devotion.

I know my place and have faithfully carried out my duty, but in my private heart I cannot deny my feelings. The world has lost all reason, and I am descending into madness along with it. What kind of a world are my actions helping to shape? What will my children and my children's children inherit? Will they ever understand the horror and suffering that their vast fortune is built upon? If they don't know the truth, how will they learn from our mistakes?

THE sun reemerged. Dancing waves lapped rhythmically as birds squawked and dove along the beach. Max slid to the sand and closed his eyes. He might have nodded off for a minute, but he wasn't sure. When he finally looked over at Tomoko, her face was a mix of unreadable emotion. "What's wrong?"

"This diary—it starts in 1942 and ends in 1947, when the prince and his family were made into . . . they were not royalty anymore."

"You mean they became commoners?"

"Yes," she continued, "and it says that during the war, Prince Takeda worked on a secret project called 'Golden Lily.' He was forced to hide stolen things for the emperor." Emotion shook her chin. "It's hard to believe this really happened."

His comforting arm slid around her shoulder. "Toshi mentioned that as well—but I don't get the part about the prince being forced to do it."

"These are his private thoughts, Max. He was following orders, but he felt very bad. His words are filled with a great sadness."

"You're telling me this dude was a humanitarian?" he said, eyes half closed. "I'm not sure I can buy that."

"I've only read a little, but it seemed he was unhappy about many things he had to do."

"So what's in there that makes the *Yakuza*—" Max threw on a jesting smile and held up both palms dramatically. "Oh, sorry, I mean the bad guys— want it so badly?"

"Don't tease me." Tomoko dug a gentle elbow into his ribs. "I'm not sure yet. The prince writes about digging tunnels and hiding 'war treasure,' but there are no details so far. I can't find any maps, but there are a lot of pages. It's big." She tapped the inch-wide spine.

Max stared out at the water. "We won't solve the problem from here. We should go back to Tokyo, and I'll go to the U.S. Embassy. I can find a cheap hotel until they give me a new passport. And maybe they can help straighten things out with the police."

"Or you could stay with my uncle in Hitachi for a while. It's close enough for me to visit on the weekends."

"That'll just delay things. It won't solve them." He shook his head, wishing he could propose a genuine solution. Every path seemed to have almost insurmountable obstacles. He looked into her eyes. Her lovely face was so close. She was holding her breath, and he could feel her desire to respond, but the moment slipped away.

She rose up and swiped the back of her jeans with her hands. "I'm hungry," she muttered. "Let's eat. If we walk a few minutes, there's a train station. We can catch it into town."

Max stood up and placed the satchel and diary back in the daypack before swinging it over his shoulder. "I could use some comfort food—eggs, toast, potatoes."

"Is your ankle all right to walk?"

"Yeah, sure, no problemo. It's almost good as new." The first steps were edged with sharp pain, but he distracted her by grasping her hand. "Hey, did I tell you that Kenji remembered a picture of Yoko and Mr. Murayama together?"

She laughed. "Nice try—proves nothing. I saw a picture of them on the office wall, but it could have been taken yesterday."

Max gestured with his free hand. "No, I mean a picture of them when

Yoko was a little girl. Kenji said it shows Mr. Murayama pushing her on a swing."

"Really? And he's sure it was Yoko?" The skin on Tomoko's forehead wrinkled slightly. "But Miki was positive Mr. Murayama didn't have any children."

Max shrugged. "Well, there's always a first time for being wrong."

SENATOR MCCLOY needed to be warned about what was transpiring, but the Washington-based satellite phone couldn't be used for the late-night call. It was a basic protocol of the Code that communication chains should never be continuous. Extensive military training and field operations had drilled the routines into Vincent Lemoine's head until they were second nature.

He dialed instead from a Georgetown pay phone and waited. It could be an FBI, CIA, or NSA number he was ringing; he would never know for sure. Several seconds passed while automated systems determined that the communication link was clean. Finally, a synthesized voice instructed him to leave a message.

"This is Lloyd Elgin. I received a call from an old friend who invited me to Japan. He's concerned about some recent business deals that have taken place. After careful consideration, I've agreed to the invitation and will be catching United 9678 to Tokyo at 10:45 a.m. tomorrow. Prepare my usual goods and have them delivered to the Shinjuku Century Hotel. You can expect another message from me within the next thirty-six hours."

CHAPTER
TWENTY-NINE

TWELVE MEN in heavy, polished boots charged up the stone stairway before making a stealthy, single-file dash under the little shrine's *Torii* gate. Racing across the blacktopped courtyard, the highly trained troops remained slightly hunched. They made a sharp left before moving along the shoulder-height cinderblock wall running alongside the Tokyo Poor House. Approaching the T-junction at the path's end, the unit commander held up a gloved hand and the group slowed to a stop. From beneath his combat helmet, the commander peered both ways down the wider laneway. It was empty.

He reached back and slipped a silver-handled collapsible device from his belt case. A single swift movement extended the metal baton to its full twenty-inch length, then he stepped around the corner and drove the sole of his boot into the front door. Wooden shards exploded as the rotting timber holding the lock in place splintered. Like a dam unleashed, the uniformed officers poured into the molding interior of the old house. Shrieks of confusion and anger filled the morning air. The creaking structure shuddered and swayed under the weight of the police and the agitation of the astonished occupants.

WITH his hands clasped behind his back, Masami Ishi paced beside the nearby police vehicles. In his left hand he gripped a day-old search warrant, obtained after visiting Yoko's office. It had taken some serious arm-twisting before the reluctant judge had finally issued the document with one caveat—there would be twenty-four hours of surveillance before any action was taken.

Twenty aggravating hours had ticked by, revealing nothing, until finally Masami Ishi's patience had worn thin. They were just a bunch of *Gaijin*, after all, and would never be able to navigate the complex judicial system. His biggest concern was how to hold the American out of sight for two weeks—if he could find him—without placing any charges.

A walkie-talkie squawked as the commander sent back his report. Masami Ishi heard the noise and approached the driver's side of a white police van. He motioned for the window to be rolled down. "What's going on?"

The young officer struggled to turn down the volume on the crackling handset. "The commander says they have four foreigners, but none match the American's description. He also says two of the foreigners' visas have expired, and one Israeli needs medical attention. He resisted arrest and is bleeding from a head wound."

"Damn it." He'd felt sure the American would be hiding in the house, cowering in his bedroom. Masami Ishi took the two-way radio. He stepped away from the vehicle, just far enough to be out of earshot of the driver. Pressing the rubber button, he spoke. "Commander—are you there?"

"Yes, sir."

"Take the Israeli to the hospital. Then bring them all in for questioning."

"Affirmative," came the quick response.

"I also want you to leave two men behind. Make the house look occupied. If the American comes, then grab him, but do not harm him."

"Yes, sir."

"And I have one special request. If your men do catch him, I want you to call me first—on my personal cell phone—before making any report to headquarters." Masami released the radio's button. The pause in communications was noticeably longer before the reply came back.

"I understand, sir."

CHAPTER
THIRTY

TOMOKO SWUNG the plastic 7-Eleven bag containing underwear and deodorant from one hand while the other grasped Max's as they walked back along the beach. "What else is in that backpack?" she asked.

"A novel, some daggers, a few bracelets," he said. "And a cell phone."

She shot him a playful grin. "Don't forget you owe me a new phone."

"Maybe I should just give you this one. Course I don't know if it belonged to the guys who robbed the office. And it had an odd text message on it."

"What do you mean? What did the message say?"

"Eight-nine-three-O-K." Max's arm tugged backward as Tomoko stopped dead in her tracks. He turned and repeated himself in response to her shocked look. "The message showed the numbers eight, nine, three, and the letters O and K. Why? Does that mean something?"

"Let me see the phone." Her voice was urgent.

"Give me a sec." He unzipped the daypack and dug around the bottom before pulling out the phone and tossing it to her outstretched hands. "It has a built-in GPS, so you shouldn't . . ."

She flipped it open and powered it up.

". . . turn it on. Or you could simply go right ahead."

Tomoko's head remained bowed over the small screen. "I just want to see the owner's name."

Max rested his weight on his good ankle while he waited.

"It belongs to Mr. Murayama." Several more beeps followed before she powered it off. "And the message is different from what you said. There are dots after the letters."

"So? So what if it's *O* dot *K* dot or the word *OK*? Doesn't it mean the same thing?"

"No, Max, it doesn't mean the same thing." She shook her head vehemently. "There's a Japanese card game called *oicho-kabu*, and in that game the worst possible hand you can get is an eight, a nine, and a three. The cards together are called *"Ya-Ku-Za."*

He looked at her, surprised that she expected him to be aware of such an obscure cultural reference. "Are you serious?"

Tomoko nodded. "And *O* dot *K* dot doesn't mean *okay*. They're initials for one of the most famous *Yakuza* in the country. His name is Oto Kodama."

Max felt stunned. "How do you know all this?"

"Everyone born here knows the meaning of Eight-Nine-Three, and Oto Kodama is famous because his father was famous. The *Yakuza* gangs are over three hundred years old, but Yoshio Kodama is called the 'Godfather of Vision,' because fifty years ago he brought many enemy gangs together into one large group. He's as well known in Japan as . . . *nanda-ke?* . . . you know, the famous American mafia man."

"Al Capone?"

Tomoko nodded. "Yes, Al Capone."

"So the message was meant to tell Mr. Murayama something about this *Yakuza* guy, Oto Kodama? But why? Who sent it?"

"It was sent at 11:41 p.m., on April nineteenth, by someone named Kazue Saito."

Max fell silent. He felt lightheaded and moved to sit down on a nearby rock. It was too much information to digest all at once. Tomoko stared at his perplexed face as she sat beside him. "What is it?"

"Kazue Saito . . ." Max thought back to the shrine murder article in the newspaper and the question he had raised. "Mr. Murayama told me he didn't know the guy."

"Who is Kazue Saito?" she implored.

"You didn't see it? In the paper? The diplomat who was killed last Thursday night."

Tomoko dropped the plastic bag at her feet as she put her hand to her mouth. "I saw the headline, but never read the story."

"The article said he died around midnight. That means Mr. Murayama lied to me. And it also means this text message was telling Mr. Murayama who his killer was." Max stared into Tomoko's fear-filled eyes. "So you still think the *Yakuza* aren't involved?"

Her hands began to shake. "Fine—whatever. You were right."

He thought back to his earlier assumptions. "You know, I could have had it all wrong. Maybe the *Yakuza* aren't looking for Prince Takeda's diary after all. Maybe they found out Kazue Saito sent a text message, and they're trying to get back the phone. Get rid of the evidence."

As Tomoko shivered, Max slid an arm around her shoulder and closed the loop with the other. "Hey—hey, don't worry. It'll be all right. We'll figure something out." She said nothing, and he tried to reassure her by lightening the moment. "Grab our high-end luggage out of the sand." He pointed at the plastic bag. "Let's go say goodbye to Mrs. Kanazawa. She's probably wondering where you are, anyway. We've been gone for hours."

MAX LIMPED slightly as he climbed the stone stairs rising up the lush, tree-covered hillside, his mind drifting, lost in a spiral of consequence and recourse. Arriving at the top, he realized they were on the property adjoining the Fairlady *onsen*. "Damn!"

Tomoko looked up from her feet. "What?"

"Wrong stairs. We should have gone around the corner on the beach. They all look the same from the bottom." Tomoko turned to go back, but Max motioned for her to follow him. "My ankle's not feeling so great. Let's find another way." He squeezed through a gap in some nearby bushes. "Come on. We can walk to the front this way."

"Are you sure?" Tomoko pressed gingerly into the space between the fence and the bushes. As they approached the front of the property, the shrubs closed in tight. Forward movement was impossible.

Max motioned for them to stop. "Looks like we're climbing over."

"Ahhh!" Tomoko swiped away a cobweb. "We should have used the stairs."

The plastic bag went over the fence first, just before Max winked and wove his fingers together, motioning for her to step into his outstretched palms. She did not appear convinced. "If I hurt myself, you're in big trouble." Stepping up, Tomoko grunted and disappeared over the fence top.

He could hear her brushing herself off. "Here, take this." Max swung the daypack over the wall before pulling himself up and over.

They were standing on the south side of the Fairlady *onsen*, with a rectangular window directly ahead. "This is Mrs. Kanazawa's office," she whispered, leaning forward. Cupping her hands to block out the sunlight, she pressed her face against the glass. But a short, sharp gasp escaped her lips as she stumbled backward and slammed against the fence. Her face twisted in soundless terror before she leaned down to vomit uncontrollably on the ground.

Max leaped to the window, tensing as he peered inside.

Mrs. Kanazawa's lifeless body was slumped forward across her desk. Her pinned-up hair hung loosely to the side of her oddly twisted head. Bright blood ran down the desk front, like a scarlet scarf draped below her vacant face. Through the partially open office door, he could see the back of Thick Neck. The killer was watching the front door while keeping himself shielded from direct view.

"She's dead!" Max gasped, spinning around to gather Tomoko into his arms, before pulling her back to the wall, away from the window. Her body was shaking with irrepressible shock, and he struggled to form his own screaming thoughts into a cohesive plan. "Sh-sh-sh-sh. You're all right. You're all right." He was hoping that saying it would make it seem more believable. Seconds ticked by as he rocked her gently and stroked her hair.

We can't stay here. These guys will kill us for sure.

His voice was quiet but firm. "Give me your keys. We have to move."

Sobbing, she dug into her front pocket.

Fear gripped Max's mind, but he was much calmer than he expected— someone had to be. "Tomoko . . . Hey, look at me . . . do you trust me?"

She sniffed an acknowledgment and wiped at her streaming eyes.

"If we stay, they'll find us. We have to go." Max kept a loose grip on her upper arm as they edged forward along the side of the building. Her sobs grew more controlled. Peering around the corner, he saw the back of their SUV parked ten paces past the sliding glass door. "If we make a run for it, we can get past the front door, into the car."

Edging out farther, he spotted the roof of a van parked at the far end of the sloping U-shaped driveway. "Damn it! They've blocked the best exit! And I'll bet that second guy is waiting in the van."

Max's foot bumped against a fist-sized rock in the flowerbed, and he paused briefly before glancing back at Tomoko's tortured expression. "I have an idea. How good is your throwing arm?"

CHAPTER
THIRTY-ONE

H IRO ADJUSTED his silver aviator sunglasses, then went back to methodically clenching and releasing his fists while pacing on the patio just back from the Izu hillside. It was clear that Jun loved being in charge—he'd been almost gleeful when snapping instructions.

Hiro turned to glance across the clear blue water of the *onsen*'s outdoor hot pool. He could see Jun in the lobby, pacing before the reception counter, keeping an eye on the front door while gruffly informing the startled hotel patrons that the pool was closed for cleaning.

The lobby's rear glass doors were propped wide open, leading into the ornate back garden with its carefully tended flowers and sculptured shrubs. The hotel owner had obviously been a gardener who loved her plants, and he felt sick thinking of her lifeless body now lying in the side office.

My father was a gang member his whole life and he never killed. This is not how it's supposed to be. The ancient principles of machi-yakko *instruct us to help the weak and oppose the strong . . . not murder them.*

Mrs. Kanazawa had steadfastly refused to divulge any guest information to Jun. Standing defiantly behind her office desk, she was tough as nails, her resolve unflinching. Finally making good on her threat to call the police, she reached for the office phone. But the *Surujin* flew with incredible speed, and the chubby woman had time to dial only a single number before the chain's weighted end wrapped around her neck, pulling her forward onto the desktop. A slash across her throat from the razor-sharp knife ended the discussion.

We've become like masterless samurai, nothing more than common criminals.

The beach below appeared empty. Hiro secretly wished the American wouldn't show up. It was Jun's turn to look the part of the fool. And it also meant that Tomoko wouldn't come to harm. Her lovely face was etched in Hiro's memory, as if he were still holding her picture in his hands.

Suddenly from behind came the crash of splintering glass. The burst of sound sent Hiro racing toward the lobby. Dashing along the pool's curving rim, he looked forward and glimpsed a lone figure streaking past the front of the hotel. Scrambling up and into the lobby, Hiro glanced to his left. Jun was charging from the office, holding a rock.

The air filled with the sound of a roaring engine.

Hiro grappled with the handle of the sliding door, finally wrenching it open just as a silver SUV shot past, heading toward the driveway entrance. From behind, he felt two fists hammer him in the back, sending him sprawling onto the stone walkway, as Jun raced past on an interception course.

The SUV slowed near the azaleas, and the passenger's side door flew open. Lying on the ground, Hiro stared as Tomoko's slender figure come to life. She dashed from the building's corner, her long black hair billowing as she dived inside the vehicle. The tires squealed, filling the air with smoky gray residue and the smell of burning rubber.

Jun's charging grunt became a hysterical shriek to stop. *"Yamete!"* He leaped forward and slammed into the vehicle's side. His hands clawed at the air before finally grasping the roof rack, and he jammed a foot into the closing door.

Bucking wildly, the SUV plowed over the driveway's curb and pressed hard against the shrubs. The thorny bushes became an army of tiny swords. Jun's guttural screams filled the air as the branches slashed at his face and arms, finally knocking him from his slender perch. Hiro watched him slam onto the driveway's hardtop, somersaulting him into a sprawling pose, where he lay still. The SUV bounced from the driveway into the street and made a sharp turn before disappearing from sight.

"OPPOSITE side of the road, Max! Drive on the left side!" Tomoko grabbed at the steering wheel while the fishtailing vehicle tore into the right lane. An oncoming delivery truck blasted its horn, then careened onto the sidewalk to avoid a head-on collision.

"Woah! Shit!" Max felt wild with fear. His eyes flicked from the road to Tomoko to the rear-view mirror and back again. His heart was racing, and his neck was as tight as piano wires. But he was pumped with exhilaration. They'd made it.

Tomoko turned to stare out the back window and her voice shook. "Are they following?"

The approaching traffic light changed to red. In front, a single mid-size sedan sat idling, its signal light blinking yellow in methodical rhythm. Heavy cross traffic flowed through the exchange. It seemed like far too many cars for a weekday lunch hour.

Max slowed the vehicle and glanced anxiously over his shoulder. "I can't see them, but they don't give up easily. You should put on your seatbelt." He drummed both hands on the steering wheel. Tomoko remained half turned in her seat. The traffic light was staying red far too long. The seconds dragged by, and when Max heard Tomoko gasp, he didn't bother looking back. Instinctively, he slammed the vehicle into a short reverse before executing a forward arc around the waiting sedan. Glancing briefly to the right, he prayed for the best and jammed hard on the accelerator, causing the SUV to jump forward into the crossroad. Horns blared as cars swerved and skidded.

The SUV raced along with the traffic. Weaving wildly back and forth, Max surged into the oncoming lane repeatedly and pushed forward one car-length at a time. Shocked drivers shook their fists in protest. Minutes ticked by while they wove an erratic path northward.

The congestion increased, the traffic flow slowing before finally grinding to a stop.

"This is bad." Tomoko's words broke Max's concentration. "We're heading into the town center. We need to go west. Away from the city." The traffic inched forward.

"I'll try, but we're not going anywhere in a hurry." Max glanced into the left-side mirror. His heart stuck in his throat. Thick Neck was on foot, charging toward them. The man's grim face wore a mask of determination, and his massive bulk swayed left and right while he pushed pedestrians aside.

He was only seconds away. Throwing the gearshift into reverse, Max crushed the bumper on the car behind.

Tomoko shrieked as the SUV shot forward onto the sidewalk. "What are you doing?"

"Surviving!" Max shouted, "Put on your seatbelt!" He pressed repeatedly on the horn as they flew along the sidewalk. Two startled teenagers stood in front, frozen like deer in the headlights. At the last second, Max jammed the racing vehicle to the left, within inches of a wrought-iron fence. Glass and plastic exploded as the passenger's side mirror blew into a million pieces, but they managed to narrowly miss the gawking teens.

Max leaned on the squawking horn. A construction site lay fifty yards down the road, but directly ahead, on the sidewalk, sat a vendor. Tomoko screamed. The gesturing owner finally abandoned his post by dashing into the street. The food stand was no match for the charging vehicle. The square aluminum frame molded to the shape of the bumper before the cart was tossed high into the air, slamming down onto the hood of a nearby taxi. *Yakisoba* filled the sky and drenched the area in sweet noodles and syrupy brown sauce.

Max groped for the wiper switch as he swerved to avoid a collision with a telephone pole. The slender spray of washer fluid fought against the brown sludge on the windshield. Fear had now changed to sheer terror. The heavy fence they were racing beside could easily shred the SUV.

Sidewalk changed to gravel as they neared the entrance to a construction site on the left. Max wrenched the wheel sharply, sending them into a sliding skid.

Max fought hard to regain control. The cab bucked and bounced over the uneven earth. Weaving to avoid the construction workers made it impossible to see anything in the rearview mirror. Beside him, Tomoko appeared apoplectic, but there was no time to console her now. His foot jammed the gas pedal with certainty. The *Yakuza* weren't likely to give up just to avoid a traffic ticket. And he was sure they were close behind, marking the same erratic path.

He shouted and waved frantically. *"Outta the way!"*

The bully on the playground wasn't just wielding his fists. This time around, death was being dealt. Kazue Saito and Mrs. Kanazawa had underestimated the threat, and it had cost them their lives. Max was resolute that he wouldn't make the same mistake.

THE police dispatcher's sweaty fingers pressed the button at the microphone's base. An SUV was racing northward toward Odawara, with a gray van in hot pursuit. The call for police support was confirmed by two black-and-whites. The first patrol car was in the area, while a second car, in the Hakone Mountains to the west, made a southern approach along a winding country road.

THE SUV burst through a metal fence and bounced into the adjoining road. A trail of torn earth, shattered equipment, and stunned victims lay strewn behind. The van was hot on the SUV's trail, having managed to gain ground.

Simultaneously weaving along the narrow hillside roads, the two nearly conjoined vehicles dodged bicycles and pedestrians. Bewildered citizens stared on as the screaming vehicles raced by on the normally tranquil roads.

The sing-song rhythms of a lone siren grew louder as the first police car finally caught the charging drag-racers—the two license plate numbers now surely being radioed by dispatch.

The van pulled into the oncoming lane and began hammering the SUV's right side, sending it dangerously close to the road's cliffside edge. Max held a vicelike grip on the steering wheel, struggling to maintain his vehicle's tenuous position. Metal panels screeched and twisted against the violent blows and counter-blows.

The battling vehicles crested a small hilltop above a four-way stop, the van riding the center line as it pushed the SUV precariously close to the roadside ditch. Ahead, a second police car blocked the middle of the intersection. Unable to change course, the van T-boned the police car, causing both vehicles to spin wildly. Shattered glass filled the air, raining down like crystal hail.

Max stabilized the swerving SUV and climbed the rising road. In the rear-view mirror, he watched the sliding van come to rest down an embankment at the same time as the first police car crested the hilltop. Next to him, Tomoko twisted backward in her seat, a look of horror painted on her face as the black-and-white vehicle tore into the already shattered remains of its sister car before flipping onto its roof.

The road through the forest ahead wound up into the Hakone Mountains. A cover of trees and houses flickered past and soon the roadside carnage disappeared from sight. It was impossible to tell if the gray van had started moving again.

Max's anxious voice filled the cab. "Are they following?"

Tomoko's response was fractured. "I . . . I don't know . . . but the police . . . must be hurt. We should . . . go back." She kept staring out the rear window.

"No way! Those *Yakuza* are probably just shaken up." He pointed to the daypack lying at her feet. "Use Mr. M's cell phone to call for help. Then turn it off again." Max could tell she was taken aback by his response, and he pulled his attention from the twisting forest road. "Listen to me. These guys aren't playing a game. They won't just threaten us. And we're not gonna die like Mrs. Kanazawa. We're not gonna die!"

CHAPTER
THIRTY-TWO

THE ARSENIC-GRAY limousine sat idling in the empty parking lot. Exhaust fumes puffed from its tailpipe and dissipated into the early morning air. Senator Andrew McCloy bit on the end of his pipe as he stared out the window at the barren park. Spring would arrive soon and with it the muggy warmth of a D.C. summer. He actually liked the cold weather. It was a nice change from the year-round Florida heat he had come to endure. But his wife loved the constant sunshine; it helped with her arthritis.

A dark blue Lincoln town car drifted into sight on the adjacent road, and he watched as a familiar heavyset man exited from the back. Even though both vehicles were registered to legitimate businesses, he knew that Ray Hylan would never risk any unfriendly eyes associating the two license plates. His covert Black Pearl Operations was quietly sheltered in a nondescript Washington office complex, and he would want to keep it that way.

Ray spoke to his driver before turning to walk the twenty yards toward the waiting limo. The April wind whipped his thinning auburn hair as it gusted between leafless beech trees and across the brown grass of the nearby field.

At the limo's rear, a tinted back window slid halfway down. "Go round the other side," the senator said.

Dissatisfaction was clearly stamped on Ray's face, and as he climbed inside he commented. "Stale tobacco and Old Spice. Two things I'd rather not smell so early in the morning."

"Hello Ray. How are you?" the senator said, unmoved by the jab.

"I'm good, Andy, and yourself?"

Smoke drifted from the senator's mouth. "Don't be smart. You know not to call me that."

Ray appeared to stifle a homerun grin. "My apologies, Andrew. I forgot how much you dislike the informal."

"With your I.Q., I doubt you forget anything, except your manners." He shook the polished walnut pipe with the three fingers on his left hand that had survived his military tour in Korea.

"I see you've switched off cigarettes. Was that by choice?"

The senator stifled a laugh. "Sylvia's been on my case for the last four decades to quit smoking. She's like a moth buzzing round the same porch light." All the years in Washington couldn't remove the Tennessee twang from his voice, try as he might. "I finally agreed to smoke this damned thing. But it just isn't like a good old pack of Marlboros."

"Please give my best to Sylvia."

"You know I won't be talking to her about this meeting," the senator chided.

"Fine, then let's dispense with the pleasantries and get to the point. What's with all the extra secrecy? Why are we meeting here?"

Andrew tapped his pipe on the door handle. "It's a bit of a bombshell, really. Lloyd Elgin called." He glanced up to enjoy what he hoped was a shocked reaction.

"You're kidding me!" The Black Pearl leader sat a little straighter. "When? What did he say?"

"Not much, really. Just that he received a call from a concerned friend in Tokyo about the murder of a Japanese diplomat and a suspicious office break-in. He made a few inquiries and thought it warranted a visit. He left for Japan a few hours ago."

Ray attempted to force a calm façade, but for all his skill in espionage the man had a lousy poker face. "I never honestly thought you'd get another call, especially after such a long silence."

"Eighteen years, to be exact."

"Let me have my folks check it out."

"No! Absolutely not. Lloyd can handle it quietly and discreetly. I don't need a bunch of your operatives stumbling around, drawing attention to something that may prove to be nothing. The last thing I need is the Japanese authorities starting an investigation."

"How can you be sure your guy can handle it? Who is he?"

"What would his real name mean, anyway? Suffice it to say I was lucky when I found him a decade ago. He's highly trained and completely ruthless."

"Andrew, if you don't let me follow up and your guy gets into trouble, there's no guarantee I can help."

The senator flicked his pipe in the air. "Bullshit! When Congress doesn't funnel you the money for all your private military firms and dirty little operations, who do you come running to? Me! You'll help out when I ask, or you'll find yourself hung out to dry."

Ray's face reddened and although he didn't speak the words, it was clear what he was thinking—*it's time for you to retire, old man, and let someone else take over The Enterprise.* "Don't kid a kidder, Andrew. You know the history of all this, what it started out as and what it's now become. You're too damn patriotic for that."

The two power brokers locked eyes.

Ray continued, "Besides, you of all people know the Cold War isn't over. It's just changed form. We do the work that nobody else wants to handle. The Black Eagle Trust and the other funds give us the means to battle dozens of private terrorist armies. Nobody has to declare war on the U.S., but they can attack us all the same, then we look like assholes when the government retaliates and fights back."

"My point exactly. If the money is so valuable to your cause, then you'll give me help—if and when I need it. Should Lloyd discover something that could be dangerous to us both, he'll do his best to put a lid on it, by any means necessary." The senator drew out the last part of the sentence before raising a single eyebrow. "If he can't handle it alone, that's when I'll get back in touch with you."

The veins in Ray's neck looked ready to pop. "I won't make any guarantees, but I'll try."

Andrew McCloy offered a good-old-boy smile. "That's all I'm asking for—just a little cooperation and reciprocity."

"What about the rest of the Enterprise council?"

"I'll let each one know by day's end.

Ray buttoned his coat. "You're playing with fire, Andrew. I hope your lone wolf can handle it."

"I believe he can."

"He'd better pull it off, because there's a helluva lot at risk here. If the flow of funds is affected at the same time as the damn bleeding-heart liberals cut the military budget, I can't imagine the chaos." Climbing back out into the cool morning air, Ray leaned in and took his final shot. "The president would go insane."

I T WAS the eighteenth hole of the U.S. Masters, and he was behind the leader by one stroke. The fairway stretched out ahead of him. A hush fell over the throng of onlookers pressed against the ropes. Eyeing the ball, he adjusted his stance and swung.

Masami Ishi sighed as the wretchedness of reality rushed back in. His ball sliced sharply to the left and dropped after seventy-five yards. Bright stadium lights had turned the field from night into day, and the ball was soon lost in the chaotic deluge of white orbs bouncing in every direction.

After setting up again, he straightened his sleeveless argyle slipover. Perched on the third level of the Meiji-Jingu Golf Range, he tried hard not to let the constant drumming of the other 122 golfers break his concentration. It shouldn't be hard to go the full 150-yard distance, he thought.

Someone stepped into the open walkway to his right; Masami heard the man stridently clear his throat. He focused harder and swung. The ball hooked sharply and hit the ground before the fifty-yard marker. Frustration swelled in his chest and he whirled around to reprimand the idiot watching him.

The police commander's mustached face was partially obscured as he bent forward from the waist. "My sincere apology for distracting you, superintendent, but you requested an update if there was any new information."

The urge to vent was unstoppable. "Next time wait until I've finished swinging!"

"Yes, sir." The younger man remained in a subordinate pose.

The Callaway gloves came off as he sat in a molded fiberglass chair and brushed his comb-over back into place. "So what's the news?" His outward attitude of cool indifference masked an intense thirst for information.

"The license plates of the American's girlfriend came up during a car chase on the Izu Peninsula this afternoon."

"Izu? What would she be doing down there?"

The commander shook his head. "I'm not sure, sir, but a gray van was also involved."

"Was anyone caught?"

"No. The American and his girlfriend got away. And the other two men escaped on foot."

"What about the van? Who owns it?"

"It's registered to Oriental Passage Pachinko and Slots, here in Tokyo." The commander paused and cleared his throat. "The *pachinko* business is controlled by Oto Kodama."

Yakuza usually only bothered with *Gaijin* when it was foreign women they were bringing into the country, Masami thought. "Put two men on a detail to follow Kodama-*san*. What could Oto possibly be up to?"

The commander appeared unsure whether to answer. "I don't know, sir, but there's more. The female owner of an *onsen* near Odawara was also murdered. Several neighbors reported seeing the same two vehicles racing away from the hotel."

Masami Ishi folded his arms across his chest. It would be a hell of a lot harder to keep the American's capture quiet if he was involved in a murder investigation. The constant drumming of clubs hitting balls seemed to grow louder during the momentary lull in conversation. "Tell me, if you were a foreigner being chased by the *Yakuza*, where would you go?"

The commander sucked in air through his clenched teeth. "I would go home to my country."

"And suppose you were worried the airport was being watched?"

"Then I would try to go somewhere as safe as possible."

"Exactly. I want you to distribute the American's picture in a bulletin. But make sure it only mentions the burglary. The press will go crazy with it otherwise."

"Yes."

"I also want a dozen men added to the guard detail near the U.S. Embassy. Double-check every person approaching the place. If the American shows up, arrest him before he gets onto the grounds."

"Yes, sir."

Masami Ishi drummed his fingers on his chubby tricep. "And remember what I told you before, commander. I'm the first number you call after you catch him."

CHAPTER
THIRTY-THREE

A
T ALMOST midnight, the stark concrete waterfront of the Takeshiba
pier stood quiet and empty. Even the ever-present seagulls had tucked
up their wings and gone to sleep. Office lights from the surrounding Tokyo
towers cast shiny, quivering fingers across the water of the dark bay.

The last employee had switched off the pier lights and gone home after
the 11:30 p.m. boat departed. The tourist vessel was on a 110-mile journey
south, to the island sanctuary of Miyakejima. It would disgorge its weary
passengers at precisely five the following morning.

Max circled the battered SUV around the same spot for the third time.
The vehicle needed to be abandoned strategically—parked illegally, close
to the pier, so the conclusion could be drawn that they had run off to the
southern islands. But the parking spot couldn't be so obvious that the police
would find the deserted vehicle before the ferry arrived at its destination. An
early discovery would give the authorities time to radio ahead. Failure would
shatter the illusion, while success could buy them some much-needed time.

Slumped in the passenger's seat, Tomoko sat unresponsive. She was
staring at a crack that stretched the width of the front windshield. It must
have started when the van was repeatedly hammering into them.

He pulled the SUV to a stop and turned off the engine. *It's my fault,* he thought, turning toward the passenger's seat. *She trusted me and now look at her.* "I'm so sorry about Mrs. Kanazawa. It's wrong—all wrong." The deadly afternoon felt fuzzy and unclear, like a distant, hazy memory that left a lingering feeling of terror. He touched her chin, guiding her pensive eyes away from the cracked glass. "Tomoko, we have to go. I need out on your side. Mine won't open."

Trancelike, she unlocked the door and slid out into the chilly breeze sweeping off the bay.

Max grabbed the daypack and crawled out behind her. "This should do. It won't get noticed right away because the good side is pointed out, but once people start arriving for work, someone will spot the damage and report it for sure. Hopefully later tomorrow morning."

She stood shivering in the wind before he pulled her toward him, guiding them away from the waterfront to the train station a half dozen blocks away. They walked in silence, his arm wrapped around her shoulder, their feet moving in rhythm. The commercial streets finally gave way to the bright lights of the approaching station.

"Tomoko, you haven't spoken in hours. Please say something."

Her voice cracked and she coughed. "I—I want to go home. See my mother."

He squeezed a bit tighter, intent on remaining calm and rational for her sake. "I know you do, but it's just not safe. Let's find somewhere to stay tonight and talk about it tomorrow."

"How will it be any better tomorrow? We still have the diary." She shivered again. "What if it's my parents who aren't safe?"

Max's voice edged upward. "That's my point. Look what followed us! Mrs. Kanazawa died because we went there. I don't want the same thing to happen to your parents. We need to be smarter. We have to stay away, at least for now. Understand?"

She half glanced at him before looking away. "I do understand, but I need to call my mother tomorrow. She's probably crazy with worry."

"Sure." Max conceded for the moment while remaining convinced it was a bad idea.

"Let's just find some place to sleep. I'm so tired . . . but I don't want to see anybody. I look awful." Tomoko wiped at her eyes and tried to straighten her frizzled hair.

The familiar clack of an approaching train could be heard as they headed into the station lobby, "Hurry, we can make this one," urged Max, fumbling coins into the ticket machines as the rumbling grew louder.

Racing through the turnstiles, they wove up the stairs and through the people exiting the train, finally squeezing between the closing doors.

Max dropped into a seat. "I have an idea where we can stay." He rubbed his throbbing ankle while carefully observing the faces of the half-dozen occupants in the train car, verifying their anonymity. "It's not far from here, and I promise they won't ask questions."

THE slender hotel looked like a handful of other six-story buildings on the narrow Meguro Street, including the glowing pink sign advertising two prices for each room, one for a "rest" and an alternative to "stay."

Max stood alone in the muted lobby light of the undersized Chez Moi Love Hotel, which he had chosen at random from a street full of similar establishments. Upon entering, he'd waited discreetly while another couple examined the only two available rooms displayed by illuminated eight-by-ten photos set within a collection of similar but dark pictures. The *Kogal* girl eyed him briefly, then ignored him. She had streaked hair and heavy makeup, while the man beside her wore an ill-fitting suit and appeared to be intoxicated. After a round of pouting and discussion, she finally pressed a button beneath a glowing picture and helped him insert his credit card. The photo went dark, and the machine automatically dispensed a card key. A shiny elevator door opened, and they disappeared through it as the woman giggled and cooed.

Approaching the photo wall, Max pressed the button of the last remaining room and inserted his cash. While waiting for the key, curiosity got the best of him. He looked at the room that the couple had selected. The histrionic reds and the cutesy Hello Kitty theme seemed odd when compared to the S&M chains hanging from the bedroom ceiling. Tomoko would not have appreciated the bizarre room, no matter how exhausted she was.

Max stepped out the hotel's front door and waved his arm. Looking up and down the dim street, he finally saw her appear from the shadows. She kept her head down and her arms wrapped tightly around herself while jogging the short distance. Darting into the lobby, she slipped into the open elevator. Max followed her and inserted the room key. The fifth-floor button blinked on, and they shuddered into motion.

"I told you that you wouldn't have to see anybody."

"*Domo arigato.*" Tomoko's teeth chattered.

Upon exiting the elevator, it was clear which of the rooms was theirs: it was the only one with a blinking pink light above the doorway.

The brightly lit room smelled strongly of cleaning products and baby powder. Startling life-sized plaster statues of Apollo and Zeus stood on either side of a heart-shaped tub to the left. A mish-mash of fake stone, fake tiles, and fake stucco adorned the walls. Against the far wall stood a round bed surrounded by Greco-Roman columns. Sheer pink drapes cascaded between the columns, complementing the matching sheets on the round mattress. Three televisions were placed strategically about the room. Muted in sound, they all displayed the same soft-core sex scene.

Tomoko's mouth hung open. "You're joking."

"This was the only room left, and believe me, it's the most conservative by far." He set the daypack down and turned to face her. "I was thinking a lot while we driving, and I have some things I need to explain."

Tomoko looked defeated. "Give me a minute." The bathroom door closed as she disappeared inside.

Max collapsed onto a dingy sofa, retrieved his soon defunct airline ticket from his pocket, and put his feet up on the faux marble coffee table. He leaned back and stared up, listening to the sound of running water as his eyes followed the path of plastic vines snaking across the ceiling. The events of the past two days settled like a lead weight. He wondered how things could go so wrong so quickly, while at the same time acknowledging gratitude that at least they were alive.

Several minutes passed before Tomoko emerged and took a spot next to him on the couch. She laid her head on his shoulder and clutched his arm.

He placed the ticket in her lap and spoke hesitantly at first, trying to figure out how to explain exactly what he had been pondering on the drive back from the Izu. "Moving someplace new and starting all over can be really tough—trust me, my family has done it enough times. But starting over fresh, coming here to Japan, was something I chose because I wanted to get more out of life—you know, learn new things and see the world from a different perspective. And along the way I discovered that being so far from home, everything feels incredibly magnified. Familiar comforts aren't there and you don't have your old friends or your family to lean on—the highs become way more extreme but so do the lows."

He paused, feeling self-conscious, unsure whether there was any point continuing until he felt her squeeze his arm, encouraging him on.

"And when I found the TPH and then started teaching Mr. M, I was on a high because I finally had friends again and a chill place to live. Of course then I met you . . . and the high got even higher." He couldn't look at her for fear that he wouldn't be able to finish. "And even though everything felt great, there was always this little voice in the back of my head warning me that a new low was coming. Nothing lasts forever. It's just a matter of time, Travers—prepare yourself." His head shook as if in denial. "And now here it is. I just can't imagine there ever being a worse day than today."

He held his lips against the top of her head, pausing before speaking with quiet conviction, recalling the argument outside Tony Roma's. "So, I want you to have my return ticket because I need you to trust that I'm not going anyplace without you. We'll get through this together." Max could feel her nodding, knowing she understood his sincerity, and he followed the urge to sit up in order to see her face. "Would you kiss me?"

Tomoko wiped at her eyes while licking away the salty tears washing over her lips. "I'm a mess. Why would you want that?"

"Because . . ." He paused before meeting her puzzled gaze. "Because I really need it."

She reached up abruptly and pulled his face toward her, breathing life into him.

OH shit, they've found us!

Max bolted upright and tried to scan the dark room. The only sound was the pounding heartbeat in his ears; nothing else. The room was silent. He had a fleeting thought that maybe it had all just been a terrible dream. His eyes adjusted to the glimmer of hallway light sneaking in around the hotel door. The Roman Colosseum wall clock glowed 4:31 a.m.

Tomoko gently touched his shoulder and pulled him back down. She whispered in his ear, "I'm sorry for waking you, but I've made a decision." She had slipped off her underwear, and her entirely naked body pressed warm against him. "I'm ready." She kissed his lips and ran her slender fingers into his blond hair.

Max, his arousal evident, tensed briefly. After months of denial, she now seemed so sure. Was she reaching out to him because of love or fear, or both? "But you said you wanted to wait. Are you sure this is what you want? I mean—"

Tomoko held two fingers across his mouth. "No more holding back. I'm sure." She kissed him harder this time as she flicked the waistband of his boxer shorts. He obliged by sliding them off.

His hands traveled the gentle curve of her hips. Fears that the actions, so long suppressed, would feel awkward were unfounded. The movements were instinctive and true, a dormancy finally awakened. The urge to lose himself in her became overwhelming.

He felt the softness of her belly pressing upward, and his head dropped down to cradle in the nape of her slender neck as a rising crescendo of pleasure washed against the moorings of the past day's terror and mortality. The moment felt overwhelmingly alive.

CHAPTER
THIRTY-FOUR

Wednesday, April 25

WHENEVER MAX neared the U.S. Embassy, he could still hear the haughty drawl of a former TPH roommate. On several occasions, the pompous guy had droned on about how ironic it was that, up until 9/11, the Soviet Embassy was inhospitable and sinister, while the U.S. Embassy was a bright place with trees, flowers, and a wide-open gate flanked by pleasant, rotund guards. Not any longer. The two embassies appeared to have switched roles. There were now dozens of police in combat gear surrounding the United States' modern ten-story Akasaka building. Riot buses were parked at every entrance. It was a dark and foreboding citadel. Demonstrations or public gatherings were banned anywhere near the grounds, and to get inside meant running a gauntlet of security. The drawn-out conclusion was that the switch between the characters of the two embassies was simply the physical manifestation of a truth that everyone knows but is afraid to admit: that America has become the shadowy invading power of a darker world. Of course, the guy had sideburns shaped like lightning bolts and a liking for pornographic *Manga* cartoons, so it was difficult for anyone to take him too seriously.

With a sense of foreboding, Max stepped from the Ginza Line subway car before pressing through the platform crowd to hug the gritty tiled wall.

He couldn't recall if the U.S. Homeland Security level was Yellow or Orange. No recent terror attacks came to mind, but then he hadn't really been paying attention to the newspaper the last few days. Being chased by madmen had that effect. He tested his sore ankle by rotating it, noticing that even with all the activity, it was finally starting to feel better. Standing between two glossy cosmetics posters, he scanned above the crowd. Nothing seemed unusual. He thought how odd it was that he could be so paranoid, even in a crowd of millions.

The city's morning commute was tapering off, but the flow of people in both directions was still unbroken. From overhead, a recorded female voice bounced off Toranomon Station's low ceiling.

Max's gaze swept the area as he moved to a stairwell. Climbing the steps, he approached the top at exit number five, mere blocks from the embassy.

Just stay on the opposite sidewalk from the police and get inside the gate. The Yakuza won't come around here, and there should be other Americans heading to work, so it'll be easier getting lost in the crowd.

He rose to sidewalk level and slowed as he peered out, but the unrelenting crowd jostling past threatened to push him onward before he felt ready to move. A patch of morning sky revealed broken white clouds on a light blue canvas. Traffic was creeping past as a construction crew hammered on the road to his left, and heavily fortified barricades could be seen several hundred yards up the road.

Max felt himself unconsciously flinch, pressing tighter against the wall at his side. Something was out of place. Twenty paces away, a dozen police officers were standing on the curving sidewalk in the direction of the U.S. Embassy. They were blocking most of the walkway, and pedestrians were being forced onto the street's edge to navigate around the group.

The group's attention was focused on a man standing directly in front of them. Max couldn't see his face, but he was dressed in a knee-length, olive green trench coat. He appeared to be addressing the officers while holding a clipboard, rotating it so all the men could see. With his free hand, he motioned in the air as if indicating the height of a tall person. The uniformed officers nodded at every statement. All of them were unusually attentive. In fact, they seemed apprehensive.

The sharp, goose-like honk of a passing truck drew the attention of the group. The truck trumpeted at a miniature car trying in vain to squeeze past the construction work. As the Japanese man in the trench coat turned his head, Max could see that he had a trim black mustache and appeared to be in his late thirties.

The shouting truck driver continued cursing out his window until an officer blew his whistle and motioned for order. The commotion seemed to signal an end to the meeting, and the mustached leader pressed the clipboard against his leg before bowing slightly. Turning swiftly, he strode toward the subway entrance. It would be mere seconds before he reached the top of the stairs.

Max flipped his hoodie up onto his head and took a couple of steps back down into the station. He wasn't sure why he felt so anxious. Maybe it was just his nerves getting the better of him, but he chose to trust his gut. Turning, he raced back the way he'd come, entering the tunnel to his right. The only place to go was the newspaper kiosk, by the far wall at the tunnel's end. He grabbed the closest magazine, opening it to shield his face as he slouched down. Seconds ticked by while he remained motionless, noticing the veins in his neck pulsing.

The guy must have walked past me by now.

Max lowered the magazine an inch and peered over the top. The olive green trench coat was standing right next to him.

Shit! His body stiffened in anticipation of an attack.

Tense seconds ticked by while a stream of people continued to pour through the lobby.

Lowering the magazine a little further, Max could now see that the man's back was facing him. He had bent over, attempting to leaf through some newspapers with one hand while being jostled by other customers purchasing cigarettes and candy bars. Frustrated with his inability to find what he wanted, the man set down his clipboard and used both hands.

Max felt his cheeks flush as a fresh wave of panic punched him in the gut. On the clipboard, staring back was a full-size photograph of his own face. He jerked the magazine up. The urge to run felt overwhelming. It screamed and rattled inside his brain, almost drowning out the little voice in the back of his head that commanded him to remain stone-still.

He stood paralyzed for what seemed an eternity, until finally the kiosk owner's angry voice forced him to lower his shield. Behind the counter, the owner was forming two fingers into a circle, demanding payment. Dropping the magazine, Max turned and scanned the busy subway lobby. The mustached man was nowhere in sight.

I was right! The police are hunting for me.

Max rushed to the nearby ticket machine, sorting hastily through the coins in his pocket while glancing uneasily around the station. His own suspicions had been confirmed, and it was a pretty sure bet that if the cops were looking for him then they were also looking for Tomoko. He needed to get back to the Love Hotel right away and warn her. They had to find somewhere safer to hide.

CHAPTER
THIRTY-FIVE

VINCENT LEMOINE dozed in a half sleep. His facemask and earplugs insulated him from the surrounding first-class passengers. Lying prone in 2A, he could feel the comforting pulse of the 777-300ER's powerful dual engines vibrating up through the flatbed seat. It was certainly a far cry from the military transports he'd taken a quarter century earlier as a young Navy Seal.

Pulled into the CIA's Black Ops program at twenty-four, he had resigned fifteen years later, having been approached quietly by Senator Andrew McCloy. The good representative from Tennessee had set forth an offer that Vincent couldn't refuse. It was an opportunity to serve God and country, but more importantly, the chance to earn a boatload of cash in just ten years. The Freedom 50 plan—retiring to the French countryside—could be a reality. And so Vincent had bitten.

In the years after World War II, General Douglas MacArthur's office had charted a shadowy network of global informants. There was always someone close to those in power willing to do the job—easy money for very little work. Each man's single task was to monitor chatter within his designated area. Anything that could threaten to reveal the past's dark secrets or blow open the unsavory actions of the present was to be reported. The informants were instructed to take no direct action. They were simply required to dispatch information to a central location. The appropriate course would be determined only after careful analysis. The Code's strict communications protocols were designed and implemented—and thus the role of "Lloyd Elgin" was born. Over the decades, the hitmen who monitored the chatter and acted on the reports each bore the same working name.

Vincent's mind ran back over his predecessor's encrypted data files. The last trip to Tokyo had been eighteen years earlier. At the time, it appeared that former Prime Minister Takeshita's fifty-eight-year-old secretary, Mr. Ihei Aoki, was getting ready to talk publicly—the prime minister had just resigned over the "Recruit" bribery scandal.

The former Lloyd Elgin had found the distraught secretary face down in a karaoke watering hole and had befriended him. After several rounds of drinks, Ihei Aoki grinned and whispered to his new American friend that he was going to change the landscape of Japanese and U.S. politics forever. He would reveal truths that would make the current scandal look insignificant.

In the early morning hours of Wednesday, April 26, 1989, the two men had stumbled from the bar together. But only one of them was actually drunk. The former Lloyd convinced the intoxicated Aoki-*san* that they should walk back to his apartment instead of taking a taxi. The remainder of the electronic file revealed an almost gleeful telling of the assisted suicide. While the American was efficient and effective, he also harbored a sadistic joy when it came to death's delivery. Back at the apartment, the drunken secretary had passed out repeatedly. Each time he was revived, a razor was carefully returned to his hand. The sympathetic voice in his ear urged him to bear responsibility for Japan's fallen leader. A death with honor was the right thing to do. After seventeen futile attempts, there was blood everywhere. A necktie and a curtain rod finished the job.

VINCENT felt a hand gently touch his shoulder, triggering him to remove his sleeping mask. Standing in the aisle next to his seat was an ANA flight attendant. She was grinning like a love-struck schoolgirl as she touched her lower lip and whispered in perfect English, "Mr. Elgin, we are going to be serving breakfast soon. Shall I bring you something now? Anything? Coffee perhaps?"

He nodded his head and then watched her walk slowly and seductively toward the airplane's cockpit. A little mile-high action would be an excellent way to wake, he thought, but he couldn't draw undue attention to himself. And besides, there was his beautiful new wife to think about. In a year's time, he would be unshackled from his work, and they would be living in a Provence villa.

Vincent stretched his muscular torso before walking the several steps forward to the lavatory.

Warm water splashed his tanned face while he mentally refocused on the job ahead. Staring into his own eyes, he whispered into the bathroom mirror, "Now is not the time to get sloppy, pal. Until you're back in Washington, your only goal is to confirm if there's a problem, and then eliminate it."

JUN'S HULKING frame paced along the stark edges of the dimly lit underground room; a single bare bulb illuminating a spot near the windowless metal entrance. The damp concrete walls were closing in all around, and he struggled to shake off the bad night's sleep on the cold floor. Besides the two thin mattresses against the back wall—Hiro lying nearly invisible on one—the only other furniture was two chairs and a wooden table in the room's center. The natural, unfinished top appeared stained, as if ink had been poured in abstract patterns over its rough surface.

Flicking his fingertips lightly over his face, Jun felt the dried blood that had formed on the field of tiny cuts. Yesterday's chase had gone from bad to worse. Not only had the *Gaijin* slipped away, but they'd had to leave Oto's van nose-down in the ditch. Hiking west into the forests of the Hakone Mountains had seemed logical at the time, at least until it grew dark and the temperature began dropping.

Finally finding a narrow country road, they had been able to direct a pickup car to their location. Within minutes, elation turned to trepidation as the driver stated that Oto wanted to see them, and he wasn't happy. Several hours later, the sedan pulled into the underground parking garage of the Yebisu Garden Terrace. But instead of being marshaled to the elevator, the driver locked them overnight on the P5 level of the complex.

Jun stopped pacing as the rusting lock on the door cranked open with a groan. One of Oto's bodyguards entered the room, followed by the great man himself, dressed in a purple velvet tracksuit. The aging leader looked as if he could have been out for a leisurely morning stroll. Oto pointed at Jun and barked a command. "Sit!"

The bodyguard dragged Hiro to his feet and shoved him roughly him into the second chair.

Oto paced in the meager pool of light. His dog-tag chains slapped against his protruding belly. "You greatly disappoint me. I gave you a simple task. 'Go and get me a book.' Is that so hard?" Saliva clung to his lower lip. "I guess so, because you let a boy pluck it from your grasp. Then I asked you to follow his girlfriend and find him . . . and the result is that you jump the wrong *Gaijin*." Oto's deep voice rose and echoed inside the cave. "And finally, I send you to the Izu for a second chance to get it back. What do you do? You kill an old lady, smash a few police cars, and abandon my van."

Even in the dim light, Jun could see the heavy veins protruding from Oto's neck. "Father, we tried—"

"Don't speak, boy! Excuses are not what I'm looking for."

The hinges on the metal door sang out of key as the second bodyguard entered the room. Bowing at the waist, he handed a dagger to Oto, then stepped back away. Sliding the simple knife from its metal sheath, Oto walked to the center of the room. He jabbed the dagger into the center of the table, where it stood upright.

"You've shamed me. You know the rules." The words resonated in the windowless room.

Without hesitation, Hiro place his right hand on the table. Palm down. His fingers were spread wide. His face remained bowed.

It suddenly became clear to Jun where the dark spots on the wooden table had come from. His troubled eyes locked on Oto's angry face as he placed his own trembling hand on the table.

"Not you! It's your *Sempai*'s responsibility to take the blame for this."

Jun snatched his hand back and held it close to his groin.

Oto pulled the knife from the table. He seemed to be drawing out the moment, as if savoring the taste of a fine wine.

"I will give you one more chance to redeem yourself. Catch the girl for me." The lone light bulb glinted off the shiny metal blade. "You can catch a little girl, can't you?"

Suddenly the blade sliced through air and bone, slamming hard against the table.

A HOWLING scream of agony tore upward, twisting and echoing its way through the parkade. At street level, a lone attendant listened and shuddered before sliding the window of his booth closed.

CHAPTER
THIRTY-SIX

TOSHI TOOK two crystal glasses from the cupboard while Max stood in the open kitchen doorway. The shaggy blond hair and pale skin were gone. He eyed his reflection in a hallway mirror while towel-drying his short brown hair, unsure of whether the right decision had been made. "I think that drugstore tanning lotion worked too well. I look like George Hamilton."

"Who?"

"Never mind."

"Changing appearances will do little." Toshi shrugged as he spoke. "You're still too tall."

"At least I won't resemble the police mug shot." Max hoped the transformation would also reduce his growing feelings of paranoia. "I really appreciate you letting us stay here tonight. I couldn't risk staying another night in a busy hotel." He leaned against the wall. "Plus, I saw the pair of cameras out front and I think this place is probably more secure."

"My father was a very cautious man. He put in security systems." Toshi cracked open a bottle of whiskey. "In the end, it did no good. They killed him in public, on the subway."

"They?" Max's head jerked up. "Who are they?"

"I have theories." Toshi handed over three fingers of amber liquid. "Drink this."

"It's only two o'clock." Max's voice registered mild surprise.

"After everything that's happened?"

"True enough. It's hard to believe that three days ago I was minding my own business, and now . . ." Goose bumps raced up Max's arms. "I never realized how violent this place could be."

"You've seen what you've been told to see: sushi, karaoke, capsule hotels, geishas, and sumo wrestling." Toshi sighed. "You haven't moved beneath the surface. This country has both good and bad. It shouldn't be a shock." He raised his glass. "Let's drink a toast . . . to understanding our weaknesses and making them strengths."

The liquid bit hard on its way down and Max was forced to take a deep breath before speaking. "Surviving this is gonna take more than just strength. It's gonna take a miracle."

Toshi stroked the vertical strip of hair beneath his lip and his eyes grew unfocused, as if he were watching something in the center of the room that was only visible to him. "Sometimes the spirits require us to do things we don't think possible. It's how we grow and find who we truly are."

"But people aren't usually dying as a result." Max's chest swelled. "Tomoko's the best thing that's ever happened to me." His words grew hushed. "If she ends up getting hurt, I could never forgive myself."

"I understand. So the question you must ask is . . . what was the single thing that set the current chain of events in motion?"

Max thought back to the moment as he crouched in Mr. M's dark office. "Going to the office and then grabbing the daypack. I should have never picked that damned thing up."

Toshi sipped his drink. "The *Yakuza* probably wouldn't have chased you, and the policeman may not have noticed you."

"I know where you're going with this, and trust me, I've thought of returning the stuff to Mr. M. But what if he doesn't believe me? What if he blames me for the robbery and all the damage?"

"But if he does believe you, he can tell the police to close the case. He may also have a way of helping with the *Yakuza*. The man was a diplomat, after all." Toshi took another sip. "If you want, you could leave the diary with me and I could return it for you."

"Thank you. That's incredibly generous." The offer seemed sincere, and the urge to seize it so tempting, but one completely innocent person was already dead. Max was resolute not to make it two. "No. You've already done way too much for us. I can't let you do that."

MIKI'S head seemed overly large on Toshi's wall-mounted fifty-inch flat-screen monitor. Still, Tomoko had been relieved to see her friend's face.

"And they killed her?" Miki was still gasping when she finally lifted her fingers away from her mouth. "You have to go to the police!"

"I know! But Max is convinced the police will charge him with the break-in." Tomoko's tear-filled eyes stared back. "And he thinks they're all connected to the *Yakuza*."

"That's just stupid." The two friends nodded together in agreement. "So where are you hiding?"

"With a friend of Max's, a Shinto priest. He seems like a good guy." Tomoko wiped her eyes with a tissue. "But I don't know what to do next. I need to make sure my parents are fine, although I'm afraid to call home. What if Max is right? What if contacting them just adds to the danger? Their phone must be bugged. It's the only way the *Yakuza* could have found us at the *onsen*. Mrs. Kanazawa must have talked with my mom and told her where I was."

"You need to go home and warn them!"

"I know." The response caught in her throat. "Max doesn't understand how much I love them. How could he? He's not close to his own family. He can't know how I feel."

"Then use my little trick." Miki leaned closer to the camera, further distending her image on the big screen. "Tell him what he wants to hear . . . and then do whatever you need to do. He'll get over it."

Silence hung in the air while the two girlfriends stared anxiously at each other. Miki finally sat back, changing the subject. "I followed up on the information you asked for."

"You found where the prince lives?"

The corners of Miki's mouth crept into a grin as she swept the blonde hair away from her face. "I know I'm fabulous, and we can talk about that later, but I have to warn you, it's not good news. Visiting Prince Takeda will be a little difficult, since he died in 1992 at the age of eighty-three."

Tomoko's head dropped into her cupped hands. She felt like crying.

Miki continued, "Prince Tsuneyoshi Takeda owned an estate in Chiba Prefecture that was sold by his family after he died. There was also one other property. It's near Osaka, in the mountains outside the old western capital city of Nara. It wasn't part of the family estate, but was transferred separately to someone named Ben Takeda. Interestingly enough, the prince had five children, but none named Ben." Miki rifled through a stack of loose papers and pressed the page with the address toward the camera.

Tomoko grabbed a scrap of yellow paper to copy the information. Something was tingling in the back of her mind, and she struggled to figure out what it was. "Did you find out any more about this Ben person?"

"How long have you known me? Of course I did. Ben was adopted by Prince Takeda in September 1947, just before the prince became a commoner. But the documents were signed only by the prince, and not his wife. The archives don't show a birthplace, but the boy was ten years old at the time. It's really strange, actually. There's nothing I can find to explain why this boy was adopted." She shrugged. "Maybe he was a child from a mistress."

Tomoko's eyes shot wide. "Or maybe . . ." She unzipped the daypack at her feet and retrieved the diary. Opening the leather jacket, she carefully scanned the last few pages.

"What is it?"

"Just a moment . . . here it is. I knew I remembered something. After the war, the prince brought back a child named Benjie from the Philippines. Ben could be short for Benjie, right?"

"Yeah. But why do that?"

"I'm not sure exactly, but his diary says that just before the prince returned to Japan, he found a child named Benjie, and he brought the boy back with him."

"Strange." Miki motioned to her watch. "I'm sorry, but I have to get back to work."

There was a knock at the office door, and Max slipped into the room. Tomoko motioned for him to come forward as she deftly switched to English. "Wait, Miki, this is my boyfriend."

"Hi, I'm Max." He leaned in and nodded to the camera.

"But his hair? The color?"

"It was my idea to change it." Tomoko ran a hand across Max's damp head. "He needs a disguise, and I think I like it."

Miki nodded. "I must go, but be careful, and remember my little trick." She giggled, effectively masking the seriousness of the parting comment. "Bye-bye."

MIKI'S face was reflected dozens of times on the surface of the multifaceted crystal drinking glass. In the semi-dark bedroom, Toshi drained the remaining drops of scotch. Reaching forward, he stopped the recorded image while he wrote down the Nara address.

Opening the house's security software, he scrolled to view the live feed coming from the office. The image on the screen enlarged and stabilized. Tomoko was handing the diary to Max, pointing and relaying the details of her conversation.

Sitting straight-backed, Toshi stroked the hair on his chin, observing the private conversation.

CHAPTER
THIRTY-SEVEN

ZOE DRAGGED a hand through her spiky platinum hair. After the previous day's violent police raid, she was in no mood for visitors. From the second floor of the Tokyo Poor House, she scowled and eyed the annoyingly persistent man at the front door, keeping her face well back from the window to avoid being seen.

Dressed in a navy sports coat, he wasn't making any motion to kick his way in, but he also didn't appear to be giving up and leaving. For the third time, his knuckles rapped on the door. She cringed as she heard a bedroom door slide open.

Zoe moved quickly to the stairs and descended. She could see the injured Israeli stop near the middle of the hallway. He slowly turned his bandaged head to look back at her. "Itzhak, go back to bed. I'll answer the door."

The man banged on the door again. It sounded as if he was using his whole fist now.

Zoe yelled over her shoulder while guiding Itzhak back to his room. "Hang on a freakin' minute." Turning and stomping down the hallway, she pulled the front door open, revealing a handsome, middle-aged man. His hair, parted straight down the center, along with his horn-rimmed glasses, gave him an odd bookish quality. "What do you want?"

"DON'T mean to disturb you, ma'am. My name is Lloyd, and I'm from the U.S. Embassy."

Zoe's eyes overflowed with distrust. "So embassy people don't have last names?"

"I'm sorry, ma'am. My last name is Elgin. Here's my card." The role of the polite, down-home American was one he'd played many times before. He didn't have to work very hard to add a Southern twang to his voice. It felt like sliding into a second skin.

She took the card and eyed it carefully before pocketing it. Her face remained defiant.

"I'm looking to speak to a Mr. Maxwell Travers."

"Concerning?"

Lloyd hunched his shoulders and wrung his hands together. "Well, ma'am, I wish I could tell you, but it's embassy business, and I'm only supposed to speak with Mr. Travers . . . unless you're Mrs. Travers."

Zoe pursed her lips and sneered. "No, I can assure you that I am not Mrs. Travers."

Lloyd was sure he knew her next response before he even asked. "So do you know where I can find him?" Using his left hand, he reached into his sport-coat pocket and removed a single black glove.

"No, I don't."

"Will he be home later today?" He slid his left hand inside. "Maybe I could wait?"

"No, Lloyd," Zoe said sharply, "I'm afraid that won't be possible. When I see Max, I'll tell him you came around."

Reaching into his right pocket with his left hand, he removed a matching glove and slid his right hand inside. "Well, I'd like to thank you for your time. And I'm very sorry for the bother."

Lloyd grasped Zoe's unwilling hand and pulled it away from her side. He shook it vigorously and gave her a little wink before disappearing around the corner and down the path running along the side of the house.

VINCENT stopped in the empty concrete courtyard at the path's end, taking a seat on a bench next to the temple grounds. He carefully removed the gloves and placed them in a Ziploc bag.

His watch read 4:36 p.m.

COLLECTOR *of* SECRETS

The sky was gray with clouds, and rain looked imminent. An umbrella would have been a good idea, but he knew he wouldn't have to wait long. The liquid sedative on the woman's skin would absorb quickly into her bloodstream. She was probably already staring at her tingling hand, wondering what was happening. Normally the drug took effect in a couple of minutes, although with the history of needle tracks clearly evident on her arm, it might take three or four. She probably had the tolerance of a bull elephant.

He felt certain that once he entered the house, he could find some drug paraphernalia to leave beside her sleeping body. That way, she'd think she had knocked herself out. Nevertheless, it didn't really matter. By the time she recovered, he would have found what he wanted and been long gone.

CHAPTER THIRTY-EIGHT

ACCORDING TO Toshi's instructions, the hospital intern was meant to be waiting at the Tokyo Catholic diocese's Tsukiji church. Max considered again how this latest plan was probably a bad idea, but Kenji's disquieting email had described Mr. Murayama's condition as grave.

He felt numb as he paid the driver, grabbed the daypack, and slipped from the taxicab. Standing before the two-story building with its six Parthenon-style pillars, he thought how it seemed so out of place. Greek architecture in Tokyo was odd enough, but the fact that this was a one-hundred-thirty-year-old Catholic church was even more bizarre. Max checked the address. It had to be correct. How many of these places could there possibly be?

Glancing up, he saw a head pop out from behind the second pillar on the left, followed by a waving arm, gesturing for him to approach. Max jogged the dozen paces to the church's entrance. As he climbed the steps, he could see the man digging into a duffel bag.

"Hi—" A white cotton lab coat sailed through the air and hit him in the chest. Startled, he managed to catch it before it dropped to the ground.

"Put it on." The twenty-something intern wasn't wasting any time. "You're late."

"The taxi driver didn't—"

"Hurry up, dude!" The agitated intern commanded as he puffed anxiously on a cigarette.

Dude? This guy looks Japanese, but he's definitely not native.

Max slipped the calf-length coat overtop his hoodie.

The intern eyed him dubiously. "I wanna make something clear. I'm doing this favor for Toshi, but if anything goes wrong in there, you're on your own. And don't speak to me once we're inside. Move with me, but not beside me. Understand?"

Max nodded. Evidently the journey would be uncomfortable as well as dangerous.

"There's a cop sitting outside the hospital room twenty-four/seven. I'll distract him while you get into the room. When we get close to the nurse's station, I'll signal by sneezing. That means I go straight and you go to the right, around the station. Make two lefts, then go into room 671. If it goes wrong, I never met you."

"What about the other patients?"

"The room's private. And another thing—I only get you in. Leaving is your problem."

Max moved to avoid the drifting cigarette smoke. "What if someone asks who I am?"

"This hospital has over two-hundred-fifty doctors. Make up some bullshit. You can do that, can't you?" The cigarette butt was crushed beneath his heel. "Now, let's go." He loped down the church steps and made two lefts after the gate.

Max raced to keep up. He could see the fifty-one stories of St. Luke's Tower looming over the ten floors of the hospital. Toshi's friend could be forgiven for being short-tempered—the guy was, after all, risking a highly sought-after internship at one of the finest facilities in the country.

Soon they descended an underground parking ramp. With the swipe of a card key, they were inside the hospital and moving fast. Pressing past orderlies and nurses, they made their way through a maze of hallways. Max tried to memorize the path, so he could follow the same way out, but he quickly lost track. Every stainless-steel corner looked the same as the last.

A petite nurse with a ponytail stood near a hallway's end. "Hi Dan. How are you?"

"Really good. Talk later." Dan pushed past her without looking back.

Her eyes trailed them as they hurried through a set of swinging doors. They appeared to be heading for an elevator straight ahead, but instead Dan entered an adjoining stairwell. He took the stairs in pairs at great speed, and his lead increased to a full flight.

Racing to catch up, Max hurried into the sixth-floor hallway and narrowly missed colliding with an elderly woman clutching a rolling IV stand. Dan was already halfway down the hall. Max heard the sneeze signal before the nurse's station came into sight. Dan was distracting the two RNs.

Max circled the station as instructed. Approaching the final left turn, his muscles tensed with expectation. A tall row of cabinets blinded him from seeing the activity in front of the room as he rounded the corner, but there was no time to stop.

The cop, gun holstered on his belt, was standing in the hallway with his back to the door, engaged in a conversation with Dan. Still, the two men seemed to be far too close. Surely the cop would hear the groan of the hinges.

Max hesitated as he approached room 671 on the right, but at the last second, he ducked inside and froze. Heart racing, he fought his heavy breathing, waiting for the officer to burst into the room.

The door pressed silently back into place. Seconds passed. Nothing happened.

It had worked.

Across the dim room, Mr. Murayama's face appeared peaceful with sleep. He looked puny and shriveled, surrounded by the medical equipment's blinking lights. Max edged toward the bed.

"I was wondering when you would come."

Max almost leaped from his skin at the sound of the familiar voice.

The paper-thin eyelids slid upward. Behind them, the pupils seemed as clear as ever—the spirit was still there. Only this time Mr. M wasn't smiling. "We need to talk."

CHAPTER
THIRTY-NINE

TOMOKO KEPT her jacket collar up and her face cast down as she stepped through the glass doors of the five-sided crystal building. It was Wednesday afternoon, and while her coworkers were busy dealing with the stress of the office, she was being chased by killers. It was a surreal nightmare, and her stomach felt twisted into a knot.

The Prada store's main floor held shoes and handbags on waist-high displays. She feigned interest in a pair of boots as her eyes roamed over the open space. A dozen other women were perusing the shelves to the sound of a disco beat. No one paid her any attention as she traced a line around the room's edge.

The building's futuristic interior was a mix of display cases, tube-shaped hallways, and angled staircases. As Tomoko climbed up each successive level, she could feel nervous tension building at the base of her neck. Finally reaching the fourth floor, she let out a frustrated sigh. Yoko was nowhere in sight. Kenji must have lied to her.

Tomoko needed to clear her brain and figure out what to do next. The surrounding space was near the peak of the glass-and-metal building, and she walked along the nearest transparent wall. Convex and concave diamond-shaped bubble windows made the surrounding city appear to flex and bow.

The wavy movement felt too much like the thoughts inside her head, and she stopped to rub her tired eyes. How would she ever explain to her mother that Mrs. Kanazawa had been murdered by *Yakuza*? The two women had spent their childhoods together, and for as long as Tomoko could remember, they had been best friends. Her mother would of course blame Max, the *Gaijin*, for the entanglement in this deadly affair.

Tomoko began descending the stairs before her muscles seized in place. Through a glass side wall, she could see to the third floor below. There was the familiar bobbed haircut. Yoko was easily recognizable, even from the back. She was running her fingers down the sleeve of a purple jacket, while Kenji stood attentively next to her, holding her purse.

Tomoko crept down the remaining stairs and ducked behind a dress rack. She waited a moment before allowing her eyes to drift over the display's top. She felt sure she hadn't been seen. A bowing attendant was leading Yoko toward the change rooms, while Kenji remained rooted to the floor.

Her plan would work only if properly timed. She edged toward the open floor, watching as the sales clerk unlocked the change-room door and held it open, motioning for Yoko to enter.

It was time to move.

Spinning around, Tomoko raced forward. The clerk had no time to react as the door was snatched from her grasp and slammed shut.

Inside, the two women collided in the closet-like space, and Yoko stumbled forward, catching herself on the padded bench. Her voice exploded. "What are you doing? Get out, you silly girl." Then her enraged eyes flashed with recognition. "What do you want?"

Tomoko turned the lock with a shaking hand. "I should be asking you the same question."

The salesgirl banged on the door from the outside. "Is everything okay?"

The air was thick with tension. Just feet apart, the two women eyed each other warily. Finally, Yoko's syrupy-sweet voice responded. "Yes, dear, everything is fine. A friend is helping me change. Come back in a few minutes."

The clerk's heels clicked as she departed.

Inside the cubicle, Tomoko spoke first. "Why—" The words stuck in her throat. She knew what she wanted to say, but the thoughts felt jumbled. "Why do you have people chasing after Max?"

"I have no idea what you're talking about."

"After your father's office was burglarized, the *Yakuza* followed me from work, then they chased Max. You must have told them about me."

"That's ridiculous!"

"Max warned me that you're a good liar."

Yoko sat back and straightened her hair. "Get your facts straight. Max is the one who broke into the office."

"Only to get back the passport you were holding."

"Regardless of his intention, he took more than that. Perhaps he's lying to you about the *Yakuza* in order to cover up the trouble he's in with the police."

"I might have believed you until yesterday." Fear and pain rushed forward. "When they murdered my mother's best friend."

"I can assure you that I had nothing to do with any murder." Yoko appeared momentarily flustered, but quickly regained her poise. "Let's be reasonable? I'm sure we can solve this misunderstanding. Why don't you have Max come to my house? He can keep his passport and bring back the things he took. I'm sure we can work this all out quietly. I can let the police know that everything has been returned and ask them to drop any charges."

Tomoko sniffed and wiped at her eyes with her sleeve. "What are you talking about? He never got his passport back." She tried to pull the conversation back on track, as she'd imagined it. "You call off the killers—the *Yakuza*—and we'll trade the daypack for Max's passport."

"I have no time for your foolishness." Yoko waved a dismissive hand. "I don't have his passport, and this . . . this . . . story has nothing to do with me. While my father is sick, I'm handling his affairs. If you don't want my help, then please leave. But stay away from my school and my students' families."

The conversation was going nowhere, and so Tomoko reached back to unlock the door. "Oh, and one more thing: that story about Mr. Murayama being your father—save it for someone else. We both know it's not true."

Yoko placed a hand to her gaping mouth.

The reaction spoke volumes. Stepping from the changing room, Tomoko sped down the stairs and outside. While charging across the plaza, she spotted Kenji moving hastily to intercept and she tried to veer away, but he was too quick. Reaching into his pocket, he pulled out a U.S. passport and shoved it into her hands. She was astonished, and meant for the reply to be louder, but only a startled murmur came from her mouth. "Thanks."

Kenji turned away without a word.

THROUGH the myopic third-story glass exterior, Yoko watched the scene unfold in the plaza below. "It seems I have a traitor in my midst."

CHAPTER
FORTY

MAX SLID into the chair next to the hospital bed and leaned forward, his voice earnest but hushed. "Mr. Murayama, I didn't intend to rob you. Honestly, I just went to get my passport, because Yoko wouldn't give it back." He eyed the hospital door warily, half expecting the police to burst through at any moment. "And there were men— real thieves—in your office . . . I didn't know what to do. A diary and some other things were in a daypack. I panicked, and took it with me when I ran."

Mr. Murayama winced as he coughed. "I know, my boy. I know."

The reply was unexpected, and Max displayed his bewilderment. "But—"

"It's not your nature to steal."

Max inhaled sharply. Finally, something seemed to be going right. "Thank you." He dropped his gaze to the floor. "That means a lot to me."

"I sent a message—asking the police not to place charges. It may take some time, but soon enough they will lose interest." He sighed. "Besides, stealing prince Takeda's diary implies ownership, but I don't own it."

The old man sipped water through a straw while Max unzipped the daypack. "They also took your cell phone."

"Why would they take that?"

"Maybe 'cause there's a text message on it," Max said with soft malice, "sent by Kazue Saito around the time he was murdered." He stopped to let the potent words sink in. "It reads 'eight-nine-three,' followed by 'O dot K dot.' Tomoko said that it meant—"

Mr. Murayama waved two fingers in the air. "Oto Kodama! No need to explain. At least now I know who came looking for the diary."

"So maybe you could tell me how to stop all this. Two people have died already."

"Two?" The tempo of the heart monitor bounced upward. "Who was the second?"

"Tomoko and I went to hide on the Izu yesterday. The *Yakuza* followed us and they killed her mother's friend, the owner of the *onsen* where we stayed. There was a car chase. We barely escaped. And now the police are looking for us both. My picture is all over town. Why do you think I snuck in here—and changed my hair?"

"I was wondering." The old man's mouth curled slightly at one corner but quickly grew somber again. "This is far worse than I expected."

"So you can see why I need help—anything, please."

"I was sure that the *kami* spirits brought you to me, in order to help return those watches. But now I know that your destiny is much greater than that." Mr. Murayama seemed to gain strength even as he spoke. "The diary has chosen you as its new guardian."

Max felt the prickly heat of distress sweep across his face. "That's nuts! First off, I don't believe in any magical spirits, and second, even if that's true, I don't want the responsibility."

"You have no choice. After decades of time, the chorus of so many who have suffered and died cannot be silenced. It's your destiny."

Max was unsure whether Mr. M. was suffering medicinal hallucinations. "Then I'll just drop the book with you and disappear."

"And leave your girlfriend to suffer the consequences? You won't. You care for her too much."

The chair squeaked as Max leaned forward. "So help me figure out what to do." He spoke each word separately. "Give . . . me . . . something."

"All right." Taking another sip of water, Mr. Murayama began. "After Kazue Saito's murder, I knew someone would come, but I didn't expect *Yakuza*."

"Who were you expecting? " Max shrugged. "And why'd you lie about knowing Kazue Saito?"

"Sometimes a person tells so many lies that it's difficult to remember the truth. Let me explain." Mr. Murayama grimaced as he shifted slightly. "A man named Tetsuo Endo was an old friend who possessed the prince's diary at the time of his death. We served together in the military, many years ago. Afterward, we both went into diplomacy. I worked in Washington. He worked here in Tokyo in the legal department. Kazue Saito was his assistant. When Tetsuo died in 1961, he instructed Kazue to bring me the diary, for safekeeping."

"Safe from what?"

"Endo-*san*, believed there must be a treasure map hidden among the pages. You see, during the war, he was Prince Takeda's private bodyguard, and for almost fifteen years, from the time he and the prince left the Philippines, he thought constantly about that map. Which is why, the year before he died, he went to get the diary. Cancer was killing him already, so there was little risk in him trying to recover it. He found the book's caretaker and took the diary from him by force."

"So, was there a map inside?"

"No, but he found something else. He found words of truth and wisdom."

"Words? That's it?" It was going to take more than words to get out of this mess.

Mr. Murayama squeezed his fingers into a fist. "Ideas contain power, Max."

"Okay, so after Lieutenant Endo died, Kazue brought the diary to you. But why?"

"To protect it for future generations. The days of the Second World War were—still are—too recent for some. There are people who would not want the public to know what really happened. It would create great political difficulties." Mr. Murayama shook his wrinkled fist in the air. "But ideals should not be allowed to die. That diary should be used to teach future generations, so they do not repeat the mistakes we made in the past."

"But Japan's not aggressive. You only have a self-defense force."

"A few years ago, I would have agreed with you. But look at your own country—there's something very wrong. Your government has forgotten about Vietnam too quickly and is repeating the same mistakes around the world. And just last year, my government passed laws forcing schools to teach patriotism again. And the Defense Agency has changed to a proper ministry for the first time since the war. Politicians are also at work altering our constitution to allow a full army again. We are already beginning to forget, Max. It's only a matter of time now. This diary is more valuable than ever."

"But the *Yakuza* wouldn't want it for its truths. They must believe it holds a treasure."

"Yes, that's a good point. Kazue must have lied to them when he offered the diary for sale. A valuable prize would increase the price he could demand."

"So if I now give the *Yakuza* the diary, and they don't find a map, then they'll accuse me of stealing it. And I can't imagine that ending well." Max cocked his head as he thought back to the words he had heard only moments earlier. "Wait a minute. If you didn't expect the *Yakuza* to come for the diary, then who did you expect would come?"

Mr. Murayama turned his face away. "I can't say. It's for your own good."

"Great—so what do I do now? How can I make this all go away?"

"You can't. I believe destiny has given you a calling." Mr. Murayama took another sip of water. "In our meetings, you've confessed to wanting more from your life."

"Honestly," Max replied with a shake of his head, "I was thinking more like getting a decent job and a nice house."

"You can be forgiven for having a young man's vices—optimism, recklessness, and a little greed. I wish you could see that money and wealth are an illusion. There is never enough, my boy . . . never enough." His wrinkled face grew focused with intensity. "If you want to be special, to do something truly important, then change history."

"But—"

Mr. Murayama raised his hand, signaling for silence, as a noisy conversation approached and then passed outside the door. "You need to find the caretaker and return the diary. Perhaps he can also help you with the *Yakuza*—explain to them that no map exists."

"By caretaker, you mean the guy who handed over the diary . . . almost fifty years ago? He's probably dead by now. And if not, then why can't I give it back to you—then you give it to him?"

"This is my journey's end." The old eyes grew watery. "I've known that I was dying for some time now."

"Don't say that."

"But truth will find a way to be spoken, my boy. It can't be hidden forever."

Max leaned back and rubbed his temples, fighting the icy panic washing over him. The conversation wasn't going the way he'd hoped, and his chest filled with a heavy breath of resignation as he asked the next fateful question. "So, who is this caretaker? Where'd he live?"

"He lives in the countryside near Nara."

For a moment, the room felt as if it were swaying. It was just a minor tremor and Max realized it was probably only in his head, but it forced him to sit up a little higher in his seat. "Did Kazue ever tell you the caretaker's name?"

The old man paused before speaking. "His name was Ben."

Benjie—the kid from the Philippines—was the caretaker?

"You mean the boy from the diary?" Max could barely believe what he was hearing. "And Tetsuo Endo took the diary away from Benjie? Which is how you eventually ended up with it?"

"Yes. Exactly."

"So, why didn't you ever return it?"

"I thought about it many times . . . but I couldn't bring myself to give it away. I like to find and keep things. Old habits . . ." Tears rolled down both sunken cheeks. "My plan was to protect it until I died—I left instructions in my will so that after my death, copies would be sent to the media and a small group of well-known intellectuals. The information would then be impossible to contain."

It's all becoming clear.

Outside in the hallway, the sound of a squeaky wheel came to a stop on the other side of the door. A female voice was speaking to the on-duty officer. From her high-pitched giggle, it sounded as if she was flirting.

"The nurse is coming. I have an appointment for tests. You need to hide." Mr. Murayama motioned with a flick of his hand. "Go into the toilet. The policeman will take a break when I'm away. Then you can leave."

"But I'm not done. We haven't finished talking."

"Hurry."

Max jumped to his feet and in one swift movement stuffed the diary into the daypack while charging into the bathroom. Pivoting on his heel, he turned back. "One more thing. Yoko—is she really your daughter?" The nurse's voice was growing louder. She was just outside the door.

"Ask President Kennedy."

"What?"

Mr. Murayama coughed. "Ask President Kennedy."

"But that doesn't make any sense."

"Hide, Max. Hide!"

CHAPTER
FORTY-ONE

D RESSED ONLY in loose cotton pants, Vincent Lemoine spun and kicked at the air. The thirty-fifth-floor hotel curtains were pulled wide open, all the better to take in the view of the dazzling city lights.

The Century Hotel's executive rooms were spacious and uncluttered, just right for a workout. He twisted again and unleashed a flurry of jabs. Ducking left, he rolled across the floor before flexing his entire body and springing back to his feet. A roundhouse kick cut the air. His torso glistened with sweat.

The self-designed routine appeared similar to the Brazilian art of Capoeira. But in fact it was much deadlier, blending Krav Maga, the Israeli military hand-to-hand combat system, with key elements of Muay Thai martial arts. Decades of training had taken him from a mere student to a master. He was both lethal and effective.

The day's visit to Max Traver's House had yielded little. The documents retrieved were spread out on the desk next to a recently opened bottle of cognac. There was a sparsely written journal, several pay stubs, and only a few photos that merited any examination. He had already noted and memorized the relevant details before sending an encrypted verbal report to Senator McCloy.

Vincent prized his almost perfect recall. Friends often commented on his uncanny ability to retain the smallest of details. Names, dates, faces, and addresses—it was a CIA skill that had saved his life on more than one occasion. Not to say that brute force wasn't necessary on occasion; but while force and firepower came in handy, information was the most powerful weapon of all. Without it, an agent became just another sharpshooter.

The kid's a nobody from a dead-end family. He won't even be missed; just another traveler who never made it home.

Long ago, he had made a conscious decision to never waste time thinking about all the people he'd killed. Whether it was Hong Kong, Seoul, Beijing, or a dozen other places, it didn't really matter. Secrets needed to be kept, security needed to be safeguarded, and those who were a threat needed to be eliminated.

There was a knock at the door. Vincent paused to admire his ripped abs in a mirror before walking to the entranceway. "Who is it?"

A male voice with a Southern drawl carried through the door. "A package for Mr. Bob Elgin."

"I'm his brother, Lloyd Elgin. Just leave it there." Several seconds ticked by before he peered out into the hallway. There was no point being too hasty. A camouflage duffel bag rested on the carpet. Glancing down the corridor, Vincent could see the courier's back as he strode away. The man was dressed in a cheap suit, but walked with a crisp authority—probably a U.S. Marine from the nearby Yokosuka military base, just making a little extra money. No questions asked.

He retrieved the bag and emptied its contents onto the bed. Everything he'd asked for was provided, right down to the two modified ASP handguns, their unique features and rounded edges made them the best covert guns available.

Vincent slung the hotel towel over his neck and felt the weight of the weapons in each hand. The moment was good, and he allowed himself to revel in it. A strong body, an exotic city, fantastic toys, and the thrill of the hunt.

He couldn't help but smile. It didn't get any better than this.

CHAPTER
FORTY-TWO

Thursday, April 26

TOSHI'S FOYER was silent as a grave, Max mused as he sat in the open hallway, clutching her note, gazing bereft at the duvet that had covered Tomoko's curving silhouette. But she was gone. In fact, the entire damn house was empty. He'd scoured the place twice after waking alone, refusing to believe, shouting noisily and banging on any door that didn't yield. He'd been abandoned at exactly the moment he believed he was finally set to do the right thing. It was quarter to six in the morning and the place was an empty tomb.

Talking things over as they drifted toward sleep, she had again raised the idea of going home, before finally conceding. *The Yakuza won't give up, and I can't go to the police—at least not yet. Finding this caretaker may be the last shot. It's my fault everything went wrong.* First, they would go to Nara and only then would they contact her parents. That was the agreed on plan. But she had lied.

Max hammered an incensed elbow backward into the wall. *How could she?*

The corner of the note resting in his hand was folded into an origami bird; something Tomoko only did when stressed or bored. The handwritten words claimed she would find him in Nara, and asked for him to wait, but was it true? Or had she simply changed her mind about their relationship?

And where the hell was Toshi?

Despite his battered ego, Max rose and descended the open staircase. In the stillness, each feather-light creak of the floor felt like an explosion of noise.

Searching for her family home would be pointless. He knew they lived in Urayasu, but nothing else. She had never taken him there. How could she have, since her parents were oblivious to his existence? He was just a foreigner after all, a *Gaijin*, an exotic fucking pet.

Adjusting the daypack, he approached the front door looming large before him. *But what if she changes her mind and comes back?* Reaching for the handle, Max bit his lip and clenched his fist, hammering an invisible tabletop. *Should I wait awhile?* It was the point of no return, and his resolve began to slip. He steeled himself against weakness as he turned to survey the two white urns resting beneath the vaulted foyer.

Mr. M's passion and remorse had weighed heavily on his mind: "The chorus of so many who have died cannot be silenced." Throughout the night, the lingering words had echoed in his dreams: "The diary has chosen you as its new guardian." Even if it were not the case, even if the old man was losing it, the power of action, any action, was better than cowering and hoping the threats would simply go away. Too many of his childhood moments had been spent sitting next to his careworn mother, praying for help that never came. A miracle hadn't happened then, and it wasn't going to happen anytime soon. Max recalled, as if it were yesterday, the small-town American preachers speaking in a rising crescendo, their pseudo-prophetic words spiraling upward to meet climactically in the air with the stinging slap of two palms: "The Lord helps those who help *themselves!*" Hallelujahs, waving arms, and thunderous applause always followed.

Nobody forced her to leave. She made her own choice.

Max slipped into the crisp morning air. Outside the sanctuary, he pulled on a baseball cap and trotted down the stairs. The trains would start soon, and there was a long way to go. Time was short, and he started to run, slowly at first, but more quickly with each passing building. Block after block, he raced an invisible enemy until his burning lungs screamed as loud as his mind, "*You have been chosen!*"

CHAPTER
FORTY-THREE

I T WAS almost eight in the morning, and the prefab suburban neighborhood was quiet. The house in the middle of the block showed no signs of life. For over an hour, Tomoko had stared at the rolled shutters of the two-story white aluminum building. From her vantage point down the street, she could easily spot any activity. A tiny patch of grass served as the front lawn, with an adjacent concrete pad for a single car. The community was well planned, orderly, and perfectly uniform; a compact version of the American dream.

Nothing seemed out of the ordinary. In fact, it wasn't unusual for her mother to spend days indoors. The regular routine had been twice-weekly grocery shopping, a flower-arranging class, and Wednesday's "Lady's Lunch." Even as a child, she had found the suburban homemaker's life unimaginably dull. She vowed that she would never be dependent, waiting each day for her man to come home.

Crouched next to a utility shed, staring through the hedge, she ached with the thought of rushing into her mother's arms. But she held back. The last few days had trained her to be wary. Nothing could be taken for granted. People were being murdered, and she would not put her family in harm's way.

Tomoko watched a FedEx Kinko's van drive slowly past. The faceless driver stopped and started several times but didn't exit the vehicle. He was probably lost in the maze of copycat streets. Reaching the T-intersection at the road's end, the van turned and disappeared from sight.

She refocused her attention on the yellow slip of paper pressed tightly between her fingertips. It held the prince's Nara address, but at the moment the edge was bending to and fro, preparing to form the wing of a crane. The folding effort usually proved a distraction, but now it was only serving to remind her of the transgressing note she had left behind and the wake of pain it had no doubt caused.

Max had returned late to Toshi's the previous evening, saying he'd gone for a long walk after his visit to the hospital. He'd seemed distracted, simply picking at the take-out dinner, claiming he didn't have an appetite and saying little else.

They had both been weary and afraid, unsure of what to do. Lying in bed, drifting off to sleep, he had coiled his arm over her, finally speaking. "We need to find the caretaker Mr. M told me about."

"But first I need to make sure my parents are okay," she'd implored, hoping he would relent. "They don't use computers, and I can't call them in case their phone is bugged."

"You don't understand, Tomoko. Mr. M wouldn't explain everything, but that diary is even more dangerous than either of us thought." He sighed. "We can't do that. At least not yet."

She burrowed her face into the pillow. She wanted desperately to scream, realizing that his own phantom-like relationship with his family would never allow him to empathize with her plight.

He was unbending. "First we go to Nara and then we'll contact your folks. Okay?"

"Yeah, sure." She thought of Miki as she forced out a culpable breath against the tightly spun cotton. "That makes sense."

Sleepy lips kissed her ear, "I'm glad you agree."

WHY did he force me to choose? Tomoko's fingers involuntarily ceased folding as sadness flooded down, but there were no more tears, at least for the time being. She couldn't stand to question her actions yet again—the choice would still be the same.

Enough time had been spent watching the house. It seemed safe enough to make a move. Standing, she shook her legs and rubbed her lower back.

Grabbing her purse, she stepped out from behind the hedge and crossed the sunlit laneway.

Her father's Lexus was in its usual spot. He would have taken the train to work early in the morning. She removed the house key from her pocket and stepped into the alcove covering the car's hood. The lock clicked open easily. Warm air escaped through the open door and pressed against her face, carrying the wonderfully familiar smells of home. Stepping inside, she scanned the central hallway. The house was quiet, but nothing seemed out of place. Habit forced her to remove her shoes.

Movement at the hallway's end made her look up as her mother's familiar figure appeared in the living room. She was dressed in a white blouse under a red sweater vest, her petite hands folded in her apron's front pocket. Tomoko rushed forward, choked with elation. Her socked feet were half sliding on the hardwood floor.

Then a shadow flickered on the living room's wall and the glint of a silver blade appeared ahead of the *Yakuza*'s massive form. Her mother looked utterly helpless cowering next to him.

Tomoko screamed and shook as the scowling man motioned with his head for her to continue down the hall. The thug thrust one paw-like hand over her mother's face, covering her mouth, and the butcher's knife in his other hand rested precariously at her throat. Her eyes blazed with horror.

"Tomoko held arms up in surrender. "Don't hurt her! Please don't hurt her! I'll do whatever you want." She crept forward, steadying herself against the wall. She wasn't sure her legs would obey the commands. Stepping into the room, she saw more clearly the scar running down the big man's face. "Momma, are you all right?"

"Silence!" The *Yakuza*'s deep voice boomed.

Glancing left, she dropped her purse as she gasped. Her father was in the dining room, dressed in pajamas, bound upright in a high-backed chair. His head was drooping unconscious over his chest.

Tattooed arms grasped her from behind and she stiffened, craning her neck to the side, struggling. The second man's face was barely visible in her peripheral vision, but she recognized him. He'd run past her in the Shibuya plaza. Tomoko braced for pain as he pressed her forward and down.

Lying against the sofa cushions, she felt her hands being bound, but he seemed oddly gentle, weaving a cloth around her wrists before binding them with rope. The incongruity made no sense as she fought back tears, trying frantically to draw a response from her mother. "Are you okay?"

"Hiro, shut her up." The muscular man yelled, while pushing her mother into a nearby chair. The older woman struggled and cried when he pulled a handkerchief from his pocket, wrenching the cloth tightly across her mouth. A bloody trickle formed at one corner of her lips.

"Stop it," Tomoko shouted, "you're hurting her!"

"Not so hard. Jun!" The smaller man said with an air of authority. "Loosen the gag."

Jun sneered and then relented, adding a paltry dose of slack to the material.

Tomoko felt herself rolled onto her back as the shorter *Yakuza* spoke. "Where is your boyfriend? What has he done with the leather satchel?"

"I don't know what you're talking about."

Jun retrieved the kitchen knife and lurched aggressively across the room, kicking the coffee table from his path. Waving the blade over her face, he made slashing motions in the air. "Don't lie! Tell us where he is."

Tomoko was desperate. "We broke up last night." She knew she needed to give them something more in order to sound plausible. "He's a stupid *Gaijin*. I hate him. It's finished."

"Jun, get her purse. It's over there on the floor."

The psychotic man stomped away while Hiro whispered at her. "You need to cooperate. Please. I don't want to hurt—"

The handbag struck the side of Hiro's head and fell to the floor as Jun chuckled fiercely. "You check it if you want to. I'll check her pants." Pushing Hiro aside, he knelt on the sofa and straddled her body. His massive frame hovered close as he sniffed at her hair, while his tongue flicked reptilian-like back and forth across his lower lip. She could see the many fine cuts covering his face, and she recalled the sharp bushes dragging him from the SUV's side.

"Do you like what you did to me?" He jammed his fingers into Tomoko's jean pockets. She tried to kick him, but he caught her knees with a single hand. The attempt made him almost giddy and he laughed harder, clearly enjoying the struggle.

"Get off her!" Hiro commanded, to no avail.

Jun's thick fingers drew the folded scrap of yellow paper from her pocket. They were going to get what they wanted, and she was powerless to stop them.

"I wonder who lives at this Nara address?" He pressed himself back to a kneeling position.

Tomoko couldn't watch. She turned her face to the side, instead focusing on her mother, trying to catch her attention, to project reassurance that everything would be okay.

Jun reached down and twisted Tomoko's jaw, forcing her gaze upward. "And now maybe we should have some fun with you, for all the trouble you've caused."

Hiro's right hand, wrapped in a bloody bandage, thumped deliberately against his left palm. "You touch her and I'll kill you."

Jun smirked insolence. "I won't touch your new girlfriend, but we're bringing her along for the ride. She may prove useful as bait." He snorted bull-like. "And as for killing me . . . go ahead and try it sometime. I dare you." He rose and stomped from the room.

STANDING in the hallway, Jun lit a cigarette and dialed the private number. The plan had been carried out and the enemy located. He inhaled deeply. Guts, the cartoon warrior, would be proud. The call went directly to voicemail. "Father, it's done. I need a fast car. I know where the American has gone."

CHAPTER
FORTY-FOUR

THE RHYTHMIC hum of the Shinkansen Bullet Train ebbed to an offbeat rumble as the high-speed locomotive broke its westerly run near Osaka.

I can't believe she left me.

He'd slept at first, drifting in and out of consciousness; perhaps it was his body's way of protecting itself from the rejection that stabbed knifelike when he was fully awake. The first-class cabin was packed, forcing Max to shift his feet to allow the young boy across from him to retake the seat beside his sister. They were playing a game using a stopwatch and Latin letters pulled from a cloth bag. It seemed the goal was to spell as many words as possible within sixty seconds. Their mother periodically shushed them when their squeals and giggles grew too loud.

Max adjusted his sunglasses and watched the streaming landscape, thinking back to his arrival at the train station. The fact that the train's coach seats had been sold out was unusual for a weekday morning. First-class tickets were more than double the price of the low-cost ones, but the next cheap fares wouldn't leave until that afternoon. There was no time to wait. He'd cursed under his breath while withdrawing the precious money from an ATM.

The reason for the crowded state of affairs became clear while he stood waiting on the train platform. Overhead, row after row of Golden Week banners hung from Tokyo Station's iron girders. Glittering letters announced the year's longest holiday period. In a work-obsessed country, it was monumental to have a stretch of four vacation days.

The yearly celebration kicked off on April twenty-ninth, Greenery Day. At least that had been the case historically. But after numerous legislative attempts, the government had finally pushed through a recent amendment. Jeff, a fellow teacher and friend, had pointed out a back-page article in the English newspaper. April twenty-ninth was former Emperor Shōwa's birthday, but the tongue-in-cheek commentary noted that beginning in 2007, the first holiday of the week would now officially be called Shōwa Day. It struck the cynical columnist as ominous that Japan would want to honor a period covering two world wars, especially conflicts they helped start. The people are forgetting the past.

He stared out the train's window. The rice fields racing by gradually gave way to houses, factories, apartments, and finally unrelenting urban sprawl. His fragmented brain barely registered the gradual decline in speed. A crushed piece of paper—printed at the train station's Internet café—was clutched in his hand, and he read it over again:

From: zoepitman69@hotmail.com
To: maxdawg@gmail.com
What the HELL is going on?
Date: Wed, 25 Apr 11:54:36

Where are you? Police raided the house yesterday. It was dreadful. Itzhak was badly hurt, but he won't go to a doctor. What am I supposed to do? I'm not a bloody nurse! They took us all in for questioning. Everything they asked was about you. What happened at your office? After six fucking hours they let us out, but the two Kiwis are gone— expired visas. Some guy from the U.S. Embassy showed up today, wanting to speak with you. A real weirdo with bright green eyes. He gave me a card—Lloyd Elgin (090-8849-1212)—but I think his story's bollocks. I got a really bad vibe from him. We need to talk, Max. Call me!

Z

It just didn't make sense that the U.S. Embassy would send someone to the Tokyo Poor House.

I never made it to the embassy when I tried. How could they possibly know I need help?

Max checked his pocket watch—9:25 a.m.—Tomoko would be home by now.

God knows what she's found.

The harder he tried to squeeze the hurt from his mind, the more it refused to budge. Not only had she abandoned him, but how could she not see that by going to her parents' she was taking the danger with her?

Finding this caretaker may be the only way out. I just hope he can help me, or else . . .

Across the aisle, the boisterous action from the kids' word game caught his attention. They noticed Max's gaze and grew louder as a result. To distract himself, he played with anagrams on the paper in his hand. The letters in Zoe's name rearranged to make "zap time on" or "at omen zip." Lloyd Elgin became "no idyll leg" or "old yelling." Max rearranged the letters once more and gasped when he saw the result. Self-consciously he glanced around, confirming that no one else had noticed his astonished reaction.

Sweat formed on his skin as he stared at the final combination of letters. It had to be a mistake. Flipping the page over, he quickly sorted the letters again, but with lines to account for each one. It was crazy and wrong, yet staring at the result he knew with growing certainty that it was no coincidence.

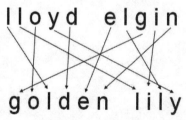

A sinister energy wrapped its arms around the compartment and squeezed tight. As bad as the situation already was, it had just grown far worse. Someone else was hunting for him, someone who obviously knew where to look.

But who is Lloyd Elgin? And where could the guy possibly have come from?

It was impossible to know, but one thing was certain, given the evil history of Golden Lily—the decades of plundering and raping Southeast Asia, the elaborate plans for hiding the emperor's stolen treasure—it seemed doubtful this new hunter would be the least bit friendly.

THE train arrived in Osaka and slid smoothly up to the platform as the surrounding passengers rose and gathered their belongings. Both kids smiled and waved goodbye as the compartment emptied.

Max stuffed the anagram in his pocket while remaining seated with his head down. It would be better to depart with the final swell of passengers to avoid police eyes. Through the window, he watched the pre-holiday passengers surge onto the platform stairs.

He had been alone in the car for only a few seconds when he heard two voices; men were approaching from the car's rear. It was a clear signal to move. The voices behind grew louder as he raced toward the car's front end. He chanced a quick look back. At most, he hoped the two policemen entering the compartment had caught only a brief glimpse of a tall, brown-haired man disappearing from sight.

CHAPTER
FORTY-FIVE

"YES, HELLO?" Yoko shouted across the open floor. The resonance of her authoritative voice bounced off the white walls and echoed in the cavernous gallery space. "Can I help you?" The man standing near the front door didn't respond. She could see only his charcoal suit coat from the back. He was Caucasian and seemed to be admiring the oversized canvas paintings. Probably a foreigner who couldn't read the writing on the sign that said the art exhibit was under construction. Kenji must have forgotten to lock the door. She'd deal with her foolish assistant soon enough.

Yoko turned to the two workers struggling to hold a mural at waist height. "Take a break, but be back in five minutes. You've been much too slow this morning." She waved the scowling men away with a dismissive hand.

Her shoes clattered on the hardwood floor as she descended the open staircase to the main floor. The mysterious man turned to watch her. The fact that he was handsome did little to alleviate her upset at the unwelcome intrusion.

"The gallery is closed. You'll need to come back on Saturday."

"How unfortunate. I'm only in town for a short time, and I'm a great fan of Jake Poyser's paintings." His voice held a refined edge.

"Really?" A well-cut suit and liquid green eyes, she thought. "Where have you seen his work?"

"New York. In 2005—his Ice World exhibit. They're very good, but I can see his style has changed since then."

Yoko adjusted her blouse and her voice took on a mellifluous tone. "I'm very sorry if I seemed rude before. It's just that we are setting up, and sometimes . . ."

The man nodded. "Please, there's no need to explain. I should go."

"No, no. Since you know the artist, let me show you the best ones." She motioned with a sweep of her arm toward the far wall, where several large paintings rested atop plastic tarps. "They're not hung but they're still wonderful."

VINCENT followed behind Yoko as she moved across the open floor. He noted her waist-hugging skirt and how well preserved she was for a woman in her late sixties. It was understandable why she'd been an effective tool more than forty years earlier. No man would have been able to resist her charms.

"The exhibit is called *Turbidity of the Soul*," she said.

They were standing before a ten-foot canvas. The colors changed from bright red near the bottom to dark brown at the top. Abstract patterns swirled across the painting's face.

"Magnificent." Vincent leaned in close. "Has he mixed wax in with the oil?"

"You do have a good eye, Mr. . . . ?"

"Elgin. Lloyd Elgin." He threw on a dazzling smile just as her cell phoned chirped. "Please take the call."

"It's just the hospital again. I'll call them back."

Vincent looked up toward the top of the canvas. Crossing his arms over his chest, he enjoyed the feeling of the dual ASP muzzles pressing against his ribcage. "Yes, it's a shame about your father."

A look of confusion swept over Yoko's face. "Excuse me?"

"Your father and his unfortunate illness."

He watched as her shoulders visibly tightened. "How do you know about that?"

"Your assistant mentioned it when he gave me directions to the gallery. He said something about an angioplasty procedure and that your father would be sedated for the day."

"Why would he tell you that?"

"I'm not sure, but he was very chatty. He also mentioned a break-in that happened a few days ago. I hope nothing important was stolen." Vincent was sure he saw a hint of anger cross her face, only to be replaced instantly with a calm, professional mask.

"Kenji should never have bored you with so many personal details."

"Actually it's quite all right. I'm in Tokyo doing research on crime statistics—meeting with the local police. It's my field of expertise. Was anything valuable taken?"

She lifted her chin slightly. "It's a private matter, and I would rather not talk about it."

A loud bang reverberated from the second-floor loft. Yoko turned and shouted at the workers. Vincent noted that she probably would have been less vulgar if she'd known he was fluent in Japanese. The upstairs chamber grew quiet.

Turning back, she motioned toward the front door. "Thank you for coming."

Vincent stared upward at the painting. The easy route he'd hoped for wasn't going to work. It was time to take control. "Did you enjoy your time living in New York and Texas? It must have been exciting in the sixties. There was a lot of promise back then."

"What? Who are you?"

He tilted his head to one side as he examined the painting from a different angle. "Do you think the red in this painting is the same color as the blood was on his shirt? You know, the blood caused by your lover. Or do you just try not to think about it?"

Yoko stepped backward toward the bench in the room's center, her words catching in her throat. "You . . . you have to leave . . . I'm going to call the police."

He turned to face her. "Your past sins can't stay hidden forever."

"I don't know who you are, but he wasn't my lover. I was too young to understand. They took advantage of me." She sat down on the bench, visibly shaken.

Vincent moved in, sensing the kill. "We all have skeletons. Things we can't erase. But we are absolutely responsible for them, regardless of age."

"What do you want?"

"I simply want to know what was stolen from your office and why."

"What does that have to do—"

"Just answer the question." Vincent's tone was harsh, and he let his anger seep through—it usually helped in these situations.

"Jewelry . . . just jewelry and a cell phone. The building manager interrupted the robbery."

"Nothing else?"

"No, nothing."

He stared at her a while, allowing the quiet room to gnaw at any composure she might still have. "I hope you're being honest." Vincent walked past her toward the entrance. "Because if I find out any differently, I'll be back. And this exhibit won't be the only thing with more red tones in it."

TERROR kept Yoko's gaze locked on the hardwood floor as her horrible dream resurfaced. The Cadillac and the dark gravel road flashed through her mind. She could almost feel the weight of the envelope clutched in her frightened young hands.

She felt as if she might stay attached to the bench forever. Staring into space, she fought against a painful haze of memories—the rifle shot, the world's collective gasp.

Time passed.

The distant thud of work boots finally made her look up. The gallery was empty. For now, the nightmare was gone.

CHAPTER
FORTY-SIX

T HE SINGLE-LANE country road continued its steep wind up the mountainside. Forests of cedar and cypress grew interspersed with dense bamboo stands.

It had been at least three hours since the streets on the outskirts of Nara had faded into the distance. Homes became increasingly sparse, and when the odd one did appear, it seemed quiet and empty. Now and then Max saw access roads cut into the forest. It was impossible to know if they led to private or public property.

He was fed up with trying to find the address copied from Tomoko's hastily written note. His feet ached, and he was tired of walking. A taxi ride would be the ideal thing, but no vehicles had gone by in the last hour. He just wanted something to eat.

It had only been a few days ago when he'd introduced Tomoko to Mr. Murayama, yet it seemed like a hundred years. So much had happened since then. Now he was wandering in the mountains, trying to save their lives by finding the former caretaker of a long-forgotten diary. Despair crept into Max's mind, and he found himself battling against the growing feeling that there would more killings in the future. *My relationship is ruined, and I'm getting blisters looking for some guy who gave up a diary almost fifty years ago . . . and who's probably been dead for decades.*

A break in the trees on the plateau offered the first clear glimpse of the valley below, stretching south to the next mountaintop. He sat down in the dirt near the roadside. A thin layer of hazy clouds blanketed the blue sky, but the sunshine sneaking through felt good.

It's supposed to be around here somewhere, but I'm never gonna find this place on my own no matter how many people I ask for directions. They're too polite to say they don't know . . . or maybe it just doesn't exist anymore.

A twig snapped noisily in the trees to his left. Max turned to see an elderly woman exit the forest about forty yards away. She was wearing tennis shoes and a loose-fitting gray kimono, topped with an olive green fishing hat. Trailing close behind her was a young girl of about ten, wearing jeans and a short-sleeved shirt. They walked briskly across the single-lane road without looking back. It seemed odd that the two of them would be out so far in the mountains with no extra clothing and no vehicle.

"*Sumimasen . . .* excuse me!" Max yelled while scrambling to his feet. He walked rapidly up the road in the same direction as the woman, who continued to march away. Behind her, the young girl glanced back. The woman motioned for her to keep up, and they both continued to move quickly. In fact, they seemed to be running away.

He followed them up the road for a quarter mile before the woman vanished into a thicket of green trees. Behind her, the girl slowed before glancing backward once more. She appeared to be laughing as if it was a game they were playing. Then she too scurried into the forest.

Approaching the spot where they'd disappeared, Max pressed aside a covering of vegetation in order to peer through. Behind the leafy façade, heading into the forest, was a well-used lane, but the woman and child were nowhere to be seen.

Trespassing? All right, one more attempt, then I'm finished. He pushed the loose branches aside and squeezed through.

As he started down the winding lane, a familiar feeling of warmth crept over him. His fingers wrapped around the watch in his pocket and he recalled the smell of liniment. This place was like the childhood trails he'd scouted at his grandpa's ranch, before the heart attack had gone and changed everything.

The forest grew tight on both sides, and the hump of brown grass in the road's center led the way between the tire ruts as he walked on for what felt like miles. His sore ankle twinged, and he was seriously thinking about turning back when the sound of barking dogs filled the air. He paused to listen more carefully. It wasn't the bay of hounds on the hunt but rather dogs crying for the attention of an arriving master.

Somebody did indeed live close by.

One more turn in the forest road revealed a straight laneway about thirty yards long. The end was blocked by the dual panels of a large front gate. As Max approached, he could see that each wooden door was about nine feet high and almost half as wide. When opened, they would easily allow a vehicle through. Each gate possessed an upper and a lower section, infilled with bright yellow bamboo shafts. The sound of the whining dogs was coming from the opposite side.

He was getting set to knock on the gate when the fence line caught his eye. Straight green lines ran into the forest in either direction. Moving closer, Max traced his fingers gently along the leaves, then pushed his hand beneath to the surface below. His knuckles bumped against solid bamboo. It was a living fence. He'd never seen anything like it.

A woman's voice shouted from the gate. *"Hanarero!"* She was demanding that he go away.

Max leaped back toward the spot where he'd been standing only moments before. A chest-high hole had appeared in the right gate, about the size of a breadbox. The old woman held it open a crack. She repeated her angry order, *"Hanarero!"* before pushing the window shut.

Please come back. He drew a deep breath and stared at his dusty shoes in defeat.

Max turned and retraced his steps down the lane while images of the past week raced through his head: hiding in Mr. Murayama's office; the *Yakuza* chasing him through the streets; Toshi taking him in; Tomoko screaming in the plaza; Mrs. Kanazawa's lifeless body; the Izu car chase; the Love Hotel; waking to an empty house.

No, no, no!

Whirling around, he charged back toward the gate. His palms slapped hard against the wood. "Please open up! Please, I need help. He stood on the spot tensed with frustration while talking to himself. "How do I ask for help?" He tried desperately to think back to his language classes as the dogs' barking grew louder. Paws scratched on the other side of the gate—they wanted at him. In a flash, he remembered. "Uh . . . *Tasukete . . . Tasukete . . . Tasukete!*"

Finally, he heard the scrape of the turning latch. A shouted word dropped the canine chorus to a whimper. The modest window swung wide open. However, this time it was the young girl gazing out. Her round face held rosy cheeks, and she was giggling.

"Hello. My name is Chiho. Your Japanese not so good."

He was elated. "My name is Max. You speak English?"

"A little." The old woman was out of view, whispering, and the girl paused to listen. "My grandmother say, 'Go away!'"

"I will. Tell your grandmother I will go away, but I'm looking for someone."

He crouched down and looked through the opening. Behind her, a collection of thatch-roofed buildings interplayed with sculpted pine trees and an arching bridge in the distance. The view was infused with serenity, like an idyllic landscape painting.

"She say you go away now. She will telephone police."

Max shook an outstretched palm. "No, no police. Tell her that I'm looking for this place." He handed the girl the yellow paper with the address on it. "I'm looking for a man named Ben Takeda." He enunciated the syllables carefully. "I need to talk. It's a matter of life and death."

The girl spoke to the hidden woman while Max stared farther into the bucolic scene. In the distance, he noticed the wind catch a red-and-white flag hanging on a slender pole. The flapping image displayed a stylized picture of the sun with three letters below it.

A man pushing a wheelbarrow appeared in the distance. He was wearing overalls and his face was hidden by a farmer's hat. He seemed unaware of the drama unfolding at the gate as he stopped to dig in the soil.

The girl spoke again. "That man go many years ago."

"Does she know where he went?"

"No, my grandmother said he not here." The girl shrugged and smiled. "Now you go."

Wrinkled hands pulled the smiling girl away from the gate. The wizened face reappeared. "*Hanarero!*" the woman shouted before the picture frame slammed shut.

CHAPTER
FORTY-SEVEN

JUN'S FINGERS squeezed the steering wheel of the Mercedes SLK 280. He imagined the euphoric feeling that would rush through his body when he crushed the American's neck. The shaking death spasms would bring a special thrill, and in his mind's eye, he played the stylized killing repeatedly. He pictured a primal scream pouring from his own lungs as he wrenched the book from the *Gaijin's* dead hands and held it high over his head, rays of piercing sunlight flaring behind him. He knelt before Father, who beamed with pleasure at seeing his prize finally recovered. Exotic women and buckets of money would be gifted to him by the ecstatic leader. Jun grinned while the fantasy played in his head.

The silver two-seat roadster was streaking west on the Tomei Expressway, chasing the setting sun. Its top speed was pegged at one-hundred-sixty miles per hour, and he was itching for a test run. Perhaps at some point during the ten-hour drive to Osaka, maybe closer to midnight, he would get the chance to really pick up the pace. Until then, an endless line of delivery trucks snaked ahead in his path.

On the empty passenger's seat beside him lay the coiled body of his *Surujin* chain. Over time, while mastering its execution, he had come to consider the weapon his only true friend. It had been given to him back when he was sixteen. Or more accurately, he'd taken it. On the wire-fenced exercise ground of the Chiba Boys' Academy, he'd watched as another boy proudly displayed the unusual weapon, a present from his uncle. Cocky and boastful, the youth allowed only his closest friends to touch it. That night, after curfew, Jun had tried to get a better look. Alerted by the noise, the older boy fought to take back his gift. It was a short but violent exchange and the reward was expulsion. From then on, life became a game of street survival, with only his wits and the prize that he'd carried with him ever since.

The blaring guitar solo from Bump of Chicken's latest single died down. The noise was replaced by the sound of a ringing bell. Jun eyed the dashboard suspiciously. An illuminated space in the console center began blinking, so he jabbed a finger at it. The words Phone Connected appeared on the screen.

"Hello, Jun," Oto Kodama's voice resonated in surround sound. The bass made it seem as if a god were speaking to him from the walls.

Out of habit, he bowed his head repeatedly. "Hello, Father. Thank you for having this car waiting for me."

"Your message said you know where the American is."

"I believe he's gone to Nara, but I'm not sure why." He hesitated. "I wanted to push the girl for information, but Hiro was too soft."

"Never mind, it's not a concern. I've left you something in the glove box. Go ahead and look."

Jun's massive hand flipped open the latch. The compartment door swung open, revealing the illuminated body of a handgun inside.

"It's a—"

Oto interrupted. "I hope you understand what I'm telling you to do?"

Jun trembled with excitement.

"The American has been enough trouble. Don't bother catching him. Just finish the job."

"Yes, Father."

"And afterward, make sure to bring my gift back. Hiro will take the blame for your action as well as for the other problems he's caused lately. Where are you now?"

"Near Nagoya. I should get to Osaka late tonight, and I'll begin looking in the morning, but it may take some time to find this address—it's in the countryside."

"I want results, not excuses. Meet the other men tomorrow and find him.

Call me again after it's finished." The tone of the deep voice grew more serious. "This has gotten out of control. I want *all* the loose ends wrapped up within the next twenty-four hours. Don't let me down."

The dashboard screen went blank, and the screaming guitars rose back to their former crescendo.

Hiro will be gone, and I will assume a proper position of authority in the gang.

The last sliver of sunlight dropped from sight while the sports car sped into the night.

H IRO APPROACHED the steel prison door on the P5 level of the Yebisu Garden Terrace. A rakishly thin figure stepped from the shadows. He was just a kid really, with flat-ironed rusty hair and a wispy goatee; eighteen or nineteen, maybe, and trying to look tough.

Hiro held out his arms. "It's just two blankets."

The sentry shrugged with indifference before opening the screeching door, motioning for him to enter. The dank concrete room with its lone light bulb hadn't changed in the last thirty-six hours. It still smelled of his blood.

Tomoko lay curled up in the inky darkness near the room's rear wall. The arch of her back was facing him, and he laid a folded blanket on her legs, which she batted away in disgust.

Turning back, he placed a second blanket on the wooden table, along with two apples. Using his good hand, he withdrew gauze, tape and a folding knife from his pocket.

A sniffling sound seeped from the back of the room. Tomoko's voice cracked as she spoke. "Why is a diary so valuable that it was worth Mrs. Kanazawa's life?"

He wasn't good with women, but he attempted to respond as gently as he knew how. "I don't know." It came out sounding gruff.

Her voice dripped with disdain. "You just do what you're told. You're a mindless zombie." Grabbing the blanket, she shook out its folds and covered herself.

The door groaned, and the young sentry motioned for Hiro's attention. "I need to take a break. I'll lock the door if you can wait outside."

Hiro spoke in a hushed voice. "Go ahead. I'll stay here."

"You want me to lock you inside?"

"Yes. I'll spend the night."

"Everyone says your crazy." The sentry shook his head as he exited. "Now I see why."

Sharp pain shot up Hiro's forearm as he re-bandaged the stump of his pinkie before moving back into the darkness to lie on the second mattress.

A moment of silence passed before Tomoko spoke. "Thank you for letting my parents go free. I promise they won't talk to the police . . . and my mother will call my office to tell them I'm sick, like I asked her." Seconds ticked by. "I know it was you who let them go. That other jerk would never have done it."

Hiro wanted to say something profound, something she would remember, but all he could stammer was, "You're welcome."

CHAPTER
FORTY-EIGHT

Friday, April 27

THE THREE letters *KKK* played havoc with Max's sleep, but his subconscious just wouldn't let go. Throughout the night, the bed sheets twisted and pulled. There was no clear answer for why such a tranquil bamboo-fenced compound would be flying the Ku Klux Klan's red flag. The paradigm was all wrong. The Klan didn't exist in this part of the world. They were relegated to history, except for a scattering of members in the southern U.S. states.

Having finally had enough of his struggling thoughts, he rose at first light and headed downstairs to the Nara hostel's dining room. Upon entering, he noted that the four round tables in the main-floor breakfast area were already uncomfortably crowded. Max grabbed a bowl of cereal before taking the only available chair with a loud group of British twenty-something's. Observing the three couples seated at the table, he silently noted he was the only loner before forcibly sweeping aside the distressing pang. *No one forced her to leave. She made her choice.*

One of the girls across the table, a petite brunette, was holding a laptop. Her chubby lowbrow boyfriend made a point of keeping his arm around her as if he was staking his property. She'd found an unsecured wireless network in the area and was regurgitating U.K. celebratory gossip.

Max tried focusing on his breakfast, but the chatty redhead next to him insisted on holding travelers' conversation. He quickly learned that her name was Maxine and that she was from Bristol, as was everyone at the table. Most of them couldn't find work, so they thought a trip seemed like a good way to piss away the time. She commented on how funny it was that his name was Max, and hers was Maxine. It was such a small world. They'd been in Japan only a few days, but had found it terribly expensive and were trying to find a cheap way to get to Thailand.

Max concentrated on his cereal. It crossed his mind that staying in bed a little while longer would have been a good idea.

Maxine continued on about how they were also planning to head to the Philippines to stay with her cousin Sarah, who was working in Manila for a British bank. It was odd that she wanted to go to Manila for a year, but then Sarah always was a little different.

Finally, Maxine took a much-needed breath, allowing Max a brief moment of silence. The conversation made him wonder whatever happened to his friend Janice from Manila. Her whole family had moved back there after she graduated high school.

Suddenly Max stopped chewing as an old yet familiar image formed in his head. He leaned across the noisy table and spoke to the cute brunette. "Could I use your laptop for a minute?"

The girl smiled and handed over the computer. "No problem." Her boyfriend's upper lip curled slightly before he smoothed his oily hair and looked away.

Maxine leaned over Max's shoulder while he Googled for information. There were millions of hits for "Ku Klux Klan," but he quickly found one that showed what he was looking for.

MIOAK STANDS for the Mystic Insignia **Of A** Klansman. Today it is most commonly known as the Blood Drop Cross. It is displayed as the patch seen on the robes of Klansmen. It is also a part of the Imperial Seal of the Klan.

THE Klan symbol wasn't at all like the one he'd seen hanging from the flagpole the day before. A second Google search used the criteria of "Philippine Flag."

It didn't take long to find a picture similar to the one he remembered hanging in Janice's former Los Angeles living room. According to the information on the screen, the Philippine flag had changed several times between 1842 and 1898.

> An 1894 Katipunan flag had the three *K*s, but also a sun that projected sixteen rays. It was the flag used during the Battle of San Juan del Monte, the first major battle of the Philippine Revolution.

Max felt an electrical charge course through his veins and he almost shouted, "It *was* Ben!" Attempting to stand quickly, his knees jolted the table's underside. A chorus of upset voices erupted as several glasses slopped liquid on the table's surface. "Damn!" He snatched the laptop from harm's way and handed it back to the giggling brunette.

"Sorry about the mess." He backed away quickly. "And good luck with your trip and the magic mushrooms and all that."

Charging from the room, the last thing he heard was the boyfriend's nasally voice. "What a bloody wanker!"

THE living bamboo fence traced a line in either direction from where Max was standing. The taxi had dropped him on the closest road, and he'd run the rest of the way, only stopping to catch his breath. His ankle wasn't throbbing much, he noticed.

What if Ben doesn't speak English? The girl—Chiho—might be gone. Max smacked his hand against the gate repeatedly. *I may still be out of luck.* He worried as he paced back and forth. It had looked like a huge compound, and since they weren't expecting guests, they might not answer. The dogs, however, heard the noise right away and barked wildly. They were the perfect doorbell.

An eternity seemed to pass before the inset window opened. A tanned, round face peered out, displaying no visible emotion. The man had trimmed gray hair and wide, flat nostrils.

"I, uh . . . hi, I'm Max Travers. It's important that I find a man named Ben Takeda." He felt like an idiot, but didn't care. He could hardly contain himself. His heart was beating insanely fast.

The man's stoic expression remained unmoving, as if cast in bronze.

"I have to return a diary that I think belongs to Ben . . . Mr. Takeda. Let me show you." Max dropped to one knee and set the daypack on the ground. He undid the zipper and removed the satchel. Reaching inside, he noticed his hands shaking with excitement as he withdrew the yellow volume and raised his head in anticipation. But the window was closed.

The face had vanished.

Max was stunned. *This can't be happening.* Failure and despair swept down like a cold wind whistling from the treetops. It was all for nothing. The twisting path had led to a forested dead end.

Where do I go from here? How do I make this stop?

He cursed and threw down the diary before punching blindly at the solid gate.

"Owww!" Max slumped backward into the rut of the dirt path. His eyes watered and his bleeding hand ached as his head hung down between bent knees. It shouldn't be this way. He'd bought into Mr. M's bullshit speech about ideas and wisdom needing to survive—but ideas don't feel pain. The book was a curse, not a treasure. He shouldn't have to suffer for it. People shouldn't be dying. He had simply wanted his passport. Was it too much to ask?

Why did I ever leave the States? I should never have come here. What was I thinking?

Max gripped the sides of his skull, pressing hard with his palms. He desperately tried to crush away the anger and self-loathing swelling inside his chest. "Dumb . . . dumb . . . dumb!"

Unexpectedly, the air was pierced by the sound of squeaky hinges. The high gateway groaned as it swung away and the same gray-haired man stepped out into the laneway. Dressed in denim overalls with a brown work shirt, he appeared to be just a little over five feet tall. He approached and motioned for Max to stand. "There's no need to be upset. I was simply putting the dogs away." The man's soothing voice had a refined, lilting accent. "I see you've hurt your hand. We can find a bandage."

The throbbing in Max's head eased slightly as he rose up and dusted off his jeans. "Thanks." He wiped at his flushed cheeks, overcome with a bloom of gratitude and embarrassment.

The tiny man retrieved the daypack and satchel, handing them over, but he held onto the diary. Cradling it between his chest and forearm, his fingertips lightly brushed the raised picture on the leather surface. "It's still so lovely." His eyes glowed, transfixed. "I haven't seen this in a very, very long time."

Could it be? It didn't seem possible. Max could hardly believe his ears.

Blinking rapidly, the man seemed to catch himself. "Mr. Travers, my name is Ben. Come inside with me."

CHAPTER
FORTY-NINE

FLUORESCENT PULSES of red light created peaks and valleys on the heart monitor's face. Outside the windowless hospital room, the police guard sat propped up in a chair, his chin resting above his protruding belly. The sedative from his coffee would wear off in an hour or two. In the meantime, the hospital staff would think he was just catching a little catnap. Nobody walking past would give it a second thought. Luckily, police reputations around the world were notoriously similar.

Vincent had observed the doctor finishing his post-breakfast rounds. It would likely be another thirty minutes before anyone came to check up on the patient again. The hum of equipment was the only noise in the room until Mr. Murayama spoke first.

"I was expecting someone to come. Are you here to hurt me?"

"Yes." The lethal green eyes stared at the shell of a man lying in the bed. "If you don't cooperate."

"Well, you have competition. I think the doctor is trying to kill me first."

Vincent came forward and stood near the bed. He straightened the sleeves of his charcoal Kilgour suit, the only thing he would ever concede that the British made better then the French. "I'm here to discuss what was taken from your office five days ago."

"My phone and some antique daggers. Nothing important. It's all in the police report, which I'm sure you've read."

Vincent exhaled sharply, not buying what was being sold. "All right, let's begin with why Kazue Saito was murdered."

Mr. Murayama coughed before speaking. "I don't know, but since his divorce, he's been gambling. I helped him with money sometimes, but it appears the *Yakuza* killed him. Probably men he owed loans to. He may have told them that he possessed a map to—" He paused to glance at the closed door. "—to something they wanted."

"So why come after you?"

"When he couldn't deliver the map, I believe he lied and gave them my name."

"And they came to your office, but took nothing important?" Vincent shook his head. "I can guarantee you if I came looking for something valuable, I would leave with more than trinkets."

"Please, I'm telling the truth."

"Then why is the prime suspect in the police report an American English teacher?"

"I . . . I don't know."

It was obvious that the old man's diplomatic mask was slipping a little, and Vincent leaned closer. "Ever since the end of World War Two, there have been rumors of someone spending considerable amounts of money to gather proof of Golden Lily, and the fact that it has become the source of the Black Eagle Trust and the M-Fund. As you well know, this evidence is something your government and mine would prefer to keep private."

"What does that have to do with me?"

"This rumored person was said to be hoarding maps, photographs, letters, waybills, contracts, tax records, insurance documents, audio tapes, and the like. There were stories of him quietly hunting and gathering for many years. But in our business, you can never be perfectly quiet. The rumor was that this collector of secrets would come forward at some point to demand a ransom for his silence." Vincent paused, watching for a reaction, before he continued. "Did you know, because of your diplomatic knowledge and extensive collection of artifacts . . . at one time you were on the list of prime candidates?"

Mr. Murayama sputtered, "I have never done anything—"

Vincent clicked his tongue in condescension. "Don't look so shocked. No, you've proven your loyalty and greed far too many times, and besides, why would someone gather evidence in order to point a finger back at themselves? Several times this elusive collector was nearly caught, but he always managed to slip away. Years ago, the trail went cold and the rumors died away." Vincent paused to let the moment sink in. He knew that fear took longer to work its way into the thick skin of an experienced diplomat.

"But then recently a strange thing happened." Vincent adjusted his gloves. "Rumors began circulating of information being offered for sale to the highest bidder. The items for sale were a very old diary and a map. A buyer came forward. Perhaps it was the *Yakuza* you mentioned, or maybe it was the elusive collector at work again. Then within the last week, Kazue Saito was murdered, and your artifacts were ransacked. To the less observant, these may seem like completely separate things." His voice deepened and grew deadly serious. "But to a mind that has spent a lifetime drawing lines between events and people, these are three dots in the same connected picture."

"Please go." Mr. Murayama said. "I've told you everything. There's nothing more to say."

Vincent straightened up and reached into the side pocket of his suit jacket. From within, he extracted a clear plastic syringe and removed the cap. He'd fully expected to use the serum, but it was always worth exploring an easier avenue.

"This little puzzle is one that I intend to solve. So you can help me either willingly or unwillingly. The choice is up to you."

A thin line of serum sprayed across the pillow's face.

Raising his hands, Mr. Murayama wiped the fluid from his cheeks. "You're insane!"

THE room was dark and warm. Mr. Murayama's eyes fluttered, then shut again. He was drifting on the edge of sleep, but Vincent was shaking his shoulder and pulling him back. "Wake up! Wake up! It's Max. Help me. Please help me."

The old man's thick tongue struggled against dry lips, and his words slurred. He was fighting to speak clearly. "But . . . but you were supposed to find Ben."

"I lost the information."

"Where are you, Max? I can't . . . see you."

"I'm so scared. Please, Mr. Murayama, help me remember what to do. I'm in so much pain."

"Ben in Nara. You must . . . Ben Takeda in Nara . . . give him the diary."

"But where in Nara?"

"I did . . ." The old body spasmed and shook.

Vincent glanced at the rhythmic squiggles on the heart monitor as they grew increasingly chaotic. Administering truth drugs, even the latest generation, was not an exact science. There was plenty of room for error. "Help me! Where does Ben live?"

"You . . . in the country . . . Nara . . . Ahhhh!"

Mr. Murayama's withered frame convulsed violently. The line on the monitor bounced, then slowed to a trickle before the alarm began screeching.

It was time to move. The information was enough to go on.

Stepping out of the room, Vincent almost collided with a youthful nurse running down the hall. Her panicked demeanor changed to a look of confusion as she raced past him into the room. The shrieking noise rose and died away as the door opened and shut.

Vincent casually made his way to the nearby stairwell. He was already thinking about the Bullet Train reservation he needed to make.

Exiting the hospital, he looked up at the crucifix above the Nursing College next door. As he dialed the Japan Rail train office, he made the sign of the cross with his right arm. "In the name of the Father and of the Son and of the Holy Spirit. Lord have Mercy. Amen."

CHAPTER
FIFTY

THE QUEEN of Korea did not go quietly. The cordial face that she initially presented in 1895 to the conquering Japanese quickly turned to irreverence and finally contempt. Her refusal to support the scheme to conquer her people ended in fiery flames. Servants watched in horror as she was set ablaze, making a desperate, screaming run through the peaceful grounds of Seoul's Gyeongbok Palace. Having had their way with her, the Japanese Black Ocean agents smirked and giggled like schoolboys with a frog as she thrashed and stumbled. She tried, with arms outstretched, to reach the nearby lake. A kerosene inferno consumed the billowing layers of her silk dress. The fragrance of the normally flowered setting lay blanketed beneath the sweet, awful stench of searing flesh. Finally her arms ceased to beat the air, and she fell forward. Her smoldering skull rang out as it struck the rocks on the pathway, while the last of the flames licked away what little exposed flesh remained.

"MY mother told my sister and me that story," Ben clutched the diary and spoke in a calm voice as they walked in the late morning sun. "The murder of Empress Myeongseong was the beginning of fifty years of death and theft. Mother told us never to forget that if the empress fought to the end, we should do the same."

"How could that happen?" Try as he might, Max couldn't stop the unsettling wave sweeping over him. The words seemed so out of place in this pastoral setting. A lush and intricate garden had been carved into the surrounding forest. Winding pathways edged the curves of the central pond. Sculpted bushes grew alone or huddled together. The main house, made of dark brown wood, stood to the northwest, its helmet of bullet-gray ceramic tiles glowing through the surrounding green leaves. Scatterings of cherry and maple trees brushed the scene with pink and smoky red. "Where's your sister now?"

"She disappeared. When I was a child, soldiers came and took her. They killed my mother when she tried to stop them. I never saw my sister again, but I hope she died quickly." Ben hesitated. "A quick death would have been better than what those men had planned for her."

Max exhaled horror, struggling to accept the statement.

"It is strange to wish death . . ." Ben whispered, "for someone so loved."

They strolled past a thatched hut next to the path, allowing the aching moment to dwindle and pass. Max still wasn't sure it was all real. Any second, he expected to wake in a tangle of sheets at the Nara hostel. "So at the end of the war—you were brought here?"

"Yes. 1945. We came in a submarine. I was eight years old and terrified."

"And you were adopted by the prince."

"I was raised with a good education and a stern British-trained nanny. This place has been my home for the past sixty-two years." Ben looked up with an odd smile. "My adoption wasn't written in the prince's diary. How do you know that?"

"Tomoko, my . . . my girlfriend. She did some research." *How can I forgive her for leaving like that?* He would have been relieved to express his angst and frustration, but the story was too personal to share with a stranger, at least so soon. Max looked away, masking his mixed emotions as he deftly changed the subject. "So didn't you ever want to go back to the Philippines? To your real home?"

"A place is only a place, Max—it's the people you are with who make it home. Prince Takeda became like a father, and then when I grew older, I met my wife, Sayuri."

"But wait a minute." The logic felt circuitous, as if the thread were looping back upon itself. "It was Prince Takeda who killed your real father . . ."

Ben continued walking with an even, rhythmic pace as he spoke. "I know it must be difficult for you to understand, because when you think of the prince, you see a tyrant. He appears a dangerous and evil man. I also thought that way once, but in time, I came to see a man torn between duty and personal conviction. He was required to do things he didn't want to do. But every chance he could, when duty did not clearly dictate, he chose the better path."

"But in the diary he confessed to burying hundreds of people alive."

"True, and my birth father was one of them. But is redemption for the sinner possible? Can a lifetime of terrible actions be erased with just a few good ones? I believe the answer is yes."

Max recalled the blood scarf trailing below Mrs. Kanazawa's head. "I don't know if I agree."

Ben appeared willing to accept a difference of opinion, and he nodded without speaking.

As they approached the wooden mast, Max pointed up. "That Philippine flag was the thing I remembered. It brought me back here."

"Don't tell my wife." Ben chuckled. "If she knew that story, it would be removed by morning."

"But why do you keep it, if Japan became your home?"

"My true father was born on August 30, 1896, the same day as the Battle of San Juan del Monte, the Philippine Revolution. He loved this flag."

Max continued staring up, feeling his guard slipping just a little, questioning his decision only a year before to leave California. "My dad loves only two things, baseball and football, the Chargers and the Dodgers. It drove my mom crazy." The memory felt like a faded photograph.

Ben stopped walking and turned, his face growing serious. "So have you come looking for treasure? For riches? For reward? Because if you have, then I'm sorry to disappoint you."

"No. Like I said, I've come for help. To make this stop. Mr. Murayama couldn't help me, but he thought maybe you could. I'm tired of running and being afraid all the time."

"You have to forgive me. I don't know who Mr. Murayama is."

"He's a friend of mine. A diplomat who once worked with a guy named Tetsuo Ando . . . no, wait, that's not right. His name was Tetsuo Endo."

Ben's face lit up. "Aaaah! Tetsuo Endo. He was Prince Takeda's personal bodyguard during the war. A greedy and dangerous man. He was the one who came and took the diary away from me. He thought it held directions to one of the 175 burial sites. I'm sure he was disappointed to find it holds no maps."

"So why did you give it to him?"

"He owed considerable loans. I can still remember his half-crazy eyes as he threatened my wife and baby. Fighting is not for me. I have seen too much death." Ben shrugged. "I gave it to him, and he simply went away."

"But Prince Takeda could have protected you."

"The prince lived his own life with his family in Chiba. By that time, I saw him perhaps once a year. I was deeply sad to see the diary go. It was my only link to the past." Ben stared directly into Max's eyes, unblinking, as if he were trying to glimpse the corners of the soul inside. "And now you've brought it back."

"Yes," Max said with foreboding. "But there are others who want it."

Seconds ticked by before a reply was forthcoming. "That is a problem."

"So could the *Yakuza*—could Oto Kodama—still think there's a map inside it?"

"It seems the most logical answer for why a man of his . . . background would desire it."

Max looked away at the sculpted trees and reflective ponds. Time felt suspended. Yet outside the protective bamboo walls, he knew that events were racing forward. Something was coming, and he needed to figure a solution fast.

"*Ojii-chan! Ojii-chan!* Grandpa!" Chiho's high-pitched shout tore ahead of her running feet. She sprang from the grove of tall trees on the north side of the clearing and raced toward them. Ben's wife also emerged from the forest. She spotted Max and stopped walking for a moment. Even from a distance, he could see her scowling face as she turned and stomped toward the two-story house.

Ben stretched out his arms as Chiho approached, and the two collided in a hug. He whispered into her ear, and she giggled a reply as Ben stood straight again.

"You will stay here tonight." Ben said suddenly with an air of authority. "It's the start of the holiday week, and all the hotels will be full. There is more to discuss. We should continue our conversation after I take Chiho home."

Max thought instantly of Tomoko's promise to find him, but before he could express gratitude Chiho grasped each of their hands, connecting them into a chain. Then she burst into song, pulling them all forward along the gravel path toward the house.

THE wooden flooring beneath Max's feet creaked. Translucent light glowed through the thin *washi* paper stretched over *shoji* screens on the opposite side of the hallway. He was viewing a procession of photographs that ran the length of the house's main corridor, straightening them as he moved along.

The pictures told the story of Ben's life in Japan, from his childhood through to his grandchildren. The voices of Ben and his wife could be heard in the kitchen at the far end of the hall. It was too distant to make out the words, even if he could speak the language, but it was clear from the strained tone that the conversation wasn't going well.

"HOW do you know he can be trusted?" Sayuri's salt-and-pepper hair was pulled into a knot, her arms folded defensively across her chest. A row of creases decorated her forehead.

"I don't know that yet," said Ben, "but he seems genuine."

"It could all be an act. I know what you're thinking, but you must not . . . it's too important to trust a stranger. He may just be a treasure hunter with a good story or even a foreign spy."

"He could be, but he may also be someone who truly needs my help."

"I have a very bad feeling about this."

"Well, Chiho likes him, and children are excellent at spotting liars. And I think he may be honorable—but that will take longer to determine."

"Yes, well . . . regardless, it's time we don't have. We need to leave, now. I'll be finished here shortly." She shook her head and turned back to the sink, returning to the task of washing the last of the bamboo shoots freshly dug from the forest floor. "Let him stay only one night."

"As you wish." Ben exited the kitchen into the hall as the wooden floor groaned and echoed.

Sayuri's voice rang out behind him. "And he stays in the guest house!"

MAX was halfway down the hall, bent over examining a photo, glad for a brief moment to focus his mind on something other than his overwhelming problems. He spoke when he heard the creaking floor grow quiet behind him. "Is this your son in this climbing picture?"

"Yes. He lives in Osaka now," Ben replied.

Max straightened up. "I love sport climbing—try to do as much as I can." He longed for the return of carefree days of harnesses, ropes, and chalky hands.

Ben smiled as he spoke. "I know only that it makes my son happy." He motioned toward the exit. "I know you are looking for answers, and I do want to help you." He seemed sincere. "We will talk again, soon, but for now I have to take Chiho to her home. I should be back this evening. Please— let me show you where you'll stay tonight."

For the smallest space of time Max paused. As hospitable as Ben appeared to be, gaining his trust would take effort, and events would move at whatever pace he chose to set. Max nodded resigned agreement, silently hoping there was enough time, still unsure if Tomoko might come, praying the gamble would pay off.

The two returned to the sunshine of the yard before turning north into the forest grove. The dense overhead canopy filtered out much of the blue sky, and a cool, lush feeling of moist air brushed past as the pathway changed to dirt. Max was puzzled but tried not to show it. Ground vegetation thickened as they approached a short slope between the bases of two enormous cedar trees. Continuing for another twenty paces, they stepped through a thicket of bushes into a great forest clearing.

Ahead, in the center of the open space sat the square base of what must have once been an Imperial castle. The gently curving walls rose at least fifty feet. Moss-covered blocks of stone made up the foundation. Stacked diagonally, they resembled diamonds rising into the air.

Max gazed up, craning his neck, and blinked with surprise. The image was astounding. "Whoa!" He turned immediately to look at Ben. The old man's smiling face revealed that he'd expected the reaction.

Perched on top of the stupendous ancient stone base was a modern, but rustic, wilderness cabin. A set of switchback stairs zigzagged up the face of the structure, soaring high before meeting a jutting veranda suspended into space.

Ben waved his hand like a vaudeville performer. "Welcome to my guest house."

CHAPTER
FIFTY-ONE

THE PEN in Yoko's hand was running out of ink. She rattled it in frustration before throwing it across the open gallery space. Overhead, powerful voices from Rigoletto's quartet, "Un di, se ben rammentomi," resonated from hidden speakers.

She searched through the desk-drawer clutter. There was so much to do and so little time. The application lying before her was for the preview showing of the fifty-second International Art Exhibition, the Biennale di Venezia. Only professionals and the press would be permitted to attend. The application would be the key to the birth of her new life. It needed to be faxed no later than the April thirtieth deadline, just three short days away.

Her future identity had arrived by courier in a sealed envelope. A week from now, she would disappear to Venice. She would wander the canals and stroll again through the palaces and palazzi. Then she would sharpen her Italian and drink in the works of the Venice Biennale before buying a space and opening her own gallery.

The terrible past would fade into distant memory once and for all. Death and debt would haunt her sleep no more. Her life would consist of rising late and sipping coffee at outdoor cafés. Afternoons would be spent with guests, ushering them through her latest exhibit. She could almost feel the warm evenings filled with operatic crescendos, rich wine, pasta, and worldly company.

The bobbed haircut in the passport photo was hers, but the new name would take some getting used to: Vera Weaver. It had an old-school movie star ring to it. She would become a new and better person. She would step into the skin of her newly acquired life and never look back.

The cell phone next to her buzzed and bounced on the desktop. The display read, "Masami Ishi." She chose to ignore until a text came through: "I know you're at the gallery. Call me."

The conjoined operatic voices reached a climax as Yoko dialed the missed call and stepped from the front door onto the concrete sidewalk. Sunlight and shadows from the surrounding buildings painted the narrow, car-lined street in wide stripes.

Her voice betrayed frustration, but she did her best to remain calm. "How did you know I was at the gallery?"

Masami chuckled. "See the tan car across the street? Did you think that I would just trust you?"

She retreated into the recessed gallery doorway. "You're a bastard."

"You will not slip away again. At least not until I get my money. Speaking of which, how is the sale of the school's shares coming along?"

Yoko wanted to lash out, but she bit her tongue instead. "Everything is on schedule. The shareholders will be meeting me at the lawyer's office tomorrow to sign the final documents. They think Max has gone traveling with his aunt. The money should be transferred within ten days."

"Excellent."

"Any news from your side? This whole process could still unravel if Max is publicly arrested."

"I'm suppressing the crime details from the media. We're also following up a lead from the Izu, but so far he's remained elusive."

"Well, perhaps your men should work a little harder."

Masami Ishi's voice rose to a shout. "*Do not* tell me how to do my job. You focus on your tasks and let me do mine."

Yoko smirked to herself. Her voice became soothing. "Of course, Masami-*kun*. I didn't mean to imply that you weren't trying very, very hard."

His snorting breath simmered down. "My officers tell me your gallery opening is tomorrow."

"Yes. I'll be bringing the shareholders here after the meeting at the lawyer's office. Make sure your men are invisible."

"They will be."

"Is that all?"

"Yes, I suppose—"

Yoko snapped the phone shut before he could finish.

Thank you again for showing your cards, Masami. My next vanishing act may require more finesse than the last one—challenging, but still doable.

She eyed the wicked car before turning back inside.

CHAPTER
FIFTY-TWO

TOMOKO WATCHED as Hiro squirmed in a hard-backed wooden chair, rubbing his eyes. Minutes had stretched into hours as he adjusted the pages of *Cry Freedom* against the shadows created by the prison cell's single overhead light bulb.

The door scraped open, and in stepped the skinny sentry. He'd brought one of Oto's bodyguards with him. "Father wants to see her." The sentry motioned with his goatee toward the room's back wall.

Hiro set down his novel. The legs of his chair screeched against the bare concrete floor. "Please do as they say. You'll be forced to go, anyway."

Silently, Tomoko rose and brushed the hair from her face, having known this moment would come. She hoped her eyes were expressionless, hiding the dread that was wrenching at her stomach. "Fine."

PRESSED into the back corner, Tomoko felt the elevator trip to the thirty-first floor would take forever. A symphonic version of "I Will Always Love You" drifted from the ceiling. As they arrived, she reminded herself that the fear of the unknown was usually worse than the pain of dealing with it, or so she hoped.

They crossed a marble foyer and entered the mansion's living room, but Hiro remained back, almost out of sight.

Ceiling-to-floor windows showcased the evening twilight and the first glow of city lights stretching into the distance. The room's sleek opulence was designed to impress.

Oto was reclining on a sofa, with the second bodyguard towering behind him. Dressed in a pure white Nehru suit, his black socks peeked over the top of his patent leather shoes. A crystal glass rested in one hand while his lecherous eyes played slowly over her form. "So good you could join us."

Standing between the entranceway and the furniture, Tomoko felt suspended in a kind of no-man's land. Her vacant eyes belied the tension in her body as she chose not to speak.

"I understand. You're giving me the silent treatment in order to show your displeasure." Oto sipped his drink. "Maybe you'll speak if I pick your parents up again and question them all over?"

Tomoko edged forward, bristling heat raking her skin as the guard behind her locked a warning grip on her shoulder. "They aren't stupid enough to return home," she spat while pushing the guard's hand away. "Don't touch me!"

Oto sat up. From his irate expression, it was clear he wasn't used to being addressed with such insolence. "So you do have a tongue. Well, perhaps you can use it to give me the information I want, so I don't need to go looking for them."

"What could I know that would matter to you?"

"Begin with the diary. We know your *Gaijin* boyfriend has it and that he's gone to Nara. Why go there?"

"You're mistaken. I left him. It's over, and I have no idea where he went." She motioned back toward Hiro. "His partner—the big ape—made the assumption Max went to Nara because of an address he found in my pocket. But in fact, it's my manager's summer home."

"We'll find out soon enough if you're lying."

"What do you mean?"

Oto ignored the question. "I also want to know if you got a look at the map."

"Map? What are you talking about? What map?"

"Don't lie to me!" The *Yakuza* leader flared as he rose and pointed directly at her with two fingers, like the barrel of a gun. "During the war, my father was a rear admiral in the Navy and an advisor to the prime minister. He knew exactly what was going on, and he swore there was a diary with a map. You and your stupid American boyfriend are not going to take what belongs to me!"

"Too bad your father wouldn't swear that you were actually his son." The moment the words left her mouth, she knew she'd gone too far. Tomoko and the guard both ducked as Oto's crystal glass sailed overhead and shattered on the wall. The *Yakuza* leader was red-faced as he screamed, "Get this bitch out of my sight!"

The guard lurched forward and wrapped his massive arms around Tomoko, running his open hands across her chest, making her gasp. She reacted by raising her right knee and driving her heel into his instep. He groaned in pain and briefly relaxed his grip. The movement freed her arm for the next self-defense move. Twisting her upper body, she hammered an elbow backward into the center of his neck. The big man gasped and swayed, giving her the chance to spin around. A kneecap caught him in his groin at the same time as his fist impacted with her right temple and she shrieked as the force sent her diving to the ground. The guard careened backward, toppling over a clear vase. Glass shards and smooth stones blanketed the floorboards.

Oto and the second bodyguard remained motionless, both men clearly shocked as Hiro raced forward to scoop Tomoko from the ground. "I'll take her downstairs." He fled to the waiting elevator, carrying her in his arms.

"You care about her so damn much? Then you can stay locked up with her." The great man's bellow echoed out into the grand foyer. "And just so you know, little girl, your American boyfriend is going to die."

TOMOKO balanced on the creaky chair with her knees tucked to her chest. A bowl of steaming water sat on the wooden table; Hiro dipped a cloth into it. Leaning forward, he attempted to pull her hands from her face, but she tensed and refused.

"You're playing a very dangerous game with Kodama-*san*."

Her muffled voice was defiant. "I'm tired of being a victim."

"If you want to live, you'll be whatever he tells you to be."

Tomoko removed her left hand from her face. She pointed at the bandage covering his pinkie finger. "You may have chosen to survive that way, but I won't."

"The difference is that I'll live."

"If you call it living."

"Call it what you want. Now move your other hand so I can see your face."

Tomoko could sense that he was serious about helping, although why he was being so kind was still a mystery. Her feet slid to the floor, and she dropped both hands into her lap. Her right eye blinked and fluttered when she opened it. Surprisingly, the vision seemed fine.

Hiro leaned in closer. The cloth turned pink with blood as he gently wiped at the wound. His sleeves were rolled up close to his elbows, and she could see the tattoos snaking down his arms. The odor of stale cigarettes floated from his mouth. Tomoko instinctively turned her head away, but his hands gently guided her face back toward the light. There was something about him that was so oddly sincere.

"You must listen to me. Being an illegitimate child is Oto's weakest spot. If he didn't think you were still a useful bargaining chip, he would have killed you for mentioning it."

Tomoko shifted in her seat. "But everyone knows his father never publicly acknowledged him and that the leaders of the other *Yakuza* gangs treat him like an outcast. They believe he should never have inherited his father's position. Oto seized power but never paid his dues. There was a magazine article about it just a few months ago."

"True, but a magazine can't describe how dangerous and volatile he is."

Tomoko bit her lip and flinched at the sting of hydrogen peroxide. "Ow!"

"He's been searching for this map since his father died more then twenty years ago. It's not just the money he wants. He believes if he discovers the map and recovers the fortune, he'll gain the full respect of his peers in the *Yakuza* community. That's the most important thing to him."

"You mean he's just a child who wants the other kids to like him?"

Hiro shrugged. "Yes, I suppose.

She could feel the bandage on his hand pressing into her hair. "I'm sorry about your finger. I shouldn't have said that."

"Don't worry." Hiro placed the final piece of medical tape into place. "That should hold until morning. The swelling will go down in a few days. You should get some rest. I'll see if I can get something for your headache."

Tomoko flinched again but this time from surprise. "How can you be so sure I have a headache?"

He turned away, tossing the water into the corner and gathering up the medical supplies. "I've been hit a few times before. I know how it feels."

CHAPTER
FIFTY-THREE

MAX WOKE with a start. A clanging bell was demanding attention. He strained to force the pea-soup fog from his sleepy brain. Sitting up, he noticed he was on a double bed pressed into the back corner of a room. The walls were cedar logs infilled with white caulking, and he recalled staring up at a cabin perched on an ancient rock base. Ben had settled him in before leaving to take his granddaughter back to Osaka. There'd been a promise that they would speak again when he returned. The remainder of the day was filled with frustrated agony, pacing near the gate and imagining every woodland noise to be Tomoko's footfall. But with nightfall's descent, the only visitors were the stars and so, despondent, he'd withdrawn back to the cabin.

I must have fallen asleep.

The piercing jangle continued unabated as Max stumbled to the desk at the cabin's front. The solid black receiver of the chrome-dialed 1950s phone felt heavy in his hand. "Hello?"

"We are not alone!" Ben's voice on the other end was burning.

Max paused. Now that the ringing had ceased, he could hear baying voices—dogs. It was the sonorous cries of animals on the hunt. "What's happening?"

"Someone's here. I can see on the security cameras. They came over the fence, and there's more than one man."

The Yakuza . . . or the police! Max felt his heart skip a beat. "I don't know how they found me." His free hand ran through his unkempt hair.

"Come through the trees and meet me by the flagpole. Use the flashlight I gave you, but be careful. They may see it." Ben's voice overflowed with urgency. "Hurry! There's no time!"

Max threw the receiver onto the desktop. He turned and lunged back to the bed. His hands shook while stuffing loose articles into the almost empty daypack. *Where's the diary?* He paused for only a second, straining to recall. *Ben's got it. Now move!* Rushing for the door, he reached for the handle, but paused as it dawned on him that the invaders could be waiting on the other side and he'd walk straight into a trap. He considered turning on the porch light, but decided against it. The darkness could work to his advantage. Max slowed his breathing and pressed himself against the strip of wall between the door and a large picture window. Inching the curtain back, he peered out onto the front deck. A dim glow drifted up from the yard light at the distant base of the stairs. The coast looked clear.

He cracked the door open and eased out into the crisp night air before edging toward the staircase. A flight of stairs led him down to the first landing. Pausing to crouch, Max stared through the handrail's slats. Far below, a shadow raced from the bushes toward the base of the rock wall. It could have been the shape of a bulky animal, but as the figure drew closer to the yard light, it clearly became that of a man. He was dressed entirely in black with broad shoulders and a slender waist—but it was his thick neck that gave him away.

Holy crap, it's him!

Max's panicked mind raced in circles. He was fairly sure he hadn't been seen yet. The problem was that the only escape route was now cut off—there was no alternate way down.

Thick Neck was almost at the bottom of the stairs when Max saw the shiny reflection of metal in his hand. It could mean only one thing.

Scurrying upward in retreat, he could feel the big man's weight vibrating from below. It would be only a matter of seconds before the killer arrived. Clambering onto the nearest handrail, Max scanned the steeply pitched rooftop. The end of a slender rope, likely used for maintenance, stretched down from the peak. He grasped and pulled with all his might, trying to move as noiselessly as possible on the asphalt shingles, praying that the line would hold his weight as he scrambled up its length.

The footsteps below reached the landing and stopped just as Max eased himself over the far side of the peak's crest and lay still. He tried to slow his rapid breathing. Both hands clutched the peak to keep from sliding backward to his death.

Suddenly, the door was kicked inward with a crashing bang. Stomping boots raced inside. He heard Thick Neck cursing in frustration. The bed frame was flipped and slammed about in anger. The room was empty, but the thug was bound to figure out soon enough that the roof was an option.

A cell phone rang and he heard the killer answer, still yelling.

Max knew he needed to do something quickly. Masked against the noisy conversation below, he slithered left toward the chimney. The stonework began at the peak and ran about three feet down the backward-sloping roofline. He peered into the darkness below.

If I stay, he shoots me. If I jump, I die.

A whisper of a thought eased into his brain—there was another possibility. Rising up, he straddled the roof's peak and slid the daypack off his shoulder. Undoing the zipper, he probed around inside, finally retrieving a dagger.

The blade cut easily through the twine-like maintenance rope.

Max forced himself to concentrate as his shaking hands fed the material through his belt loops. Using what little light was available, he struggled to join the two loose ends together with a fisherman's knot, making sure to leave an eight-foot loop of loose rope. The result was the makeshift ring of a lineman's belt attached to his waist. Standing up, he secured himself by easing the loop over the chimney top's four corners—he was attached.

All I have to do is climb onto the outside of the chimney and stay hidden till he's gone.

Below, the two porch lights snapped to life, illuminating the cabin's front and the surrounding canopy of trees. Frozen in place, Max stared down onto Thick Neck, who strode into plain view. The man had his broad back to the roof as he moved to the balcony's front. He rested his handgun on the railing before lighting a cigarette.

Max's muscles burned hot, and he struggled to remain absolutely still.

Don't turn around. Don't turn around. Please, don't turn around.

Smoke curled slowly into the air, dissipating into the dark sky as Thick

Neck leaned against the handrail, drawing repeatedly on the burning ember dangling from his lips.

Max held the painful pose as the seconds ticked past, biting his lip, swallowing a groan.

Finally, Thick Neck's cigarette flicked outward into space and then, without warning, he turned and looked straight up at the rooftop. The two men held eye contact for a split second as the big man grinned maliciously and spoke a single word—"Tomoko"—while drawing a line across his throat with a bulky finger.

No! She can't be dead!

The air exploded with action as Thick Neck dove toward the gun. Grasping it, he spun and fired repeatedly. Max dropped, hugging the roof, scarcely avoiding the bullets ripping past. He could feel the projectiles' searing heat as they screamed past his skull.

Springing forward, the big man clambered onto the handrail, which groaned under the immense load. As he struggled to pull himself onto the roof, he lost the grip on his pistol, cursing its fall into the dark bushes below.

Max grasped the chimney and pressed the toe of his shoes between the stones. Reaching around the far side, he gripped the rock and prayed the rope would hold as he swung out into space. The loop tugged at his waist but held firm against his body's weight. Every limb shook, and he prayed for strength while clinging precariously, inching his way around to the outside edge.

Thick Neck screamed curses as he struggled to reach the chimney, but his voice fell silent when he reached the daypack resting on the peak. Max understood enough Japanese to know that the man was muttering, "Where is it? Where is it?" Moments later an angry cry preceded the sound of the pack clattering down to the deck. The killer was now reaching around the chimney, grasping. He grunted as he tried to catch Max's arms. Each swipe missed by mere inches, before the attempts ceased.

Max listened for sounds of movement, his mind reeling. *It can't be true. Tomoko can't be dead.*

The rattle of a chain preceded a hammering weight crashing violently into the chimney over his head, causing him to shout and duck. Bits of rock and dust rained down, choking the air.

What the hell?

The metal ball slammed again, even closer this time.

Shit! Max listened to the rattle of the links being retracted. He knew the device would get him eventually and his mind spun desperately. A fresh burst of adrenaline coursed through his veins.

You're gonna pay, you bastard!

Max edged back the way he'd come, and waited.

The weight smashed into the rock a third time. Closer yet, it brushed the hairs on his head, while shards of rock bounced against his face.

He reached a hand around the stone corner and leaned back against the lineman's belt, releasing a roar as he swung hard away from the chimney, back in the direction he'd come, kicking his legs horizontal. His feet struck Thick Neck squarely in the shins, breaking the man's single-armed grip on the chimney's top, sending him reeling backward before he slid down the roof's back slope.

The sudden force of weight tested the limits of the lineman's belt as Max dropped hard, crashing into the chimney's side. The collision hammered the wind from his lungs, and he could taste blood. He gasped for air. But even as he hung against the rope, his hands and feet instinctively struggled for a hold. Using every ounce of remaining strength, he clawed back up the stones, barely noticing the *Yakuza's* screams for help as he collapsed back onto the asphalt rooftop, gasping.

Looking up, he saw that Thick Neck had slid down to the roof's back edge. The top of the thug's torso was flat against the shingles, but his feet and waist were kicking into empty space over the sixty-foot drop. He was using friction to slow his gradual slide downward as he shouted for help. *"Tasukete! . . . Tasukete! . . . Tasukete!"*

Max hugged his aching ribs as he stood up straight, straddling the peak. He freed himself by pulling the rope back over the chimney's top.

"Tasukete!"

Reliving the image of Thick Neck drawing a finger across his throat, Max spat blood as he shouted his greatest fear. "Did you hurt her?"

"Tasukete!"

"I'll kill you, asshole! *Itsu?*—when did you see her?"

Thick Neck's eyes were wild with fear. "Tomoko—okay."

"Okay? You're sure she's okay?" Max was struggling to free the rope from his waist, intending to toss the end down.

"Okay—Tasukete! . . . Tasukete!" The deep voice shifted to a whimper as

the *Yakuza* slid farther over the edge.

Suddenly the absurdity of his good intention hit home. *Help you? Are you joking?* "What am I doing? You expect me to save you? After everything you've done? After killing Mrs. Kanazawa?" He rose to his feet. "Go to hell." Turning, he lay flat, edging down to the cabin's front before swinging to the deck below. As he gathered up the daypack and turned off the deck lights, he heard the bloodcurdling scream of Thick Neck plunging to the ground.

Rage and exhaustion washed over Max.

Sayonara, asshole.

MAX stuck close to the shrubs as he crept from the trees on the north side of the central garden. There was enough ambient moonlight to navigate without the flashlight. Following the eastern boundary, he was on edge, focused, watching closely for any signs of movement.

Before long, he could see the thatched hut near the flagpole. He dashed to the building and hugged the perimeter as he scrambled around to the opposite side. Crouching, he tried to calm his labored breathing.

Ben materialized from behind a bush. "Where have you been?"

"One of them found me. The same guy who chased me in Tokyo." Max licked at his bleeding lip. "And he told me Tomoko is dead!"

Ben gripped his arm in solidarity. "I am so sorry."

"But then he changed his story and said she was okay, so I don't know what to believe. What if she's been caught? How do I save her?" Max asked helplessly, certain now that there was nothing anyone could do to stop the spiraling descent into madness.

A half-dozen heart beats passed before Ben replied, "Wait here." He turned and vanished inside the hut.

Max listened to the trees and the wind and his own rushing blood, thinking how angry he'd been on the train and then imagining Tomoko abducted by the *Yakuza*, realizing with regret that it was his own stubbornness which had forced her into such a difficult dilemma. She'd been willing to challenge the norm, and he'd admired her for that, encouraging defiance of the way things had always been done, but then when she'd asked for help to uphold just one tradition—caring for her parents—he'd dismissed the request without a thought. *I should have listened. I should have paid attention.*

Ben rematerialized a few feet away, one arm full. "There are still at least three men. You're not safe here. You have to go. Here—take this with you." He pressed forward a wrapped cloth bundle.

"Aren't you coming?" Max took hold of the offering reluctantly. "Where's your wife?"

"We're not leaving our home."

"But they have guns. They'll kill you!"

"We know where to hide. Now listen. Inside here is the yellow diary, and also its companion."

"What?" Max couldn't believe what he was hearing. "Another diary?"

"Yes, but only the prince and few select people knew about the second one. You need to take them both. It's the only way you can help Tomoko." Ben's voice wavered. "I don't wish your story to be the same as mine."

Max opened his mouth, about to speak, when the realization struck hard. "Oh my God—you mean like your sister."

"Yes . . . so listen!" A silent figure could now be seen exiting the trees on the garden's north as Ben pressed on. "This is a continuation of the prince's life story. The secrets in it are powerful. You must take great care. Many have died to keep it safe."

"I don't understand. What do I do with it?" He wanted to believe the books could make a difference, but it didn't seem possible.

"Go to Okinawa. Use them to find what you need."

"You mean the Southern Islands?" Frustrated, Max ran a hand through his hair. Little of what he was hearing made any sense. "Why? What's there?"

A second figure emerged from the forest, behind the first.

"I'm sorry. There's no time to explain. Go to Okinawa Island. The blue diary is written in English—read it and find what it shows you."

"I can't. It's too risky." He held out the bundle. "I can't do it, Ben."

"You must use it to save her . . . it's your destiny."

The intensity of the moment felt overwhelming and he closed his eyes. Only days earlier, Mr. Murayama had uttered the same fateful words. Images of the Korean Queen, and the past week, and Tomoko's smiling face flew by like a slideshow. Finally he spoke, astonished to hear himself agreeing. "All right . . . I'll try."

"Good man." Ben placed a reassuring hand on his shoulder. "But remember one thing. Make sure to guard the real treasure until the time is right." Ben's head flicked up, and Max followed the direction of his gaze. The two silhouetted figures had been joined by a third, and the group was moving down to the pond and across the arching bridge. "You'll know what I mean when the time comes." He pointed south. "Now go through the trees. Walk straight. When you come to the main road, go across it and back into the forest. The hill will drop, and you'll find a stream. Follow the water's flow. It will lead you to town."

"Thank you, for everything."

"You're welcome." Ben motioned with both hands. "You must go. Quickly!"

Max dashed into the trees before stopping to peer back. He watched the old caretaker vanish into the shadows. *Good luck, Ben.*

CHAPTER
FIFTY-FOUR

Saturday, April 28

"YOU CALLED for me, sir?" The mustached police commander respectfully stood at attention.

"Come in." Masami Ishi continued to gaze out the window at the morning sunlight. "Do you have a girlfriend, commander?"

"Not right now." The man muttered, his eyes puzzling over the personal nature of the question.

"That can be fixed once you return from Nara." He turned to face the room. "I have just the girl for you to meet. She is extraordinary."

"Thank you." The commander adjusted his wrinkled shirt. "Did you say I'm going to Nara?"

"Yes. You're here because I'm sending you on a special assignment—a hunt for the American."

"But shouldn't the matter be handled by the regional police bureau for that area?"

Masami Ishi knew he was exceeding his jurisdictional mandate, but he'd be damned if a mere boy was going to rob him of his chance to retire in luxury. This truth could never be revealed, so a lie would have to do, and the popular media had supplied him with all the ammunition he needed. He walked around and half sat on the desk's front edge. "I'm going to tell you something that you need to keep only between us."

The commander stood a bit straighter.

"I've been coordinating with the Public Security Investigation Agency. They've had Max Travers under surveillance for a while. It appears that he's working with one or more terrorist groups in this country." He patted a fake file lying thick on the desk. "In fact, they were just getting ready to arrest him when the burglary incident occurred."

"Why would he be working with terrorist groups?" The commander seemed skeptical, but Masami Ishi could tell that he wanted to believe.

"Money."

"Are the burglary and the Izu incident both related to this?"

"At this point, it's unclear." Masami Ishi punched a fist into his open hand. "But if we can get him alone, we may be able to get some details—names, places, dates, that sort of thing. And this all has to be done very quietly, so the other terrorists don't get spooked."

"What about the American government?"

Masami Ishi laughed. "If their government can keep prisoners indefinitely at Guantanamo Bay, then they'll have little cause to complain about us holding Mr. Travers for a short period before laying formal charges."

"Yes, I understand, sir. But why Nara?"

"A phone call came in this morning. There was an attack at a private residence just outside the city last night. The woman of the house reported it, and she gave Max Travers' name. It looks like he was there, along with several *Yakuza.*"

"But that doesn't add up. The gangsters appeared to be chasing him on the Izu Peninsula."

"I'm sure it will all make sense in time." The conversation needed to be wrapped up before many more questions could be asked. "Perhaps once we catch him, we can figure it out. An airplane is being readied to take you to Osaka. Find him!"

"And my team?"

"No. Too many of us arriving at once could draw the attention of the local authorities. Only you will go for now. We need to keep this under wraps. I'll inform my counterpart in Osaka when the time is right."

"Shouldn't the Public Security Investigation Agency have men working to find him? It's a very unusual request, sir. I'm not sure that—"

"Stop!" Masami Ishi pushed up from his half-seated position, his eyes bulging far more than normal. As he stepped forward, his comb-over slid down his forehead, adding to his semi-crazed look. "Are you questioning me in a matter of national security?"

"Of course not!" The commander bowed low.

"Good! Now get some clothes and get on the damned plane." He moved closer to the younger officer. "And if I hear that you've spoken of this to anyone, I'll have your head on my desk."

"I understand." The commander bowed again.

"Oh, and once you're back, I'll make that introduction. Trust me. You'll like her."

THE NARA community police office was showing its age. A cluster of creaky metal desks, piled high with paper, were pressed one against another. Chipped linoleum tiles covered the floor, and the walls hadn't seen fresh paint in a decade.

In tourist brochures, the city was celebrated as the first capital of a unified Japan. The reality was that thirteen hundred years had passed since then. Regardless of the UNESCO World Heritage stamp, it was a quiet little backwater town in a country filled with dazzling mega-cities.

The plainclothes officer excused himself from the smoke-filled central room. Heading for the toilet, he slipped out a side door and down the lane. Pulling a calling card from his pocket, he eased into a nearby telephone booth.

A growly voice picked up on the second ring. "Yes."

"I have information that will be very valuable to your boss." He paused briefly before continuing. "And I was hoping I could get paid more this time."

The response was brushed with disdain. "Listen, I don't make those decisions."

The policeman was silent.

"Are you still there? If not, I'm going back to sleep."

The officer sighed while he stared from the booth at a half-dozen kids riding by on bikes. "All right. A woman came into the station this morning to report a late-night break-in. She said that several men invaded her country home. It appears that one of the men was involved in a fight—and he lost. She turned in a bloody wallet. The identification gave his name—Jun Hirano."

"And where is Hirano-*san* now?"

"I don't know. Officers have gone out to the house, but they haven't reported back yet."

"Is that all?"

"Yes. But please make sure to tell Oto that this time I could really use more money."

"Yeah, sure." The man's snort was cut off by the buzz of the disconnected line.

CHAPTER
FIFTY-FIVE

THE MASSIVE eight-hundred-year-old Nandaimon Gates welcomed the most recent band of visitors pouring off a seemingly endless stream of air-conditioned coaches. Two immense *Niomon* Guardians, their snarling faces and bulging muscles carved from wood, towered over the flow of people coming and going. A bright procession of orange-robed priests moved single file down the wide stone walkway leading up to the Todai Buddhist Temple. The rare display resulted in a touristic frenzy of jostling, gawking, and picture-taking.

Vincent pulled unnoticed into the slipstream of a group of Germans. Many of them were smoking unfiltered cigarettes, and there was a great deal of finger pointing as they approached the curving dual eaves of the world's largest wooden structure.

The group moved into the temple through the gaping left entrance, while Vincent broke away and stepped over the threshold of the entrance to the right. A forty-five-foot bronze Buddha rose above the group's tour guide, who was frenetically trying to pull his flock back together. His Germanic shouts echoed in the cavernous chamber but were ignored by the amateurs circling the 550-ton statue, each photographer searching for the perfect shot.

Vincent strolled among the temple's shops before stepping past the clearly marked No Entry sign. He made his way out of the building's side door, undetected.

It had been a stroke of early-morning luck when he'd begun a conversation with an elderly man sitting on a bench outside the city's tourist office. The octogenarian informed him that "Old Ben Takeda wouldn't be at home on a Saturday morning." The man spoke between puffs on the stem of a bamboo *Kiseru* pipe. "Takeda-*san* teaches painting classes. Today I think he's on the lawn behind Todai-ji. Nice view, and not so many annoying foreigners getting in the way."

Just ahead of Vincent, a set of stairs led down to the temple's back lawn. Standing at the top, he counted at least twenty-five people scattered on the grass below, parked behind matching easels. Their heads intermittently peered over their work as they gathered glimpses of the imposing structure.

Vincent placed an oversized wad of chewing gum into his mouth and descended the steps. He focused his mind back to the blue-collar accent he'd been practicing earlier that morning. It was important to get this impersonation over with as quickly as possible—less time for questions. Approaching one of the female painters at the front of the group, he made sure to speak in rapid English between smacks on the gum.

"Hey there! I'm looking for a Mr. Ben Takeda. Do you know where I can find him?"

The woman shrugged, her face clearly conveying a lack of understanding.

Vincent knew it was important to appear ignorant of the obvious signals, so he raised his voice while over-enunciating on the second attempt. "Ta-ke-da-san! *Ben Ta-ke-da!*"

"Aaaaah!" The women smiled with recognition and motioned toward a slight man at the back of the group. He was hunched over a canvas, providing instruction to a nodding student.

The small man eyed Vincent warily before straightening up. "I'm Ben Takeda."

Vincent sidestepped his way past the whispering members of the class. As he approached, he stuck his arm straight out and formed the biggest grin he could make. "I hate to interrupt your class, but I could sure use your help."

Ben vibrated from the vigorous handshake. "What can I do for you?"

"My name is Charles Travers, and I'm looking for my son. I heard he may be visiting you."

"Max is your son?"

"Yes, he is. I came all the way from California looking for him." Vincent chewed his gum, noting a slight flexing in the man's shoulders.

"What a pleasure." Ben said. "Max mentioned to me once that you're a fervent soccer fan."

"Absolutely! Best sport going."

"Yes, yes. American football is good, but soccer is much better."

"I couldn't agree more." Vincent tapped his watch with his index finger, unclear where the small man was going with his strange banter. "I hate to change the subject, but it's urgent I find Max. I've been to his house in Tokyo and talked with his roommates. I've also visited his school and spoken with a Mr. Murayama. Nice older man. He told me that I might be able to find my boy here, with you."

The slight man eyed him blandly. "May I ask why you're looking for him so urgently?"

"We haven't heard from him in weeks—his mama and me—and, well, Martina's taken ill. If he comes home, it would really make his mama very happy. It may be her last wish."

"Well, I can tell you he was here, but he left yesterday."

"Dammit! I need to find him, Mr. Takeda. Do you know where he was going?"

"Back to Tokyo." Ben crossed his arms. "I'm sure if you return, you will find him there."

"I knew I should have stayed and waited for him. Thank you very much." Vincent stepped forward, grasping him in a bear hug, triggering snickers from the surrounding students. "Thank you very much." He kept his hands attached to the Ben's shoulders as he pulled back. "Tokyo. You're sure he said he was going back to Tokyo."

Ben's reply was flustered. "Yes . . . yes. That's what he told me."

"All right, then." Vincent let go and straightened up. "Sorry for interrupting your class."

"Not at all."

VINCENT slid into the driver's seat of his Avis rental car. A flick of his fingers pushed the blanket from the passenger's seat to the floor. He plugged a gray metal box into the cigarette lighter and connected it to his laptop through

241

the USB port. As he inserted an earbud into his left ear, he powered on the receiver. This latest UHF circuitry wouldn't be on the market for another five years or so. The advanced technology provided drift-free operation along with excellent range.

You're a liar, Ben Takeda.

The monitor on the laptop blinked awake, invoking the digital scanning tools, causing the earpiece to crackle. Within moments an outside conversation burst forth. The silver pen resting in Ben's jacket pocket was doing its job.

Vincent listened.

"You're doing much better this week. The brush strokes are showing more feeling."

"Thank you, *Sensei*. It's easy to paint in such a powerful place."

"But remember that purpose comes from within. Never be afraid of your own power."

"Yes, *Sensei*. I won't forget."

CHAPTER
FIFTY-SIX

M AX'S HAND found his face as his bleary mind pulled itself awake from the nightmare; which of Thick Neck's stories was the truth?

A uniformed station attendant was kicking at his feet, forcing him to lift his cramped neck away from the wall where he'd drifted off. Every muscle in his body ached, and he was exhausted. Following the serpentine flow of the river into Nara had taken most of the night. The flashlight's battery had given out after a few hours. He'd stumbled into ruts and fallen over logs. The cuts, bruises, and dirt on his forearms and shins gave evidence of the journey. But at least he was alive.

The chubby station attendant was vocalizing his displeasure. He kicked Max's feet again.

"Yes. Yes," Max said, groaning. "*Wakarimashita!* No sleeping here. I understand."

He stood to his full height as smarting ribs joined in to accompany the pain from his throbbing ankle. The station attendant backed away warily and watched as he shouldered the daypack.

The Osaka Station corridor disappeared into the distance in either direction. It didn't really matter which way he walked. He just needed to get some food and kill time until the travel agencies opened. Calling the airlines directly hadn't worked. Nobody on the domestic travel desk could speak enough English.

The holiday week was in full bloom, and it seemed the entire country was on the move. The corridor teemed with travelers, families with children in tow, and cooing couples off for some holiday fun. In fact, it was so busy that there were no seats available on any southbound Bullet Trains for the next two days. Using local trains for the journey would take much too long. The ferries to Okinawa were also jammed full. The situation was growing increasingly desperate.

The trailing attendant eventually lost interest and vanished as Max limped away.

Soon, a deserted side room with public telephones appeared. His paranoia had reached new heights, and he glanced suspiciously around for any police before moving into the dead-end space. He dialed the Okinawa number and slid to the floor, listening as the number rang repeatedly. On the fourth ring, he sighed, knowing the call was headed for the answering machine again.

Suddenly there were sharp scuffling sounds as if the receiver on the other end was being dragged across gravel. Muffled cursing could be heard. Jeff's froglike voice whispered into the line, "Has there been a death I should know about?"

Max gripped the receiver tighter. "Jeff! Man, I can't believe I finally got you."

"Maaaax." A raspy cough followed. "Bro—how's it going?"

"Not so great." Just speaking the words to a friendly ear brought relief.

"Really? Was that you calling here this morning?"

"Yeah. Why didn't you answer?"

"We hit this great beach party. So, what's up, bro?"

"It's a long story, but I'm in trouble, and I need your help."

"Sure, man."

"I need to stay with you for a while."

"Great, but I have to warn you that my domicile is what one might call cozy. Objectively speaking, man, it's kinda cramped, but you're more than welcome."

In the background, Max could hear sheets rustling, followed by a giggling female voice. "Thanks, buddy. I'm in Osaka right now. Trying to get a ticket to Okinawa is almost impossible."

"Yeah, the Golden Week curse." Jeff's voice pulled away from the phone. "Hang on, babe, I'm talking here." The distant giggling continued.

Max wanted to unload the ordeal of the past few days, but the timing was wrong, Jeff was clearly distracted. "I'll keep you posted once I get a ticket—let you know my arrival time."

"Sounds cool, brother." Jeff's voice pulled away again. "Hey . . . hey . . . don't touch the phone!" A woman's voice could be heard.

"You sound busy. I'll let you go."

"Okay, buddy. Keep in touch."

The call ended with a raucous surge of high-pitched laughter. Max reached up, replacing the receiver, and suddenly, abruptly, he missed Tomoko very, very much.

IT would be another half hour before the travel agencies opened, and Max desperately needed a distraction. Unzipping the daypack, he retrieved the second diary. The exterior was bound in a simple dark blue cloth, very different from the leather splendor of the first volume.

While examining the book's spine, a folded paper slipped out and drifted to the tiled floor next to him. It was yellowed with age, and the inside surface displayed three separate grids with a line of numbers running along the bottom and another down the right side of each grid. The look was similar to the mathematical game of *Sudoku* that had people hunched over in coffee shops and on trains, but it wasn't exactly the same. It was impossible to tell if the paper even belonged with the diary, or if it had simply been Ben's bookmark. Max flipped it over. Numbers and letters were also written on the four outside edges:

N 26° 11' 13" – E 127° 40' 36" – N 26° 11' 9" – E 127° 40' 30"

A shiver shook his shoulders and spiraled down his backbone. They looked like coordinates, but to what? Could this be what he had been sent to find?

He knew he'd have to get to the Internet to find out what the numbers meant—Google Earth could help—but it would have to wait until later, maybe after the travel agency. Max stared at the paper before folding and reinserting it between the pages. He flipped to the beginning of the diary and read.

TWO and a half years have passed since the emperor surrendered. On August 15, 1945, the Imperial voice crossed the airwaves in order to stop the terrible bombs that slaughtered our innocent countrymen in Hiroshima and Nagasaki. The wounds are still exposed and infected. The horror is too dreadful to think on.

I have seen firsthand the destruction inflicted on Tokyo. The once beautiful streets and gardens now lay in ruins. The city's heart is burned out. Noble veterans in shaggy uniforms line the streets, armed only with begging bowls. Gangs of children with dirty faces run between the shacks bordering the muddy streets.

Existence has become difficult. Shortages of food and scarcity of electricity have left most citizens cold and hungry, while sitting in the dark. Even now, survival for many is not guaranteed. Thankfully, my wife and children have been spared much of the hardship that has befallen my cousins.

I am no longer royal. The title for me is gone, but the flesh and the former deeds remain the same. My nights are still haunted by the voices of the past. I have no means to lay them to rest. There is no way I can think of to right the wrongs.

General MacArthur's tentacles, with the blessing of America's President Truman, have spread and infected every corner of this country. The octopus has captured the fish and is slowing consuming it.

Military trials are done, and the new constitution has been approved. Large corporate groups have been made to divide.

A Socialist coalition government was elected last year. The new prime minister is Christian—in a country where Shinto and Buddhism are the common beliefs.

But I still have old friends in high places, and they have been whispering to me, telling me things that should not be revealed. Golden Lily has been found. The earth is giving up her secrets. The emperor's grand plan is being used against us. Ideals are being bought and sold. Lies and corruption are everywhere. Bribes are making the new politicians and bureaucrats rich. Elections are being controlled. Even as I write this, a secret campaign to purchase generations of compliance is being forged.

USING the travel agent's telephone, Max left a message after the sound of the beep. "Toshi, it's Max. I need help. It's a long story. I found the diary's caretaker, but the *Yakuza* followed me. I don't know how, but they did it. I'm stuck in Osaka, and I need to get to Okinawa fast. All the flights are sold out. I was hoping you might know somebody at the airlines who could help me get a ticket. Anyway, I'll try to call again later."

The travel agent took back the phone and re-cradled it. Her perfume was overpowering, which was probably good, since he badly needed a shower. He was purposefully dragging out the meeting, hoping for a little luck. "So, you're sure there's nothing? No flights today or tomorrow? Maybe something came free in the last few minutes."

The agent sighed. "Very sorry, Mr. Ma-ku-su. Everything full."

It was the fourth agency he'd been to, and the answers were all the same. His sense of panic grew larger. The warm office air pressed in around him; he needed to get outside. Squeezing through the crowd of people gathered in the tiny space, he finally made it to the door and onto the sidewalk. Pacing back and forth, he took deep, controlled breaths. It seemed pointless to try a fifth.

If only I knew Tomoko was safe, then I could lie low and go to Okinawa in a few days.

A thumping sound made his raw nerves jump. Turning round, he saw a shaggy-haired boy slapping a palm against the inside of the window, waving for him to return.

Pushing his way back inside, Max could hear the agent's voice. "Come, Mr. Ma-ku-su."

His hopes soared. The crowd parted, and he stumbled through the sea of arms and legs before catching himself on the desk's edge. "You found something?"

The agent held out the receiver, a quizzical expression on her face. "Telephone for you."

The situation felt strange, and he hesitated before speaking. "Hello?"

A woman's soft voice sounded in his ear; her diction perfect. "Mr. Travers, I'm Toshi's secretary. He asked me to return your call."

"Is Tomoko safe!" Max blurted. "Is she there at the house with you? Is she okay?"

"I don't know sir. I'm at the office," the woman explained with cold efficiency. "However, I was asked to pass along a message. Toshi has a plan to help you, but he stressed that you must be aware of the potential risk."

"I'm desperate!"

"Then write down this address—it's the airport you need to go to."

CHAPTER
FIFTY-SEVEN

THE TORA-FUGU Fish Company delivery truck swerved erratically through the freeway traffic. Brakes screeched and horns blared as it squeezed into the fast lane between a red sports car and a minivan. The *Yakuza* driver was struggling to keep up with Oto Kodama's Mercedes sedan, which was rocketing westward.

SEALED inside, Tomoko watched as Hiro kicked his foot against the metal side of the truck's cargo hold. He was shouting in vain, trying to be heard over the engine's gunning noise. "Stop driving like an idiot!" He staggered sideways as the driver made another unpredictable lane change.

Stacked boxes formed descending layers along the cargo area's front wall. They vibrated and jumped with each swerving motion. The odor of seafood permeated the confined space.

Tomoko crouched against the opposite wall, trying to stifle her involuntary moans each time the vehicle lurched violently. Her white-knuckled hands clutched the free end of a secured rope—it was the only thing keeping her from tumbling across the rancid floorboards. The bump on her head was pulsing, fueled by her racing heart, and it was just a matter of time before she vomited.

"Keep hanging onto the rope," Hiro yelled. "We should be out of city traffic soon."

Tomoko raised her sarcastic voice against the rumble. "Thanks for the advice."

Along the front wall, a wide box groaned as it slipped from its place and tipped precariously on edge. Tomoko caught the movement from the corner of her eye, turning in time to see the heavy cargo plummeting straight for her.

Hiro attempted an interception as the truck executed another unpredictable swerve. His feet caught up, sending him stumbling to his knees. His injured right hand collided with the floor and he shrieked in pain, instinctively clutching the wound to his chest, causing his face to hammer hard against the wooden floor.

Attached to the rope, Tomoko swung her slender frame away, barely missing the box as it crashed down and tumbled past, finally coming to rest against the rear door.

Swinging back into place, she exhaled a sigh of relief while her moaning captor lay fetal on the floor, motionless. He should have been the object of her hatred for what he'd done. Yet surprisingly, she found herself moved by his pain. He seemed different from the other *Yakuza*, thoughtfully intelligent, and even aware of his own parasitic place in society. The hoodlums who formed the base of the group's pyramid structure didn't place great stock in kindness or literacy. It was no wonder the others disliked him.

Soon, the vehicle's motion smoothed out. Presumably, the traffic had lightened. As Hiro predicted, they must have finally reached the main highway between Tokyo and Osaka.

Moving onto all fours, Tomoko crawled across the shuddering floor. She touched his shoulder, and felt him tense. "Come on. Sit up. Let me look at your hand."

"I'll get up on my own." The wiry *Yakuza* kept his right arm clutched to his chest as he twisted himself into a sitting position.

Tomoko gasped at the sight of the open gash on his left cheek. The fall on the rough floor had torn away a ragged inch-long strip of flesh. A bloody trail ran along his face.

"What's wrong?"

She did her best to hold back another wave of nausea. "Nothing . . . you've just got a cut. Let's move over to the boxes." Tomoko held herself against him as they cautiously crouch-stepped their way toward the front of the hold.

Hiro settled onto the floor. Resting his back against a box.

"Do you have any medical supplies I can use?" she asked.

He opened his mouth, then suddenly stopped, staring into her eyes as though he was seeking an answer. Finally he spoke. "I have a knife and bandages in my back pocket."

He shifted his weight, allowing her to lean in close and wrap herself around him, one arm grasping while the other worked as an anchor. Anyone unexpectedly opening the truck door would have sworn they'd caught the two in a lovers' embrace. Tomoko suddenly became aware of the fact that she hadn't bathed in three days.

Her fingers slipped between the layers of denim. "Got them." She leaned back quickly. "I need something to wipe away the blood." Opening the box next to her, she pulled out a swath of heavy brown packing paper. It would have to do. "If I do this right, the scar will be small."

His eyes remained downcast as he spoke. "Thank you, but it won't matter, anyway."

"What are you talking about? Of course it matters."

"I'm not . . ."

Tomoko tore open the plastic pouch holding the bandage. She could tell that he wanted to say something. "What? Tell me what you were going to say. It's not like I'll pass it on to anyone." She made a sweeping motion to illustrate the empty compartment.

There was a pause before Hiro spoke. "I'm not going to live for long, so don't spend time worrying about a scar."

She wrinkled her brow, confused. "I thought I was the one worrying about survival."

"Your chances are better than mine."

Gingerly, she applied the bandage. The truck's shuddering made it a difficult task. "How do you know that?"

"I overheard Oto's guards talking to the sentry. The plan is for me to take the fall for the problems we've had in retrieving the diary." Hiro scowled. "Once it's found, I'll be killed. Then the police can blame me for everything, and Oto can walk away."

"'Problems'? That's how you describe murder?" Tomoko felt her chest grow tight as her eyes welled with tears. "Mrs. Kanazawa was my friend!

Her death isn't just a 'problem' that needs to be solved." She forced herself to concentrate on smoothing the bandage's edge. "It's all insane. This whole thing is crazy."

"I'm very sorry. My *Sempai* Jun is not—"

Tomoko's voice filled with righteous anger. "I mean, how can you kill and . . . and steal . . . then go home and read books like *Cry Freedom*? Stories of people with courage who take risks—who try to do something with their lives."

"I never killed your friend!" Hiro's eyes flared. "I've never murdered anyone. The fact that I'm *Yakuza* and what I have to do . . . those things were dictated to me. I have no choice. My path was laid out since before I was born into a *Yakuza* family."

Tomoko picked up the knife and slapped the remaining supplies together, tossing them into his lap. "That's a nice, clean excuse. People fight to change their lives every day. You may be tough on the outside, but maybe it's your inside you need to worry about. Instead of just reading about courageous people, you should try being one sometime!"

"I tried to change once." He said feebly.

The truck swayed as Tomoko turned and crawled back to the loose end of the rope. Parking her back against the wall, she pulled the frayed yellow fibers over her shoulder.

Hiro lowered his face again. "It's too late now, anyway."

"Look at me. *Look at me!*"

He lifted his head a bit.

"Anyone can change, even you. It's never too late to try."

Hiro nodded back.

She couldn't be sure that it wasn't her imagination, but for the first time she could recall, the edges of his mouth seemed to tilt slightly upward.

CHAPTER
FIFTY-EIGHT

STEPPING GRACEFULLY from the elevator, Yoko eyed the cheaply tiled floor in the windowless corridor and thought that it would have been nice to hire legal counsel with a better location. A display of opulence always made people more comfortable when they were handing over large cash sums.

Nevertheless, the paralegal work was being done for half the usual rate, and all of the shares had been presold to her "ladies," anyway. Getting the signatures was just a formality when the group arrived in thirty minutes.

Halfway down the hall, she turned into the women's washroom. She checked her appearance in the full-length mirror. The new cobalt-blue Versace suit looked fabulous, and she knew it. Her hands smoothed the skirt and she made a last-minute adjustment to her blouse. A shiver of excitement crossed her shoulders.

In a few hours, this deal will be closed. The gallery will be filled with smiling people drinking champagne, and I will be congratulated on my latest triumph.

Behind her, a lone figure stepped into view. Yoko could see the old woman in the mirror's reflection. A simple flowered scarf covered her head.

That face . . . it can't be . . . she's dead!

The vision dragged time backward. Her mother's words were sharp and stained with worry. She was wielding a brush through Yoko's hair. "Pull yourself together. This is not the time to act like a vain schoolgirl. Focus on staying in character. Remember to leave the door slightly open when you exit his hotel suite. Once you go out for dinner, I'll come in and take the jewelry. We need this money to take care of our family and pay down the debt your father left behind. Don't make a mistake, child. Our survival depends on it."

Yoko blinked and the stern maternal figure was gone. Instead, she found herself staring at the withered face of the building's cleaning lady.

The woman edged away from the doorway. "I'll come back later."

Yoko turned. "I'm finished here." She shook off the mental cobwebs and stepped around the cleaning pail at her feet.

This is the last job. Get it done, and you never have to play this game again.

Continuing to the end of the hall, she came to the two-room office of Ito & Ito. An engraved plastic sign was glued to the metal door. Mr. Ito Sr. had passed away in the late nineties, and Mr. Ito Jr. was the only lawyer now occupying the space. He had a skeleton-like appearance befitting a mortician, with sunken cheeks and dark circles around his eyes.

Yoko tried the door handle, but oddly it was locked. Turning an ear, she noted voices inside. They sounded raised and angry. Nonetheless, her manicured finger pressed the buzzer, and soon the pinprick of light coming through the peephole went dark. Seconds later, the door cracked open and a harried-looking Mr. Ito Jr. slipped out into the hallway. He was wringing his hands and looking paler than usual.

"Hello, *Sensei*. It's good to see you."

His protruding Adam's apple drew her eye. It always seemed so vast on his slender neck. But there was no time for his idiosyncrasies. Her tone was demanding. "Why is your office door locked?"

"Well . . . we seem to have a situation."

"What situation? It's critical for everything to go as planned. My ladies will be arriving soon and I have a gallery opening taking place at six." She could feel her blood pressure rising. "If you're holding out for more money—"

The lawyer waved his slender hands in the air. "No, no! You misunderstand me. Several guests have arrived early, and they have in their possession a letter that has . . ." He appeared to be struggling with phrasing the sentence. ". . . it has upset them very much."

"A letter from whom?"

"It's a translation, but the original letter was written by one of your English teachers named Max. It contains serious accusations against you." Mr. Ito's head dipped like a thief caught with a hand in the cookie jar.

"But how?" She suddenly felt as though an earthquake had struck the building. "Did you tell them the letter is full of lies?"

"I tried, but they seem convinced that it's true."

You're a pathetic excuse for a man.

Yoko straightened her posture and inhaled sharply. "Then I'll have to persuade them to believe otherwise. They are my ladies, after all. They will believe whatever I say."

"Please, you don't understand."

"Step aside!" She pressed past the simpering man, opened the door, and strode into the office. The picture inside stopped her in her tracks. Almost a dozen women and their husbands lined the waiting room's walls, some sitting, some standing in clusters. Several women looked as if they'd been crying, while the accusing eyes of all the others fell directly upon her.

Palpable hostility pierced the air as Mr. Ito's voice whispered from behind her, "Their husbands also came for support. I tried to warn you."

One man stepped forward from the group. He thrust a single sheet of paper into Yoko's hand. "You have some explaining to do!"

The room was filled with hushed breathing as she skimmed the document. Her raised plea broke the silence. "This is clearly fabricated! Max was caught stealing from me. The police are looking for him. I didn't want to worry anyone until he was found." The expressions in the room remained stoic and several heads continued shaking their betrayal.

This can't be happening. These are my ladies. I have to get them to believe me. They can sway their husbands. Masami Ishi will want his money. I cannot go to jail.

Another man stepped forward and spoke up. "I checked the invoices my wife paid over the last three years." He raised an open hand. "On five occasions you charged us for English classes while we were away. Other times we were double or triple-billed."

"I . . . I'm sure it was a simple mistake. Every business makes a few errors. I'll refund the money." She scanned the hostile room. "*I'm* not the bad person." Yoko shook the paper. "These are all lies from the mouth of a thief!"

A third man spoke. "It doesn't matter. That *Gaijin's* letter was just the catalyst. We've compared the stories you've been telling our wives. There are too many inconsistencies and half truths. I've spent enough time in business to spot a con artist. You won't be getting any more of my money." He barked an order to his wife. "Let's go."

Mr. Ito Jr. scuttled away from the door.

The strain registered in Yoko's anguished voice. "Your children's welfare is at the center of everything I do." *I need my new life.*

The women gathered their coats and handbags as a stream of silent couples exited the room. Yoko moved from one familiar face to another. She searched desperately for allies, but found none. Downcast eyes refused to meet her gaze. "I've cared for your children like they were my own. Please don't do this. I can get you copies of the police report. Please believe me." The room soon emptied and the sound of footsteps faded away.

FROM her position in the hall, a mop in one hand, the cleaning woman watched through the office doorway as the elegant lady in blue collapsed to the floor.

CHAPTER
FIFTY-NINE

THE COMMANDER'S shadow stretched across the cracked tarmac. He watched the coral sun begin its slide below the western horizon. Dusk was settling on Osaka's Yao Airport. A cell phone rested against his ear as he waited to speak to a taxi dispatcher. Beside him, a Cessna's engine pinged and popped, cooling off after the short hop across the country.

The Class Two private facility was quiet, probably since its dual runways could at most accommodate light jets.

The pilot climbed from the cabin with a dark-blue duffel bag. He apologized again for the mechanical delay that had kept them waiting on the ground in Tokyo for over six hours.

The commander acknowledged the excuse before entering the adjacent hangar. The waiting room at the building's front was empty. Setting the duffel bag on the nearest bench, he retrieved a brown case from inside and glanced around before withdrawing his police-issued handgun. There was no point needlessly drawing anyone's attention. It slid smoothly into the leather harness inside his jacket.

Moving outside, he lit a cigarette and paced like a caged animal. His thumb and forefinger rubbed nervously along the twin sides of his mustache. The day was not going as planned. He should have picked up his rental car and been in Nara hours ago.

THE commander's second cigarette was almost down to the filter when the taxicab finally appeared. Pulling into the darkening lot, the car's back door popped open as the cabbie apologized for the delay.

The duffel bag went in first. "I've had a day full of excuses. Just drive."

The two-lane access road hugged the wire fence running along the airport's perimeter. The commander stared steadfastly out the cab's window. A jet plane had landed, and he watched its outline as it approached the end of the concrete runway. It pulled onto the taxiway before rotating 180 degrees to sit facing back the way it had just come. The white, pointy nose was just back from the edge of the runway's blast pad.

Squeezing the muscles in his shoulders, he glanced ahead and watched as the outline of a man appeared, walking on the grassy edge of the road. And he thought how odd it was that someone would be walking toward the airport in the dark. The high beams briefly illuminated the lone figure before dropping him back into shadow.

The commander let out a short, astonished grunt and spun around in his seat. Hastily unzipping the duffel bag, his hands dug inside. He yelled for the driver to turn on the light as his fingers groped for a folder. Yanking it from the bag, he scanned the single sheet of paper inside. The American's headshot stared back at him.

He pounded his fist against the glass while grasping for his gun. "Stop! *Stop* the damned car!"

MAX heard the taxi's tires screech behind him. Without slowing his pace, he snapped his head around to see the red taillights fifty yards back. Something wasn't right. The car was glowing from the inside, and he thought he could see someone staring out the back window.

His ankle complained as he increased his pace to a jog.

The straining, high-pitched whine of the car's engine signaled that it was backing up quickly. Brakes squealed while it executed a three-point turn. Max broke into a sprint. Up ahead, the road veered to the left, and he could see the airport's fence line.

I won't be able to keep this up for long.

The car was now racing toward him. Its headlights illuminated the galvanized poles of the fence's perimeter. Max cut to the right and slammed into the meshing at full force. He could hear the car door opening behind him. A hostile voice shouted for him to stop.

His fingers gripped the cool metal while he struggled to get a foothold, and he cursed as his foot slipped from the fence and hit the ground. He jammed it harder the second time. From behind, the angry voice was drawing closer. The fence was only six feet high, but a line of barbed wire stretched across the top. Max managed to slip his hands between the razor-sharp barbs, and he got one foot on the shaky wire before chancing a backward glance. The silhouette of the shouting man was twenty yards back. He was bathed in the car's bright headlights. Max watched with shock as the man dropped to one knee and raised both his hands.

Oh shit—not another gun!

There was no warning shot as a bullet punched into the fence. Max felt himself hurtling forward, spinning, before the daypack bore the impact in the tall grass. Piercing pain shot up his spine, but there was no time to stop. A second bullet kicked up a nearby dirt plume. He scrambled to his feet and ran. Behind him the fence rattled as the stranger struggled to climb over.

The Christmas lights on the taxiway ahead drew him on, toward the plane.

Learjet 40XR—please be the right one.

His ankle was screaming as he raced across the grass toward the back of the parked jet. Charging along the plane's side and ducking under the wing, he narrowly missed a third bullet, which ricocheted off the concrete near his feet.

Ahead, the plane's front hatch sat open. Max vaulted the two steps before tumbling inside and smashing into the far wall. He lay in a heap on the floor, struggling to catch his breath.

A flight officer stepped from the cockpit. Max stared up at his round face and saucer-wide eyes.

He doesn't know me. I'm in the wrong plane!

The idling twin turbines revved louder and the jet crept forward as the officer closed the exterior door. When he turned back, he spoke the single word "seatbelt" before retreating into the cockpit.

Max crawled into a beige leather seat. Blood was streaming from his left hand as he struggled with the metal clasp at his waist. Miraculously, he had escaped the bullets, but the barbed wire had torn a gash down the center of his palm. He pinched the wound closed and held it. Peering cautiously out the side window, he searched the darkness. The gunman was nowhere in sight.

The aircraft picked up speed before rising swiftly into the air. It banked sharply to the south, its left wing dipping dramatically.

Max could hear Toshi's reassuring voice shouting from the cockpit. "Sorry. We took off against the air traffic—had to get out of the way. I'll have trouble explaining that to the aviation officials." Toshi was grinning from ear to ear as he stepped into the main cabin. "I'm going to put that into a video game." The grin vanished instantly from his face. "You're hurt!"

"I'm okay, really."

Toshi grabbed a nearby towel and wrapped it around the injured hand. "Who was the man chasing you?"

"I can't be sure. He saw me walking toward the airport and just came after me." Max shook his head, exhaling frustration. 'But I couldn't see his face."

"Hold the pressure while I bandage it."

"It's not only the *Yakuza* and the police looking for me now."

"Who else?"

"I'm not sure, but the guy is American—someone named Lloyd Elgin. Also, one of the *Yakuza* caught up with me in Nara—he told me Tomoko was dead, but then he said she was okay."

Toshi pulled gauze from an emergency medical kit. "Well, they did drive away with her."

"What?" Max bolted upright, his voice erupting. "How do you know?"

"Two days ago, when Tomoko left the house early, she triggered the motion sensors. I was very concerned for her safety, so followed to her parents' house." He paused to cut a strip of tape. "I couldn't return for you, otherwise I would have lost her trail. I was hoping you would wait for me to return before you left for Nara."

Max rubbed the ball of his good hand against the center of his chest, his fear crystallizing like a massive, crushing weight.

Toshi continued. "I was watching from a delivery truck. At the beginning, everything seemed all right. But eventually two men drove away with her in a Mercedes. I tried following, but they were lost in traffic."

Max's anguished face stared up at the cabin's arching roof. *This can't be happening.* "Turn the plane around! We have to go back and find her!" He could barely stay seated.

Toshi was still kneeling, and he pressed his hands together as if in prayer. "Where would we go, Max? Where would we start looking? You know how vast Tokyo is. It will not work, I guarantee. You will never find her unless they want you to." He shook his head. "There has to be another way."

A wave of nausea raced from Max's stomach to his chest. He squeezed his eyes shut and blew out great puffs of air, allowing the feeling to pass. "I have to stop this. I have to make this right."

"I understand your pain, I truly do, but your best action is to continue forward." Toshi stood. "If you go to the *Yakuza* with the diary but no map they could harm you both. What you need is to have something ready to exchange for her—and the more valuable, the better."

Max pondered the chilling words, letting them settle before he spoke again, unsure if he wanted to hear the answer to the question in his head. "How long do you think they'll hold onto her?"

"The risk becomes greater with time. My guess would be four, maybe five days, but it's just a guess. I have no way of knowing the criminal mind." Toshi shrugged and glanced forward to the cockpit. "I'm sorry, but I have to attend to some things. My copilot will finish with your wound."

"Just leave me the tape." Max shook his throbbing head. "You've already done so much. I owe you big time."

"I had planned a business trip to Taiwan, anyway. It's just a short detour." Toshi gave a tiny wink as he backed toward the cockpit. "Next stop—Okinawa."

CHAPTER
SIXTY

S ENATOR ANDREW McCloy's plaid slippers shuffled across his kitchen floor. The aroma of freshly brewed coffee wafting through the Washington, D.C., apartment had awakened him from a deep sleep. He poured a cup and took a seat at the kitchen table. Pressing a button on the telephone opened a secure connection to his encrypted voicemail.

Saturday's newspaper displayed the carnage of another bombing beneath a screaming headline, **DOZENS DIE IN BAGHDAD ATTACK**. He pushed the paper away. It was too early in the morning to stomach another story just like the one the day before.

Savoring the chicory in his coffee, the senator closed his eyes and listened to the first message. Vincent's voice was providing an update. Progress was being made, although it was slow. So far he had killed only once. The matter-of-fact tone could have been that of someone describing a trip to the grocery store. The man was a methodical machine without a conscience, built for the job. The message terminated with a single critical request.

The senator deleted the message and then proceeded to make a call of his own. He glanced dispassionately at the early morning hour displayed on the Swiss wall clock.

Ray Hylan's sleepy voice answered. "What do you want?"

"I just received an update from my guy in Japan. Do you remember that conversation we had about possibly needing your assistance at some point?"

"Yeah, sure."

"Good—because I believe that moment has arrived—and I need it fast."

S AYURI TAKEDA'S voice rose over the sound of creaking floorboards as Ben climbed the stairs to the second story. "Are you coming to bed?" she demanded.

"Just a moment." Ben's words echoed along the upstairs corridor. He pressed apart the paper-white *shoji* doors, backed out of his slippers, and entered the sparsely decorated bedroom. "The house seems so much emptier without Chiho's sweet voice, doesn't it?"

"Yes . . . and without the *Yakuza* as well." She was cocooned in her bed; the slim mattress with a generous duvet lay on the floor next to his.

BEN concentrated on changing into his nightclothes. He wasn't going to let Sayuri goad him into another argument about the previous night's excitement. And he certainly wasn't going to tell her about the strange American who had come looking for Max earlier in the day.

He moved a nearby ceramic bowl a bit closer and emptied his pockets. Dry paint flecks and slender brushes clattered into the container, along with a silver pen. Ben picked up the shiny object, noting its solid feel. He wasn't sure how it had arrived in his jacket pocket.

"Are you listening to me?"

"I'm sorry. I was trying to figure where this pen came from. It looks expensive." He laid the mysterious object next to the bowl before resuming the process of changing his clothes

Sayuri clicked her tongue in annoyance. "You never told me if you gave anything to the American boy," she said.

Ben sighed. She wasn't going to let him sleep until he confessed. His shirt slid over his head. "Yes. I let him have Prince Takeda's diary back—on loan. Are you satisfied?" There was no point making things worse right now by mentioning the second diary.

Her tone was sharp. "I knew it. How could you? There's so much at stake."

"Because, unlike you, I want to believe that some people in this world are good."

"You're too trusting."

Ben's voice rose almost to a shout. "And you do not trust enough. I would never do anything against the prince's plan. It's out of our hands now. If that boy can use the diary to save one girl's life while still guarding the secrets, then I believe Prince Takeda would approve. Remember, I know the pain of watching someone I love taken before my eyes. I don't wish that sentence upon anyone else."

Sayuri's voice grew subdued, chastened. "Then you sent him to Okinawa?"

"Yes." He finished changing before approaching her mattress and kneeling down. Her watery eyes gazed up at him as his fingers adjusted the duvet under her chin. "You are a wonderful wife for your concern and care." His palm stroked her flowing hair lying loose about her head. "If you don't trust Max, then please at least trust me."

Her chin nodded in silent consent. Ben leaned down and kissed her forehead.

A SHORT mile away, Vincent sat in a dark car. He smirked to himself and removed his earbud.

Okinawa, is it? I pegged you right, you liar.

He opened the driver's side door, allowing the night breeze from the mountain to flow inside. Vincent gathered the electronics off the passenger's seat and added them to the contents of the two duffel bags in the trunk before signaling a flashlight at the nearby line of trees.

Within moments, two brawny soldiers materialized near the car, both dressed in military fatigues. The taller man spoke. "Can we help you, sir?"

Vincent pointed down. "Pick up this kit and follow me."

Using the flashlight, he made his way to the nearby ridge top. On the wide-open plateau beneath a sea of bright stars sat a CH-53 Sea Stallion heavy-lift cargo helicopter. It was definite overkill for moving just him and his equipment. The Stallion could carry up to fifty-five troops at a time. Nevertheless, his message to the senator had asked for transport, and it had been provided.

My boss has influence.

The grass on the ridge bent low from the immense rotor swooping to life. Vincent charged underneath a wash of air and leaped up into the side doorway. The two camouflaged men nodded, wide-eyed and grinning.

Vincent shrugged his shoulders and shouted over the growing noise. "What?"

The taller one spoke. "We just aren't used to a Jody—I mean a civilian—being so agile. You're ex-military, right?"

Vincent realized his actions were betraying his cover, and his cold green eyes locked them in a stare. "Focus on the task at hand. Tell your pilot we're going to Okinawa—the main island."

The soldiers bristled with formality. "Yes, sir."

"I'm going to get some sleep. Wake me when we arrive."

Vincent made his way to the back of the thirty-foot cabin. The mission was now into its fourth day, exceedingly long for a Lloyd Elgin operation. Andrew McCloy would soon be growing angry and impatient. It was time to box in the quarry and end the game.

CHAPTER
SIXTY-ONE

Sunday, April 29

MAX CHECKED his pocket watch for what felt like the hundredth time; it was 1:07 a.m. The taxi driver had assured him that the address was correct, and for the exorbitant price charged, he hoped the guy was right. Knocking on the front door had produced no result. The house was dark and quiet. Shōwa Day had officially begun, and there was still no sign of Jeff.

He could smell the nearby ocean's salty tang, even if it wasn't visible. Sitting on the ground beneath the single outdoor light, he swatted at the bugs buzzing around in the muggy, semi-tropical air. His shirt was stuck to his back where it pressed against a concrete post. He watched a spider perched in an elaborate web suspended between the bungalow's exterior wall and a twenty-foot palm tree.

A maroon sedan drew his interest as it crawled past the house. Max stood and limped to the driveway's end. He was sure he'd seen that same car drive by thirty minutes before. Even if it was just his imagination playing tricks, he needed to stretch his stiff legs. Sitting on the stoop was causing his muscles to tighten. It was also providing too much time to conjure up a variety of horrible fates for Tomoko. In the distance, he observed the car's taillights turn and vanish from sight.

Looking back at the house, Max watched with surprise as the opaque vertical windows on both sides of the front door suddenly grew bright. He glanced up and down the silent street. That was odd, since nobody had come in from the road. The only other way in was the beach.

He walked up to the door and banged loudly. A slurring voice from inside yelled in response. "Come in, babe. I unlocked it already."

Turning the handle, Max stepped into a rectangular room housing both a kitchen to the left and an adjoining living room at the far end. Beyond the sofa were two plate glass windows looking over the illuminated waters of a kidney-shaped swimming pool. The butt of Jeff's shorts protruded from an open refrigerator. He was wearing an untucked shirt and no shoes. Max felt lightheaded with hunger as he watched his friend push plastic containers around in an obvious quest for food.

The voice reverberated inside the open fridge. "I know you're mad, baby, but every guy at the party was looking at her. She was barely wearing anything, and—" He turned and stopped in mid-sentence. His bloodshot eyes stared blankly for a moment before a wide grin spread across his surf-tanned face. "Hey, buddy!"

Despite the painful embrace, Max relished the incredible sense of relief as he felt himself locked in a bear-hug grip.

"Sorry, bro. I thought you were Rina. We had a scrap at a beach party, and she left. But she'll calm down in a couple days." Jeff stepped back. "So what? I move away three months and you go all *J-rock* on me with that short brown hair?" He laughed heartily. "When did you get in?"

"A couple of hours ago."

Jeff took a couple of tottering steps before steadying himself against the counter. "Why didn't you tell me? You could have come to the party. There were so many beautiful babes, although Tomoko might not have been too happy." He adjusted his shell necklace and placed a hand on his curly red hair, which was pulled into a ponytail, the ends bleached white from the sun.

It was clear that explaining the past few days would be pointless until a little sobriety took hold. But indulgence was par for the course with Jeff; he was brighter than most but lived completely and absolutely in the moment. "The flight was kind of . . . sudden," Max replied.

"Well, you're here now. Hey, put your bag down, 'cause I need to show you something. Follow me, bro." He turned and led the way through the living room and onto the outside patio, past the swimming pool. A waist-high gate sat in the middle of a concrete fence that ran along the property's back. The rusting hinges squeaked on opening. Continuing down a path carved through a dense grove of trees, he descended a short, steep trail that changed to sand at the bottom.

"Where are we going?" Max called out, struggling to keep up in the darkness.

"Have faith, amigo."

The salty breeze grew stronger as they made their way along a sandy path between patches of tall grass. Ahead, the beach glowed, illuminated by the homes running along its length. Jeff picked up the pace as they approached the water. Max raised his voice against the sound of the lapping surf. He could do without this game, whatever it was. "Where are you going?"

Jeff was laughing while dropping the shirt off his tanned back. "I hate to tell you, bro, but you stink—for real. And here's the biggest bathtub in the world." Hopping from foot to foot, he pulled off his clothes and raced naked into the black surge.

Max looked up and down the empty night beach. It had been days since he'd bathed.

Jeff's disembodied voice mocked him from the dark surf. "Afraid of the ocean? Didn't you do some scuba diving back home?"

Max noticed that his jeans were hanging loosely on his hips, making them easier to remove. Jeff continued to spout taunts at him as he charged into the tepid water. Salt water bit at the wound on his hand and stung his scrapes and cuts, but the pain passed quickly. The ebb and flow of the surging water felt almost healing.

"I'm telling you, buddy, you should quit your Tokyo job and move here. It's a way better life."

"I'd need to work out a few things first." Max straightened upright and briny water washed into his mouth. He spat it out. "Hey, are there sharks around here?"

"Bro, there are sharks everywhere. You just have to relax and learn to swim with them."

"Yeah." Max rotated onto his back again. "I'm learning that the hard way."

"THEY found me in Nara. They can find me here." The bitter recounting was sharp, but short lived, replaced by exhaustion. Max's head pressed back onto the sofa and as he spoke, his mouth felt detached from the rest of his body. "And since there's no map to the Philippine treasure, I need something other than just the diary to give the *Yakuza* in exchange for Tomoko. That is, if she's still alive." The words stabbed even as he spoke them.

"Don't talk crazy, man. She could be back home already. You may be worrying for nothing."

"I tried calling. There's no answer at her place."

"Even so, she's smart—that girl can talk her way into or out of anything." Jeff held out a fresh beer. "Here you go, buddy."

"I don't know, man—this is scary—on a whole new level." Max instinctively reached out, then stopped with his hand in midair. The bottle swung like a tempting pendulum, promising to numb the ache in his soul.

"It's cool and refreshing."

Max snapped his hand into a retreating fist. It wasn't the time to lose what little control he had left. "No, no thanks. I've had enough."

"Suit yourself." Jeff dropped back into his plush chair and pushed their recently cleaned plates and a half dozen empties to the far edge of the coffee table to make room for his feet. He was holding both diaries. "Bro, it's unbelievable what you've been through—*Yakuza* car chases, murder, a rooftop duel—all for these little books." He drank down the first beer and started on the second while slowly leafing through the pages. Noticing a protruding edge of loose paper, he pulled it free and opened it. "Is this your *Hanjie* puzzle?"

"Huh?" The reply was groggy.

Jeff extended his leg and tapped Max's knee with his toe. "Come on. Sleep time. We'll figure things out in the morning."

"Okay." Max peeled himself off the sofa. He swayed on his feet but managed to stay upright. "Even if I get rid of the *Yakuza*, what about the police? And what about Mr. Golden Lily?"

"Let it go for now." Jeff grabbed an arm, guiding the way to the adjacent room. "Don't worry, bro. Remember that you're talking to the dude who likes to swim with sharks."

Max fell forward onto the partially made bed, his mumbling lips barely moving. "Gonna remind you . . . you said that."

OUTSIDE, a male figure slipped from the passenger's door of a maroon car before sinking into the shadow along the front edge of the bungalow. Hundreds of cicadas chirping in the trees masked the sounds of his movement. Approaching the outdoor porch light, he unscrewed the bulb with a gloved hand, plunging the front yard into darkness.

Crossing the inky driveway, he knelt beside the motorcycle. His fingers squeezed through the bike's frame, attaching a stamp-sized magnetic device to the underside of the gas tank. Unless a complete overhaul was performed, the owner would never notice the ultra-small radio transmitter. The broadcast range was short, but it would have to do.

The man peered cautiously around before rising and jogging away unseen, swallowed by the night.

CHAPTER
SIXTY-TWO

TOMOKO'S RUMBLING stomach woke her from a half slumber. She felt so hungry that she barely noticed the reek of rotting fish infusing the truck's stale air. Hiro's shoulder was pressed against hers, beneath the heavy fibers of a single blanket. Together, they were nestled against the stack of boxes.

A brief, uncontrollable shiver ran through her body. She'd initially resisted sitting so close to Hiro. Yet somehow, he seemed more pathetic now that he was also a captive. He had become sullen and withdrawn, like a wounded animal waiting to die.

The truck had been parked for hours in the cool night air, and the temperature in the cargo box had plunged. Tomoko fought it for as long as she could. Cold and exhaustion finally forced her to relent and climb beneath the blanket. A few days earlier, she would never have believed it, but now she understood how anything was possible in perilous times.

A metallic latch groaned and the truck's back door notched open. Two plastic bottles rolled inward, before the door slammed shut again. Grabbing them, Hiro stuck one to his mouth and handed the other to Tomoko. The water felt miraculous sliding down her parched throat, even if it did taste mildly salty.

The truck rumbled to life and began to move. It was impossible to figure out where they were going, since they didn't know exactly where they were. Several times during the long night, they'd heard the sound of ambulance sirens, but it didn't help in determining their location. The Osaka area was home to eighteen million people. They could be almost anywhere.

"Talk to me!" Tomoko tucked the blanket back in where it had pulled out.

His voice, a muffled whisper, could barely be heard above the engine. "What?"

"I shouldn't have been so insensitive. Changing your life—any life—is hard. I've read articles about *Yakuza*—but that doesn't mean I know who you are."

"And yet you were right." He studied the ceiling for while. "I read stories about great adventurers, and think constantly about making another break, and still I stay in the same place."

She shrugged. "We all have regrets."

"I should have at least died trying." His words hung ominously in the air.

"I'm sure you had your reasons for staying."

The road smoothed out as the truck accelerated up a ramp. They were on a freeway again

"What do you regret, Tomoko?"

"I . . . uh . . ." She felt unsure whether to answer. He'd never actually spoken her name before. She turned to look at his hawkish face, at the bandage she'd so carefully applied. The words rushed out before she could stop. "My girlfriends all said that dating a *Gaijin* was a mistake. They said I would only get hurt. And I listened to them and never told my parents—my father is so very traditional. We were always sneaking around so they wouldn't find out, and I know that bothered Max. Then, a month ago, he confessed that he loved me, but I didn't . . . say it back. We never discussed it, but I know he was hurt." A feeling of embarrassment swept over her. "I'm sorry. You can't possibly be interested in all this."

"Don't apologize—I asked." Hiro glanced at her. His thin lips edged upward and his yellow teeth showed through, but it was a true smile nonetheless. "Do you love him?"

"Yes." Tomoko felt warm and slightly relaxed, and an unconscious blush painted her cheeks. "I must sound like an immature school girl. We're in a terrible position, and I'm whining about my relationship—or former relationship. I'm not sure." Her eyes felt paralyzed, staring at a single spot on the floor. She recalled leaving the note on the pillow. It felt like a lifetime ago.

The truck rumbled on for a few miles before Hiro spoke again. "I did try to leave once."

"When?"

"I was twenty-five, and my father had just died. It seemed a good time to break free, but I was captured and brought back. Oto was as cruel then as he is now. My whole family suffered. I lost my first finger and also my status. It took more then a decade to regain some trust. I could never put my mother and sisters through that again."

"I'm sorry you didn't escape." Tomoko let out a sigh. Her head was growing heavier, and the cargo bed appeared to flutter. Glancing over at Hiro, she noticed he was fighting to stay awake.

The truck came to a halt, and they heard the driver's door slam shut.

His words were slurring. "You should live the way you want to, not how tradition forces you."

She was moved by the unexpected moment, but it was short-lived. The truck's back door swung open. Morning light poured into the box.

The familiar voices of Oto's two bodyguards echoed simultaneously in the chamber. "Get out."

Tomoko crawled out from beneath the blanket toward the open door. She wavered as her feet touched the ground. They were at an airstrip of some kind. A service crew was attending to a nearby plane. A Mercedes was parked next to it, and she could see the backs of two men climbing on board. The surrounding city was pressing in from all sides, but the buildings were still a long way off.

Oto's bodyguard tugged her away from the truck. His face was swimming in her vision, but she could see a sweeping bruise on his throat. He was evidently the one she'd hit.

The second bodyguard opened his jacket, revealing a gun tucked into his belt. "Just move toward the plane."

Hiro stumbled so close to the guard that he seemed to be laying his head on the bigger man's chest. "You tell me where we're going, and I'll walk quietly onto that plane."

The guard shrugged indifferent agreement. "The cops let Father know about her boyfriend's recent trip to Okinawa. So we're all heading off on a tropical vacation."

Tomoko's legs felt as if they were turning to jelly. "Why is he . . . in Okinawa?" She felt the bodyguard's arms slid beneath her as she spoke. "That bottle. There was something in the water." The vision in front of her warped and twisted. She saw Hiro stumble and drop to his knees. Her head lolled backward. *Why is this happening?*

The last thing she recalled was seeing a wide blue sky.

CHAPTER
SIXTY-THREE

H IS BODY felt weightless as he drifted up the cave-like stairwell into the familiar corridor. The only open route led to the office, directly in front of him. He entered and crossed to the far wall. Framed photographs of all shapes and sizes hung between the waist-high cabinets and the ceiling. The slipstream of time reversed as he drifted toward the back of the office. Decades of faces floated past. Near the room's rear wall, his eyes focused on a modest copper-framed picture. The hair on the back of his neck stood on end. A voice directly behind him whispered in his ear, "Ask President Kennedy."

Max bolted upright. He was shaking, and his bruised ribs cried out.

The curtains on the bedroom's ocean-side windows were flung wide open. Sunlight poured into the room. He collapsed back onto the mattress, Mr. M's parting words still ringing in his head.

It was just a dream. Just a stupid dream.

AS Max shuffled into the living room, he was greeted with a picture of Jeff sprawled out on the sofa. The two diaries lay on the coffee table, nested in a field of empty beer bottles. Lunging forward, he grabbed the diaries from their resting place. Bottles fell like bowling pins, and he used his legs and elbows to stop them from rolling off the table.

Jeff stirred. "Morning, bro—what's going on?"

Max checked over the yellow and blue coverings. "Nothing— I just didn't want the diaries to get beer-stained."

Jeff closed his eyes. "Hey, I'll make some coffee in a minute." He was asleep again, mouth half open, as soon as he finished the sentence.

The clock on the wall displayed 9:15. Max dropped into a nearby armchair. He flipped to the center of the blue diary. Page after page of entries, dated from 1948 through 1990, documented the transfer and disbursement of billions of dollars among dozens of private bank accounts. The currency values grew increasingly large as the entries described in detail a string of backroom arms deals, political buyouts, vote tampering, covert operations, death squads, and assassinations. Most names were unfamiliar, the participants probably long dead along with Prince Takeda.

This is unbelievable. The wealth of information in his hands was staggering. *If the media ever get ahold of this . . . bloody hell! No wonder people have died for this book.*

ONE familiar name did catch his eye: President Richard M. Nixon, the thirty-seventh president of the United States. In entries dated during the 1960's, the diary told of Nixon's deal to return a massive pool of money to Japan's Liberal Democratic Party in exchange for supporting his bid for the U.S. presidency. The M-Fund was valued at over thirty-five billion when its control was transferred. Nixon narrowly won a 1968 election victory.

It would be worth at least ten times that much now!

Max leafed through the pages. It was riveting material, but would take months to read and comprehend. The clock now read 10:30 a.m. It was time he clearly didn't have.

Pulling out the loose "bookmark" page, he opened it.

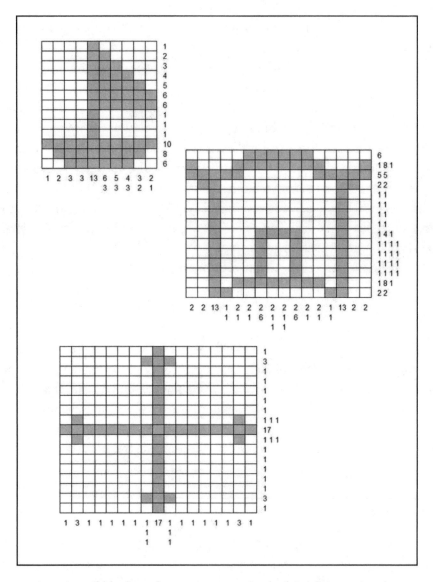

A series of blackened squares were marked in the previously empty grids. Max kicked the sofa. "Hey, did you do this?"

Jeff started. "What?"

Max jumped to his feet. He waved the paper and his voice grew demanding. "Did you do this?"

"Yeah, bro, *Hanjie* puzzles are my thing." Jeff sat up and vigorously rubbed his nose between the knuckles of both hands. "You want some coffee?"

"What's a *Hanjie* puzzle?"

"You remember paint-by-numbers?" Jeff yawned as he took the paper.

"Kind of."

"Well, it's similar, except what you do is fill in the squares based on the numbers beside the horizontal and vertical axis. You see, this row has the number one beside it. That means only one square in this row is black. This one here has a combination of one, four, and one. There are three sections in the row to be filled in— the first is a single square, the second has four squares, and the third section has one square. The brutal part is that you have to simultaneously solve both the horizontal and vertical numbers." He hesitated before continuing. "This puzzle is truly weird."

"Meaning?"

"I need to make coffee." Jeff shuffled around the sofa and into the open kitchen. "Once you're finished, it's supposed to form a picture. Like an apple with a worm or a dragon breathing fire."

Max was pacing. "You still haven't answered why this one is weird."

"Look at it, bro. It's three things that don't make any sense together. A sailboat, a Buddhist tomb, and . . . I don't know, maybe a Christian cross? Usually there's a common theme. This doesn't make a cohesive picture." He shrugged.

Max pointed at the paper. "Did you see the markings on the back of the page?"

"No." Jeff flipped the coffeemaker's switch, sending it gurgling to life.

"They look like coordinates. Maybe . . . maybe it could be a guide to one of the Golden Lily burial sites in the Philippines. If I can figure it out, possibly I can use this to barter with Oto Kodama."

"You mean one of the 176 burial sites from the first diary?" The sound of Jeff's voice was muffled by the open refrigerator door.

"You can read Japanese?"

Jeff lifted his head and stared smugly. "I hope so, since it was my major in university."

Max continued to pace. "Right, I forgot. But no—wait, you're wrong."

"Bro, I think I should know my own major."

"Not that. There were only 175 burial places, not 176. Ben told me himself."

"Well, then, his mind is getting old, cause I counted them myself last night—and there are definitely 176."

Jeff dropped a cereal box on the counter. "Come on, eat something. Then we'll check out those coordinates on the Internet." He grabbed a carton of milk and closed the refrigerator with his foot. "You can't save the world on an empty stomach."

MAX was cinching up his belt when he walked into the undersized home office. "Your clothes fit me pretty well."

"And they give you some much needed style."

"Yeah, yeah!" He chuckled. "No bias in that opinion."

Jeff shifted a surfboard to an adjacent wall. "Grab a chair from the kitchen."

The vivid blue Google Earth image defied gravity, hanging suspended in the monitor's center. It spun on its north-south axis. The U.S. rotated away to the right as the image flew along the equator. Jeff stopped it just over Indonesia and zoomed in before turning on the grid function. A matrix of lines leaped onto the globe. "Let's start with longitude first."

"All right." Max sat down and rotated the *Hanjie* paper in his hands. "E 127° 40' 30" and E 127° 40' 36"."

Jeff entered the digits, then stared perplexed at the screen. "Well, it's close to the Philippines, but in the middle of the ocean, off the east coast. Maybe there are small islands. You sure that's right?"

"That's what it says."

"Give me the latitude."

"N 26° 11' 13" and N 26° 11' 9"."

The image followed the increasing numbers northward. It zoomed in closer, revealing the terrain of hills, rivers and cities. Jeff spoke in a flat voice, as though he didn't believe the words coming out of his mouth. "Bro, those coordinates are for *here* . . . for Okinawa."

Max nodded, amazed. "I guess Ben did have a reason for sending me here." He leaned in closer. "But where exactly?"

"South of here—fairly close."

"This whole island is sixty miles long and a couple of miles wide. Everything's close."

Jeff pointed at the screen. "It's in Tomishiro City, next to the airport you landed at last night."

"So what are we waiting for?"

"Nothing, I guess." Jeff retrieved a web search engine and typed in the words "Yamashita's Gold." Over three-hundred-thousand hits appeared on the screen.

Max squinted. "What's that?"

"General Yamashita was the dude who led the Japanese forces defending the Philippines. After World War Two, he was hanged as a war criminal."

"What does this have to do with anything?"

"We can talk about it later. Just have a quick read. I'll hide the diaries and grab a shower. Then we'll roll."

MAX hesitated, listening to the distant splash of running water before pressing the CALL button to start the Internet conversation. Within moments, Kenji's spiked hair came into view on the computer monitor. His familiar chubby cheeks grew animated with recognition. "Where are you?"

"Kenji—I'm really sorry for taking your office key. I shouldn't have done it."

"It's all right. I understand why you did. But since then, everything has gone bad for Yoko. The investors read your letter. They rejected buying the school's shares." The head on the screen flicked around in short, jerking motions. "I'm finished with this job anyway. She was going to fire me, so I quit."

Max felt a pang of remorse, although he didn't regret writing the letter. "What will you do?"

"Maybe work at my family's restaurant." Kenji continued. "Hey, did Tomoko give you the passport?"

"What?" The office chair squeaked as Max edged forward on the seat. "When did you see her?"

"Wednesday afternoon. I gave it to her after she argued with Yoko."

"She saw Yoko? That means . . ." Max slumped backward and rubbed his temple. *That was our last night together. She could have given it to me, but she didn't.* The thought of her body pressing next to his while she secretly held his passport made him shudder. Waves of remorse collided against a prickly feeling of betrayal.

"What's going on?"

"I'm not sure exactly. I can't explain it all."

Kenji seemed willing enough to accept the answer as he lowered his head and took a great gulp of air. "I have to tell you something else . . . Mr. Murayama is dead."

"*What?*" Max shot to his feet, knocking the chair back, sending it clattering onto its side. "No!"

"He died on Friday."

The small room pressed in as Max thrashed about, quaking in disbelief.

"The police told Yoko it was a heart attack—just old age." Kenji hesitated for a moment. "But they also said a foreigner—a man with bright green eyes—was seen in the hospital."

Colossal loss flooded the room, forcing Max first to the wall and then to the ground, his forehead in his hands. Salty tears rushed to the tip of his nose on their way to the floor. Was it another murder? *Could it have been Lloyd Elgin?* He lost himself to the moment, listening to the sound of his own grief.

"Are you all still there?"

I have to end this insanity.

"I can't see you, but I hope you can hear me." Kenji's sympathetic voice whispered from the speakers. "In the past, Mr. Murayama had many teachers. But he told me you were his favorite, Max . . . you were his friend." There was a pause. "He said you were brought to him for a special purpose."

"Oh? Yeah, I am the chosen guardian, after all." Max lifted his head and laughed aloud before wiping his face with his palms. "Leave it to him to come up with something crazy like that."

"I don't know why he thought so, but he was sure it was true."

Max pulled himself from the floor and righted the fallen chair. It seemed pointless to argue with a ghost. He swallowed the lump in his throat. It would be necessary to lie in order to get the call over with. "It was just a shock. I'm fine. Everything is fine." Max blinked repeatedly before leaning closer to the pinhole camera. "Is anyone else there?"

"No. It's just me."

"Good. I need one more favor." He stared at the machine resting next to a snorkel mask on the desk's corner. "Write down this fax number. You'll need it."

"Hold on—let me get a pen." Kenji's sympathetic face flickered as the transmission struggled to keep up with the motion. "Go ahead."

Max read out the digits. "Now, I need you to go to Mr. M's office and locate a small copper-framed picture of President Kennedy."

CHAPTER
SIXTY-FOUR

A N ON-DUTY nurse checked the clipboard hanging outside the Osaka hospital room. Her supervisor's morning call had been unexpected, and the scowl on her face indicated her displeasure. An unplanned holiday staff shortage meant that a serious number of patients were not receiving proper attention.

The man in room 398 was a John Doe. He'd been brought in the day before in an unconscious state, with no identification. Twigs and leaves had been removed from his wounds, apparently from a yew bush. Emergency treatment had patched him up with more than twenty stitches and several units of blood. Whatever he'd been up to, he appeared to have been injured while doing it outdoors.

His claim of amnesia was clearly a lie. The tattooed patterns covering his muscular frame told the story of who he was and why he didn't want to reveal his identity.

Scanning his chart, the nurse was intrigued to see that he was type O. Of all the blood types, it was her favorite, since it meant he would likely be outgoing, driven, and passionate. He would have a warrior's spirit. The day seemed to be looking up just a little.

She entered the quiet room. Her white rubber soles squeaked as she strode toward the window. "It's time to get up." She snapped the curtains open, and light filled the orderly room. "We need to give you a bath and get you moving around." Her forehead wrinkled when she noticed the unusual contour of the blankets on the bed.

Hauling back the sheets, she let out a gasp. The bed was covered with a hastily arranged stack of pillows. Pushing the disguise aside, she could see the flower-like patterns of dried blood and plasma on the sheets.

The "warrior" had vanished.

CHAPTER
SIXTY-FIVE

THE COMMANDER pressed his way down the chaotic sidewalk of Naha City, Okinawa's capital. Kokusai Street was surging with people enjoying the sunshine. Crowds of tourists streamed from a department store, past the teeming Starbucks and through a never-ending flow of taxis and buses. He thought it an interesting coincidence that, as he passed an Army/Navy Surplus store, a squadron of U.S. fighter jets roared by in the hazy sky. Their thunderous sound drowned out Bob Marley, who blared from the speakers of a nearby T-shirt shop. Startled tourists craned their necks for a look, while locals displayed their blasé attitude to the everyday racket overhead.

As he approached the street's western end, his eyes swept across the busy road, scanning the crowd. Masami Ishi had finally relented to his request for assistance but had allowed him to bring only his best officers, thereby minimizing the risk of attracting local police attention.

The four hand-picked men were not hard to spot; they were huddled together beneath the Island Brothers marquee. Their floral-print Hawaiian shirts made them stick out of the crowd like a blinking neon sign. The commander rubbed his forehead as he shook his head in mild disbelief. Crossing the traffic-jammed street, he approached his team.

The men all bowed in unison, but he motioned for them to stop.

"I told you to dress like you were on vacation not going to a luau. Let's get off the street before more people see you in those ridiculous shirts." Tapping the folder he was carrying, he continued. "Plus, we have some material to review."

ON the empty second floor of a nearby coffee shop, the commander recited his encounter with the American at the Yao Airport. At the same time, he distributed an information package to each of the men. The cover photo of Max had been altered to darken the hair.

"He's changed his appearance and he seems to have some powerful friends."

The group's most senior member spoke. "So how does Oto Kodama fit into all this? We were told that he was spotted arriving here within the last few hours."

"It's still unclear. The *Yakuza* were chasing Travers-*san* and his girlfriend on the Izu, but Oto's men may have been working with them during the home invasion near Nara." The commander brushed his mustache. "All I know is, it's our job to catch him before more innocent people are killed."

"But if we can't ask the local police for help, how are we supposed to find him?" The senior man threw a questioning glance at the others. "There are over a million people on this island, and thousands of them are American military. It won't be so easy to pick him from a crowd."

"You're right, it won't be easy, but my plan is to have a patrol here on Kokusai Street as well as the markets at the East End, a continual sweep from morning to night. He may feel that the other foreigners will lend him some anonymity."

The men nodded in unison.

"A second man will cover the main stations on the monorail system, while a third will take the downtown bus terminal. Those are the two fastest and easiest ways around this island. He'll likely use one of them at some point. And finally, two of us will cover the *Yakuza*."

The commander took a drink of his coffee and continued. "We will locate and tail Oto Kodama. If he's looking for the American, then he has a much larger network of men to do it than we do. But if they are working together, then they'll likely meet at some point. Either way we should be able to locate Max Travers."

The men grunted and nodded before one of them spoke. "Excellent, sir."

"Let's congratulate ourselves only after we've completed the job." He pointed to the team's three youngest members. "You look after this street, you take the monorail, and you the bus terminal."

Clasping the most senior man by the shoulder, he spoke again. "And *we* will go hunting *Yakuza*." The man acknowledged the honor with a seated bow.

"But first," the commander said, leaning back in his chair, "we need to do something about those crazy shirts."

CHAPTER
SIXTY-SIX

S PEEDING SOUTHWARD, the red KLR motorcycle tore down the highway toward Naha City. Max wasn't used to riding, and every time the bike unexpectedly sped up or changed lanes, he felt his muscles involuntarily flinch and tighten his grip on Jeff's rib cage. Leaning forward, he tried to speak, but the wind tore his words apart.

Jeff throttled down the bike, pulled into the slow lane, and edged up his visor. "Don't be nervous, bro," he yelled. "Just relax."

"It's not that," Max shouted back. "We're being followed." The motorcycle wobbled slightly and he gripped even tighter before Jeff steadied the course. "It's a couple cars back—maroon with tinted windows. Drove past your house twice last night."

Jeff peered in the rearview mirror. "Okay, let me try something. Hang on."

The bike pulled back into the fast lane before accelerating hard. Max tried not to stare at the stream of pavement flying past his feet. Instead, he watched over Jeff's shoulder as the speedometer increased from fifty-five miles per hour to sixty-five, then finally nudged seventy-five.

The distance between them and the car widened to a quarter mile before the maroon car pulled into the fast lane and accelerated in pursuit.

Dexterity was on their side, or so Max hoped, trying to remain calm while the anxious voice in his head agreed with Jeff—they were in big trouble.

Weaving through an increasing volume of Sunday afternoon traffic, the bike entered the city on the north side. Traffic jams were usually an annoyance at best, but Max found himself hoping for one now. The bike could slip along the roadside while the pursuers were stuck in a sea of crawling vehicles. He leaned forward to speak. "Can we find someplace with a lot of congestion?"

"Exactly what I'm thinking, bro."

They sped onward, charging past delivery trucks and slow-moving cars. Their route took them past the city wharf and onto the high-flying bridge on the west side of downtown.

"At least they haven't started shooting." Max yelled into the wind. He racked his brain trying to figure out who was following them. Surely the police would be in a marked vehicle—which left only the mysterious Lloyd Elgin or possibly the *Yakuza*. It was impossible to know.

Cresting the bridge's lofty arch, the motorcycle raced forward and slipped between two semi-trucks traveling in tandem. Max said a prayer under his breath; he could feel the swirling ocean air buffeting them while they rode the line between the two hefty vehicles. The pursuit car, blocked from squeezing through, blasted its horn in frustration.

The bike quickly exited the seaside road, taking a path that crossed beneath the monorail. Row after row of streets flew by as congestion increased before they finally turned onto the west end of Kokusai Street. It had the look of a parade in full regalia, except that nothing was moving.

Cars, buses, and jaywalking tourists clogged the road ahead. An orchestra of rumbling engines blended with the rhythmic musical beats coming from the shop fronts. Farther down the block, a police officer strolled through the shoppers overflowing the crowded sidewalk.

The bike came to a halt behind a row of taxis strung bumper to bumper. Jeff edged his visor up and cursed as he bounced on the seat. "That next street—I want to turn there, ahead on the right. But there's a cop standing just before the turn." Jeff glanced into the rearview mirror. "That damned car just turned the corner. Cop or not, I'm going anyway."

"You sure it's a good idea?"

The reply was prickled with frustration. "Got any better ones?"

Max recalled the Yao Airport and bullets ripping into the ground. "Go for it."

"Hang on, bro. This may be bumpy."

The bike revved and growled, following the solid line down the road's center. Dodging car mirrors on both sides, they covered the distance in short order. The intersection ahead was snarled with traffic. Jeff blew the squeaky horn as he veered in front of a car crawling toward them in the opposite lane. The motorcycle bounced up onto the sidewalk and shot into the crowd.

Like parting waters, people screamed and scattered, opening a pathway forward. A flurry of shopping bags and footsteps mixed with the shriek of a police whistle.

From the side, the beat cop came racing to intercept. Instinctively, Max's leg kicked out, knocking over a passing café table, catching the man in the shins. The motion sent him tumbling to the ground, just feet from their spinning tires.

The motorcycle wobbled precariously as it flew off the far curb onto the side street. Max craned his neck to see the carnage behind as the crowd surged back into the path they'd cut, but the bike picked up speed and he lost the view within moments. The wail of sirens in the distance told him the chase was only beginning.

Jeff continued on a southern course using a jagged, broken route on side streets and alleyways. Managing to avoid the circling sirens, they crossed a bridge connecting Naha to Tomishiro City. Within minutes, they had skirted the mangrove forests of Lake Manko. Jeff turned onto a narrow road and climbed through a series of switchbacks leading up a steep hillside. Nearing the top, he pulled to the side, in front of a derelict house, and announced their arrival. "We're here, and it looks like we lost the chase car."

Max climbed from the bike and pulled off his silver helmet. "I thought my heart was gonna stop when you drove onto that sidewalk. Thank God nobody was hurt."

Jeff shook his head while he undid his chinstrap. "Yeah, but that cop you knocked over probably isn't very happy."

"Damn! I can't believe I did that."

"Me neither. What happened to the law-abiding guy I knew?" Jeff laughed.

Max grinned and then looked around puzzled. "Where exactly are we? This just looks like residential houses."

Jeff pointed up the road. "Those coordinates on the back of the *Hanjie* puzzle pointed here. This also ties into the first image of the puzzle—the boat."

"Even I can see we're nowhere near any water."

"This was the Navy's underground headquarters during World War Two. Japanese troops dug tunnels into the rock below this hill—by hand—when they were preparing for attack by the Allies. It's been open to the public since the seventies."

"So you've been here before?"

"I brought some friends here once, although I wasn't feeling my best—a bit of the twenty-six-ounce flu—so I just hung out in the parking lot at the bottom of the hill. But we can't leave the bike there, it's too public. "Should be okay here for a while. Let's go have a look underground."

"So if the puzzle is right, we're looking for a tomb or a cross inside the tunnels?" Max asked.

They both paused, listening to the distant wail of police sirens as Jeff's normally laid-back style grew serious. "I don't know, man, but whatever it is, I hope we find it fast."

Entering a modernist glass structure at the hill's peak, they purchased tickets in the hushed marble lobby and descended the ninety-foot whitewashed staircase into the heart of the tunnels.

"So, Yamashita's Gold? What's that all about?"

Jeff's voice echoed up the stairwell as they approached the bottom. "From what I read, conspiracy theorists have been talking about it for decades. Golden Lily was the project that buried all the stolen goods during the war, and Yamashita's Gold is the name given to the same loot by the treasure hunters who've been trying to find it. They're opposite ends of the same story, bro."

With the *Hanjie* puzzle in hand, they traced a path through the catacombs, along every intersecting corridor and passage, hunching now and then to make it through low archways. The few tourists they encountered spoke in whispered tones.

Max glanced up and down the main tunnel and finally threw up his hands in frustration. "This can't be right. There's nothing that matches any of the shapes from the puzzle. All the walls are blank. There must be something we're overlooking."

Jeff's fingers brushed the pick-axe cut surface. "Maybe I made a mistake." He crouched down, concentrating on the puzzle and its odd images, while a raucous group of children descended into the tunnel and thundered past, their shrill voices echoing and bouncing.

An inquisitive boy stopped. He looked to be about six or seven years old. Max wanted to shoo him away, but the pensive face was filled with youthful anticipation as he said hello in English.

Jeff returned the greeting without looking up or breaking his focus.

The boy pointed at the first puzzle, pronouncing "boat," before pointing at the second, grimacing. He seemed to be struggling for the English word, and when it didn't come, he resorted to Japanese: "*Soto.*"

Jeff's head snapped up, "Outside! Did you just say outside?" He sprang to his feet. "Of course!"

The child's eyes inflated with surprise and he dashed away into the next chamber.

"Nice work. Scaring the little kids . . ."

But Jeff wasn't listening, charging away up the long, sloping tunnel toward the exit. "I don't know why I didn't think of it before," he shouted. "Thousands of people died in here at the end of the war. If there's no graveyard inside, then there must be one nearby."

Max raced to catch up. Reaching the outside world, they exited onto a columned and tiled patio. A thin layer of clouds drifted overhead, muting the noontime sun. They turned to the right and crossed the winding length of a promenade, quickly reaching the staircase descending to the visitors' parking area far below.

Jeff pointed excitedly to the hillside next to where they stood. Four enormous tombs were inset into the rock. Surrounded by flowering trees, the paint-chipped monuments were camped together, shoulder to shoulder. Each was fronted with a ballroom-sized concrete plaza that needed to be crossed in order to reach the mustache-shaped awning capping the tomb's front wall. Set within the smooth faces were recessed waist-high stones, each one marking a burial chamber's entrance.

Max took hold of the *Hanjie* puzzle as Jeff spoke. "Look, the second image shows the tomb's curving roofline and the entranceway."

"But which one is the right one?"

"The puzzle's third picture—look for a tomb with a cross on it." Jeff was already jogging away before he finished his thought. He waved back. "You start on the right one, and I'll start on the far left."

"Sounds good." Max scanned the waist-high concrete pony wall while crossing the first tomb's plaza. Time had worn most of the paint off the exterior, leaving only splotchy gray and black patches on the surface. Faded flowers lay near the entrance to the tomb, next to a porcelain dish filled with the ashes of burned incense. He ran his fingers along the marble wall, scrutinizing it. Names of the deceased were engraved on a stone slab near the tomb's front. Otherwise, the surfaces were flat and smooth, with no noticeable markings. Moving on, he glanced around surreptitiously before scaling the pony wall into the next tomb's plaza; there was no time to go around the proper way. Then his eye caught movement in the parking lot below, and he watched in astonishment as the maroon car cruised out from behind a parked school bus.

Shit! Max dropped to a crouch. *How'd they find us?* He rose up enough to peer over the pony wall's top, waving first with one arm, then with both, but to no avail. Two gravesites over, Jeff was oblivious, absorbed in his own search.

Half hunched, Max raced to the front of the next tomb where a hasty search revealed nothing. Finally, vaulting over another pony wall, he scurried toward the third marble exterior.

Seeing Max stooped over, Jeff stopped what he was doing. "What's going on, bro?"

"Get down! *Get down!*" Jeff dropped just as Max reached him. "That car is in the parking lot!"

"Impossible! Man, there's no way they could have followed us."

"Yeah, well, they did. I don't get how, but we have to go. I haven't found anything. You?"

Jeff shook his head. "No. Nothing even remotely resembling a cross. But it's a Christian symbol. I wouldn't expect to find it in a Japanese graveyard."

"Let's leave."

"No." Jeff's ponytail shook as he swung his head from side to side. "We've come this far. Let's go around the other side of the tunnel's exit. If there's nothing, then we leave."

Max felt locked in place by fear. *That's three dead now—how many more will it be?* Every time he had tried to escape, he'd been found. Maybe it was time to stop running and instead walk calmly down to the parking lot and hope for the best.

Jeff rose to a half stance and snapped his fingers for attention. "Listen—I know this whole thing has been rough, but you have to do it for Tomoko—and for yourself."

"If she's still alive." Max took a deep breath before finally nodded agreement.

Regaining the promenade, they took shelter behind a pillar overlooking the parking lot. The maroon car had pulled to a stop and they watched as a single man climbed out the passenger's side. A blue military cap hid his downturned face. It was impossible to get a good look at him.

Jeff flicked his head, indicating a desire to get moving. Crouching in a half run, they returned back the way they had come. Reaching the promenade's opposite end, he pointed down a lengthy staircase that made a ninety-degree left turn beneath the decking of an overhead bridge. "Let's try here." They sprang down the stairs and around the corner.

Emerging from the trees under the bridge, they slowed. Max could see a laneway twenty feet below, and off to the far left, in the distance, was an open amphitheater. To their immediate left was a small grassy plateau. The remains of a decaying, moss-covered tomb stood half swallowed by the hillside. Jeff leaped onto the grass and moved along the wall. "Keep an eye out."

The first two sites were bare of any markings, and they moved to the third burial site while keeping a wary eye on the laneway.

The final moss-covered tomb was clearly the oldest. Snaking vines and tree roots hung over the edges of the encroaching hillside, covering the tomb's top. Crumbling pieces of wall lay on the ground, mixed with dead leaves and discarded water bottles. The stench of urine filled the air. "A homeless shelter," Jeff said wryly. "Hey—help me move these vines."

Working from opposite sides of the battered wall, they yanked back overhanging vegetation, unearthing blank surfaces along with an excess of dirt and startled insects. With each tug, Max's voice overflowed with frustration. He spat dirt from his mouth. "Nothing—nothing—nothing—noth—"

His last pull yielded something different. High on the wall, rising out of the tomb's face, was the stylized shape of a sixteen-point chrysanthemum. The Imperial symbol. He pointed at the spot. "That's the same image as on the diary's satchel!" His voice rose an octave. "This is it!" He stood on his toes and ran his fingertips across the plate-sized symbol.

"It's the Japanese royal crest . . . but what to we do now?" Jeff sounded perplexed. "It's not a cross, and the *Hanjie* shows a picture of a cross."

Max's face pressed against the rough rock wall while his fingers probed around the image's outer edge. "I can feel a space between the petals and the wall. It's not carved from the wall; it's been inset into the surface. They feel like they'll move."

"Maybe—maybe we have to push the four that form the shape of a cross . . ."

"It's worth a shot!" Max nodded with excitement.

"But we don't know what order to push them in." Jeff was pacing on the grass now. "I'll bet there's a specific order."

Their heads jerked in unison when the brakes of an aging truck squealed in the laneway below them. It crawled over a speed bump before driving away.

Turning back, Jeff shook his head. "We'd better hurry. Just push the top one and then go around the symbol clockwise."

"All right." Max stretched his arm up, but paused as he heard Jeff muttering the words, "North, east, south, west." His hand stopped in midair. "What did you just say?"

"Uh . . . first push north, then east, south, and west. Why?"

Max flashed back to Mr. M's office, and he recalled seeing the top of the wooden box as it was pressed four times. "That's it!" He felt a rush of excitement as his outstretched fingers pushed the eastern petal first, then the bottom one, followed by the left, and finally the top.

Jeff grabbed him by the shoulder. "Why in that order?"

"*Mahjong* winds—east always goes first." The waist-high burial stone slid quietly backward.

Jeff let out a whoop and clapped his hands before fumbling in his jacket pocket. He produced two hikers' headlamps. "I thought these might come in handy at the underground museum."

Max grinned with anticipation, feeling sure they were close to a breakthrough. He slipped the elastic strap over his head before flicking on the light. "I knew you must have been a Boy Scout."

"Yeah, right!" Jeff laughed. "Let's roll—hurry up, before it closes."

At that moment, Max spotted the maroon sedan pulling into the laneway's end. "The car!" He dropped to his knees and scrambled forward, brushing away cobwebs. "You think they spotted us?"

"I don't think so," Jeff replied as he followed hastily.

Inside the narrow passage, the headlamps cast pale glowing beams. Just ahead was a metal lever jutting from a split in the rock wall, and Max gripped it as his voice echoed. "Here goes."

He slammed the lever down, sealing them within—it seemed not a moment too soon.

CHAPTER
SIXTY-SEVEN

H ER PURSE sailed through the air and crashed into a shelf, scattering its jumbled contents onto the industrial carpet. Yoko stared from her office chair at the room that had held her secret dreams of freedom. She listened to the silence, amazed to find that she actually would have preferred the chorus of children's laughter in the classroom next door. It had always seemed like such an annoyance, but now without it, the place felt like a hollow husk.

Armani, Lauren, and Versace had been replaced by sweatpants, a baggy T-shirt, and white sneakers. Her normally immaculate bobbed hair was disheveled.

She picked up the legal documents on her desk and read again from Murayama-*san*'s last will and testament. The old man had left everything to Max.

How could she not have foreseen? She had been too blinded by her own ambitions to notice everyone conspiring against her. Max had transformed so quickly into Brutus. Her mind raced a wild course, consumed with betrayal. She struggled to find the pivot point when everything had turned.

There would be no new gallery. The palazzi of Venice would no longer welcome her with open arms. One selfish boy had washed away years of painstaking work.

Pools of moisture gathered in her eyes, threatening to roll down her cheeks, but she dabbed them away. Her mother's haunting voice whispered over her shoulder, urging her to run and hide, to begin anew. But the thought that troubled her most: is there time enough to start again?

She wasn't young and beautiful anymore, and she couldn't risk taking much when she left—Masami Ishi's men were parked in a van on the street below.

Luciano trailed her as she stomped from the office down to the third floor. The costly art prints would go with her. Since the gallery exhibit was technically still underway, it shouldn't raise questions from Masami's men. Glancing around, she attempted to locate a cardboard tube. As her eyes swept the long, pictured wall, they stopped on a gap. An empty space stared back. She knew the spot well—a picture was missing.

Yoko gasped.

Rushing to the wall, she prayed that the photo had somehow fallen from its hook. Her eyes scanned desperately, but it was nowhere in sight. Turning around, she finally saw it on the corner of the desk. The slim copper frame was lying face down, the paper backing torn open.

Almost simultaneously, she saw pages in the fax machine's bottom tray. A receipt slip showed they had been sent only hours before. On the cover page, the From box was blank, while the To box simply said, "Max."

Luciano rubbed against her leg, and he hissed as she kicked him away.

Yoko's hands shook uncontrollably and a tear finally escaped its prison, snaking its way down her cheek. She recognized Mr. Murayama's handwriting on the pages. Dropping into a chair, she studied the first paragraph of the guilt-filled confession, but there was no point reading it all. She knew it as her own story, or more accurately, their story. The voices in her head grew to a screaming crescendo. They told her to be strong, to get up and flee, and to not stop until she was far away.

But from this . . . there was no place to run or hide.

She laid her head into folded arms and wept. Forty years of tortured thoughts and haunted nights burst forth. Tears from her uncontrollable sobs soaked the pages and blurred the ink.

Only a single way out remained.

CHAPTER
SIXTY-EIGHT

M AX CRAWLED into the forbidding gloom, drawing in the tomb's dank musty air. Goose bumps slithered over his exposed skin. The wet black walls, cut straight but unfinished, pressed in around him. He hated confined spaces. Slender drainage canals ran down both sides of the narrow passage. Even so, stale water lay in shallow pools on the ground. Twenty feet inside, light from the headlamp allowed him to view the rising ceiling. He desperately wanted to take the weight off his aching knees.

Several paces back, Jeff's voice rang forward. "That door better open up again."

Max turned his head back, momentarily blinding them both.

"Bro! Point that thing at the floor." Jeff threw up a hand to block his eyes.

"Sorry." Max rose to a half stance. "Hey, it's high enough to stand up. Whoa!" His right foot shot forward, and he bridged his hands between the walls to keep from falling. "Careful—it's slippery."

Jeff guffawed while standing. "We're crawling around inside a tomb. I think falling on my ass is the least of my worries."

Max swiped cobwebs from the path and edged forward with determination. "This whole mess is my fault."

"Ease up, bro—it's not like you planned it. Let's just find what we need and get outta here. This place gives me the creeps."

Walking single file, they advanced a dozen paces. The slender passage joined a foyer-sized room at right angle to a ramp—ten feet wide—descending farther into the stone hillside. Opposing handrails allowed them to simultaneously navigate the slick incline.

Trailing behind, Jeff lost his footing and let out a shout as he slipped the last few feet, dropping hard onto the smooth floor. "I'm okay, I'm okay!"

Max took a couple of tentative steps forward, barely noticing Jeff's echoing voice. "Look at this room!" The chamber they were standing in was fifteen feet wide and extended another twenty feet before a steel door blocked the way. The oval-shaped door was embedded in the center of a curving wall that arched up and forward before meeting the high ceiling above them.

Jeff whistled his astonishment. "Amazing!"

"No kidding." Max walked slowly toward the door. "After you mentioned the extra burial site in the Philippines and we found that the *Hanjie* coordinates pointed here, to Okinawa, there were only two things I thought it could be." His voice rose with excitement. "Either it was the location of a map for the 176th treasure, or else it was the treasure itself—somehow moved here after the war ended—Yamashita's Gold!" He touched the curving wall's vulcanized rubber surface. "Maybe it really is the treasure. Maybe I will have something valuable to bargain with after all."

"Look here, this floor is dry." Jeff held a hand on the smooth ground. "The granite must be heated—it's slightly warm—and there's writing."

Max moved back toward the incline's base. "Can you translate what it says?"

"It's a Haiku-style poem. Basically it says:

I kill an ant
And realize my three children
Have been watching.

Jeff's lips moved silently, reading it over again. "I think . . . whoever built this place was concerned about his kids learning to murder innocents based on his actions."

"Three innocent people have already died in just the last few days." Max bent down to stare at the inset letters. "I just hope for Tomoko's sake . . ." He wanted to finish the sentence, but the words caught in his throat, and he fell silent.

"Don't worry, man, we'll get her back. As a matter of fact, what are we waiting for?" Striding forward, Jeff spun the round metal handle in the center of the steel door, then heaved on it. The door groaned and opened, revealing a chamber the size of a closet and an identical steel door on the opposite side. They each tried the handle of the second door but it refused to budge, so Jeff sealed them inside the airlock while Max again tried the handle. The door swung outward easily, and he had to catch himself from falling forward as fresh, dry air rushed in.

High above, at the apex of the arching ceiling, a fluorescent light clapped on, followed by another equally noisy light, then another and another until at last a row of more than two dozen lights blazed overhead, stretching seventy yards into the distance.

Max stared at his friend, whose childlike astonishment mirrored his own. "It's a freakin' warehouse!" His shouting voice echoed and bounced.

A ten-foot-wide central corridor stretched ahead, the length of the bunker, looking almost canyon-like as it carved its way down row after row of multilevel storage tiers that filled the room's width and rose fifty feet to the curved ceiling. A jumble of wooden crates of all shapes and sizes filled the visible shelf space to overflowing. At the front, on either side of Max and Jeff, ran a string of dozens of gray filing cabinets. Directly ahead sat a table, upon which rested a square black television, a Betamax video player, and a lone cassette case.

"What is this place?" Jeff massaged the tension from his neck. "How could this be built without anyone knowing?"

Max shook his head. "I have no idea. Check that TV—maybe there's a message." He walked to the left and opened the first cabinet's top drawer. It was stuffed with documents. Unwedging a single beige folder from its hanger, he fingered through the papers. "These are all written in Japanese, but they look like receipts or government documents."

Jeff was puzzling over the old-fashioned video equipment. "Let's see what this thing has to say." He pressed the power button, then popped up the tray on the suitcase-sized machine before breaking the seal on the cassette case and inserting the videotape.

The image of an elderly Japanese man blinked into view. His thinning hair appeared glued to his skull, and he was seated in a straight-backed chair. A midnight blue kimono wrapped around his protruding belly. Dark, intelligent eyes stared directly from the screen as the stilted delivery of his words betrayed the fact that he wasn't used to speaking before a camera.

A few moments passed before Jeff motioned at the screen. "He said he's Prince Takeda."

"Max moved closer to get a better look at the withered face. The man on the screen looked so frail, not at all like the powerful picture he'd formed while reading the second diary. "What's he saying?"

"He's talking about responsibility for the past."

"What about the map? Did he say anything about the extra burial site in the Philippines?"

"Bro—" Jeff pressed the pause button and placed the palms of his hands together. "Go check out the warehouse and give me a few minutes here. By the time you're back, I may have more info."

"I get it." Max moved off down the main corridor, before turning down the second side row. The face of a massive, snarling dragon had caught his attention. He touched the statue's polished neck and muttered in wonder when his hand barely reached the bottom jaw of the intricately carved stone.

Wooden crates rose on the shelves towering overhead. The video voice whispered in the distance as he turned back into the main corridor and continued away from the sound. Trolling up and down the museum-like rows, he followed the oversized yellow numbers painted on the floor. Turning out of row 6, Max stopped cold. Just ahead, in the reflection of a shiny metal container, he could see the outlines of two men standing in the next row. *No!* He threw his back against the closest crate, fighting to quell his raging panic.

It can't be! How did they get in here?

He'd seen only two men, but there could be others. How many more were lying in wait? Impulse and experience yelled for retreat, escape. But in the clarity of the brief, still moment, staring up at the crates rising overhead, he realized running was no longer an option. *This is my responsibility now.* It was up to him to face the enemy directly. Max slowly filled his lungs through his nose, clenched his jaw, and charged silently around the corner with fists raised high.

He bravely faced the terracotta soldiers standing rigid inside a Plexiglas case. It took but a moment for the realization to register in his brain as a feeling of grateful relief washed over him. Stumbling backward, he dropped to the floor, collapsing against a crate, and laughed aloud.

What would I have done if they were real?

He jumped up and shook off the moment, finishing his sweep of the main corridor. The last row, aisle 10, looked the same as the first: crates and storage units with unreadable descriptions printed on the sides. He glanced at his pocket watch and quickened his pace as he turned and headed back toward the entrance. By now, maybe Jeff had some answers to the burning questions that remained.

Jeff looked up from the documents he was examining and motioned for Max to join him. "The video directed me to a cabinet with this binder inside. It contains a floor plan." He pointed to the open page. "The rows are organized by area—Korea, Singapore, Taiwan, China, the Philippines, and so on."

"You mean all the countries that were invaded?"

"Exactly. After World War Two, Prince Takeda spent over forty years gathering stolen objects, things that had disappeared into private collections. He knew they'd never be seen again unless he did something about it. According to him, the stuff in this room is just a drop in the bucket compared to what was actually looted."

"So, if this isn't Yamashita's Gold," Max motioned to the cabinets, "then which of these holds the map to find the gold?"

Jeff set the binder down on the video machine. "Bro—he didn't say anything about a map."

"But . . . but there must be something," Max sputtered. He walked to the nearest cabinet and slapped his palm hard against the thin metal top.

"I didn't say there wasn't a map, but just that the prince didn't mention it."

"It'll take a hundred years to find it if we have to look through everything." Max leaned on his elbows and rested his face in his hands. "You know anyone who can help us search this place?"

"For sure. I've got some friends who can help." Jeff nodded. "But my phone has no signal here. I need to go back outside to call."

THEY exited the same way they had come, but this time neither friend spoke while they retraced their steps, grunting their way back up the slick ramp. Leading the way, Jeff peered out before climbing from the tomb. "There's no maroon car. It seems all clear."

The sun was sitting much lower than when they had entered.

Cautiously, Max crawled out into the fresh air, a frown on his face. In his mind, even the discovery of the bunker couldn't overcome the overwhelming feeling of failure. "Oto Kodama is expecting a map to a treasure of gold—we'll never find it in there. Not in time."

A nearby voice shouted, *"Stop!"* The military man leaped out from behind the crumbling wall. "Hands up!" He waved a gun directly at them.

"What the fuck?" Jeff stumbled back against the stone wall.

Max slowly complied, noticing the man wasn't wearing a military hat as he'd first thought, but a pilot's cap instead.

Unexpectedly a second man rounded the far corner and slowly removed his blue cap. As he lifted his face, Max felt his cheeks flush with betrayal. He stared at the familiar face and the distinct stripe of hair running down the man's chin. "But why?"

"Please turn around and go back inside." Toshi's face appeared grim. "Both of you. I insist!"

CHAPTER
SIXTY-NINE

VINCENT REMOVED the wrenches and soldering equipment from the toolbox and set them on the floor in the back of the van. He downed the last of his soda and mused again on the fact that even the NSA didn't know everything. It had taken the all-powerful information agency more than half a day to locate detailed information on Max Travers' only known Okinawa associate—a former roommate named Jeff Moreau.

Vincent slipped on his sunglasses and stepped from the back door of the Toto Plumbing van, zipping up his olive-colored overalls. The beachside rental house was directly across the quiet suburban street. Nobody was home—he'd been watching for more than an hour. The only activity so far had been the appearance of a young woman with vivid purple stripes running down both sides of her long dark hair. She had arrived on a scooter and pounded angrily on the door. Circling the house for several minutes, she'd peered into all the windows. It seemed Mr. Moreau was suffering from a bit of female trouble.

Vincent straightened his ball cap and crossed the road. Less than five seconds at the front of the house and he was inside as smoothly as if he'd had a key for the place.

The kitchen sink sat filled with dirty dishes, and the living room beyond was no better. A half dozen empty beer bottles covered the coffee table. Back issues of *Playboy* were stacked next to a picture window that looked out onto a kidney-shaped swimming pool. An overgrown dieffenbachia occupied the room's far corner; the cannabis plant growing at its base was barely noticeable.

Vincent picked up a daypack lying on the living room floor. He unzipped it and dumped the contents onto the sofa. Dirty clothes were mixed with a bag of silver bracelets, a paperback novel, several ornamental daggers, and a cell phone. Turning on the unit, he scrolled through the menu to find the owner's name: Takahito Murayama. This was indeed Max's daypack, but it contained nothing useful.

They must have hidden the diary or taken it with them.

Stuffing the contents back inside, he set the bag back in the exact spot he'd found it.

The office alcove across from the kitchen was overflowing with sports equipment. There was no need to turn on the computer. The NSA report had already told him that the most recent activity from Jeff's PC was a Google Earth search of Indonesia, the Philippines, and Okinawa, and also a Skype session. It would be several more hours before he'd receive a written transcript of the online conversation, but Vincent had played the game long enough to know that the water was warming slowly. He just needed to make sure he was in the right place when it boiled.

A search through the papers on the desktop provided him with the cell phone number he was looking for. He retrieved a prewritten text message on his own phone and added the new number before hitting Send.

Retrieving the toolbox, he removed a brick-shaped object. Even though he'd already double-checked the device, he checked again to make sure the motion-sensitive detonator was secure before sliding the package beneath the sofa's frame. When and if Max returned, he wouldn't survive for long.

Vincent-the-plumber finished his service call and made sure to lock the door on his way out.

CHAPTER
SEVENTY

RADIANT WARMTH from the floor was a welcome relief, but Max's tailbone still throbbed from sitting on the hard ground for so long. In fact, he ached all over. And from the scowl on his friend's face, Jeff didn't appear too comfortable, either.

The copilot with the gun, seat against the wall, appeared to be dozing.

Max took the opportunity to whisper, "You never told me what was in all those cabinets."

"Evidence." Jeff's voice was barely audible. "According to the video, it's evidence of all the illegal activities documented in the second diary—stuff like letters, contracts, photographs, videotapes, interviews. The prince knew that without it, his revelations could be dismissed as the ramblings of a lunatic. He wanted future generations of Japanese, and the rest of the world, to know what really happened . . . so he spent decades and most of his fortune gathering everything in that room as proof. Some people collect coins, but Prince Takeda was into collecting secrets—secrets that could blow open the horrible past."

"Richard Nixon wouldn't have been too happy to hear that."

"What are you talking about?"

"The second diary said that Nixon returned billions—called the

M-Fund—back to Japan in exchange for funneling back corporate donations to help get him elected."

"Are you serious? Damn! No wonder people are hunting for that book."

"And believe me, from what I read, it's just the tip of the illegal iceberg." Max rubbed his ankle. "So what about all the crates and containers?"

"The prince couldn't do anything about all the wealth stolen during the war." Jeff paused, visually checking the guard before continuing. "He seemed remorseful about his role in hiding some of the loot in the Philippines, but he also stated that wealth can be rebuilt, while history can't. He hired people to help him trace statues, paintings, scrolls, porcelain—basically anything he could find, and he brought everything he could get his hands on back here. The plan was to return it to each country, as a gesture of forgiveness, when the full extent of Golden Lily was revealed to the world."

"So why didn't he do it before he died?"

"No idea. All he said was that he didn't think the time was right to tell the world. That it would be the responsibility of future generations to figure out when that time would be." Jeff stretched slowly onto his back on the heated floor. "The videotape was dated 1989. Since Emperor Hirohito was still alive at the time, maybe the prince was afraid of the impact on the royal family. He could have wanted to wait until the next emperor was crowned. You know . . . let more time go by."

"But Prince Takeda lived until 1992."

"He looked pretty frail on the tape." Jeff shrugged. "Maybe he was too sick. I don't know, bro."

"Still, it's just not fair that the emperor should get away with so much theft, not to mention starting the war in the first place." Max switched from rubbing his ankle to massaging his ribs. "*He* should have been held responsible, don't you think?"

Jeff propped himself up on his elbows. "Yeah, you're right, and I'm not defending his actions—but let me ask you this, Maxie—do you know what was in his head at the time Japan entered the war? Was it conquest, or was it fear of his generals and the giant corporate heads? Maybe if he hadn't agreed to go to war, they would have just killed him and done it anyway. What if the emperor's decision was based on concern for his family? Even if the safety of his family meant the death of thousands or millions of innocent people, isn't that what most people try to do—protect their loved ones?"

"Sure," Max's voice rose to an irritated hiss, "but I'm not talking about intention. I'm talking about taking responsibility for the results."

"I understand, and it's an extreme case, but my point is people make choices they regret later, and often it's impossible to see the outcome in advance—good or bad—we weigh the pros and cons and take our best shot. Would you have gone to Mr. Murayama's office if you knew all this would happen?"

"No, of course not." Max's voice trailed off as he pondered the insight, recalling the last night at Toshi's, wondering if Tomoko regretted choosing to leave or harbored any guilt over her decision to hold onto his passport.

"I didn't think so," Jeff replied. "So, let's just find a way to get out of this and get your girl back safe." He held out a straight arm with a fist on the end, and Max bumped it lightly with his own fisted knuckles. "We can debate the rest later, over beers."

"Agreed."

ANOTHER thirty minutes ticked slowly past before the round handle on the steel door spun open. The dozing copilot leaped to attention, training the headlamp and the gun on his hostages.

Entering from the antechamber, Toshi motioned for the man to put the gun away. He walked to the center of the room and sat down on the Haiku lettering embedded in the center of the floor. Clearing his throat, he said, "I'm sure that you are angry so please listen before judging."

Traitor! Max's chest felt tight. He wanted to lash out at Toshi's duplicity, but chose instead to wait for the justification, skeptical that any reason could possibly explain the messed-up situation.

"I come from royalty."

"Of course." Max's shook his head, recalling the first meeting on the train when Toshi had handed him the business card. "Your ring is the royal symbol—I should have known."

Toshi nodded. "My parents rarely spoke of it, but my mother was very proud of her heritage. Since they were murdered, my actions have tried to honor them. It's why I became a priest—for my mother." He appeared to be struggling to find the right words before he continued. "Can you imagine my shock when you came to my door with Prince Takeda's diary? I needed to find out if the things it said were true or not. Then when you were sleeping on the airplane, I looked at the second diary. The things in both books could do great harm to the royal family . . . my blood. I thought that if the stories were lies, or could not be proved, then it was my duty to destroy the diaries." Toshi glanced back toward the steel door. "But there is so much evidence in there. My parents would want me to serve truth, not bloodlines."

Max struggled to absorb the words he had just heard. Could they really be true? He remembered his relief at finding a safe haven after the robbery, and the elation of escape as Toshi's jet carried them into the sky. *He arranged for me to see Mr. M one last time.* "So why didn't you just talk to me. Why not tell me?"

"After you came to my house, I consulted with the *kami* spirits. Their guidance told me to help you when I was asked, but not to interfere. The answers would come when the time was right."

Jeff climbed to his feet. "Wow! Spiritualism with a bullet. I feel so much better." He motioned to the ramp. "So, are we still hostages or can we leave?"

"You are free to go. Please accept my humble apology."

As Toshi began to rise, Max reached out and grabbed his forearm. "Wait."

The gun snapped up and took deadly aim.

"Put that away!" Toshi shouted, forcing the copilot to slink backward.

"Thanks." Max started breathing again, his anger melting away. "I think your parents would be proud of your decision."

Toshi responded by helping Max to his feet.

"So that's it?" Jeff snorted. "You hold us here, this guy points a gun at me, and now all is forgiven—we're all best buds?"

Max gripped Jeff's shoulder. "He can help us get Tomoko back."

Toshi nodded. "Especially since Oto Kodama is on the island."

"*What?*" The room echoed as the two friends shouted together.

Toshi continued. "His jet landed here before noon today. Another pilot, a friend of mine who works at the airport called to inform me—and I found the hotel Oto is staying at."

Max tried to stay calm, but the strain in his voice betrayed him. "Was Tomoko with him?"

"My friend saw a woman matching her description being escorted from the plane to a car."

"She's alive!" Max shouted, shaking two clenched fists in the air before pressing them against his forehead and exhaling hard.

"So how do we get her back?" Jeff interjected.

Max paced around the semi-dark chamber. "After talking to Ben, I think Oto believes there's an actual treasure map in the diary that points to Golden Lily burial sites. That's why he wants it." He motioned to the steel door. "When we found this place, I thought it might have a map that I could barter with, but even if there is one, we couldn't find it."

Toshi took his time before responding. "But why do you need a real map?"

A brief silence ensued before Jeff spoke. "That's brilliant, dude! Why didn't we think of that?"

"Because Tomoko's life is at stake." Max paused. "Because I want her back in one piece."

Jeff slapped the back of one hand into the open palm of the other. "But Oto won't know what a real map looks like. So we give him a bogus one, get her back, then make a run for it."

Max paused to think. "It would need to be an incredible fake."

"Remember all the posters in my living room in Tokyo?" Toshi suggested slyly.

The air hung silent while the statement settled.

Max drew a sharp breath when the realization finally dawned. "You have company artists—people working for you who make those posters?"

"Yes."

"Could they make a map convincing enough to fool the *Yakuza*?"

An impish smile crept across Toshi's face. "It would fool Prince Takeda himself."

THE four exited under a deep blue evening sky. The sun was a slender, vanishing glow on the horizon.

"How soon can you get working on the fake map?" Max asked, aware of the danger of time pressing in.

"Possibly tonight, but tomorrow morning at the latest. My people should have it ready in twenty-four hours."

"I just hope that's fast enough."

Jeff's phone, which had received no signal inside the hill, trilled loudly, indicating that a text message had been received. He rested against the crumbling wall and scrolled through the menu. Within seconds, he sprang back to his feet. "Uh—bro—there's someone wanting to meet you ASAP."

Max stopped talking and turned around. "Who?"

"According to the text I just received, it's Lloyd Elgin."

CHAPTER
SEVENTY-ONE

Monday, April 30

THE TAXI screeched to a halt next to a red single-story building. Vincent tossed money to the driver and climbed from the back without a word. Looking around, he took in the lay of the land. Heavily treed grounds encircled the five-hundred-year-old fortifications of Shuri Castle. Curving outer walls surrounded the higher inner walls, which served to guard and protect the numerous rebuilt structures inside the hilltop expanse.

It was almost 10 a.m. Buses had been arriving for the last hour. The Shurijo Park visitors' lobby was swarming with tourists, and Vincent figured that was exactly what Max wanted when he'd insisted on the meeting place. It was a naïve and sometimes deadly mistake of amateurs to convince themselves that nothing bad could happen in a public forum. And, yet, he couldn't help but be mildly impressed with Max. The kid had made it this far, after all.

Vincent serpentined through the slow-moving crowd blanketing the park's main causeway. The path ran beneath numerous arching gates on its way to the hilltop. The hike would take about five minutes. Within the first dozen yards, he noticed he'd picked up a tail. A curly-haired Caucasian man with sunglasses was standing near a tree, keeping an eye on the entrance. He was trying to remain undetected by keeping his distance, but his tie-dyed shirt was a dead giveaway. A best guess placed him as Jeff Moreau.

Arriving at the hilltop, Vincent bought a ticket for entry to the castle's main courtyard. In the open plaza, an audience was gathering beneath a tent to watch a group of *Ryukyu* performers dressed in traditional costumes. Drums beat as dancers swayed in time. The tie-dyed shirt hovered nearby on the crowd's edge.

Ignoring the activity, Vincent climbed a short staircase and entered directly into the expansive brown-and-white tiled Una plaza. Blood-red pagoda-style buildings surrounded him on all four sides. The most elaborate structure was that of the Seiden, straight ahead. The double-roofed, two-story wooden building was sheathed in red clay roof tiles and fronted with a colorful four-columned marquee.

He could see no blond hair in the plaza, but the agreement had been to meet inside the Seiden, near the throne. The entrance to the surrounding buildings was up the stairs to the right.

Removing his shoes, Vincent entered the hushed building. He placed his footwear in a plastic bag provided by an elderly woman. Looking ahead, a half dozen people were turning left at the far end of the otherwise empty corridor. Vincent glanced sideways, out the sliding glass entrance, in time to see Jeff and his shirt-of-many-colors entering the plaza in hot pursuit. *Amateurs.*

Moving swiftly down the hundred-foot corridor, he could see there was construction occurring at the far end. Outside light glowed through milky plastic sheets hanging from the rafters, where the far wall of the corner should have been. As he turned left, a voice spoke from behind him.

"Lloyd Elgin?"

Vincent stopped, but only his head and shoulders pivoted round. "Yes." He could see a young man with brown hair just out of sight, at the turn in the corridor. He was standing in front of the plastic sheet. "Max Travers, I presume?"

"Yes."

Taking two steps backward, Lloyd put on an easy smile and spun around, reaching out as if to shake hands. Then suddenly, unpredictably, he formed a fist that drove hard into the side of Max's neck. Lloyd felt the satisfying muscle spasms and watched the eyes flutter and roll back into the skull. He stepped forward to slow Max's fall while using his own momentum to slip them both behind the loose plastic curtain. Ushering the body to the ground, he checked for a pulse.

The thud of sock-covered feet pounded down the carpeted hallway. Lloyd watched a blur of muted colors move past. Within seconds, Jeff's voice, uttering profanities, disappeared into the next building.

MAX could feel someone slapping his right cheek. Through a fog, he could hear construction equipment humming nearby. An impatient voice was urging him to wake up. Stabbing pain pierced his brain as he opened his eyes and the room came slowly into view. He found himself propped against a stack of burlap sacks on a dirt floor, groaning as he tried in vain to sit up. He tried again, but managed only to twist his upper body slightly. Panic set in. "I can't move!"

"Motor function loss accompanies a blow to the sterno-cleido-mastoid muscle. Movement should return in time . . . assuming you live."

Dressed in khaki pants and a blue dress shirt, his assailant was staring out the only window of the tiny work shack they occupied. A column of dusty morning light angled into the window. Max closed his eyes again, hoping to reduce the painful throbbing in his head. "Why'd you do that?"

Lloyd's voice was deep and monotone, almost machinelike. "You have a diary that I want. Give it to me or die. Those are your only options."

"If I give it to you, you'll kill me anyway," Max responded while Lloyd drew close and crouched down next to him. Just inches away, he could clearly see the man's face, and he recalled Kenji's comment about the nurse spotting a foreigner with green eyes. "You were the one in Mr. Murayama's room. You did kill him!"

Lloyd's gaze remained cold and rigid.

Max coughed. "You're not the only one searching for the diary, you know."

"But I'm the only one who'll get it."

"Who are you? CIA?"

Lloyd grabbed Max's face and compressed the skin in a vicelike grip. "Where—is—the—diary?"

"I have it."

"Clearly, but the question was, where?"

"I need your help."

Lloyd stifled a mocking laugh. "We're done." He slipped a gun from its holster and held the barrel to the side of Max's head.

"No, no, no . . . *Please!* I really need your help. Then I'll give it to you."

Max fought to control his stuttered breathing. "I never wanted it."

"So what *do* you want, Mr. Travers?" The mockish tone parodied a deranged therapist.

He can't kill me or he would have done it already. Max could feel the smooth metal against his temple. "The *Yakuza* have my girlfriend. I need you to help me get her back."

Lloyd's chin rocked slowly back and forth. "I'm not in the charity business. First I'll kill you, then your buddy in the hippie T-shirt—then I'll get on a plane and go home. Job done."

"Neither of us have the diary with us."

The gun jammed harder against his head. *Don't freak out, Max.*

"Then who has it?"

"Another friend, but he knows about this meeting." Max felt a strong tingling in his feet and hands. Sensation was slowly returning. "You can go back to the States, but whoever you work for won't be very happy about not getting the diary." He prayed he was right.

"You're lying."

I have what he needs. A steely calm descended over Max, and he could scarcely believe the words coming from his own mouth. "Shoot me, and I guess you'll find out."

The crunch of gravel and sound of voices could be heard outside the shack. Lloyd moved quickly to stand next to the window. Squeezing into the shadow cast by the wall, he peered outside as the noise moved past without stopping.

Max struggled to move as Lloyd turned back, aiming the gun's glowing red laser on his chest. The game was over—finished. He waited for the bullet.

"If the *Yakuza* are looking for the diary and you're giving it to me, what will you give them?"

"A map." Max caught a glimmer of confusion on Lloyd's face before continuing. "They don't want the diary—they want the treasure map they think is inside."

"Is there one?"

"No."

"So like I said, what are you giving them?"

"A fake."

Lloyd's smirk held a hint of admiration. "Trailer-park boy makes good.

Maybe you're working in the wrong profession, Mr. Travers." He thought a moment before sliding the gun back inside its holster and cracking open the shed door. "Arrange a meeting with the *Yakuza* on the cliffs—east side of the Memorial Peace Park—at the end of the dirt road—seven tonight. You meet me at 6:15 at the Naha bus terminal. If this fails, and she dies, you still give me the diary."

"But that's not enough time. The map won't be ready."

"Draw faster. Your lives depend on it." Lloyd jerked the door closed as he exited, rousing a dust cloud that twinkled in the window's light.

Minutes ticked by before Max could pull Jeff's cell phone from his pocket. He dialed Toshi and relayed the instructions. His throbbing head slumped back. Exhausted, sweating, he studied the exposed wooden planks above his head.

I've climbed into the cage with the tiger.

CHAPTER
SEVENTY-TWO

LOCKING HIS gaze on the carpet, the timid hotel concierge adjusted his mint-green suit jacket. He was rooted to the floor near the twelve-person boardroom table in the Royal Suite. He could see the tapestry of tattoos blanketing Oto Kodama's back, shoulders, and arms, and he found it difficult not to stare. He nervously cleared his throat and waited.

Oto growled through the face-hole in the collapsible massage table. "What do you want?" The slender young woman kneading his back muscles lifted her tawny arms away, and Oto moved a hand to grasp her upper thigh. She let out a gasp, but remained in place.

The concierge stepped forward and bowed from the waist. "I apologize for the disturbance, but there is a man in the lobby who says he has critical information for you. He refuses to leave—and he's dressed rather unusually."

"Who is he?"

"He says he knows an American who took a book of yours, but he wouldn't identify himself."

Oto gave a walrus-like moan as he rolled onto his side. "Bring the mystery man up."

"Yes, sir." The concierge bowed repeatedly while making a hasty exit.

TOSHI stood with his eyes closed, palms pressed together at chest level, his wide sleeves hanging loose below his arms. Directly behind him was the first set of doors to the hotel's Royal Suite. He struggled to keep his mind in the moment, but it continued to drift back to his dead parents. What would they think of his putting himself into harm's way like this? He pictured the two of them sitting together as the terrorists unleashed the odorless Sarin gas into the subway car. The look of shock on their faces as they felt blood seeping from their noses; chests seizing while they clung together in their final dying moments. Toshi rotated his shoulder blades and forced his mind back to the present. His armpits were slick with nervous sweat, but it was important not to let this show. A chain of comma-shaped beads dangled between his fingers, and he flicked through them one at a time while chanting softly.

The two beefy guards standing before him were dressed in matching black suits. He could tell that his priestly robes were making them nervous. This was a good sign; the flowing, pure-white layers of fabric were having the planned effect.

Toshi slipped from his black laminate clogs and walked into the suite. A long dining table was just ahead, in front of a bank of windows overlooking the Pacific Ocean's blue waters. The guards motioned for him to turn to the right.

Rounding the corner, Toshi could see Oto Kodama seated in a plush chair at the room's far end. Clad in a striped housecoat, the *Yakuza* leader was running a comb over his oily black hair.

Oto's eyes flared as he took in the Shinto priest's image. "Is this a joke?"

Toshi tried to maintain an expression of placid calm while returning the dark-eyed stare. "I'm simply here to deliver a message."

"Don't think your costume will intimidate me." The irritation grew on Oto's face. "Were you hired to do this?"

"I am simply a humble messenger."

Oto snapped his fingers. "Then get on with the message."

Toshi removed a piece of paper from the folds of his left sleeve. "An exchange is proposed for tonight—the girl for the map." He fought his nerves as the paper shook. He'd memorized the message, anyway, so he lowered his hands.

The deep lines in Oto's tanned face barely moved when he spoke. "Where?"

"At seven—the end of the unpaved road near the cliffs to the east of the

Memorial Peace Park."

"Have you seen the map?"

Toshi nodded. "I was the one who discovered it inside the lining of the diary's back cover."

"You?" Oto raised a single eyebrow.

"I noticed the lining was pulling away, and while trying to fix it, I found the map."

Oto stared out at the sunlit turquoise water. "Priests are *not* supposed to lie."

"Yes, I'm aware of that."

A silent moment passed before the *Yakuza* leader spoke again. "Tell the American it's a deal."

Toshi felt a modicum of tension leave his shoulders. "So his girlfriend is well?"

"She's breathing and in one piece, if that's what you're asking." Oto stood and adjusted the housecoat over his protruding belly. "Now go and deliver your message."

Toshi turned quickly. He didn't need to be asked twice. Sliding his feet back into his wooden shoes, he exited into the hallway and made his way to the elevator.

THE commander was seated on a sofa in the bustling hotel lobby, ruminating on the fact that none of the stakeouts had produced any results so far. Masami Ishi's angry phone calls were becoming routine.

Attempting to appear engrossed in a newspaper, he skimmed the headlines yet again. From the corner of his eye, he saw the hotel concierge touch his nose and then point discreetly at a Shinto priest exiting through the hotel's front door. Rising from his seat and tucking the newspaper under his arm, the commander followed the white-robed man out to the curb and watched with curiosity as a hotel valet brought around a maroon-colored Maserati Quattroporte.

The priest tipped the valet before disappearing behind the vehicle's dark-tinted windows. The engine purred before the car shot down the driveway, then roared again while disappearing into the traffic on the adjacent street.

Re-entering the lobby, the commander strode to the concierge's desk. "I asked you to let me know when Oto Kodama or his men leave or arrive. What was that all about?"

"Very sorry, sir—I was busy with other guests." The young man behind the desk reddened. "But that priest—he was meeting with Kodama-*san*."

The commander leaned his fists onto the desktop. His newspaper clattered to the floor. "Why?"

"He was delivering a message from an American, something about a book that was taken."

The commander slapped both palms on the desktop before charging out the front door. But even as he ran down the hotel driveway, he knew it was futile. The moment had slipped from his grasp.

CHAPTER
SEVENTY-THREE

TOMOKO PULLED her T-shirt down to cover the patch of exposed skin at her lower back. She could feel the lusty eyes lingering on her body through the slot in the door. The guard could have easily checked on the room in a few seconds, but he was working the job as if it were a peep show. She was lying on a futon mattress in the center of the room, with her back facing the doorway. Flies buzzed around a tray of barely touched food at her feet. The hinged slot squeaked when it closed, followed by the sound of footsteps fading down the empty hallway. He would be back in another fifteen minutes.

She sat up and looked toward Hiro. He was resting against the wall, his head hanging between his knees. The air was muggy and close. Tomoko rose to her knees, but she paused as Hiro lifted his head and held a finger to his lips. She tried listening, but could hear only the distant sounds of traffic and seagulls. More than once in the past thirty hours, since waking from the drug-induced coma, he'd sensed unexpected sweeps by the guard.

Their cell appeared to be an old office. Peeling white paint, yellowed with time, covered the walls, while half the checkered floor tiles were torn away. Solid wooden panels covered the windows that ran the room's length.

Hiro gave an all-clear, and together they sprang back into action. Moving in unison to the left-most window, Tomoko grasped the bottom edge of the wood panel while Hiro stepped onto a chair.

Only two more rusty screws separated them from the outside world. Tomoko watched as he inserted a shard of scrap metal into the slotted head, then struggled to make a single turn. He puckered his face and twisted again, but his hand shot away and slammed into the wall. "Aaaaah!" He bit his lip to stifle a scream.

Tomoko pressed a palm against his back. "Are you all right?"

He nodded and managed a muffled reply, but his face was anguished.

"Rest for a while? We can always try again later."

Hiro flared his nostrils. "There is no later. Get ready to hold the board when the first screw comes out."

Reinserting the metal, he twisted until he was red-faced. Unexpectedly, it budged slightly, then moved a bit more. The two exchanged a brief smile before another try. The rusty thread gave a final squeak, and the screw dropped to the floor. Tomoko swayed from the weight pressing down on her.

Hiro moved to the last screw. "You all right?"

"Uh-huh," she grunted.

The last screw proved easier, and as it clattered to the floor, he hopped from the chair. Sunlight poured through the dirty window when they lifted away the four-foot-square panel.

Hiro wrenched the window's clasp open, allowing the top of the pane to pull inside while the lower edge swung outward. Tomoko felt like crying as her lungs filled with the sweet ocean breeze rushing into the room. She turned and embraced him. He stiffened and held his arms near his sides.

"I'm sorry. I was just happy that—" She stepped back and blushed.

He shook his head while staring awkwardly at the floor. "No, no, I should have . . . it's just that we don't have much time. Be careful as you climb out onto the ledge. It's not very wide."

She hated heights but it was the only way to freedom. "All right." Taking a deep breath, she wished for courage.

Once outside, they glanced around, trying to stay low while gathering their bearings. In front, in the distance, was a high-flying freeway bridge, but it was too far away to signal for help—the drivers would never see them. Three stories directly below, a moored fishing boat bobbed in place on the open blue waters of a U-shaped wharf.

Dropping to his stomach, Hiro peered over the edge. His head snapped back up almost immediately. "There's a man and a huge dog down there walking a patrol."

"What do we do?"

Hiro moved as he spoke. "Let's get to the end—see if we can find a way down."

Tomoko struggled to keep up while they shuffled quickly along the slender gravel outcropping. The combination of height and speed was giving her severe vertigo, and she fought to keep her eyes up and forward. Reaching the building's edge, they discovered a featureless concrete wall dropping to the parking lot. The fall would mean broken legs for sure. Hiro cursed. "We'll have to try the other end. Turn around. Hurry!"

Less than halfway back, her heart sprang into her throat. A head popped out of the window they'd opened. The guard shouted and pulled himself onto the ledge. A second window swung out not ten feet from where they stood, trapping them in the middle.

There's only one route left. She knew what had to be done.

Clasping Hiro's hand, she stepped away, out over the indigo water, turning in time to watch his eyes change from fear to panic to sheer terror as they fell from the building's roof.

"*Noooooooooo . . .*"

The water foamed and bubbled when they plunged beneath the surface.

Rising almost instantly to the top, instinct drove Tomoko's powerful strokes as she swam toward the wharf's open end. Her wet clothes felt like lead. A dozen strokes into it, she noticed she was swimming solo. Her head spun around and she saw why. Hiro was thrashing in the water, his arms flailing as he sank and resurfaced.

She wanted to escape so badly, but she also couldn't let him die, not after he had freed her parents, not after the rescue from Oto. Racing back, she dove beneath the cool water and came up behind him. Just in time, she hooked an arm around his neck as his body went limp. His face rose to the surface, accompanied by a gasp and the noisy sucking of air. "It's all right. You're all right. I've got you," she yelled while struggling to keep them both above the waterline.

Three guards were standing above on the mooring's edge. The crazed dog was barking feverishly.

Hiro fought to break the grip she held around his neck. He coughed and thrashed, yelling, "Leave me! Swim away!" A guard tossed out a coarse line of rope and he grabbed it, sputtering, as she kept her hold on him.

Just above them, Oto Kodama's tanned face and threatening scowl came into view. "Have a nice swim?" He laughed cruelly.

Tomoko screamed in anger and tried in vain to splash water up the wall.

Oto was unflinching. "Get cleaned up. We're going out tonight."

AS he turned to stroll back inside, the *Yakuza* leader couldn't help chuckling to himself. "Suicide Cliffs—perfectly named for what's about to happen to the two of you."

CHAPTER
SEVENTY-FOUR

MAX STAYED low as he slipped past Jeff's pool in order to peer through the window. The place looked empty, but as he'd learned lately, appearances could be deceptive. He crept into the living room, leaving the door open, and paused to listen before moving cautiously toward the kitchen. A knife would be necessary in order to pry up the floorboard and retrieve the hidden diaries.

As he edged past the office, the fax machine beeped softly. Max recalled the web chat he'd had with Kenji. He slid into the room and loaded blank paper into the machine's tray. It whirred to life, generated three pages, and then fell silent. He quickly stuffed the pages into his pocket while taking a letter opener from the desktop.

Returning to the sofa, he gripped it from behind and pulled. On the wooden floor, the legs easily slid backward a few feet. Max's eyes were searching for the correct floorboard as he walked around the sofa's arm, noticing the bricklike object lying exposed on the floor. He gasped as an ominous red light on the brick's face began to blink, slowly at first but then increasing in pace.

What the . . .

He lunged forward, kicking frantically at the device, sending it out the open patio door and into the pool, just as a deep-bass rumble shook the very foundation of the house.

The ferocious blast shattered the picture windows, driving them inward. Max dove behind the sofa, narrowly avoiding the shards of glass that flooded the room like swarming locusts. Anxious seconds passed as he lay fetal on the floor. He could hear the blood pulsing through his veins.

Who put that there?

Cautiously rising up, he shook debris from his hair as he surveyed the carnage. Pool water and glass covered everything. The room was a mess.

Max clenched his fists and shouted in frustration, *"Shi-i-i-it!"* The momentary release felt good, but he knew he needed to get out before anyone came to investigate. Moving quickly, he located the correct floorboard and pried it open. To his relief, the diaries were unharmed. Tucking them under his arm, he ran for the street.

THE copilot accelerated the Maserati Quattroporte into the fast lane on a course back to Toshi's rented downtown condo. Max's ears were still ringing from the poolside blast as he fingered the fax pages. He didn't want to read them, but he knew he had to, if only to satisfy morbid curiosity.

Please let me be wrong. Don't let what I'm thinking be true.

Mr. Murayama had been more than a friend; he'd been a mentor and guide. The man had lived an incredibly full life. He'd dined at the White House and traveled the world. Spending afternoons with him had felt like a time warp, like a master's lesson in history, archaeology, and anthropology combined. Nobody had ever taken such a keen interest in sharing the picture of a bigger world. And now, all that was gone. Mr. M was gone.

The handwritten words on the pages were Mr. Murayama's, as proven by the signature and the personal seal. The pen strokes changed slightly every few paragraphs—evidently the text had not been drafted in one sitting.

Max blinked rapidly, fighting to keep his eyes clear.

REMEMBER as you read this, there is a difference between a man's honor and loyalty to one's country. I did my duty because of the latter and despite the former. I was a fool.

In the spring of 1963, I received a diplomatic package from Tokyo headquarters. In it were instructions that have haunted my mind ever since.

First, let me go back. During the early time of the Second World War, I became friends with another soldier, Lieutenant Tetsuo Endo. He was older, and he became my *Kohai*, training and helping me. More then once he saved my life.Nine months after the war with America began, Endo-*san* received a "top-secret" position. Meanwhile, I maintained employment as a junior clerk in Manila. I watched the powerful trading companies working with the military. They were shipping gold, diamonds, and artwork back home. Only senior officers knew the details of what was happening, and so I quietly did my work and asked no questions.

Endo-*san* and I met again in 1950. We both joined the government. He became a lawyer, and I a diplomatic trainee. He was married with two daughters, the younger of whom was named Yoko. The first time I met her was at a picnic in 1951 when the cherry blossoms were blooming. She was just a little girl.

A few years later, I was posted to the embassy in Washington. It was a great honor for me.

Then, in the summer of 1960, Endo-*san* called me and asked for my help. His daughter Yoko had graduated high school and wished to work in the United States. I arranged for a visa and found her a job with a friend's company, first in New York, then in Dallas, Texas.

Not long after, Tetsuo Endo grew ill from cancer, and when he died in 1961, his assistant, Kazue Saito, came to see me in Washington. He delivered a gift from my old friend. It was a diary, but not his own. I was shocked to see that the words were written by Prince Takeda. It described a war project code-named Golden Lily. This was Endo-*san*'s secret: one time while drinking, he revealed to me he had been Prince Takeda's personal guard.

The enemy troops controlled many of the shipping lanes, and it had been growing difficult to move items back to Japan. The Golden Lily project was created to hide and protect the emperor's war treasure. After reading the prince's diary, the memory of what I had seen firsthand in Manila began to make more sense.

The prince's diary described how the Americans discovered the treasure soon after the end of the war, but the U.S. government and the military leaders, led by Douglas McArthur, kept it a secret—they wanted to use it for themselves.

In years past, I heard whispers and stories, at parties and from senior

colleagues, but until the diary, there was no proof to support the theories.

In 1961, John F. Kennedy became United States' president. He seemed to be a man of courage, with a dream of change that could carry his country. He was trying to make the world better; he was a man worthy of admiration and respect. Then the diplomatic package came from Tokyo in 1963, and the world did change, but not for the better.

The instructions were simple: deliver an envelope to Yoko Endo and have her pass it to a man named Lee Harvey Oswald. She was not to open the package or talk with anyone about it. Her only task was to make the delivery, for Mr. Oswald was expecting it.

At our meeting in Dallas, Yoko was upset to hear I had learned of her secret friendship with Mr. Oswald (although she never questioned how I knew she'd met him at a Christmas party the year before). She begged me not to tell anyone, so that her mother and Mr. Oswald's wife would not find out. She feared her family would force her back to Japan and she would have to give up her American life. I promised to be quiet if she delivered the package with no questions. She quickly agreed.

On November 22, 1963, I heard the terrible news. President Kennedy was dead, shot in Dallas by Mr. Lee Harvey Oswald. That single moment is burned like a bright light in my memory. I will never forget. I closed my office door and lay on the floor, realizing with sadness that many hands had held that rifle, including my own.

When I delivered the package to Yoko, I knew in my heart it was evil, but I kept my eyes down and tried not to see. My action was the same as when I watched the ships departing from Manila Harbor, loaded with stolen cargo. Duty to my country was always the most important thing.

Years later, I discovered what I believe to be the true reason for JFK's death: he had learned of Golden Lily and the huge fortune that was funding bribery, corruption, private armies, and secret Cold War operations. He was planning to end it by telling the public. But the world's true rulers, the richest families and the U.S. military leaders, would not allow it to happen. They took his life instead.

But for me, that is not the story's end.

Yoko lied to the Warren Commission investigators before returning to Japan. You see, her father, Tetsuo Endo, had left behind vast debts from bad investments, and his family suffered. They tried to survive and pay back the loans. Mrs. Endo died in 1971, leaving Yoko with the burden of the debt. Loans to *Yakuza* do not go away with death, but pass to the next generation.

When I returned to Japan in 1984, Yoko came to greet me with blackmail. She was desperate with fear, convinced that the police were preparing to arrest her for conning money from several wealthy suitors and yet still unable to keep up payments to the *Yakuza* who were threatening a fate worse than prison. She requested that I give her my last name, pay off her debt, and buy her an English school. This would guarantee her silence about the JFK time.

She had little to lose, and I had no desire to retire to a jail cell, so I agreed.

Every day since then, when I look at her, I don't see a scheming, heartless woman. Instead, I see the youthful tear-filled eyes that stared at me when I pushed the envelope into her frightened hands.

President John F. Kennedy was an honorable man, and I deeply regret my part in his death. I wish only for this true story to someday be told.

Takahito Murayama

MAX barely stepped through the condo's door before Toshi, beaming with pride, handed over the phony treasure map. The tan parchment was the size and texture of a handkerchief.

"You guys did it already?" He felt a sudden and overwhelming wave of gratitude.

Jeff was grinning from the plush comfort of a sofa chair. "We used chemicals to age the paper faster."

"It looks real, at least to a novice like me, but will it fool them?"

Swinging his feet off the arm of the overstuffed chair, Jeff pointed to the fake. "Look here, bro—Toshi's artist incorporated old-style war symbols into the markings. We also tried to make it look more authentic by water-staining this one corner . . . and most importantly, it has to be viewed with a mirror to match an actual area in the Philippines—on the island of Luzon. Apparently the reflection trick was used during the war, for secrecy."

Toshi sat thoughtfully, resting his chin on his hands. "But is the water stain dark enough?"

The question launched a spirited debate, allowing Max time to walk to the window. He considered telling Jeff about the explosion back at the house, but there was nothing that could be done now. The more important thing was keeping everyone alive. *But if John F. Kennedy lost the fight against Golden Lily, how will we survive?* Max stared at the cars and buses crawling up and down the street, thirteen stories below. The sun was beginning its hazy slide toward the horizon. *It's not enough just to fool the Yakuza and Lloyd Elgin. Someone has to tell the world about all this.*

"Earth to Max." Jeff's voice grew louder. "Bro!"

Max looked up. "Guys, I think the map is great. You did an awesome job, really." He attempted a smile, but he knew it looked insincere. "So what about the backup? Is everything ready?"

Toshi nodded. "Yes, Plan B is in place—everything hosted on independent global servers, just like we talked about."

Max thought back to the hospital, to Mr. M's bedside words—*I left instructions so that after my death, copies would be sent to the media and a small group of well-known intellectuals. The information would be impossible to contain.* He exhaled sharply. "I just hope it's enough." He interlaced his fingers, stretching his arms high over his head. Try as he might to resist, the tension was definitely getting the better of him.

Jeff piped in. "The guy's probably old-school, bro. He'll never see it coming."

"I sure hope that's true." Max paused. "And you'll be on standby with the yellow diary, right?"

"Of course. But once you have Tomoko, you should focus only on getting away. I can do the rest. Being a priest has some benefits."

"Like risking your own life instead of mine?" Max responded emphatically. "I appreciate your help, but no way."

Hours before, Toshi had raised the same point with a similar result. This time, however, he appeared to accept the decision with a simple nod. "Fine. There's enough pressure already. I don't want to argue." He pointed to the kitchen. "You should eat."

"I will. But I need to use the phone first." Max fumbled in his pocket. "I got the two diaries and also something else." He retrieved the folded fax pages, handing Mr. Murayama's confession to Toshi as he headed for the master suite. "Read that. It explains a helluva lot."

MAX half regretted dialing the familiar number. The phone in Yoko's office rang three times before being picked up. It felt like years since he'd heard her refined dusky voice, although it now seemed unusually subdued. *"Moshi-moshi."*

"Hello." He waited for the line to disconnect, but surprisingly, it didn't.

Her reply was tense and formal. "Why are you calling?"

"If you'd only given me my passport when I asked, none of this would have happened."

"Did you call just to tell me that?"

"No . . . I read Mr. Murayama's confession. The assassination of a president!"

She sighed. "It wasn't my fault. I was young and thought it was love. They used me as a courier—a pawn—I didn't know what I was carrying."

Max's voice edged louder. "Nothing is ever your fault, is it? What about the money you've been stealing? You weren't just a pawn in that game."

"You don't know what you're talking about. This was a legitimate school, and you destroyed everything."

He was sure by Yoko's angry tone that she was getting ready to hang up, so he spoke quickly. "I plan to let people know what's in that letter. As much as you've done wrong, you at least deserve to be warned."

"Do as you see fit." Her voice grew quieter as the sound of utter defeat seemed to echo through the line. "I had dreams once, you know, just like you, but life doesn't always cooperate."

The last thing Max heard before the dial tone was the sound of Luciano purring in his ear.

CHAPTER
SEVENTY-FIVE

TWO ROUND, polished lenses focused on the hushed wharf below. Forklifts and cranes sat idle next to stacks of weathered cargo containers; the parking lots were empty. It was a quiet holiday Monday.

The commander's binoculars had to be angled down to avoid the glare from the setting western sun. Within the field of vision, a guard with an alert dog paced back and forth, while a second man leaned on a stack of concrete blocks.

He was positioned strategically on the overpass walkway, not far from stairs that dropped thirty yards to the secondary road below. Oto Kodama's Mercedes was parked next to a long warehouse that was bordered by the water on one side. Several hours had passed since the *Yakuza* leader had disappeared inside.

The binoculars swung on the commander's neck as he retrieved his vibrating cell from a pocket. He glanced at the display with dread, hoping it wasn't another one of Masami Ishi's increasingly demanding calls. It was the phone number of his man at the bus terminal.

He shouted to be heard over the thunder of traffic. "What's happening?"

The man was panting heavily. "Sir . . . I've spotted . . . Max Travers."

The commander jerked upright. "Can you catch him?"

"I'm trying, but I think he saw me. He's running and—" Clattering, scraping, and the din of a roaring engine replaced the voice.

"Are you there? Hello?"

Below him, the commander saw a white van move from its parking spot to the entrance of the warehouse. He raised the binoculars while keeping the phone to his ear, watching while an escort hustled a slender girl with long black hair into the back of the windowless vehicle. Her hands were tied in front of her. Following quickly was a second escort, who was having trouble with his prisoner. The bound man tripped his captor before striking with his tied hands. The nearby guards pounced and dragged the kicking man to the van, pummeling him with violent blows in the process. Oto strolled from the building. His driver held the door of the Mercedes as he climbed inside, ignoring the scuffle taking place nearby.

The voice on the phone returned. "Travers-*san* got away. Another *Gaijin* in an olive-colored Range Rover picked him up and headed south."

The commander raced toward the stairs. "Contact the other two and get to your car. I'll call you back and explain." He hung up and hit the speed dial just before he descended the metal steps, two at a time.

The police officer parked in the car below answered. *"Moshi-moshi."*

"Start the engine," the commander barked. "Kodama-*san* is active. He should be coming out the driveway any moment. Don't let him see you."

The response was crisp. "Yes, sir."

"We can't afford to lose him. Things are moving, and something big is about to happen. I can feel it."

CHAPTER
SEVENTY-SIX

MORE THAN ten thousand lives were sacrificed in 1945 to Mabuni Hill at the southern tip of Okinawa Island. The ninety-day Typhoon of Steel drove Japan's troops and civilians to the island's end, until at last they could go no farther. Fertile green land, along with the jungle-like cliff, had been bombed into a moonscape, pock-marked and barren from weeks of relentless shelling. Fear, desperation, and misinformation spurred soldiers, along with their wives and children, to fling themselves 270 feet to the exposed reefs below the clifftops.

Max could easily have done without the history lecture while the Range Rover charged south. He was seated in the back, feeling light-headed, trying not to stare at the driver's seat, but Lloyd Elgin was too magnetic a draw. Was the guy a stone-cold killer? Or were collateral deaths simply an acceptable byproduct of his work?

Lloyd's cold green eyes suddenly flicked to the rearview mirror. His orders were calm, as if he'd given them a million times before. "Get down on the floor. Stay there until I tell you otherwise."

Max hesitated, queasy stomach tensing. Was it a trick?

Sarcasm dripped from the front seat. "We're near the War Memorial. If you want any *Yakuza* posted on the road to see you, then please continue to sit where you are."

Max felt his breath catch as he struggled with the seatbelt release. Throwing himself to the floor, his ribs strongly objected. He winced and lay still, listening to the gloating chuckle floating in the air. "If you and your girlfriend want to live, you'll do whatever I say."

A minute later, the Range Rover slowed and turned, leaving the main road behind. The pavement ended soon after that, as evidenced by the vehicle's washboard action. Lloyd's voice rose over the increased noise. "You can get up now."

Clambering onto the backseat, Max gazed around. The view surprised him. It seemed as if they'd left the civilized world behind and entered a wild jungle. On either side, stands of bushes and untamed grass rose higher than the vehicle's roof, while farther back the branches of tall, leafy trees could be seen. Looking ahead, he saw that the dirt road's two tracks were almost completely overgrown. "Where are we?"

"East of the meeting place." The vehicle bounced forward until it was blocked by a metal gate. "We walk from here." Lloyd killed the engine and climbed out while adjusting his khaki pants and hunting shirt. "This is Kevlar, which means I can take a bullet. Keep that in mind if you're planning to do anything stupid." A belt loaded with grenades and canisters appeared in his hands, drawn from beneath the front seat. His mid-length jacket swung open as he fastened the device around his waist, revealing a pair of handguns holstered to his chest.

Max felt an instant rush of panic, and he grasped the Range Rover's door frame for support. *The enemy of my enemy is my friend.*

Lloyd was already several paces away before he turned back to glare. "Are you coming?"

Max hurried to catch up. *I'm the guardian, the new guardian. Just keep telling yourself that . . .*

Fifty yards down the trail, they came to a wide dirt clearing surrounded by a circle of thick bushes and dense, tall trees. On the far side, just off to the right, a barricade had been placed, blocking a split in the soaring leafy wall. The dark blue waters of the horizon were visible above the graffiti-covered, waist-high concrete.

Max moved to the open edge and looked down the steep southwest cliff face. Exposed rock dropped a third of the distance to the ocean before meeting a heavy blanket of trees covering the more gradual descent to the bay. Ocean waves rolled relentlessly against a distant reef, creating a foam line where the water met the land. It was hard to imagine so many lives ending in such a beautiful place.

Glancing back to the clearing, the questions running through Max's brain must have been written on his face. Lloyd answered without being asked. "I have my reasons for picking this place, and yes, we simply wait." His head flicked suddenly left and right; eyes scanning the clearing's perimeter. It wasn't evident what he was sensing, but his voice took on an ominous tone. "It won't be long now."

The sun was preparing to sink below the horizon. It was seven o'clock, and Max was working hard to quell the agonizing tension in his neck. It was a Mexican standoff—and it was about to begin.

Voices could be heard coming down the path and he followed Lloyd's lead by turning to face the approaching noise.

Two barrel-chested men swaggered into view. Dressed in dark suits, each was brandishing a machine gun. Max guessed they must be Oto Kodama's henchmen. Scurrying in their wake was a rumpled, scholarly-looking old man in a brown blazer.

Close behind came the intimidating figure of the *Yakuza* leader himself. Sporting slicked-back hair and a scowling face, he was shorter than expected. His black suit matched his round sunglasses, and he strutted with an air of pompous authority.

Max's anger flared. *If it wasn't for you this wouldn't be happening; we wouldn't have to be here.* He envisioned seizing Lloyd's gun and finishing the job, avenging the murder of Mrs. Kanazawa. The world's criminal count would be down by one, but what about the cost? *Then who would be the killer?*

JUN'S seething eyes stared from behind the bushes surrounding the clearing. He had endured heat and stinging insects while lying in wait, but it was worth the pain. The troublesome *Gaijin* was again within striking distance, straight ahead and a just a few steps to the right.

However, the presence of the other, older American was unsettling—an unknown threat—but Jun reassured himself that with so much firepower on their side, it wasn't a concern. In the end, the map would be obtained, with Hiro taking the fall for what would now be two dead foreigners.

Father had blessed the sneak attack, but not before they had the map well in hand. The blood and horror would be spectacular, and in his mind he allowed the cartoon carnage to unfold: snapping bones, screams for mercy, and finally the dramatic, wrenching fall to the rocks below. Jun, the hunter, trembled and flexed with anticipation, watching Father's entourage enter the clearing to his left.

THE commander pressed his shoulder close to the tall grass while making his way on foot down the winding dirt road. His men were strung out in a single line behind him, guns drawn.

Dropping to a crouch, he motioned for the group to catch up. He pointed ahead at the parked vehicles coming into sight: Oto's Mercedes, the white van, and a Range Rover were parked twenty paces ahead. The young officer behind him whispered, "It's the vehicle that picked up the American."

"Masami Ishi was right, then. Oto and the American are working together."

From around the van's far side, a slender man appeared. Dressed in jeans, with long, flat-ironed hair, his tattoos showed beneath rolled-up sleeves. He was smoking a cigarette while practicing his golf swing with an imaginary club.

The commander knew he needed a game plan to quietly get past the sentry, a reason to be walking in the lane. Grabbing a discarded whiskey bottle he began a staggering walk forward.

"Get out of here!" The thug's thin arms hung loose at his side.

The two men were only feet apart when the commanders struck, delivering a hammering blow to the young man's jaw. The cigarette popped from the *Yakuza*'s lips like a cork from a champagne bottle, as he dropped to the ground.

Signaling his men forward to join him, the commander slipped between the vehicles and under the metal gate before creeping quietly up the darkening trail.

CHAPTER
SEVENTY-SEVEN

O TO KODAMA removed his sunglasses, revealing cold, hard eyes. He snapped his fingers, sending the scholarly old man in the blazer marching toward the center of the clearing. Stopping after a dozen steps, the old man held out a hand before uttering in broken English, "Give-u me map-u."

Max shifted forward to stand shoulder to shoulder with Lloyd. "No deal. I want to see Tomoko first." He tried hard to project confidence in his voice.

The nervous scholar translated the words back to Oto, who in turn bellowed a gruff call into the air. Men appeared from the bend in the path, shoving their two prisoners from behind. Max felt a surge of elation course from his head to his toes—*thank God she's alive*—only to be replaced by the painful sting of seeing her hands bound. Mr. M's grandiose thoughts for a higher purpose seemed absurdly ridiculous at this point. Surviving was all that mattered now.

Tomoko's steely expression softened when she spotted him, tears escaping down her cheeks. Even from a distance, he could recognize the flex in her jaw as she pursed her lips together, controlling her urge to cry out. The bound *Yakuza* next to her looked a mess. He was limping with each step, blood seeping from a deep wound on his forehead.

As soon as the prisoners entered the clearing, the old scholar came closer yet, holding out his hand, shaking his empty palm. "Give-u map-u."

Pulling up a grimy pant leg, Max retrieved the soft paper from inside his sock, saying a silent prayer before unfolding the edges to present it. The fake was good, but if the guy was any kind of historian, there was only one way the charade could possibly end.

Take your time, why don't you, Max thought, as the detail was scrutinized.

The old man finally refolded the map and carefully placed it in his blazer pocket, acknowledging authenticity by raising both arms over his head into a circle.

Then, without warning, reality imploded as Lloyd dropped to the ground, sweeping his left leg backward and catching Max painfully in the shins, sending him hurtling forward.

What the hell—

As the ground rushed toward his face, Max heard the snap of branches followed by the distinct pop of gunfire. A volley of bullets sailed overhead, exactly where he'd been standing. He looked up and caught a glimpse of Thick Neck bursting from the bushes, racing forward, gun waving, screaming like a maniac. Max slammed hard into the ground, his mind reeling.

Impossible! That guy fell off Ben's roof. He's supposed to be dead!

A single bullet from Lloyd caught the big *Yakuza* in the shoulder, spinning him backward and away from Max, who flinched as the first smoke grenade detonated with a flash in the clearing's center. He looked to his right just in time to see Lloyd rolling away, tossing spewing canisters, before disappearing into the thickening white haze.

THE commander heard the unmistakable crackle of gunfire and explosive snaps. He motioned for his men to split apart as they raced forward. Ahead, a smoky fog rolled toward them, and seconds later Oto's two guards stumbled from the cloud, wiping at their eyes. They raised their machine guns at the sight of the five men crouched facing them as the commander shouted surrender over the barrel of his hoisted gun.

A raging voice rose from the billowing smoke. "Get back in there and kill everyone! Get me that map!" Oto emerged just as the first machine-gun blast broke the air.

The volley of returning gunfire burst like fireworks. A bullet slammed hard into Oto's leg, and he staggered backward, vanishing from sight.

HIRO heard Tomoko scream as Jun rose up, just feet away, and renewed his charge forward, vanishing into the rolling cloud. All around, shadows raced through the burning mist while voices shouted against the thunder of exploding gunpowder. The air burned his mouth and nostrils.

Beside him, Tomoko collapsed to her knees, shoved roughly from behind by her escort.

"Don't touch her!" Hiro sputtered as he spun into retaliatory action. A driving kick from his good leg knocked the first man backward, allowing him to wrench free the man's baseball bat. Clutching it in his bound hands and swinging madly, he delivered a lethal series of silencing blows. The second escort scrambled backward before disappearing in a frenzy.

Hiro tossed down the bat and slumped purposely to the ground, keeping his face low in an attempt to draw in better air. Blood drained into his right eye from the gash in his forehead, making it difficult to see, but he refused to give up. Tomoko had peered inside his soul and seen him for who he could be, and not what he was. She had given him something he'd never expected, and his gift in return would be her freedom.

Working his bound hands free, he found her huddled form. Grabbing her wrists, he tore frantically at the knots in the rope, ignoring the pain from his missing finger.

POSITIONED on all fours, Max fought to gather his bearings. Estimating distance or direction was impossible in the cloud of surrounding chaos, but he knew it was critical to move fast. He closed his eyes against the stinging air and rushed in what he hoped was Tomoko's direction. Abruptly, he felt a crashing weight of bone and flesh slam hard against his left hip. The impact drove him back to the ground as Thick Neck tumbled overtop. Max ignored the shooting pain and struggled back to his knees, darting ahead into the thick white soup as the thud of Thick Neck's feet closed in behind him.

Then there she was, chalk-colored but clearly alive.

But the smaller *Yakuza* was holding her hands, keeping her captive. Max sprang at the man, who responded with ferocious speed, and before he could blink Max found himself pinned.

Between hacking coughs, Tomoko barked at them to stop as she pulled her hands free. She grabbed the *Yakuza*'s shoulder, and Max's mind reeled with confusion as he watched the battered man obey her command and move back.

Max rose to his feet and pulled her close, feeling her hesitate before squeezing hard in return. The painful splendor of the moment flooded his senses as he kissed her perfect dusty lips and her tears spilled down, mixing with dirt and running onto his cheeks. But there was no time. Gunfire and the clapping flash of another grenade brought them instantly back to the moment.

"We need to go." He squeezed her hand and pulled. Together, they staggered through the fog in what he hoped was the right direction.

To his amazement, the barricade at the cliff's edge appeared and then the distant rolling sea. Night was falling fast. The last rays of sunlight cut shimmering lines across the rolling water. The clear air was fighting a back-and-forth battle with the manmade fog.

Looking back, Max saw that Tomoko was holding the injured *Yakuza*'s sleeve, pulling him along like a bloody, unwilling accomplice. "What are you doing?" He shouted, making no effort to hide his shock and anger.

"Hiro's not evil. I can explain—" Tomoko's partially finished sentence twisted in terror as a scream replaced her words.

Max turned to follow her horrified gaze. From the barricades' opposite end, out of the smoke, Thick Neck's bald head came fully into view. His lips twisted into a demonic grin as the rest of his massive bulk followed. Flexing his hands with anticipation, he moved calmly beside the clifftop barrier. Max edged backward keeping Tomoko sheltered behind him. His eyes flicked around wildly, hoping for a miracle, but the only two places to go were toward the smoky gunfire or over the steep cliff's edge.

POSITIONED at the back of the group, Hiro leaned into Tomoko's ear, speaking so that only she could hear the words. "You were right that I need to show courage. Now save yourself." Hearing the calm in his voice she felt a swell of panic as she tightened her grip, knowing what he was about to do. "No!" But his sleeve slipped from her grasp as he charged from behind, throwing himself at his former apprentice.

"*Noooooooo!*" Her scream rang out while Max struggled to block her from joining the uneven battle. The vicelike grip of Jun's massive hands clamped around Hiro's neck and lifted him into the air, his legs thrashing as his fists swung wildly at his opponent's face.

The huge arms flexed and twisted, followed by the sickening crackle of bone— and the kicking ceased almost instantly. Distant machine-gun fire masked the body's fall to the ground as she watched the open, lifeless eyes staring skyward.

CHAPTER
SEVENTY-EIGHT

L OST IN a private world of self-pity, Yoko wandered down the bare service hallway toward the exit at the end. She barely noticed when the rain-soaked wind yanked the rooftop door from her hands, slamming it violently against the building's exterior.

Forty stories below, the twinkling lights of Tokyo made her dizzy, and she caught her breath. It was almost enough to make her change her mind, but she knew this was the only option left, and she hoped it wouldn't be painful. Reaching into her handbag, she clutched her cell phone. A finger hovered over the speed-dial button while cold, wet spray swirled in from outside.

Her mind flew back to the moment she'd stepped on the plane bound for America. That day, so many decades ago, had also been rainy and cold. Was it an omen of things to come? If only she'd never gone to Dallas, but had instead turned and run for the safety of home. It was the wish for a larger life—a world filled with excitement and glamor—that had been her undoing. She'd tried her best, but the deception and negligence of others had ultimately doomed her. She'd worked to build a good life, but instead had fallen victim to unfair people and unjust circumstances. It wasn't her fault.

Lifting the phone to her ear, she waited until Masami Ishi's voicemail asked her to leave a message. The tone of her voice conveyed her unreserved hatred. "The game is over, Masami-*kun*. You've lost again, and the only prize you'll be receiving is the recording I took of you and me speaking in my office. The video has been delivered to the National Public Safety Commission. I think they'll be very interested in the evidence of your illegal activities. Good luck with your retirement. You may not need as much money as you expected." She powered down the phone.

Water was pooling in the gravel on the sidewalk-wide ledge; it splashed as she stepped outside. Raindrops bit at her exposed cheeks and soaked into her Chanel suit. She edged sideways with her back pressed against the building's exterior. Fear suddenly overwhelmed her, and she considered turning back. But the wind grabbed the door, slamming it shut, locking her onto the ledge.

It was surely a fateful sign.

Her last hope was that Max felt badly for his betrayal. Closing her eyes she leaned forward, dropping like a dark meteor toward the thick shrubs at the building's base. This was usually the moment when she would stir in bed and the nightmare would abruptly end, but this time it was real, and there would be no awakening.

CHAPTER
SEVENTY-NINE

DRUNK WITH power, Thick Neck stepped over Hiro's shattered body while slipping the *Surujin* chain from a pocket and began to spin it, slowly at first, but then with increasing speed.

Half standing, half crouching, clutching a broad stick he had found in one hand, Max braced for the inevitability of the moment. He heard himself shouting to Tomoko, *"Run!"* But the sobbing noise behind him wasn't moving. He wanted to turn and hold her, to relieve her incomprehensible pain, but he knew he didn't dare break his concentration. Thick Neck seemed to be reveling in the moment, savoring the attack. The chain whistled as it picked up speed.

The deadly weighted end shot forward. Max ducked his head while striking violently upward with the stick. The wood splintered into a thousand pieces, the metal ball grazing his skull as it arced back along its path for another try. The chain shot forward once more and the ball crashed against the remaining stick, blasting his only defense and impacting violently against his skull. He cursed and stumbled sideways, momentarily blinded from the blow, catching himself against the concrete barricade.

Thick Neck's rumbling voice taunted him. *"Itaime-ni?"*

Pain tore savagely at Max's head, but he managed to look up. It would only be a matter of moments before the final driving lunge. The man's enormous muscles flexed in preparation. Then, astonishingly, the ball and chain slipped to the ground and rolled into the dissipating mist. Thick Neck screamed as he clutched first at one leg, then the other. Through blurry vision, Max watched the gangster drop to his knees, his eyes growing saucerlike, staring at the blood surging between his fingers.

Lloyd Elgin stepped from the misty cloud, both guns leveled at the *Yakuza*'s head. He leaped masterfully into the air and delivered a bone-jarring roundhouse kick to the face. The big man's head wobbled before his eyes rolled upward in a faint, and he slumped to the ground.

"Pathetic." The cone-shaped filter covering Lloyd's mouth and nose muffled his voice. He pulled the mask down to his chin. "Enough play. We're getting the hell outta here."

Max watched in stunned awe as Lloyd rolled more canisters across the ground. The smoke grenades exploded, strengthening and pushing out the edges of the white cloud. He could still hear distant gunfire and although he was disoriented, he wondered who was doing battle if Lloyd was standing right next to him.

"Police," Lloyd said, his trained ears evidently having picked up the approaching sound of sirens long before anyone else heard them. Max barely acknowledged the warning as he moved forward and knelt down. Tomoko was huddled, weeping over the dead *Yakuza*'s shattered body. She held the wounded face and gently kissed his forehead.

Has she lost her mind? Max found himself wrapping an arm around her shaking shoulders. "Tomoko! We've got to go. Please!"

Lloyd twisted furiously and blasted both guns into the dense haze. A man's voice cried out and then fell silent with a groan. The guns pointed back in their direction, accompanied by an expression of rigid determination. "You get her moving, or else."

"She'll go—just give her a second." Max pulled Tomoko upright despite her sobbing resistance. Moving back into the smoke, they followed Lloyd, who was squeezing into the bushes ringing the cliff's edge. The branches clawed and scratched, but they pressed on for a dozen steps until the rocky edge of the Suicide Cliffs lay before them.

Lloyd stood inches from the rim. Cracking a chemical glow stick, he tossed it to Max. "Give me some light, but keep it low." Lying on the ground, he reached over the edge and hoisted up a hidden duffel bag. From inside, he retrieved a length of rope and three harnesses. "Get these on, quickly."

Tomoko's hands shook as she took the device and stared at the buckles and loops. Her tears cut vertical trails through the white powdered residue on her face, lending it a sad *Geisha*-like quality. "I—I don't understand. Who are you? What is this?"

Max already had his harness half on. "I think I know what we're doing. You have to put it on. There's no time." He looped the buckle at his waist. "We're going to rappel. It's a backdoor escape."

"No, *no!*" Tomoko's voice rose and she gripped Max's arm in a vice. "It's too high up! I can't."

Lloyd growled while fashioning "draws" into a makeshift anchor. "Either she's ready by the time I am, or we leave her behind."

Max calmed his breathing and held open a single leg loop. "This man is Lloyd Elgin," he whispered hoarsely. "I don't know where he came from, but the letters in his name rearrange to spell the words Golden Lily."

Lloyd was busy attaching carabineers to the anchor.

Max continued, "He knows about the prince's diary, and he wants it. The deal was that we get you back in exchange. If we don't go with him . . . he'll kill us both."

Tomoko met his eyes. He could see she wanted forgiveness, and his voice suddenly became fierce. "I don't care what's happened. I'm not leaving you here."

Twigs cracked and leaves rustled in the bushes back toward the clearing. Somebody was still hunting. Tomoko stared intently into Max's face, searching, before finally lifting first one foot, then the other, placing them through the harness's leg loops.

Lloyd tossed the rope over the edge and attached an unusual-looking metal device before activating and passing over two more chemical sticks. His green eyes seemed to glow with superhuman intensity as he spoke. "Squeeze here to drop down. Release pressure when you need to stop. We'll all be close together, so once you find the bottom, get out of the way fast. Who's first?"

"Me. I'll show her how to do it." Max stepped forward and clipped the device onto his harness as he peered into the black abyss, hoping the fear he was feeling wasn't showing on his face. He swallowed hard before beginning to rappel down the uneven stone wall, slipping quickly below the cover of the tree line before vanishing altogether.

Waiting at the bottom with a glow stick as the only light, Max pondered running as soon as Tomoko arrived, but the darkness, rocky landscape, and heavy foliage made him reconsider. They would need Lloyd's help to make it the rest of the way down the cliff to the ocean.

But can we get away from him alive?

Tomoko descended in short, jerking motions, and Max helped guide her down the last few feet and pulled her to the side. "Everything's all right." He embraced her.

"Tell me again, once I start breathing."

Lloyd zipped quickly down the unobstructed line. Arriving at the bottom, he pulled on night-vision goggles. "Both of you follow me."

It was apparent that the underbrush had recently been slashed from the trail, and as they clambered over jagged rocks, Max wondered how it was possible for one man to have planned and executed this mission all on his own. The obvious but unexpected answer was waiting at the bottom.

Finally reaching the coral plateau, Lloyd led them toward the white edge of the ocean. The glowing full moon overhead provided decent light, but still they stumbled through shallow pools of water on the long walk. A warm breeze picked up as they moved farther out. Looking up and back, Max could see lights flashing in the distance. Lloyd had been right—the police had arrived.

Tomoko tripped, but Max caught her. "I'm so tired. I just want to lie down," she complained.

"Me, too, but keep going—just a bit more." It seemed like a silly reply, given that he had no idea what was coming next, but there was little else to say.

Just before they reached the rolling water's edge, Lloyd pulled a gun and turned menacingly. His face was shadowed, but his voice was clear. "My part is done. Now, where's the diary?"

Max stared down the barrel and pressed Tomoko behind him. "O-Jima Island. Up the coast about five miles." Max felt his skin crawl, but he stepped toward the barrel so it was snug against his sternum. "Let her go. I'll take you there myself."

"Max—*no!*"

Lloyd didn't answer, but instead pulled out a cell phone. He spoke into the receiver. "I'm in place. We're heading to O-Jima Island . . . and we have company."

From nowhere, an obscure bump on the horizon increased in size as it came toward them. A distant hum morphed and changed into the throaty drone of twin outboard motors. Only feet from the coral's edge, a black inflatable boat dropped its throttle and rotated ninety degrees before edging sideways. One of the two men on board leaned out. His muscular arms held a paddle over the rubber-sided craft to keep the surf from pushing it against sharp outcroppings.

Lloyd waved his gun. "Get in. Hurry up."

Both men on the Zodiac were dressed in camouflage, their faces painted in matching stripes of olive and brown. Tomoko jumped first and Max followed suit, warily eyeing the men's machine guns. He shivered from the ocean breeze and the mercenaries' silent gaze.

As Max passed the driver's seat, he noticed the handle of a machete jutting from beneath. It was clear now that the two had created the cliff trail earlier in the day. *This whole island is crawling with military.* The thought that Lloyd might be one of them only made the situation worse.

Tomoko moved quickly to the far rear corner, pressing her back into it and pulling her legs toward her chest before dropping her head. Max moved to take a seat just inches away.

The boat turned away from the reef and headed for open water. The rigid front bounced when it crested the first swells, but as the speed increased, the movement evened out into a flattened, rhythmic thud pounding over the wavetops.

Max pulled his knees in close, in imitation of Tomoko, who was retreating into her own world. Cautiously slipping a new cell phone from his pocket, he blinked into the wind, glancing around to ensure he wasn't being watched. The three men standing at the midpoint of the boat seemed focused on the forward horizon. With his thumb, he quickly spelled out the word *boat*—it was the most that he dared write—followed by the Send command.

Arrival by water had never been considered. *I hope Toshi and Jeff are prepared for what's coming.*

CHAPTER
EIGHTY

"GET READY!" Toshi's voice crackled in Jeff's Bluetooth headset. "I can hear a boat approaching. I think it's them." Cell phone reception on O-Jima Island was poor, even if it was only a couple of hundred yards from the mainland.

Jeff clutched his motorbike helmet while standing on some rocks, attempting to get a better look. The expanse between him and the concrete pier to his right was the length of a football field. Half the distance in the opposite direction, a group of teenagers were clustered around a beach campfire. Repeated rounds of animated cheering were followed by the clinking of beer bottles and shouts of *Kampai!* He wondered how long the beachfront homeowners would put up with the noise.

In the distance, Toshi's priestly white robes glowed in the moonlight at the end of the pier. Set against the backdrop of twinkling houses rising up the mainland's hillside, the scene looked almost prophetic: a sacred, luminous beacon waiting to deliver the innocent from danger. "I'll leave the phone line open. Remember the plan. If this goes wrong, call the police. Do not try to help."

Jeff agreed with haste, knowing full well that he couldn't stand by and do nothing if his friends were in peril. He watched, transfixed, as a dark shape pulled alongside the pier and a single figure leaped from the boat.

FORCED to kneel against the Zodiac's rubber side, with a machine gun pressed to the back of his neck, Max wondered if it would hurt to die. *What was I thinking? Lloyd will never let me walk away. My fate will be the same as Mr. M's.* And what would happen to Tomoko? None of this was her fault, but in the end that wouldn't matter. She was kneeling next to him, forced into the same awkward position, deathly fear stamped upon her face.

He watched as Lloyd jumped from the boat, moving swiftly, ominously, into Toshi's personal space, seemingly unfazed by the sight of a halo-white Shinto priest. "You'd better have what I want," he growled.

Toshi's voice quivered but his face remained a calm façade. "Yes, I have it." He stepped back and extended the billowing sleeve covering his left arm. "Please take the prize yourself." His head dipped in an outward display of respect.

Lloyd holstered one of his guns and reached inside the folds of cloth, withdrawing the yellow diary. "So this is the troublesome book?" A smirk flickered quickly across his lips as he examined Prince Takeda's red *Hanko* seal and looked randomly through the pages. "Excellent."

"And now if you would kindly complete the transaction."

"Naturally." Lloyd snapped his fingers and the two mercenaries hoisted an obviously relieved Tomoko up onto the pier's edge. As Max followed behind he glanced back to the boat, focusing on the trigger finger of the shorter mercenary twitching in anticipation, ready to respond. It was clear that the man was waiting for a signal to shoot, and in Max's aching mind, there was no choice—as dangerous as it would be, Plan B would have to be played out. Beads of perspiration formed on his forehead, and he could feel his muscles tremble as the two groups quickly converged. It was time.

Lloyd strode past without stopping as Tomoko rushed forward to embrace Toshi.

Max was sure it would only be a matter of moments before the mercenaries started shooting once Lloyd was out of the line of fire. He held up a clenched fist of solidarity in front of his chest—the predetermined sign for Toshi to flee—as he gripped Tomoko's shoulders from behind, leaning forward to whisper in her ear. "Go, now. You have to run." He pushed her onward. "Hurry!"

Tomoko's eyes grew large and her lips fell open, but no sound came forth as Toshi turned and ran, pulling her away, his robes billowing.

She knows I still love her. She understands.

It was now or never. Sweat covered his body, yet his skin felt cold as ice. *I am the new guardian!* His eyes sprang wide and he returned the way he'd come—toward Lloyd—toward what would likely be the end. "One final thing, Mr. Elgin."

The green-eyed devil was almost at the boat when he turned in response, his back facing the black ocean.

Max's voice held steady, despite his gripping fear. "The diary you're holding has been scanned and dozens of secure copies have been placed on servers around the world. Daily codes must be entered to prevent the copies being released on the Internet. If you harm any of us—"

For a moment Lloyd appeared stunned, then his face erupted into rage as he surged forward, delivering a violent punch to the stomach, followed by a driving blow to the jaw. Max felt the excruciating impact of the combined force lift him off his feet, tossing him backward to the ground.

"You two stop!" Lloyd roared as he fired his gun high into the air. The mercenaries jumped from the boat to the concrete pier with their weapons trained forward.

Gasping, grimacing in agony, rolling from side to side, Max clutched his gut. He could hear the sound of Tomoko weeping—it seemed so distant.

Lloyd wrenched at Max's blood-stained shirt, pulling him up, lifting him closer to his own menacing face. The gun's smoking barrel jammed against the flesh of his neck, triggering a moan. Lloyd's words came slow and evil. "It's a bluff. You idiots have no idea who you're screwing with, do you?"

Max struggled to rise above the pain. Mucus trailed beneath his nose and down his chin. He could sense part of a tooth resting against his tongue and he spat it out. "We . . . we know the kind of people you are." His voice shook, but the rage inside forced the words out in gasping breaths. "You would never . . . leave us alone without a reason."

"And you believe holding copies of the diary is enough of a reason?"

"Unless . . . failure is an option."

Forty feet away, Toshi began shouting and waving an arm towards the beach. "No! Don't come. Stay away! Don't come!" He was standing between Tomoko and the boat, acting as a shield, with his right hand pressed to his ear.

"Don't come?" Lloyd stood and shouted. "Who the hell are you talking to?" His hand suddenly pointed. "Dammit. Get that thing off his head."

One of the mercenaries charged forward, tore away the earpiece, and crushed it beneath an oversized boot.

Lloyd knelt back down. "Digital documents on the Internet and people eavesdropping on our meeting. You've really got this whole spy bull*shit* worked out, haven't you, Mr. Travers?"

"Take your miserable fucking diary!" Max lay still on the ground. The warm taste of blood swam in the back of his throat. "We're not going to talk about this, 'cause we know revealing Golden Lily would mean death." He observed Lloyd's face as the machinelike man mulled their fate. "You won't gain anything by killing us . . . except the world discovering your secret. Take your prize . . . leave us alone and we all live."

The moment was broken by a sudden burst of machine-gun fire searing the air.

"Sir, a group of people are moving up the beach toward this position. There's a man wearing a motorcycle helmet leading them."

Lloyd paced, glaring downward with burning eyes. "You had better be telling the truth about holding onto those copies. At least for the next year." He waved his gun in emphasis. "After that, I don't give a rat's ass. You can deal with the next 'Lloyd' if you're stupid enough to change your mind."

"Understood." Max nodded and wiped at the blood on his face. "We just want to live."

"I'll be watching and listening. One slip, one peep, and you won't even see death coming." He snapped his fingers. "It'll be over." Lloyd backed away, then paused. For just a brief instant, it appeared that he might change his mind, but he turned and jumped into the boat, followed by the two mercenaries. The dual engines roared to life as the maneuverable craft spun around before tearing away into the night.

MAX barely regained his feet when he felt himself enveloped in a hug. Toshi was laughing hysterically. "You did it!"

"Owww! My ribs."

"*Gomen*! Sorry." The grip released instantly.

"It's okay. It's okay."

Tomoko approached quietly from the side and Max reached out a shaky arm. He wiped the tear-mark trails from her cheeks with his dirt-stained thumb. "Hey, I know you." He took her hands in his. There was so much for them to talk about, so much to explain. "You're tired. Let's take you home so you can sleep."

She smiled, eyes raw. "I need to call my parents. Make sure they're all right."

"Yes, absolutely."

Her voice grew soft like a child's. *"Domo arigato."*

The sounds of distant shouting grew louder. Jeff, accompanied by the teenagers, was charging up the pier to meet them. Toshi pointed toward the raucous group. "We should leave quickly before the police come."

Max chuckled and then flinched in pain, clutching at his side, thinking of the flashing lights on the Mabuni clifftop. "Don't worry. I'm pretty sure that the cops have their hands full right now with Oto Kodama."

CHAPTER
EIGHTY-ONE

Tuesday, May 1

M AX'S CHIN rested on his forearms, which were perched on his bare knees. Frothy ocean water lapped against the golden beach sand, rolling back and forth within inches of his toes. The warm morning sun felt good on his back after a swim. He could already feel his battered body regaining strength.

The rusty gate squeaked from behind, and he turned to watch Tomoko emerge from the trees to descend the trail. She looked great, dressed in rolled-up jeans and one of Jeff's T-shirts, her hair still wet from a shower. *What would I have done if she'd been lost forever?*

"Morning," she said, her voice cracking slightly.

Max took the coffee from her outstretched hand. "Thanks."

She appeared tense, sipping quietly from her cup while settling into the sand a few feet away.

Max glanced up the beach to her right, toward a twenty-foot white vessel resting on the shoreline. He gestured for Tomoko to look. A fisherman, with a towel for a headband, was loading supplies over the boat's side. His wife, who was already on board, sat with her face hidden beneath a large-brimmed cap.

Tomoko watched, her eyes widening. "That can't be the same boat we saw in Izu?"

"I thought the same when I came out a half hour ago, but I think they're a bit younger." He was glad for the conversational ice-breaker. "Plus the Izu guy was a better singer."

"Do you want me to ask if having a simple life makes them happier?"

Max shook his head, self-consciously recalling his former question from what seemed like so long ago. "No. Did you talk to your parents?"

"Yes. They were hiding at my uncle's house." She blew over the top of her steaming cup. "And, they were happy to know I'm safe, but—" she paused. "My mother heard about Mrs. Kanazawa's death, so she cried a lot."

The fisherman pushed the boat into the lapping surf before leaping on board. He made a point of waving, then started the motor and turned toward the open water. As Max waved back, he broached the nagging question, working to quiet his own jealousy. "Last night, why did that *Yakuza* guy sacrifice himself? You said his name was Hiro. You . . . you were *upset* over him. Did something happen between you two?"

The reply was quick. "Please . . . I can't talk about that." Tomoko kept her face turned away. "Nothing happened . . . maybe later . . . not now."

"Fine." He believed her, but his hurt rushed out, uncontainable. "I can't believe you left. People who love each other don't just leave without saying anything!"

"You're right," she replied softly. "Can you forgive me?"

Max rose and stepped closer, thinking of his passport and how she'd held back giving it to him. But it would be best discussed when the sting of painful memories was more distant. He dropped back down in the sand beside her. "All I know is that I've never felt so alone as when I was on that Bullet Train." Directly before them, over the water, a pair of seagulls floated on the wind, diving and twisting around each other. Max continued. "I thought I'd lost you—I don't think I can handle that again."

She wiped at her moist eyes with the back of her hand. "Thank you for rescuing me."

"There's no need . . . you should never have even been involved. You wouldn't have been in that situation if I hadn't gone to Mr. M's in the first place, and if I hadn't been so pig-headed about checking on your parents."

"You don't know that for sure."

"Trust me, I do know." A handful of sand filtered through his open fingers as he spoke.

Tomoko nodded. "So, besides needing therapy to deal with everything, are you and me okay? Her hand reached over and brushed his damp brown hair. It was already growing blond again at the roots. "I'm so sorry."

He watched her look into his eyes, recognizing the doubt recede like the tide. "It's in the past." Max kissed her cheek as her hand ran along the edge of his swollen jaw and down to his neck.

"You have a huge bruise." She touched his shoulder. "And look at all your scratches!"

He laughed as his arms formed a circle around her, holding them both in the moment, wishing it would last forever.

There was a long silence before he spoke again. "What do you think about taking a short trip? Toshi offered us the use of his jet. He suggested a week in Cambodia, but only if you're cool with it." Max felt confident that this time her desire was the same as his—to get away, to drift anonymously in a crowd of people, without fear of being stalked or chased. To eat good food and grow tired of idle relaxation and sleep. To be someplace where there were no *Yakuza* and no diaries; a place to heal. "The Angkor Wat temples are supposed to be amazing—some of the greatest in the world. We could chill, take a few pictures."

"And when we come back, will you please talk with the police?"

"Of course. I have to clear my name if I'm gonna stay here."

"Sounds perfect."

"Good. I'll phone Toshi when we go back up to the house. But there is one thing I need to show you before we leave the island," he suggested slyly.

Tomoko's brow furrowed. "What?"

"No, no, don't worry. It's nothing bad. In fact, I think you'll be quite amazed. Trust me."

She didn't look entirely convinced as he kissed her forehead, and nose, and cheeks, and lips.

CHAPTER
EIGHTY-TWO

THE POLICEMAN'S tension wrench slipped easily into the lock. His experienced fingers worked until the click of the cylinder signaled its defeat.

Hazy light filtered in through the sheer curtains covering the single window in the back office. Stepping through the doorway, the stench of death bit at his nostrils. Holding his breath, he made a quick sweep of the room—cheap furniture, shelves, and industrial carpet—before returning back to the hallway.

A single button on his cell phone connected him to Masami Ishi's waiting ears. The superintendent of criminal investigation had sounded stressed when he'd called early in the morning. "Well, what did you find?"

"There's nobody here, sir. It appears she's abandoned the premises."

"How did you draw that conclusion?"

"Her cat's dead body. It appears to have been poisoned."

"Damn it."

"Should I call animal control?"

"Absolutely not! Just look for clues to where she might have gone. Then lock up and leave quietly. Let me know if you find anything."

"Yes, sir." Slipping the phone back into his pocket, the policeman held his nose and went back inside.

MASAMI Ishi stared down on the crowd of hundreds gathered in the street below his office. Their fists pumped the air in unison. Lettered banners and colored streamers waved and shook in the morning breeze, while the barking voice of a chanter blasted from enormous speakers mounted on a parked van. The annual May Day labor rally was in full swing.

A persistent knock at his office door finally drew his attention away from the window. The Office Lady apologized and bowed as she opened the door and stepped inside. "There's a call from the chief of police in Okinawa. He's phoned several times already. I tried to take a message, but this time he's insisting that you speak with him." She folded her hands in front of her slender waist. "And . . . he sounds very angry."

Masami Ishi sighed and let the sweeping strands of hair slide down his forehead. "All right." The morning was going from bad to worse.

"And one other thing, sir."

He raised his eyebrows in exaggerated frustration, while stomping back to his desk. "Yes?"

"The head of the National Public Safety Commission left a message a few minutes ago. He's on his way over to meet with you."

Masami Ishi's mind blanked for a moment, and he steadied himself before sitting slowly back into his chair. Yoko's voicemail had spoken the truth, after all. The betrayal of his authority had indeed been caught on tape. The moment's irony was not lost as the blood drained from his cheeks; his own indictment would mean the American's acquittal.

An awkward moment passed until the OL cleared her throat. "That's everything, sir."

"Yes. Go." Ordinarily he would have admired her form-fitting skirt as she turned around, but on this occasion he simply pressed his palms flat against the desktop and stared at all ten of his shaking fingers.

CHAPTER
EIGHTY-THREE

JEFF LED the way, crawling on all fours. Close behind, in the musty air, Tomoko followed him, then Max, whose voice echoed along the rock passageway.

"I forgot how much this kills my knees."

"Stop whining, bro. You're the one who wanted to come back here." Jeff rose to his feet and issued a warning by shaking his headlamp back and forth. "Tomoko, be careful here, the ground is slippery. Grab the walls."

"What do you mean, 'come back here'? Where are you guys taking me?"

Max had been playing coy all morning, and he wasn't about to spoil the surprise when it was so close. "Like I said, it's kind of hard to explain. That's why we need to show you."

After edging down the wide ramp, they stepped inside the closet-sized metal chamber.

Max locked them inside. "You ready?"

"I really don't need any more surprises," sighed Tomoko, "but okay."

Jeff spun the handle on the second door before pushing it open with his foot. The string of high fluorescent lights clapped into brilliance as Tomoko stared into the vast room. She turned back, and Max saw the same look of wonder that he knew had crossed his own face only two days earlier.

She raised her overflowing voice. "What is this place?"

"Prince Takeda built it." Max and Jeff glanced significantly at each other before Max finally continued. "He spent forty years collecting valuable items stolen by the military. His plan was to give it all back to the rightful owners."

"*Wau!* This is unbelievable! What about the cabinets?"

Jeff chimed in. "Documented evidence of Golden Lily and its aftermath. The plan was to reveal the global corruption at the same time the stolen goods were returned." He motioned to the television. "Prince Takeda left a video, if you want to watch it."

"So why didn't he finish the plan?"

Max shrugged. "We don't know. Maybe he got scared or sick. We're not really sure." He removed his day pack and retrieved the second diary along with a paper-clipped copy of the first. "I'm planning to return these to Ben, but I want to leave them here, for safe keeping while we're away."

"I'd like to watch the video . . ." Tomoko took the documents from his hands, "and I'll find a place to put these, for now."

Max smiled. "Great. Toshi said he needed a couple more hours to get the plane ready, and I want to show Jeff a few things, since we didn't have much time to look around before."

"Go ahead." Tomoko wasn't paying attention as her neck craned and her eyes roamed the high ceiling and far walls.

Max took his time moving down the central corridor. The pain killers he'd taken were helping but there was no need pushing any harder than necessary. "You have to see this amazing dragon statue . . . and the terracotta warriors."

Jeff adjusted his ponytail as they walked along. "So, what do we do about this place?"

"Nothing, for now." Max said matter-of-factly. "Exposing it would get us all killed. We simply need to wait a while longer. But we will tell the world what really happened. I guarantee it."

"You think we could open a few crates?" Jeff asked.

"No." *I am the new guardian.*

Behind them, emanating from the television, Prince Takeda's regal voice echoed in the cavern.

RISING to twenty-eight thousand feet, the Learjet 40XR soared on its flight path over the Pacific Ocean. Toshi motioned to the copilot to take over as he exited the cockpit and moved back into the main cabin.

"Everyone comfortable?"

Max nodded but saw that Tomoko was simply staring out the window. Silver-gray clouds floated overhead, while pure white clouds below made the reflected sunlight appear to be glowing upward from beneath the aircraft. She appeared lost in thought.

They were seated in high-backed leather chairs that faced each other, two on each side of the aisle. Toshi took the fourth empty space across from Jeff. He leaned over and tapped Tomoko on the knee. *"Daijobu?"*

"I'm fine." She turned her head and smiled. "I was just thinking."

"About what?"

Her face grew a guilty mask as she looked at the three men staring back at her. "Well, when we went to Prince Takeda's bunker today, I took the diaries . . . "

Max sat straight up. "You told me you'd found a place for them in the cabinets."

"I did, and I also watched the prince's video to the end. He told where to find a book that explained the file organization. There was a space already reserved for the diaries. It was a metal box and—"

The three men spoke simultaneously. *"And?"*

Tomoko retrieved her purse lying on the floor next to her seat. Her cheeks flushed red. She unzipped the bag and removed what looked like a tan piece of cloth. Reaching across the aisle, she handed it to Toshi, who immediately unfolded it on the tabletop next to him. They all gathered around, staring down at the faded lines of mountains, rivers, and strange symbols.

Max couldn't contain himself, finally blurting out what he was sure everyone was thinking. "Is this really it? The 176th map?"

"I think so!" Tomoko gripped his arm, her voice pulsing with excitement. "It was in the box."

The cabin erupted in a chorus of shouting and laughter, causing the startled copilot to rush stumbling from the cockpit, a look of surprise and fear etched on his face.

Jeff held up a waving hand. *"Daijobu!* Don't worry. Everything is fine."

Toshi echoed the reassurance before dropping back into his seat. He rubbed the hair on his chin while staring out the window. Finally, he turned and looked directly at Max with a mischievous spark in his eyes. "Shall we make a detour to the Philippines? Do a little treasure-hunting?"

For a moment the air in the cabin hung still, unmoving; each person eyed the others' reactions. The only evident noise was the powerful sound of the humming engines. Then Tomoko broke the silence with a veiled phrase. *"Trunk-u hitotsu dake de."*

"Romantic Airplane"—it was their song, and the message being conveyed was clear.

Max squeezed Tomoko's hand before leaning over to kiss her. "Interesting idea, Toshi, but for now, there'll be no detour. We need to stay on our present course."

THE END

About the Author

Richard Goodfellow spent two years teaching English in Japan in the early 1990s. A software consultant and self-described road warrior, he penned the majority of *Collector of Secrets* on airplanes and in small towns throughout Oregon, Texas, Florida, and everywhere in between. After completion of the novel's first draft, he returned to Japan for a month of further travel to lay fresh eyes on the locations of the novel, almost every one of which is real. Visit him online at www.collectorofsecrets.com or at @rgfellowauthor.